A Touchstone Book

By Nikos Kazantzakis:

FICTION:

> *The Rock Garden*
> *Saint Francis*
> *The Last Temptation of Christ*
> *Freedom or Death*
> *The Greek Passion*
> *Zorba the Greek*

POETRY:

> *The Odyssey:* A Modern Sequel

PHILOSOPHY:

> *The Saviors of God*—Spiritual Exercises

TRAVEL:

> *Spain*
> *Japan-China*

SAINT
FRANCIS

A NOVEL BY

NIKOS
KAZANTZAKIS

TRANSLATED FROM THE GREEK BY P. A. BIEN

A TOUCHSTONE BOOK PUBLISHED BY
SIMON AND SCHUSTER
NEW YORK

ISBN 0-671-63190-X
ISBN 0-671-21247-8 PBK.
LIBRARY OF CONGRESS CATALOG CARD NUMBER 62-9606
MANUFACTURED IN THE UNITED STATES OF AMERICA

5 6 7 8 9 10 11 12 13 14

21 PBK.

Dedicated to
the Saint Francis of our era,
DR. ALBERT SCHWEITZER
N. K.

PROLOGUE

If I have omitted many of Francis' sayings and deeds and
if I have altered others, and added still others which did
not take place but which might have taken place, I have done so not
out of ignorance or impudence or irreverence, but from a need to
match the Saint's life with his myth, bringing that life as fully into
accord with its essence as possible.

Art has this right, and not only the right but the duty to subject
everything to the essence. It feeds upon the story, then assimilates it
slowly, cunningly, and turns it into a legend.

While writing this legend which is truer than truth itself, I was
overwhelmed by love, reverence, and admiration for Francis, the
hero and great martyr. Often large teardrops smeared the manu-
script; often a hand hovered before me in the air, a hand with an
eternally renewed wound: someone seemed to have driven a nail
through it, seemed to be driving a nail through it for all eternity.

Everywhere about me, as I wrote, I sensed the Saint's invisible
presence; because for me Saint Francis is the model of the dutiful
man, the man who by means of ceaseless, supremely cruel struggle
succeeds in fulfilling our highest obligation, something higher even
than morality or truth or beauty: the obligation to transubstantiate
the matter which God entrusted to us, and turn it into spirit.

NIKOS KAZANTZAKIS

FATHER FRANCIS, I who take up my pen to-
day to write your life and times, unworthy that I am:
when you first met me, remember, I was a humble beggar, ugly, my
face and head covered with hair. From the eyebrows to the nape
of the neck I was nothing but hair. My eyes were frightened and
naïve; I stuttered, bleated like a lamb—and you, in order to ridicule
my ugliness and abasement, you named me Brother Leo, the lion!
But when I told you my life story you began to weep; you clasped
me in your arms, kissed me, and said, "Brother Leo, forgive me. I
called you 'lion' to ridicule you, but now I see that you are a true
lion, because only a lion has the courage to pursue what you are
pursuing."

I had been going from monastery to monastery, from village to
village, wilderness to wilderness, searching for God. I did not
marry, did not have children, because I was searching for God. I
would hold a slice of bread in one hand and a fistful of olives in the
other, and though I was famished, I always forgot to eat, because
I was searching for God.

I walked so much that my feet became swollen; I asked the same
question over and over again until hair sprouted on my tongue!
Finally I grew tired of knocking on doors and holding out my hand,
first to beg for bread, then for a kind word, and after that for salvation. Everyone laughed, called me a visionary, and chased me away
—pushed me until I arrived finally at the edge of the abyss. I was
weary; I began to blaspheme. I'm human after all, I said; I'm tired
of walking, of going about hungry and cold, of knocking on the gates
of heaven and seeing them remain closed. And then, as I was on the
verge of despair, one night God took me by the hand; He took you

by the hand also, Father Francis, and brought us together.

Now I sit in my cell and watch the springtime clouds through my tiny window. Below in the courtyard of the monastery the heavens have descended: there is a fine drizzle, and the soil is fragrant. The lemon trees in the orchards have blossomed; in the distance a cuckoo calls. All the leaves are laughing: God has become rain and is raining on the world. O Lord, what joy! What happiness! Look how earth, rain, and the odors of dung and the lemon trees all combine and become one with man's heart! Truly, man is soil. That is why he, like the soil, enjoys the calm caressing rains of spring so very much. My heart is being watered. It cracks open, sends forth a shoot—and you, Father Francis, appear.

All the soil inside me has blossomed, Father Francis. Memories rise up, time rolls back its wheel, and there, brought back to life, are the sacred hours we spent journeying together over the face of the earth, you in front and I following timorously in your footsteps. Do you remember where we first met? I was so hungry that night, I staggered as I entered the celebrated city of Assisi. It was August and the moon was immense. I had already enjoyed this noble city many times, glory be to God, but that night Assisi was something else entirely: it was unrecognizable. What miracle was this? Where was I? Houses, citadel, churches, towers: all were hovering in the air, floating in a pure white sea, beneath a purple sky. It was dinnertime when I entered the city through the newly built Saint Peter's Gate. The moon was just rising—full, brilliantly red. It was gentle, like a kindly sun; and from high up on the citadel, the Rocca, a serene waterfall spilled down onto the bell towers and housetops, filling the ditches with milk until they overflowed, flooding the narrow lanes, which ran like brooks, and making the faces of the inhabitants so radiant that everyone seemed to be thinking of God. I stopped, swept away by the sight before me. Is this Assisi? I kept asking myself, making the sign of the cross. Can these be houses and people and bell towers, or is it possible that, while still alive, I have entered Paradise? I held out my hands; the moon filled my palms, a moon sweet and gelatinous, like honey. I felt the grace of God running over my lips, my temples—and then I understood. I uttered a cry. Some saint—yes, without a doubt some saint had come this way. His smell was in the air!

Sloshing through the moonlight, I climbed the twisting lanes until I reached the Piazza San Giorgio. It was Saturday night and a large crowd had gathered. There was singing and raucous shouting, mixed with the sound of mandolins and the intoxicating aroma of fried fish, jasmine, rose, and cabobs sizzling on the coals. My hunger increased beyond bounds.

"Hey, good Christians," I called, approaching one of the groups of celebrants, "who in this renowned city of Assisi can give me alms? I just want to eat, sleep, and then leave in the morning."

They looked me over from head to toe, and laughed.

"And who do you think you are, my beauty?" they answered, guffawing. "Come closer and let us admire you."

"Maybe I'm Christ," I said to frighten them. "Sometimes He appears on earth like this, like a beggar."

"You had better not repeat that, not if you know what's good for you, poor fellow," one of them said. "We won't have anyone spoiling our party. Quick now, move on! Otherwise we might rise up, every single one of us, and crucify you!"

They laughed again; but then one, the youngest of the group, felt sorry for me.

"Pietro Bernardone's son Francis, old 'Leaky Palms': he's the one who'll give you alms. And you're in luck. Yesterday he returned from Spoleto with his tail between his legs. Go and find him."

At that point an ugly, gawky giant jumped forward. He had a mouselike face, a jaundiced complexion, and was called Sabbatino. We met again a few years later when he too became one of Francis' disciples and, barefooted, we journeyed together over the roads of the world. On this night, however, the sound of Francis' name made him cackle maliciously:

"Why do you think he went to fight at Spoleto, all fitted out in his gold and plumes? It seems he wanted to do great deeds, have himself invested as a knight and then come back here to play cock of the walk. But the Almighty knows what's what. He gave him a bang square on the head, and our proud rooster returned home with his feathers plucked."

He jumped into the air, clapping his hands.

"We even made up a song about him," he said with a chuckle. "Ready, lads—all together now!"

15

And suddenly they all began to clap their hands and sing at the top of their voices:

> *He went to Spoleto, la-la, la-la,*
> *He went to Spoleto for wool,*
> *He went to Spoleto, ta-ra, ta-ra,*
> *And got himself sheared to the full!*

The sight of the wine and tidbits made me feel faint. I leaned against a doorpost, gasping for breath.

"And where is this 'Leaky Palms,' this Francis—may God protect him! Where can I find him so that I may fall at his feet?"

"Go to the upper part of the city," the young one directed me. "You'll see him there under a window, serenading his lady."

I set out, perishing with hunger, and began to climb up and down the narrow streets. I could see smoke rising from the chimneys. People were cooking—all sensible people—and I smelled the odors. My entrails were drooping like naked grape stems despoiled by birds and mice. Unable to endure it any longer, I began to blaspheme: "Oh, if only I wasn't looking for God," I murmured in a rage, "if only I wasn't looking for God, how I'd loll in the lap of indolence! What a joy that would be! I'd do nothing but eat gigantic slices of white bread, and roast pig, which I love so much, or rabbit smothered in oil and garnished with scallions, bay leaves, and cumin. And to cool my insides I'd down a jugful of red Umbrian wine. Then I'd visit some widow and let her warm me: people say a widow's warmth is the sweetest in the whole world. Certainly a brazier can't compare. . . . But what am I to do since I'm searching for God!"

I was walking as fast as I could in an effort to get warm. With a sudden impetus I broke out into a run in order to breathe clean air again, to save myself from the temptations, from the odors and the widows. Finally I reached the heights of the citadel, the famous Rocca. The proud walls had been thrown down, the doors reduced to charcoal; nothing remained but two crevassed towers. The weeds had already climbed over them and were protruding from the spaces between the stones. The people had revolted a few years before, unable any longer to endure their lords, and had

16

charged this hawk's nest and destroyed it. I felt like circling the ruins in order to enjoy the misfortune of these rulers who had gorged themselves with food and wine (until our turn had come), but a bitter, smarting wind was blowing, and I felt cold. I descended at a run. The lamps in the houses had been extinguished; the people were snoring. They had eaten well, drunk well, and now they were snoring. These respectable homeowners had found the God they were seeking, found Him on earth, just as they wanted Him: their own size, complete with children, wives, and all the best things of life—while I, the visionary, roamed the streets of Assisi barefooted, hungry, shivering, and beat on the doors of heaven, cursing one moment and lustily repeating the Kyrie eleison the next in order to keep warm.

Toward midnight I heard guitars and lutes in the vicinity of the bishop's church. Probably some young men serenading their sweethearts. One of them was singing. I approached on tiptoe and hid in a doorway, glued to the wall. There were five or six youths outside of Count Scifi's mansion. One of them, much shorter than the others, a long plume in his cap, was standing with crossed arms, his head thrown back, his eyes pinned on a grated window. He was singing, while the others around him, enraptured by his voice, accompanied him on their guitars and lutes. And what a voice that was! O God, how sweet, how passionate; how it implored and commanded! I don't remember the song and can't record it here to preserve it for posterity; but I do remember well that it was about a white dove that was being pursued by a hawk, and that the youth was calling the dove to come and take refuge in his bosom. . . . He sang softly, tranquilly, as though afraid he might wake the girl, who must have been sleeping behind the grated window. You couldn't help but feel that he was singing not to the girl's body, which was asleep, but to her soul, which was lying awake. My eyes had filled with tears. I was troubled: where had I heard that voice before—the sweetness, the entreaty, the command? Where and when had I heard that invitation: the hawk in screeching pursuit, the dove twittering in terror; and, far far away, the sweet, inviting voice of salvation?

Slinging the guitars and lutes over their shoulders, the youths got ready to leave.

"Let's go, Francis," they called laughingly to the singer. "What are you waiting for? You think your little countess will throw you the rose, do you? She hasn't opened her window until now, and she isn't going to tonight, either!"

But the singer, without answering, set off before the others in order to turn the corner and go down to the square, where songs from the open taverns could still be heard. At that point I darted out in front of him. I was terrified at the thought of losing him, for I had suddenly felt that my soul was a dove, and the hawk Satan, and that this youth was the bosom in which I could find refuge. Removing my tattered, threadbare robe, I spread it beneath his feet for him to walk over. His entire body emitted an odor, a fragrance like honey, like wax, like roses. I smelled it and understood: it was the odor of sainthood. When you open a silver reliquary, that is how the saint's bones smell.

He turned and looked at me, smiling.

"Why did you do that?" he asked in a low voice.

"I don't know, sir. How do you expect me to know? The robe left my shoulders of its own accord and stretched itself on the ground for you to walk over."

He remained standing where he was. The smile had left his face.

"Did you see some sign in the air?" he asked me, leaning forward, troubled.

"I don't know, sir. Everything is a sign—my hunger, the moon, your voice. Better not ask me. I'll begin to weep."

"Everything is a sign," he murmured, looking about him uneasily.

He held out his hand. His thick lips moved as though he wanted to question me but could not make up his mind to do so. His face had melted away under the strong moonlight, his hands had become transparent. He took a step forward, coming closer to me. I leaned over to hear what he was about to say, and felt his alcoholic breath in my face.

"Don't look at me like that," he whispered angrily. "I have nothing to say to you. Nothing!"

He began to walk again, quickening his pace. He motioned me to follow him.

I trotted behind him in the moonlight, looking at him. He was dressed in silk, with a long red plume in his velvet cap and a carnation in his ear. This man isn't searching for God, I said to myself; his soul is wallowing in the flesh.

And all at once my heart took pity on him. I held out my hand and touched his elbow.

"Excuse me, sir," I said, "but there was one thing I wanted to ask you, and it was this: You eat, drink, dress yourself in silks, sing beneath windows. Your life is one continuous party. Does this mean you lack nothing?"

The youth turned abruptly and drew his arm violently away to prevent me from touching him.

"That's right, I lack nothing," he replied with irritation. "Why do you ask? I don't like having people question me."

"Because I pity you, sir," I said in reply, fortifying my heart.

When the youth heard this he tossed his head arrogantly.

"*You*, you pity *me!*"

He laughed, but a moment later, in a low, panting voice: "Why do you pity me—why?"

I did not answer.

"Why?" he asked again, leaning forward and gazing into my eyes. "Who are you — dressed like that, like a beggar? And who sent you to find me here on the streets of Assisi in the middle of the night?"

He grew furious. "Confess the truth! Someone sent you. Who?"

Then, receiving no answer, he stamped his foot on the ground:

"I lack nothing! I don't want to be pitied, I want to be envied. . . . I lack nothing, I tell you!"

"Nothing?" I asked. "Not even heaven?"

He lowered his head and was silent. But after a moment:

"Heaven is too high for me. The earth is good, exceptionally good —and near me!"

"Nothing is nearer to us than heaven. The earth is beneath our feet and we tread upon it, but heaven is within us."

The moon had begun to set; a few stars hung in the sky; the sound of impassioned serenades came thinly from the distant neighborhoods; down below, the square was buzzing. The air of this summer night was filled with aromas and with love.

"Heaven is within us, my young lord," I repeated.

"How do you know?" he asked, giving me a startled look.

"I suffered, went hungry, thirsty—and learned."

He took me by the arm. "Come home with me. I'll feed you and give you a bed to sleep on. But don't talk to me about heaven—it may be within you, but it's not within me."

His eyes flashed with anguish; his voice had grown hoarse.

We went down to the market place, where the taverns were still roaring. Drunken young men were streaming in and out of one of the low houses, in front of which was a small red lantern. Donkeys laden with vegetables and fruit had begun to arrive from the villages. Men were setting up tables and arranging bottles of wine, brandy, and rum on them. Two tightrope walkers had started to drive in poles and stretch their string. The preparations for the Sunday bazaar had already begun.

Two drunks spied Francis in the moonlight and began to laugh clandestinely. One of them removed his guitar from his shoulder. Glaring at Francis derisively, he started to sing:

> *You build your nest so high in vain:*
> *The bough will break,*
> *You'll lose the bird,*
> *And be left with only the pain.*

Francis listened, motionless, his head bowed.

"He's right," he murmured, "he's right."

Courtesy demanded I remain quiet, but, bumpkin that I am, I opened my mouth and asked: "What bird?"

Francis turned and looked at me. So much suffering was in that gaze, I could not keep myself from clasping his hand and kissing it. "Forgive me," I said.

His expression sweetened. "What bird? Is it possible I know?" He sighed deeply.

"No, I don't, I don't know," he groaned. "Stop asking me questions! Come!"

And he grasped my hand tightly, as though afraid I might leave him.

But I, how could I leave him? Where could I go? From that moment on, I was constantly at his side. Father Francis, was it you I had been seeking year after year? Was that why I had been born: to follow you and listen to you? I had ears, but no tongue—so I listened. You told me what you told no one else. You took me by the hand, we went into the forests, scrambled up mountains, and you spoke.

You used to say to me, "Brother Leo, if you weren't with me I would tell it all to a stone, an ant, a tender olive leaf—because my heart is overflowing, and if it does not open and spill forth, it may break into a thousand pieces."

I know things about you, therefore, that no other person knows. You committed many more sins than people imagine; you performed many more miracles than people believe. In order to mount to heaven, you used the floor of the Inferno to give you your momentum. "The further down you gain your momentum," you often used to tell me, "the higher you shall be able to reach. The militant Christian's greatest worth is not his virtue, but his struggle to transform into virtue the impudence, dishonor, unfaithfulness, and malice within him. One day Lucifer will be the most glorious archangel standing next to God; not Michael, Gabriel, or Raphael—but Lucifer, after he has finally transubstantiated his terrible darkness into light."

I listened to you, mouth agape, thinking what sweet words these were and asking myself if this meant that sin, even sin, could become a path to lead us to God; if even the sinner, therefore, could have hopes of salvation.

I am the only one, also, who knows about your carnal love for Count Favorini Scifi's daughter Clara. All the others, because they are afraid of their own shadows, think you loved only her soul. But it was her body that you loved earliest of all; it was from there that you set out, got your start. Then, after struggle, struggle against the devil's snares, you were able with God's help to reach her soul. You loved that soul, but without ever denying her body, and without ever touching it either. And not only did this carnal love for Clara not hinder you from reaching God, it actually helped you greatly, because it was this love that unveiled for you the great secret: in what manner, and by what kind of struggle the flesh becomes spirit. All love is one; it is exactly the same whether it be for wife, son, mother, fatherland, or for an idea, or God. A victory, even though on love's lowest rung, helps form the road which will lead us to God. So, you fought the flesh, vanquished it mercilessly, then kneaded it with your blood and tears and after a terrible struggle which lasted many years, transformed it into spirit. And didn't you do exactly the same with all your virtues and all your vices? They too were flesh, were Clara. Weeping, laughing, tearing your heart in two, you turned them into spirit. This is the road; there is none other. You led the way and I, panting, followed you.

One day as I watched you rise from the bloodstained rocks, moaning, your body one great wound, my heart took pity on you. I ran to you and clasped your knees. "Brother Francis, why do you torture your body so?" I cried. "It too is one of God's creatures and must be revered. Don't you feel sorry for your blood, your blood which is being spilled?"

But you shook your head and answered me, "Brother Leo, with the world in the state it is today, whoever is virtuous must be so to the point of sainthood, and even beyond; whoever is a sinner must be so to the point of bestiality, and even beyond. Today, the middle road is no more."

And on another occasion when in desperation you looked to the earth and it wanted to devour you, to heaven, and it refused to help you, once again you turned to me, and I shuddered when I heard your words:

"Listen, Brother Leo," you said. "I'm going to tell you something very grave. If you cannot bear it, lamb of God, then forget it. Are you listening?"

"I'm listening, Father Francis," I answered. I had already begun to tremble. You placed your hand on my shoulder as though trying to steady me and prevent me from falling.

"Brother Leo, to be a saint means to renounce not only everything earthly but also everything divine."

But as soon as you uttered those blasphemous words, you became terrified. Bending down, you seized a handful of dirt and thrust it into your mouth. Then, placing your finger over your lips, you glared at me in horror. A few moments later you cried:

"What have I said? Did I speak? . . . Quiet!"

And you burst into tears.

Every evening beneath the light of the lamp I took aim at each of your words, each of your acts, and pinned them down securely one by one so that they would not perish. A single word from your lips, I said to myself, may save a soul. If I fail to record it, fail to reveal it to mankind, that soul will not be saved, and I will be to blame.

I had taken up my quill to begin writing many times before now, but I always abandoned it quickly: each time I was overcome with fear. Yes, may God forgive me, but the letters of the alphabet frighten me terribly. They are sly, shameless demons—and dangerous! You open the inkwell, release them: they run off—and how will you ever get control of them again! They come to life, join, separate, ignore your commands, arrange themselves as they like on the paper—black, with tails and horns. You scream at them and implore them in vain: they do as they please. Prancing, pairing up shamelessly before you, they deceitfully expose what you did not wish to reveal, and they refuse to give voice to what is struggling, deep within your bowels, to come forth and speak to mankind.

As I was returning from church this past Sunday, however, I felt emboldened. Had not God squeezed those demons into place whether they liked it or not, with the result that they wrote the Gospels? Well then, I said to myself, Courage, my soul! Have no fear of them! Take up your quill and write! But I immediately grew fainthearted once again. The Gospels, to be sure, were written by Holy Apostles. One had his angel, the other his lion, the other his ox, and the last his eagle. These dictated, and the Apostles wrote. But I . . . ?

I had remained hesitant in this way for many years, carrying about your sayings faithfully transcribed one by one on skins, scraps of paper, the bark of trees. I kept repeating to myself, Oh, when shall I grow old? When, unable to walk any more, shall I settle down in a monastery and in the calm of my cell receive from God the power, Father Francis, to arrange your words and deeds on paper as a Saint's Legend, for the salvation of the world!

I was in a hurry because I felt the words coming to life and jostling each other on the bits of skin, the scraps of paper, the bark of the trees. They were being smothered, and had begun to revolt in an effort to escape. I felt Francis too, felt him prowling outside my monastery, homeless and exhausted, his hand outstretched like a beggar's; felt him slip into the cloister, unperceived by anyone but me, and enter my cell. Just the other evening, as I was bent over an ancient parchment reading the lives of the saints, I felt someone in back of me. The north wind was blowing; it was cold, and I had lighted my earthenware brazier, the Holy Superior having given me permission to keep a bit of fire in my cell because I had grown old, and lost my endurance. The saints' miracles had encircled me, were licking me as though they were flames. I no longer touched the earth; I was hanging in the air. It was then that I felt someone in back of me. Turning, I saw Francis huddled over the brazier.

"Father Francis, have you abandoned Paradise?" I cried, jumping to my feet.

"I am cold, I am hungry," he answered. "I have nowhere to lay my head."

There was bread and honey in the cell. I ran quickly in order to give him some and calm his hunger. But when I turned, I saw no one.

It was a sign from God, a visible message: Francis roams homeless over the earth; build him a home! But once again I was carried away by fear. I struggled within myself for a long time and then, having grown weary, leaned my head against the parchment and fell asleep. I had a dream. It seemed I was lying under a blossoming tree with God blowing over me like a fragrant breeze. The tree was the tree of Paradise, and it had blossomed! As I gazed at the sky through the flowering branches suddenly a group of minute birds, just like letters of the alphabet, came and perched in the tree, one on each branch. They began to chirp, at first singly, one by one, then in pairs, then three together. Afterwards, hopping from branch to branch, they formed groups of two or three or five and twittered away ecstatically. The whole tree had become a song, a sweet tender song full of passion, desire, and great affliction. It seemed as though I were already deeply buried beneath the spring-time soil, my arms crossed upon my breast, and that this flowering tree were issuing from my bowels, the roots invading my entire body and suckling it. And all the joys and sorrows of my life had become birds, and were singing.

I awoke. I still felt the chirping within my bowels; God was still blowing over me.

It was dawn. I had slept the entire night with my head on the parchment. Rising, I washed and changed to clean clothes. The bell was ringing for matins. I made the sign of the cross and went to the chapel, where I glued my forehead, mouth, breast to the floor, and received the sacrament. When Mass was over I scampered

24

back to my cell, not speaking to anyone lest I soil my breath. I flew: angels were holding me up. I did not see them, but I could hear the rustle of their wings to my right and left. I took up my quill, crossed myself—

And began, Father Francis, to record your Life and Times.

May the Lord help me and be my guide!

I SWEAR I shall tell the truth. Lord, aid my memory, enlighten my mind, do not permit me to utter a single word I might later regret. Arise and bear witness, mountains and plains of Umbria; arise, stones sprinkled with his martyr's blood, dusty, bemired roads of Italy, black caves, snow-covered peaks; arise, ship that took him to the savage East; arise, lepers and wolves and bandits; and you, birds who heard his preaching, arise— Brother Leo needs you. Come, stand on my right, on my left; help me to tell the truth, the whole truth. Upon this hangs the salvation of my soul.

I tremble, because many times I find I cannot distinguish what is true from what is false. Francis runs in my mind like water. He changes faces; I am unable to pin him down. Was he short? Was he immensely tall? I cannot put my hand over my heart and say with certainty. He often seemed squat to me, all skin and bones, with a face which bore witness to his penury—scant chestnut-colored beard, thick protruding lips, huge hairy ears erect like a rabbit's and listening intently to both the visible and invisible worlds. His hands, though, were delicate, his fingers slender—indications of descent from a noble line. . . . But whenever he spoke, prayed, or thought he was alone, his squat body shot forth flames which reached the heavens: he became an archangel with red wings which he beat in the air. And if this happened at night when the flames were visible, you recoiled in terror to keep from being burned.

"Put yourself out, Brother Francis," I used to cry. "Put yourself out before you burn up the world."

Then, lifting my eyes, I would watch him as he headed directly for me, calm and smiling, his face once again characterized by human joy, bitterness, and penury. . . .

I remember once asking him, "Brother Francis, how does God reveal Himself to you when you are all alone in the darkness?"

And he answered me: "Like a glass of cool water, Brother Leo; like a glass of water from the fountain of everlasting youth. I'm thirsty, I drink it, and my thirst is quenched for all eternity."

"God like a glass of cool water?" I cried, astonished.

"And what did you think, Brother Leo? Why be alarmed? There is nothing simpler than God, nothing more refreshing, more suited to the lips of man."

But a few years later when Francis was a doubled-over lump of hair and bones, devoid of flesh, nearly breathing his last, he bent forward so that the friars would not hear him, and said to me, trembling, "God is a conflagration, Brother Leo. He burns, and we burn with Him."

As far as I can gauge his height in my mind, I can say only this with certitude: from the ground trodden by his feet, from there to his head, his stature was short; but from the head upward it was immense.

There are two parts of his body, however, which I do remember with perfect clarity: his feet and his eyes. I was a beggar, had spent my entire life among beggars, had seen thousands of feet which passed every day of their existence walking unshod over rocks, in dust, mud, upon the snow. But never in my life had I seen feet so distressed, so melancholy, feeble, gnawed away by journeys, so full of open wounds—as his. Sometimes when Father Francis lay sleeping I used to bend down stealthily and kiss them, and I felt as though I were kissing the total suffering of mankind.

And how could anyone forget his eyes after having once seen them? They were large, almond-shaped, black as pitch. They made you exclaim that you had never viewed eyes so tame, so velvety; but scarcely had you completed your thought when the eyes suddenly became two open trapdoors enabling you to look down at his vitals—heart, kidneys, lungs; whereupon you discovered that they were ablaze. He would often stare at you without seeing you. What did he see? Not your skin and flesh, not your head—but your skull. One day he caressed my face slowly with the palm of his hand. His eyes had become filled with compassion and sweetness, and he said,

"I like you, Brother Leo, I like you because you leave the worms free to stroll over your lips and ears; you do not chase them away."

"What worms, Father Francis? I don't see any worms."

"Surely you do see them when you are praying, or asleep and dreaming about Paradise. You see them but do not chase them away because you know full well, Brother Leo, that they are emissaries of God, of the Great King. God is holding a wedding in heaven, and he sends them with invitations for us: 'Greetings from the Great King, who awaits you. Come!' "

When Francis was among men he would laugh and frolic— would spring suddenly into the air and begin to dance, or would seize two sticks and play the "viol" while singing sacred songs he himself had composed. Doubtlessly he did so to encourage his companions, realizing perfectly well that the soul suffers, the body hungers, that man's endurance is nil. When he was alone, however, his tears began to flow. He would beat his chest, roll in the thorns and nettles, lift his hands to heaven and cry, "All day long I search for Thee desperately, Lord; all night long while I am asleep Thou searchest for me. O Lord, when, when, as night gives way to day, shall we meet?"

Another time I heard him cry, his eyes pinned on heaven: "I don't want to live any more. Undress me, Lord. Save me from my body. Take me!"

Each dawn, when the birds begin to sing again, or at midday when he plunged into the cooling shade of the forest, or at night, sitting in the moonlight or beneath the stars, he would shudder from inexpressible joy and gaze at me, his eyes filled with tears. "What miracles these are, Brother Leo!" he would say. "And He who created such beauty—what then must He be? What can we call Him?"

"God, Brother Francis," I answered.

"No, not God, not God," he cried. "That name is heavy, it crushes bones. . . . Not God—Father!"

One night Francis was roaming the lanes of Assisi. The moon had come up fully round and was suspended in the center of the heavens; the entire earth was floating buoyantly in the air. He looked, but could see no one standing in the doorways to enjoy the great miracle. Dashing to the church, he ascended the bell tower and began to toll the bell as though some calamity had taken place. The terrified people awoke with a start thinking there must be a fire, and ran half-naked to the courtyard of San Ruffino's, where they saw Francis ringing the bell furiously.

"Why are you ringing the bell?" they yelled at him. "What's happened?"

"Lift your eyes, my friends," Francis answered them from the top of the bell tower. "Lift your eyes; look at the moon!"

That was the kind of man Blessed Francis was; at least that was the way he appeared to me. I say this, but I am really not sure. How can I ever know what he was like, who he was? Is it possible that he himself did not know? I remember one wintery day when he was at the Portiuncula, sitting on the threshold sunning himself. A young man arrived, out of breath, and stood before him.

"Where is Francis, Bernardone's son?" he asked, his tongue hanging out of his mouth. "Where can I find the new saint so that I may fall at his feet? For months now I have been roaming the streets looking for him. For the love of Christ, my brother, tell me where he is."

"Where is Francis, Bernardone's son?" replied Francis, shaking his head. "Where is Francis, Bernardone's son? What is this Francis? Who is he? I am looking for him also, my brother. I have been looking for him now for years. Give me your hand and let us go find him!"

He rose, took the young man by the hand, and they departed.

That night when we first came together in Assisi how could I possibly have known what this youth was destined to become—this youth whom I had found serenading his lady, the long red feather in his cap? He held me tightly by the hand and we strode hurriedly across the city until we reached Bernardone's house.

We entered holding our breath lest the ogre hear us. Francis gave me food and I ate; he made up a bed for me and I slept. Awakening at dawn, I opened the front door noiselessly and slipped outside. It was Sunday. There was to be a High Mass at San Ruffino's and I went there in order to beg.

I seated myself on top of the stone lion, the one to the left as you face the church, and waited for the multitudes of Christians to appear. They had Sunday souls today. Heaven and hell were passing through their minds: they had fears, expectations—and they would open their purses to give to the poor.

I had removed my cap. From time to time coins fell into it with a tinkle. A half-crazy, aristocratic old lady bent over and asked me who I was, where I came from, and if I had seen her son. The Sienese cavalry—curse them!—had captured him during the wars.

But as I was about to open my mouth to answer, there in front of me was Sior Bernardone, Francis' father. I had known him for years, and never in his life had he given me anything. "You have arms and legs," he would scream at me. "Work!"

"I'm searching for God," I answered him one day.

"May the devil take you!" he thundered, and his clerks broke into peals of laughter.

Accompanied by his wife, Lady Pica, and advancing at a slow, majestic pace, he was coming to church now to attend the service. Good Lord, what a ferocious beast he was! He had on a long silk robe, dark scarlet with silver borders, a skullcap of black velvet, and black shoes with long, pointed toes. His left hand was raised to his breast, where it played with a cross which hung from a delicate golden chain. He was well preserved, vigorous, large-boned, so tall he scraped the ceiling, and had a heavy jawbone, double chins, a fat, crooked nose, and eyes that were gray and cold, like a hawk's.

As soon as I saw him I curled up into a ball so that he would not catch sight of me. Following behind him were five mules overloaded to the point of collapse with expensive merchandise: silks, velvet, gold piping, marvelous embroideries. The five muleteers who led them were armed because the roads had become thick with brigands. In other words, Bernardone was coming to church together with his goods so that they too could attend Mass, be seen by the statue of Saint Ruffino and thus be known to the Saint should they subsequently fall into danger. As was his custom before every journey, Bernardone was going to kneel before the Saint and haggle with him—you give me such and such and I'll give you such and such in return: you protect my merchandise, and I'll bring you a silver lamp from Florence, a heavy embossed one which will make you the envy of the other saints, who have nothing but tiny lamps made of glass.

At his side, walking with a proud gait, her hands crossed upon her abdomen, her eyes lowered, her hair covered with a sea-blue veil of silk, was Lady Pica, his French wife. She was beautiful, cheerful, sweetness itself; her face was the kind that gives alms. I held out my hand, but she did not see me—did not see me, or else was so afraid of the ogre at her side that she dared not give me anything. Husband and wife crossed the threshold, entering the church through the large central door, and disappeared.

Years later, when we were setting out one morning for a trip around the villages to preach love, Francis recalled his parents and sighed: "Alas, I still have not managed to reconcile them."

"Who? Who are you talking about, Brother Francis?"

"About my mother and father, Brother Leo. The two of them have been wrestling inside me for ages. This struggle has lasted my whole life—I want you to realize that. They may take on different names—God and Satan, spirit and flesh, good and bad, light and darkness—but they always remain my mother and father. My father cries within me: 'Earn money, get rich, use your gold to buy a coat of arms, become a nobleman. Only the rich and the nobility deserve to live in the world. Don't be good; once good, you're finished! If someone chips one tooth in your mouth, break his whole jaw in return. Do not try to make people love you; try to make them fear you. Do not forgive: strike!' . . . And my mother, her voice trembling within me, says to me softly, fearfully, lest my father hear her: 'Be good, dear Francis, and you shall have my blessing. You must love the poor, the humble, the oppressed. If someone injures you, forgive him!' My mother and my father wrestle within me, and all my life I have been struggling to reconcile them. But they refuse to become reconciled; they refuse to become reconciled, Brother Leo, and because of that, I suffer."

And truly, Sior Bernardone and Lady Pica had joined together inside Francis' breast and were tormenting him. But outside their son's breast each had his own separate body, and this Sunday, one next to the other, they had just entered church to do worship.

I closed my eyes. From within the building I could hear the fresh voices of the choirboys against the sound of the organ pouring forth from the heights of the choir loft and convulsing the air. This is God's voice, I was thinking; God's voice, and the severe, all-powerful voice of the people. . . . I continued to listen, happy, my eyes closed; and thus, astride the marble lion as I was, it seemed to me that I was a horseman entering Paradise. What else can Paradise be but gentle psalmody, sweet incense, and your sack filled with bread, olives, and wine? What else—because I, and may God forgive me for saying so, understand nothing of what the wise theologians declare about wings, spirits, and souls without bodies. If so much as a crumb falls to the ground, I bend over, pick it up, and kiss it because I know positively that this crumb is a little bit of Paradise. But only beggars can understand this, and it is to beggars that I am addressing myself.

While I was ambling through Paradise astride the marble lion, a shadow fell across me. I opened my eyes and saw Francis standing before me. The Mass was finished. I must have fallen asleep: the mules with their precious merchandise had vanished from the square in front of the church.

Francis stood before me livid, panic-stricken, his lips trembling, his eyes filled with visions. I heard his hoarse voice:

"Come, I need you."

He went in the lead, supporting himself on an ivory-hilted cane. From time to time his knees gave way beneath him and he had to cling to a wall.

"I'm ill," he said, turning. "Hold me up so that I can reach home and lie down. And stay near me; I have something to ask you."

In the square the tightrope walkers had finished driving their poles and stretching out their ropes. They were dressed in motley and had pointed red caps with bells. Today being Sunday they were preparing to display their skill and then to pass the hat. Old men and simple peasant women, their baskets in their laps, were sitting cross-legged on the ground and selling chickens, eggs, cheese, medicinal herbs, balms for wounds, amulets against the evil eye. One crafty graybeard offered to tell your fortune by means of a white mouse he had in a cage.

"Stop and have your fortune read, Sior Francis," I said. "I've heard these mice come from Paradise—even Paradise has mice, you know, which explains why they're white. They know many secrets."

But Francis was clutching one of the poles, breathing with difficulty. I supported him on my arm and we reached Sior Bernardone's house.

Good Lord, how can the rich bear to die! What marble staircases, what rooms, all with gilded ceilings, what sheets of linen and silk! I laid him down on his bed and he closed his eyes at once, exhausted.

As I bent over him I saw alternate flashes of light and shadow cross his pale face; his eyelids kept fluttering as though being wounded by an intense brightness. I had a premonition that some terrifying, visible presence was above him.

Finally he uttered a cry, opened his eyes, and sat up in bed, horror-stricken. I quickly got a feather pillow which I placed behind him as a support for his back. I had begun to part my lips to ask him what was wrong, what had frightened him so, but he reached out his hand and placed it over my mouth.

"Quiet," he whispered, and he thrust himself into the feather pillow. He was shivering. The pupils of his eyes had disappeared; the eyeballs had rolled downward and were gazing fearfully into his very bowels. His jaw was trembling.

At that point I understood at once. "You saw God," I cried. "You saw God!"

He seized my arm and gasped in anguish: "How do you know? Who told you?"

"No one. But I see how you're shaking, and I know. When a person shakes that way it means he's either seen a lion in front of him, or God."

He pulled his head forcefully up from the pillow. "No, I didn't see Him," he murmured. "I heard Him."

He looked around him with frightened eyes. "Sit down," he said to me. "Don't put your hands on me, don't touch me!"

"I'm not touching you. I'm afraid to touch you. If I had been touching you at that moment my hand would have been reduced to ashes."

He shook his head and smiled. The pupils of his eyes had reappeared. "I have something to ask you," he said. "Has my mother returned from Mass?"

"Not yet. She must be chatting with her friends."

"So much the better. Shut the door." He remained silent for a moment, but then repeated: "I have something to ask you."

"I'm at your command, sir. Proceed."

"You told me that your whole life you've been searching for God. How have you done this? By calling, weeping, singing songs, fast-

33

ing? Each man must have his own special route to lead him to God. Which route did you take? That is my question."

I lowered my head in thought. Should I tell him or shouldn't I? I had meditated on this many times and knew which my route was, but I was ashamed to reveal it. To be sure, I was still ashamed before men at that period, because I was not yet ashamed before God.

"Why don't you answer me?" Francis complained. "I am passing through a difficult moment and seek your aid. Help me!"

I felt sorry for him. With agitated heart I made the decision to tell him everything.

"My route, Sior Francis—and don't be surprised when you hear it—my route when I set out to find God . . . was . . . laziness. Yes, laziness. If I wasn't lazy I would have gone the way of respectable, upstanding people. Like everyone else I would have studied a trade—cabinetmaker, weaver, mason—and opened a shop; I would have worked all day long, and where then would I have found time to search for God? I might as well be looking for a needle in a haystack: that's what I would have said to myself. All my mind and thoughts would have been occupied with how to earn my living, feed my children, how to keep the upper hand over my wife. With such worries, curse them, how could I have had the time, or inclination, or the pure heart needed to think about the Almighty?

"But by the grace of God I was born lazy. To work, get married, have children, and make problems for myself were all too much trouble. I simply sat in the sun during winter and in the shade during summer, while at night, stretched out on my back on the roof of my house, I watched the moon and the stars. And when you watch the moon and the stars how can you expect your mind not to dwell on God? I couldn't sleep any more. Who made all that? I asked myself. And why? Who made me, and why? Where can I find God so that I may ask Him? Piety requires laziness, you know. It requires leisure—and don't listen to what others say. The laborer who lives from hand to mouth returns home each night exhausted and famished. He assaults his dinner, bolts his food, then quarrels with his wife, beats his children without rhyme or reason simply because he's tired and irritated, and afterwards he clenches his fists and sleeps. Waking up for a moment he finds his wife at his side, couples

34

with her, clenches his fists once more, and plunges back into sleep. . . . Where can he find time for God? But the man who is without work, children, and wife thinks about God, at first just out of curiosity, but later with anguish. Do not shake your head, Sior Francis. You asked and I answered. Forgive me."

"Speak on, speak on, Brother Leo, don't stop. It's true then, is it, that the devil hoodwinks God, that laziness hoodwinks God? You're very encouraging, Brother Leo. Speak on."

"What more can I tell you, Sior Francis? You know the rest. My parents had left me a little something; I exhausted it. Then I took to the road with my sack, began going from door to door, monastery to monastery, village to village, searching for God, asking 'Where is He?' . . . 'Who has seen Him?' . . . 'Where can I find Him?' as though He were some ferocious beast I had gone out to hunt. Some laughed, some threw stones at me, still others knocked me down and beat me to a pulp. But I always jumped to my feet again and set out once more in pursuit of God."

"And did you find Him, did you find Him?" Francis gasped. I felt his warm breath upon my skin.

"How could I possibly find Him, sir? I asked every kind of person: sages, saints, madmen, prelates, troubadours, centenarians. Each gave me advice: showed me a path, saying 'Take it and you'll find Him!' But each showed me a different path. Which was I to choose? I was going out of my wits. A sage from Bologna said to me, 'The road which leads to God is that of wife and children. Get married.' Someone else, a madman and saint from Gubbio, said, 'If you want to find God, don't look for Him. If you want to see Him, close your eyes; to hear Him, stop up your ears. That's what I do.' Having said this, he shut his eyes, stopped up his ears, crossed his hands, and began to weep. . . . And a woman who lived as a hermit in the forest ran stark naked under the pine trees striking her breasts and shouting, 'Love! Love! Love!' That was the only answer she was able to give.

"Another day I came across a saint in a cave. Excessive weeping had blinded him; his skin was all scales, the result of sanctity and uncleanliness. He gave me the advice that was both most correct and most frightening. When I weigh it in my mind my hair stands on end."

"What advice? I want to hear it!" said Francis, seizing my hand. He was trembling.

"I bowed down, prostrated myself before him, and said, 'Holy ascetic, I have set out to find God. Show me the road.'

" 'There isn't any road,' he answered me, beating his staff on the ground.

" 'What is there, then?' I asked, seized with terror.

" 'There is the abyss. Jump!'

" 'Abyss?' I screamed. 'Is that the way?'

" 'Yes, the abyss. All roads lead to the earth; the abyss leads to God. Jump!'

" 'I can't, Father.'

" 'Then get married and forget your troubles,' he said, and stretching forth his skeleton-like arm he motioned me to leave. As I departed I could hear his lamentations in the distance."

"Did they all weep?" murmured Francis, terrified. "All? Those who had found God as well as those who had not?"

"All."

"Why, Brother Leo?"

"I don't know. But they all wept."

We remained silent. Francis had buried his face in the pillow; he was breathing fitfully.

"Listen, Sior Francis, it seems to me that I did see a trace of Him once or twice," I said in order to comfort him. "Once, when I was drunk, I caught sight of His back for a moment. It was in a tavern where I was having a good time with my friends, and He had just opened the door to leave. Another time I was going through the woods; there was rain and lightning, and I just managed to catch a glimpse of the edge of His garment as it was illuminated by a lightning flash. But then the flash expired, the garment vanished. Or was it possible that the lightning itself was His garment? Still another time, last winter in fact, I saw His footprints in the snow atop a high mountain. A shepherd came by. 'Look, God's footprints!' I said to him. But he replied with a laugh: 'You're out of your mind, poor fellow. Those are a wolf's tracks; a wolf passed by here.' I kept quiet. What was I to say to this thickheaded bumpkin with his brain filled with sheep and wolves? How could he ever understand anything higher! As for me, I was certain those were God's footprints upon the snow. . . . I've been pursuing Him for

36

twelve years, Sior Francis, but these are the only signs I've found. Forgive me."

Lowering his head, Francis plunged deep into thought. "Do not sigh, Brother Leo," he murmured after a moment. "Who knows, perhaps God is simply the search for God."

These words frightened me. They frightened Francis also. He hid his face in his hands.

"What demon is speaking within me?" he growled in despair.

I didn't breathe a word, but stood there trembling. To search for God, was that God? If so, woe unto us!

Neither of us spoke. Francis' eyes had rolled in their sockets again; I saw only the whites. His cheeks were flushed, his teeth chattering. I covered him with a thick woolen blanket, but he tossed it aside. "I want to be cold," he said. "Leave me! Don't stare at me; do your staring somewhere else!"

I got up to depart, but his expression grew fierce. "Where are you going?" he said to me. "Sit down! Do you plan to leave me all alone like this when I'm in danger? You spoke, you found relief. Now I want to speak, I want to find relief. Where's your mind—on food? Eat then, go to the larder and eat. And drink some wine. What I'm going to tell you is very unpleasant. Fortify yourself so that you'll be able to listen. Do not desert me!"

"I have no need to eat or drink," I answered, hurt. "What do you think I am, nothing but stomach? To listen—that's what I was born for, I want you to know; just for that: to listen. So go ahead and speak. No matter what you say, I'll be able to bear it."

"Give me a glass of water. I'm thirsty."

He drank, then leaned back on his pillow, cocked his ear, and listened intently, his mouth half open. The house was silent, empty. A rooster crowed in the courtyard.

"I think none but the two of us is left in the world, Brother Leo. Do you hear anyone inside the house, or outside? The world has been destroyed and only the two of us remain."

He was silent for a moment, but then he said, "Glory be to God," crossed himself, and looked at me. I felt his gaze pierce deep down into my soul. After another silence he reached out and grasped my knee. "Bless me, Father Leo," he said. "You are my confessor; I am about to confess."

Seeing me hesitate, he said in a commanding tone, "Place your hand upon my head, Father Leo, and say, 'Francis, son of Bernardone, you have sinned: confess, in God's name. Your heart is filled with sins. Empty it that you may find relief!' "

I remained silent.

"Do what I tell you!" he said, angrily this time.

I placed my hand on his head. It was a burning, smoldering coal.

"Francis, son of Bernardone," I murmured, "you have sinned: confess, in God's name. Your heart is filled with sins. Empty it that you may find relief!"

Then, remaining calm in the beginning but as he proceeded growing more and more agitated until finally he was gasping for breath, Francis began his confession:

"My life until now has been nothing but banquets, revels, lutes, red plumes, clothes of silk. All day long—business. I gave short measure, cheated the customers, amassed money and then squandered it with both hands—which is why I came to be called 'Leaky Palms.' Business by day, wine and singing by night: that was my life.

"But yesterday after we came home in the middle of the night and you fell into bed and slept, a great weight began to press down upon me. The house grew too constricting; I felt suffocated, so I went quietly downstairs, slipped into the yard, opened the street door like a thief, and dashed out into the road. The moon was about to set; its light had already waned. There wasn't a sound. All the lamps were out: the city was asleep in God's bosom.

"I spread my arms and took a deep breath. This made me feel a little better. Then I began climbing, going from street to street. By the time I reached San Ruffino's I was tired, so I sat down on the marble lion that guards the entrance to the church, just exactly where you were sitting to beg when I came upon you this morning. I stroked the lion slowly with my palm and, reaching his mouth, found the tiny man that he is eating.

"This frightened me. What is this lion? I asked myself. Why was he placed here to guard the church door? Eating a man as he is, who can he be: God? Satan? How can I know? Who can tell me whether he is God or Satan? Suddenly I felt a chasm to my right, a chasm to my left, and I was standing between the double abyss, on a piece of ground no wider than a footprint. I became dizzy. The world around me was whirling; my life was whirling. I uttered a cry: 'Is there no one to hear me? Am I all alone in the world? Where is God? Doesn't He hear; doesn't He have a hand to hold out over my head? I feel dizzy. I am going to fall!' "

Francis had spread his arms wider and wider as he spoke: he was suffocating, unable to breathe. He had also raised his eyes and was now staring out through the window at the sky. I started to take hold of his hand in order to calm him, but he sprang back and growled in an agitated voice: "Leave me alone. I don't want to be soothed!" Then he rolled up in the corner of the bed, panting. His voice had grown hoarse:

"I called, first God, then Satan, not caring which of the two would appear, just so I could feel I was no longer alone. Why had this fear of solitude come over me so suddenly? I was ready at that moment to surrender my soul to either of them. I didn't care which; all I wanted was to have a companion—not to be alone! And as I waited, gazing desperately at the heavens, I heard a voice—"

He stopped, unable to catch his breath.

"I heard a voice—" he repeated, the sweat suddenly beginning to run in thick drops over his face.

"A voice?" I asked. "What voice, Francis? What did it say?"

"I couldn't make out the words. No, it wasn't a voice; it was the bellowing of a wild beast—a lion. Could it have been the marble man-eating lion I was sitting on? . . . I jumped to my feet. The first sweet light of dawn had begun to shine. The voice was still rolling about within me, rebounding like peals of thunder from my heart to my kidneys, from one cavern of my bowels to another. The bells began to sound for matins. I continued on, headed for the heights of the citadel. Soon I was running, and, while I was running, I found myself suddenly bathed in a cold sweat. I heard someone behind me calling: 'Where are you running, Francis? Where are you running, Francis? You cannot escape!' I turned, but saw no one. I began to run again. After a moment I heard the voice once more: 'Francis, Francis, is this why you were born—to sing, make merry, and entice the girls?'

"This time I was too afraid to look behind me. I continued running in an effort to escape the voice. But then a stone in front of me began to shout: 'Francis, Francis, is this why you were born—to sing, make merry, and entice the girls?'

"My hair stood on end. I ran and ran, but the voice ran with me.

39

And then at last I understood clearly: the voice was not outside me. No matter how much I ran I would never escape it, because it came from within. Someone inside me was shouting. Not Bernardone's son, the libertine; no, not me, but someone else—someone inside me, better than me. Who? I don't know. How can I know? It was just someone else. . . .

"Gasping for breath, I finally reached the citadel. At that very moment the sun emerged from behind the mountain, and it warmed me. The world about me grew light, and it too was warmed. Someone within me began to speak again, but this time very softly, in whispers, as though confiding some secret to me. I lowered my head upon my breast and listened. Father Leo, I swear to you I am telling the truth, the whole truth. 'Francis, Francis,' I heard, 'your soul is the dove, the hawk pursuing you is Satan. Come into my bosom.' These were the very words I myself had composed and set to the music of the lute. Each midnight I had stood beneath a window and sung them. But now, now for the first time, Brother Leo, I understood why I had composed those words and what their hidden meaning was."

He remained silent for a moment, a smile upon his lips. Then, as though in a trance, he bowed his head and repeated in a whisper: "Francis, Francis, your soul is the dove, the hawk pursuing you is Satan. Come into my bosom."

Once more he fell silent. He had grown calm; I felt I could touch him now without being burned. Leaning forward, I took his hand and kissed it. "Brother Francis," I said, "every man, even the most atheistic, has God within him deep down in his heart, wrapped in layers of flesh and fat. It was God inside you who pushed aside the flesh and fat and called to you."

Francis closed his eyes. He had lain awake the whole night and was sleepy.

"Go to sleep, Francis," I said to him softly. "Sleep is one of God's angels; you can surrender yourself to it with confidence."

But he drew himself up with a start. "What am I to do now?" he asked in a stifled voice, his eyes protruding out of their sockets. "Advise me."

I felt sorry for him. Hadn't I been roaming for years now in the very same way, seeking advice?

"Keep your head against your breast and listen to your heart,"

I answered. "This 'Someone Else' inside you will definitely speak again. When He does, do what He tells you."

I heard the street door being opened quietly, then firm footsteps echoing in the courtyard. Lady Pica was returning from Mass—alone. I sighed with relief. Sior Bernardone must have mounted his horse and was probably already on the road to Florence. "Your mother is back, Francis," I said. "Go to sleep. I'm leaving."

"Don't go. The old man is away. You'll sleep here. Don't leave me alone, I tell you!"

He seized my hand. "Don't leave me alone in danger!" he shouted.

"You're not alone any more, Francis. You know that! A mighty companion is within you; you heard His voice. What are you afraid of?"

"But don't you understand, Brother Leo? It's precisely Him I'm afraid of. Don't go."

I placed my hand on his forehead. It was burning. His mother entered, smiling.

"I bring you greetings from the statue of the Virgin, my child. May they be a comfort and bolster to your soul."

This said, she placed a sprig of basil in his palm.

HOW MANY DAYS, how many nights did Francis' sickness last? I am able to measure everything, but not time. All I remember is that the moon grew small, grew large and then small again—and Francis still had not left his bed. You felt he was wrestling in his sleep. One moment he would cry out in a rage and spring up; the next he would shrink into one corner of the bed, shivering. Later, when he became well, he informed us that during his entire sickness he had been struggling, first with the Saracens—he saw himself entering Jerusalem, clutching the Holy Cross on his shoulder; then with demons that rose from the soil, descended from the trees, darted out from the bowels of night, pursuing him.

His mother and I were the only ones who remained at his bedside. Lady Pica would get up at intervals, hide herself in a corner, and weep. Then she would wipe her eyes with her tiny white handkerchief, sit down again, take up a fan of peacock feathers, and cool her son, who was burning with fever.

One night the patient had a dream. He related it to us the next day, not in the morning—the disturbance still upset his mind—but in the evening, after the cool darkness had fallen and the bronze oil lamps were lighted and the world about us had grown sweet. He had dreamt he was dying. As he lay in the throes of his final agony the door opened and Death entered. He wasn't holding a scythe, the way Francis had seen him depicted on paintings, but a pair of long iron pincers like those used by wardens to catch rabid dogs. "Get up, son of Bernardone," he cried, approaching the bed. "Let us go!"

"Where?"

"Where? Need you ask? You had time but you squandered it in parties, extravagant clothes, serenades. The hour of reckoning has come."

He held out the pincers. Francis huddled against his pillows, trembling. "Let me have one year," he whined. "Just one year! Give me time to repent."

Death laughed, and all his teeth fell out onto the sheets of linen and silk. "Too late. You lived your life, the only one you have. You gambled it and lost. Now come!"

"Three months only . . . one month . . . three days . . . one day!"

But this time Death did not answer. Holding out the pincers, he caught Francis around the neck—but then, uttering a heart-rending scream, the dreamer awoke.

He looked around him. The canary that Lady Pica had brought from her room to keep the patient company was singing from its place by the window, its beak lifted to the sky.

"Glory be to God!" Francis shouted happily, sweat running down his forehead. He touched the sheets, the iron bedstead, then began to explore his mother's knees.

"Is it true?" he murmured, turning to me, his eyes shining. "Is it true? Am I alive?"

"Have no fears, my young lord," I answered. "You are alive and flourishing."

He clapped his hands. His face was resplendent.

"In other words, I have time. Praise the Lord!" Laughing, he began to kiss his mother's hands.

"Did you have a dream, my son?" his mother asked. "I hope it was a good omen."

"I have time," he murmured again, carried away with emotion. "Praise the Lord! I have time!"

The whole of that day, until evening, he did not speak again. Closing his eyes, he fell into a deep sleep. His neck and entire face were flooded with light.

Lady Pica continued to fan him with the peacock feathers. Suddenly she parted her embittered lips. Remembering how she used to lull her son to sleep when he was a baby, she began to sing to him in her native tongue, softly . . . sweetly . . .

43

> *Sleep, who taketh every babe,*
> *Come down and take my own.*
> *I give him to you tiny, tiny,*
> *Return him to me grown.*

She sang softly in this way for a long time, fanning her child; meanwhile, I leaned over Francis and gazed at his face. How it gleamed! Little by little the wrinkles around his mouth and between his eyebrows vanished, his skin became as firm as a tiny infant's. His whole countenance glittered like a stone which is swept over by a cool, calm sea.

Toward evening he opened his eyes. He was rested and tranquil. Sitting up in bed, he looked around him as though seeing the world for the first time. When his gaze fell upon us he smiled and began to tell us his dream. But while he was relating it, the old fear began to take possession of him again, and his eyes filled with darkness. His mother took his hand, caressed it, and he grew calm.

"Mother," he said, "just now as I was asleep I had the feeling I was a baby and that you were rocking me and singing me a lullaby. It seems to me, Mother, that you have given birth to me all over again!" He took her hand and kissed it. His voice had become like a child's: hungry for caresses.

"Mother, Mama dear, tell me a story."

He had begun to lisp. Suddenly his whole face resembled an infant's. Lady Pica became frightened. One of her brothers, a celebrated troubadour at Avignon and a *bon vivant* and spendthrift just like Francis, had lost his reason by virtue of excessive drink and song. Overcome by the delusion that he was a lamb, he crawled about awkwardly on all fours, bleated, went to the fields to graze. . . . And now here was her son who appeared to have returned to infancy and was requesting her to tell him a story! Was it possible, she asked herself, begging God's forgiveness for her presumption, was it possible that her blood was tainted, besotted?

"What story, my child?" she demanded, touching his forehead to cool him.

"Any one you want. A story from your country—about Peter, the wild, barefooted monk."

"Which Peter?"

44

"The heresiarch of Lyons."

"But that isn't a story, it's true!"

"You used to tell it to me very often when I was a boy, and I always thought it was a story. I was just as afraid of that saintly monster as I was of the bogeyman. Whenever I did something wrong —don't you remember?—you used to threaten me by saying, 'Now the monk will come and get you!' and I would huddle under an armchair and not breathe a word, scared he might find me and carry me off."

"You told stories about Peter of Lyons, the celebrated monk?" I interrupted at that point. "Did you know him, Lady Pica? So many things are said about him—incredible, amazing things. Madam, I pray of you, humble beggar that I am, tell us if you ever saw or met him? What was he like? I myself set out to find him once, but I arrived too late. He was dead."

Francis smiled. "She threw away her sandals," he said to tease his mother. "Apparently she wanted to follow him, barefooted and all, but they didn't let her. Instead, they shut her in the house, married her off, and she had a son and forgot about everything. You see, she was looking for a son, and not for God."

He laughed. But Lady Pica was annoyed.

"I never forgot him; it's just that I have other worries now," she said with a sigh. "How can I forget him? I still dream about him often."

"Tell us how you first met him, Mother," said Francis, leaning back against the pillows. He had slept the whole day and his body felt deliciously rested. He closed his eyes.

"I'm listening. . . ."

Lady Pica had turned red as fire. She remained silent for some time with her head inclined upon her breast, her eyelids fluttering like the wings of a wounded bird. It was evident that this monk was deep down within her, buried in the darkness of her heart, and that she neither dared nor desired to hoist him up into the light. At last she asked her son imploringly, "Wouldn't you like me to tell you a real story, my child?"

Francis opened his eyes.

"No! Tell us about Peter," he said with a frown. "I don't want anything else! How you first met him, when, where, and what he

45

said to you, and how you escaped. I've heard a great many things about him, but I don't believe them. Now the time has come—I want to know the truth!"

He turned to me.

"Everyone has a hidden period in his life," he said. "This is my mother's."

"Very well, son, I'll tell you everything," said Lady Pica in a voice which betrayed her agitation. "Quiet down now."

She laid her hands in her lap. Her fingers, which were slender and graceful like her son's, began to fidget nervously with the white handkerchief she held between her palms.

"It was evening, Saturday evening . . ." she began, speaking slowly, as though struggling to remember. "I had been strolling in the courtyard of our house watering the plants—the basil, marjoram, marigolds. A red geranium had blossomed that afternoon and I was standing in front of it and admiring it when suddenly someone gave a strong push to the street door and entered. I turned, frightened, and saw a wild-looking monk standing before me. His robe was patched and tattered, a thick rope served as his cincture, and he was barefooted.

"I began to open my mouth to scream, but he placed his palm over my lips. 'Peace be to this house!' he said, lifting his hand and blessing the house. His voice was heavy, savage; but somewhere in its very center I felt an inexpressible tenderness. I tried to ask him who he was, what he wanted, why he was so out of breath, who was pursuing him, but my throat was pinched tight and no sound came out.

"'Yes, I'm being pursued,' he said—he had divined my question from the movements of my lips. 'I'm being pursued by the enemies of Christ. Haven't you heard of me? I am Peter the monk, the one who raised the tattered banner with the white lilies—Christ's banner; the one who goes the rounds of cities and villages, barefooted and hungry, and who took the scourge from Jesus' hands and uses it now to drive all fornicators, liars, and cheats out of God's temple.'

"He was still talking when I heard a great uproar in the street. A large crowd was passing by, banging on doors, hooting, threatening. The bell of our parish church began to ring furiously.

"Clenching his fist, the monk turned toward the street door and

46

contorted his lips sarcastically. 'They've smelled Him in the air,' he growled, 'smelled Christ, their great enemy, and now they're running like mad to crucify Him again. Hey, you Pilates, you Caiaphases, He's coming, He's coming; the Day of Judgment is at hand!'

"The mob went by, not daring to knock on our door, then headed for the bridge and disappeared. I remained all alone with the monk in our yard. He was staring at me, a strange anger and tenderness in his gaze. Trembling, I kept my eyes glued on the red geranium. A force gushed out of this savage monk, and I was unable to bear it. All of a sudden he seized the geranium and gave it a twist which sent all its petals to the ground. I cried out and my eyes filled with tears, but he only knitted his thick brows:

"'Aren't you ashamed to lose your soul by regarding the creatures instead of the Creator? All the beauties of the earth prevent us from seeing the Invisible, and thus they must perish.'"

Francis had been listening with lowered head up to this point. Now he looked up suddenly. His cheeks were on fire.

"No, no, no!" he shouted.

He turned toward me.

"What do you think, Brother Leo?"

"What can I say, sir? I'm a cloddish sort of fellow and to believe in anything I have to see, hear, and touch it. Only after I've seen the visible can I imagine what the Invisible is. If there were nothing visible, I'd be doomed."

"Beauty is God's daughter," said Francis as he gazed out through the open window at the yard, the vine arbor, the scattered white clouds that were cruising in the sky. "Beauty is God's daughter: that I'm sure of. The only way we can divine the appearance of God's face is by looking at beautiful things. The geranium that was despoiled of its petals by your monk, Mama, is going to hurl him into hell."

"But he did it to save my soul," Lady Pica objected. "What is a geranium next to a human soul? My monk, as you call him, is going to enter Paradise with that red geranium in his hand, simply because he saved my soul."

"What? He saved your soul?" said Francis, staring at his mother with surprise. "But didn't your father come along and throw him out, putting an end to everything? That's what you told me before, and now— Why didn't you tell me the truth?"

"Because you wouldn't have understood when you were a child, and if I had told you when you grew older you would have laughed. But now that you've fallen ill and the ardor of your flesh has been subdued a little, my child, you can hear God's secret messages without laughing. That is why I have decided to tell you now."

"Speak, Mama, speak," said Francis in an agitated voice. "No, I am not going to laugh. I may even begin to cry. The moment has come—yes, you're right, Mama—the moment has come for me to hear."

Scarcely had he finished these words when he burst into tears.

"Why are you crying, my child? Why are you trembling so?" asked his frightened mother, embracing him.

"Because I feel your blood inside me, Mama, your blood . . ."

Lady Pica took her handkerchief and wiped the sweat from her temples and neck. She glanced at me, hesitating for a moment as though not wanting to speak in front of me. I got up.

"Would you rather I left, madam? I'm going."

Francis extended his hand commandingly.

"Stay. You're not going anywhere! Mother, don't feel ashamed. Speak."

I looked at Lady Pica. Her eyebrows quivered. She threw a cutting glance at me: she was weighing me in her mind.

"Stay," she said finally. "I have nothing to be ashamed of. My heart is pure: I shall speak."

"Well . . . ?" said Francis, looking at his mother impatiently.

"The monk placed his hand on my head and I felt a flame descend to my brain, invade my throat, burn my entrails. What was this flame? It made me feel like bursting into tears, like beginning to dance in the middle of the yard, or rushing out into the street, throwing away my sandals and taking to the road, never again to return to my father's house. I was burning. What was this flame? He must be God, he must be God, I shouted to myself. This is the way God enters men."

Lady Pica's cheeks and throat were afire. Rising, she got the crystal decanter of water that was on the window sill, filled a glass, and drank. Then she refilled the glass and drank again, as though trying to extinguish the flames within her.

"And then?" asked Francis, unable to contain himself any longer.

Lady Pica bowed her head.

"Then, my child, I took leave of my senses. My father's house wasn't big enough for me any more, and when the monk opened the door and stood there and motioned me to come, I threw my sandals into the middle of the yard and ran behind him."

Francis stared at her with protruding eyes. He attempted to speak, but was unable to. I watched him anxiously, trying unsuccessfully to determine what was exciting and contorting his face so. Was it fear, or joy, or scorn—or all three, one following upon the other? Or was it all three simultaneously that made his face turn livid one moment, the flames extinguished, and the next begin to burn and smoke again, fiery red?

At last he managed to move his lips and speak. "You left? You went with him, abandoned your home?"

"Yes," replied Lady Pica in a voice that was calm and relieved. "I was sixteen years old at the time. My heart was open, ready to accept all miracles, and that evening God appeared to me, appeared to me in the form He wished. To some young girls He appears in the guise of a handsome young nobleman; to me it was as a mendicant monk, savage and barefooted. I ran behind him as we made a quick tour of the villages. He spoke to me of poverty, chastity, of heaven and hell, and the earth fled from under my naked soles: I gave it a kick and, together with the monk, mounted to heaven.

"We climbed up mountains, climbed down mountains; we entered the villages, the two of us, like great conquerors. He would stand in the village square, hop onto a stone, raise his arm, and hurl curses upon the heads of all the atheists, cheats, and rulers of the world. And when night came, I would stand in front of him and illuminate his terrible face with a lighted torch so that the villagers could see it and be overcome with fear.

"In the meantime my father had dispatched knights who combed the villages and mountains in every direction until they found me. My brother was among them. He seized me, lifted me onto his horse's rump, and brought me home."

Lady Pica stopped for a moment, looked at her son, and smiled at him.

"A few days later I was married."

Francis closed his eyes. Neither of us opened his mouth to speak;

and then, in the great silence, we heard the canary singing rapturously, its head thrown back toward the sky. It must have been chirping the whole time its mistress spoke, but we had not heard it: our minds had become filled with a panting, barefooted girl as she ran behind her savage monk.

Suddenly Francis opened his eyes.

"Go away, both of you! I want to be alone." His voice had become hoarse, grating.

Without breathing a word, his mother and I got up, opened the door, and left.

That whole night Francis allowed no one to enter his room. We could hear him sighing and, from time to time, rising to open the window and get some fresh air.

In the morning I heard him calling me: "Brother Leo!"

I ran and found him stretched out supine on the sheets, throbbing convulsively. His face was waxen.

"I'm doomed, Brother Leo," he said without turning to look at me. "On my right is God's abyss, on my left Satan's. Unless I grow wings, I'm doomed. I shall fall!"

"What's the matter with you, Francis?" I asked, clasping him in my arms. "Why are you quivering?"

"My mother's blood," he murmured, "my mother's blood . . . Didn't you hear? Madness!"

"It wasn't madness that prodded her, Francis. It was God."

"Madness! The whole night long I dreamt that I too had thrown off my sandals in my father's courtyard and that I was plummeting downward. I held out my hand to catch hold of something, but all I grasped was thin air!"

He had jerked his arms above his head and was opening and closing them, embracing the air.

I caressed his forehead, rubbing it slowly. He grew calm little by little, and leaned his head upon his breast like a wounded bird. Soon he was asleep.

I watched him, trying to divine what was parading in and out of his heart now that sleep had opened all the doors. Why did his face become altered from moment to moment? Sometimes his eyebrows rose in astonishment; sometimes his lips sagged in an expression of unspeakable affliction; sometimes an effulgence fell over his entire face and his eyelids fluttered as though incapable of enduring such brightness.

Suddenly he reached out his hands and clutched my arm, terrified.

"Brother Leo, is that you? Did you see him?"

"Who?"

"He dissolved into the air just now. He's still in the room!"

"But who, sir? It must have been a dream."

"No, no, it wasn't a dream. Brother Leo, does something exist which is truer than truth itself? That's what it was!"

He sat up in bed and began to rub his eyes.

"You think I was asleep, don't you? I wasn't asleep. The doors were closed but he entered, groping like a blind man, his arms stretched out in front of him. He was dressed in rags, thousands of rags with thousands of patches; and he smelled of rotting flesh. He reached my bed, searched, found me:

"'Are you Sior Bernardone's pampered son?'

"'I am,' I answered, trembling.

"'Come then, get up, undress me, wash me, give me something to eat.' He wasn't imploring; he was commanding.

"'Who are you?'

"'First undress me, wash me, give me something to eat.'

"I rose and began to undress him. What rags, good God, what patches, what a stink! And his body, now that he was naked and I could see it, how shattered it was! And the feet: swollen and covered with hundreds of wounds! His head was thrust in a hood which I took off, revealing the temples, which were furrowed with lines made by a white-hot iron. And on his forehead he had a red wound shaped like a cross. But what horrified me the most were the large, bloody holes in his hands and feet. 'Who are you?' I asked again, staring at him with disgust and fear. 'Wash me!' was his answer. I went and heated water, washed him. Afterwards, he sat down on the trunk, the same one you're sitting on now, and said: 'Now I want to eat!' I brought him a large plate of food. He bent down, took a fistful of ashes from the hearth, threw them over the food and began to eat. When he had finished he got up and clasped my hand. His face had grown calm; he gazed at me with tenderness, compassion. 'Now you are my brother,' he said. 'If

51

you bend over me you will see your own face; if I bend over you I shall see my own face. You are my brother. Farewell.'

" 'Where are you going?'

" 'Wherever you shall go! Farewell, until we meet again!'

"As soon as he said this he vanished, dissolved into thin air. His smell is still in the room! Who was he? Who? . . . What do you think, Brother Leo?"

Without answering, I shifted my position on the trunk for fear I might touch the invisible visitor. Who could he have been—a messenger from the dark demons? A messenger from the luminous powers? There was only one thing I felt sure of: in the air around this rich young man a great battle was taking place.

Three more days went by. The blood started to flow up into Francis' pale cheeks, his joints grew firm, his lips reddened, the flesh began to hunger and ask for food. And as his body was set on its legs once more, so was his soul, and with it, the world. The yard, well, vine arbor, the utensils around the room, the voices outside in the street, the constellations in the sky at night—all reappeared and arranged themselves in the places given them by time and God. The world, together with Francis' blood, was returning to its normal order.

The fourth day, at dawn, the bells of San Ruffino began to ring, and Lady Pica started for church, followed by the old nanny. Sior Bernardone had not yet returned from his tour. The bells rang festively because this day, the twenty-third of September, was the feast of San Damiano, the beloved saint of Assisi. His tiny church lay outside the city on the slope leading to the plain. It was falling gradually into ruins now, but once it had been in its glory, and each year on this day a rollicking festival had taken place there and the saint's statue had been covered with gold and silver offerings. Now the walls were tottering, full of gaping holes. The only thing that remained intact was the crucifix, a large Byzantine cross with a bloody, pale-green Christ hanging on it. There was something strangely sweet about this Christ, a sadness that was not divine, but human. You sensed He was weeping, dying like a human being, and thus the faithful who knelt before Him shuddered at the sight, for they felt it was they themselves who were suspended upon the cross, convulsed with pain.

I had entered Francis' room early in the morning. Lady Pica had set aside, as long as her husband remained away, a tiny room where I could sleep and be near her son, because he asked for me continually during his illness and did not want me to stray far from his side. Today I found him sitting up in bed. He was happy. His eyes pinned on the door, he had been waiting for me.

"Come in, come in, lion of God," he called as soon as he saw me. "I see you've combed your mane today and twisted your mustache in a most lion-hearted way. And you're licking your chops. You've eaten, I take it."

"Your mother, God bless her, sent the nanny to me with bread, cheese, and milk before she left for church. . . . Yes, my young lord—how can I describe the feeling to you?—I *am* beginning to turn into a lion, so help me God."

He laughed.

"Sit down," he said to me, pointing to the delicately carved trunk next to the bed.

The canary began to sing again. The sun had struck it, and its throat and tiny breast had filled with song. Francis gazed at it for a long time, not speaking, his mouth hanging half-opened, his eyes dimmed with tears.

"The canary is like man's soul," he whispered finally. "It sees bars around it, but instead of despairing, it sings. It sings, and wait and see, Brother Leo: one day its song shall break the bars."

I smiled. Would that the bars could be broken so easily!

But when Francis saw my smile, he grew bitter. "What? You don't believe me?" he said. "In other words, it never occurred to you to ask yourself whether the body—bones, hair, flesh—really exists, or whether perhaps everything is soul?"

"Never, Francis, never. Forgive me. I am a cloddish sort of man, I tell you, and my mind is cloddish too."

"Such a suspicion never occurred to me either, Brother Leo, until now, during my sickness. God pulled you and brought you near Him by way of laziness; in my case, I think, it was by way of sickness—and not during the day, but at night while I was asleep and unable to resist Him. In my dreams I kept asking myself if perhaps there is no such thing as the body, if perhaps only the soul exists and what we call body is simply that part of the soul which we are able to see and feel. Each night of my sickness as I began to fall asleep I felt my soul hovering buoyantly, tranquilly above my bed. It would leave through the window, promenade in the courtyard, perch on top of the vine arbor and afterwards hang in the air, undulating back and forth over the rooftops of Assisi. It was then that I suddenly discovered the great secret. The body does not exist! Yes, Brother Leo, there is no such thing as the body; nothing exists but the soul!"

He sprang up in bed, his face resplendent.

"And if nothing exists but the soul," he shouted happily, "if nothing exists but the soul, just think, Brother Leo, how far we can go! When the body is no longer here to hinder us, with one leap we shall be in heaven!"

I kept silent. My mind did not understand his words very well, but my heart understood them all. He continued:

"And I took this leap in my dreams—look, like this!" He thrust his arms vigorously up toward the sky as though they were wings. "When you dream, there is nothing simpler, nothing easier. But I shall also do it—you will see; yes, I've made the decision; inside me my mother's blood is crying out—I shall also do it now that I am awake. It will be difficult, very difficult. Brother Leo, I need your help!"

"I want to help you, Brother Francis, and I would with pleasure —but how? My schooling isn't worth mentioning, and my brain isn't very extensive either. The only thing I have is my heart, but what can you do with that? Poor thing, it's unhinged by nature, and proud as a cock, too, miserable beggar that it is! Better not place your trust in it. . . . So you see, how can I help you?"

"You can, you can—and quickly too. Listen: tomorrow I'll be able to get up. I want you to take my arm and support me so I don't fall. We're going to San Damiano's."

"San Damiano's!" I exclaimed in astonishment. "You know, today is Damiano's feast. Didn't you hear the bells?"

"Today!" exclaimed Francis, clapping his hands. "Then that's why . . ."

"What do you mean?"

"I had a dream; I saw him in my dream. Last night he came to

54

me in my sleep. He was ragged, barefooted, leaning on crutches, weeping. I grew frightened and ran to help support him. 'Do not weep, Saint of God,' I said, kissing his hands. 'What has happened to you? You're in heaven, aren't you? Does this mean there is weeping even there?' He nodded his head. 'Yes, there is weeping even in heaven,' he answered me, 'but it is for those who are still crawling on earth. I saw you stretched out peacefully on your rich featherbed and felt sorry for you. Why do you sleep, Francis! Shame on you! The Church is in danger.'

" 'The Church in danger? But what can I do? What do you expect me to do?'

" 'Reach out your hands; place your shoulder against it. Do not let it fall!'

" 'I? I, Bernardone's son?'

" 'You, Francis of Assisi. The world is crumbling to ruins; Christ is in danger. Rise up, support the world on your back so that it does not fall. The Church has descended to the state of my little chapel: it is a tottering ruin. Build it up!'

"He grasped my shoulder and gave me a strong push. I awoke, terrified."

Francis bared his back.

"Look," he said. "You should still be able to see his fingermarks on my shoulder. Come close."

I went up to him, but immediately stepped back in terror and made the sign of the cross.

"Angels of God, defend us!" I murmured, trembling. On Francis' shoulder I could clearly discern several black and blue marks like fingerprints.

"They are Saint Damiano's fingers," said Francis. "Don't be afraid."

Then, a moment later:

"Do you understand now why we are going to his church? It is ready to crumble. The two of us, Brother Leo, shall build it up with stones and cement; and we shall fill the extinguished sanctuary lamp with oil so that the saint's face may be illuminated once more."

"Was that all he wanted, Francis, all he instructed you to do? Or could it be that—"

"No, no, that was all!" said Francis, placing his hand over my mouth as though terrified I might go further. "Quiet! Let's begin with that."

I kept quiet, but my heart was throbbing. I sensed that this dream had been sent by God, that it contained a terrible hidden message. I knew that when the Almighty seizes a man He no longer has any mercy, but tosses the victim from peak to peak even if he break into a thousand pieces. That was why, seeing Francis rise joyfully from his bed, I was overcome by fear.

The next morning I found him already up. Leaning on his mother's arm, he was taking his first tentative steps throughout the house. With joyful, protruding eyes he had been viewing the spacious rooms as though for the first time—the carved trunks, the pictures of the saints on the triptych; and at this particular moment he was standing in the doorway which led to the courtyard and admiring the stone statue in the corner next to the street door, a representation of the Virgin of Avignon holding the infant God in her arms; also the well with its marble brim surrounded by the fragrant potted plants—basil, marjoram, and marigolds—which reminded Lady Pica of her beloved, sun-drenched homeland.

"Welcome, lion of God," he said with a laugh as soon as he saw me. "This is the lion that goes to the lambs and instead of eating them, asks for alms."

He turned to his mother.

"Mother, which of the Evangelists had the lion as his companion? Luke?"

"No, my child, it was Mark," answered Lady Pica with a sigh. "You go to church so seldom, how could you be expected to know!"

"Well then, I am Mark and here is my lion," said Francis, coming to my side and leaning on me. "Let's go!"

"Where are you going, my child?" the mother cried. "Don't you realize you're still hardly able to stand on your feet?"

"You need have no fears, Mother. I have the lion with me, don't you see?"

He took me by the arm. "In God's name!" he said, crossing himself and proceeding as far as the street door.

"Mother, what day is it today?"

"Sunday, my child."

"But what month, what date?"

"September twenty-fourth, my child. Why do you ask?"

"Go inside, Mother, take the triptych, and write on back of the painting of the Crucified: 'On Sunday the twenty-fourth day of September in the year 1206 after the birth of our Lord, my son Francis was reborn.' "

WHAT A DEPARTURE that morning! What were the wings that brought us through the narrow lanes of Assisi! We reached the Piazza San Giorgio, passed through the fortress gate and started along the road which leads down to the plain.

It was a perfect autumn morning. A light mist hovered above the olive trees and vineyards. The grapes hung down awaiting the vintagers, some clusters even touching the ground. The last figs were ripening to the consistency of honey upon the fig trees, above which the golden orioles circled hungrily. The olive trees were heavy with fruit, and a drop of light quivered on each tiny leaf. Below, the plain was still asleep: the tender morning fog had not yet risen. The fields were gilded with mown wheat, and between the stalks the last poppies glistened, dressed in purple like queens, each with a black cross at its heart.

What joy! How our hearts leapt! And not only our hearts, but those of the whole world.

Francis was unrecognizable. Where had he found such strength, such glee! He had no further need of my support, but led the way himself, singing troubadour songs in his mother's native tongue. As lithe and buoyant as an angel, he was viewing the world about him for the very first time.

Two sacred oxen passed, swinging their gleaming necks coyly to the left and right and licking their moist nostrils with rough tongues. They were spotlessly white, had fat, powerful necks, and were crowned with ears of grain. Francis was astonished; he halted to admire them, and held out his hand in greeting.

58

"What nobility!" he murmured. "What great warriors they are, these fellow workers of God's!"

Approaching them, he patted their wide, snow-white rumps. The oxen turned and gazed at him gently, benevolently, like humans.

"If I were the Almighty," he said to me with a laugh, "I would install oxen in heaven along with the saints. Can you imagine heaven without donkeys, oxen, and birds, Brother Leo? I can't. Angels and saints aren't enough. No, heaven must also have donkeys, oxen, and birds!"

I laughed.

"And a lion: you, Brother Leo!"

"And a troubadour: you, Francis," I said, and I stroked the long hair that flowed over his shoulders.

We started walking again. The downward slope aided us, and we began to run.

Suddenly Francis stopped. "Where are we going?" he asked with surprise. "Why are we running?"

"But my young lord, aren't we going to San Damiano's? Have you forgotten?"

Francis shook his head. His voice now was bitter, melancholy:

"And I thought we were running because we had set out to deliver the Holy Sepulcher."

"Just the two of us?" I asked waggishly.

"We are not two," Francis objected, his face suddenly catching fire. "We are not two, we are three."

I shuddered. It was true: we were three. That explained why we felt so much joy and assurance. And it also explained the assault—because, so help me God, this expedition was not a peaceful one; instead, it seemed that war had broken out, that we were an army —the rich young lord and the beggar—and that with God in the lead we were running to the assault.

How many years have passed since then! Francis has risen to heaven, but I still have not been deemed worthy of quitting this life. I have grown old. My hair and teeth have fallen out, my knees have swelled, my arteries are as hard as wood. At this moment my hand trembles as it holds the quill; the paper is already smudged and covered with the tears that have been flowing from my eyes. But even so, now that I recall the departure that morning I feel like springing to my feet, taking my staff, and climbing up the hill to ring the bells and rouse the world. . . . Truly, Father Francis, you are right: there is no such thing as the body. The only thing that exists is the soul—it is in command. Rise up, my soul, recall that morning when we flew toward San Damiano's, and relate everything. Everything, without being afraid of cowardly unbelievers!

As we were running we suddenly heard the squeals and laughter of young girls. We quickened our pace and arrived at the ruins of San Damiano's. The walls were leaning outward; the yellow starwort had already embraced the stones, shifting them; the tiny bell tower had collapsed and its blocks still lay in the courtyard, the small, mute bell next to them. We heard laughter and shrill voices on all sides, but saw no trace of a human being. Francis turned and cast a look of surprise at me.

"The whole ruin is laughing. There must be angels here."

"And what if they're devils?" I asked. I had begun to grow uneasy. "Come, let's go back."

"Devils don't laugh like that, Brother Leo. They're angels. You wait here. I'll enter the church by myself if you're afraid."

"No, I'll come with you," I said, ashamed. "Brother Leo is not afraid!"

The door was hanging off its hinges. We crossed the grass-covered threshold and entered. Two pigeons darted out through the tiny windows and disappeared. At first we could see nothing in the half-light, but soon we made out a huge, ancient cross hanging above the altar, and on it we divined, we did not see, a pale body, floating buoyantly—like a ghost. At its feet stood the image of San Damiano, and a glass lamp, unlit.

We advanced slowly, with difficulty. The air seemed to be filled with wings.

"San Damiano is going to appear now on his crutches," Francis said softly. He wanted to display his hardihood, but his voice was shaking.

We advanced further. Through the narrow transom of the sanctuary we were able to perceive greenery: evidently the church's tiny garden. We smelled rosemary and woodbine.

"Let's go out into the garden," said Francis. "We'll suffocate if we stay here."

But the moment we were about to cross the threshold we heard panting behind the altar, and the rustle of silk clothes, or—as it seemed—of wings. Francis clutched my arm.

"Did you hear? Did you hear? It seemed to me like—"

But before he was able to finish his thought, three young girls dressed in white sprang out from the rear of the sanctuary, where they had been hiding, darted in front of us like three lightning flashes, leapt through the doorway, and flew into the courtyard, screeching.

There all three began to laugh. It seemed they realized how afraid we were, and wanted to tease us.

This disturbed Francis. Suddenly he too flew out into the courtyard. I ran behind him.

The girls saw us, but were not frightened. Apparently they knew Francis, because the oldest of the three blushed. As for Francis, he leaned against the doorpost and started to wipe the sweat from his face.

The girl kept coming closer to him. She was gay, ebullient; an olive branch laden with fruit crowned her hair.

Francis took a step backward: he seemed afraid.

"Do you know her?" I asked in a whisper.

"Quiet!" he answered. He was livid.

The girl gathered up courage. "Welcome to our humble home, Sior Francis," she said tauntingly.

Francis looked at her without answering, but his lower jaw began to tremble.

"This is San Damiano's house, missy," I replied in order to cover Francis' silence. "How long ago did you take possession?"

The other two girls approached slowly, their palms over their mouths in order to smother their giggles. They were a little younger—about thirteen or fourteen years old.

"This morning," answered the oldest. "We're going to spend the whole day here. This is my sister Agnes, and this is our neighbor Ermelinda. We've brought a basket of food with us, and also some fruit."

She turned to Francis once more:

"If Sior Francis will be kind enough to eat with us, we welcome him to do so. He has come to our house; we shall offer hospitality."

"I'm glad to see you, Clara," Francis said softly. His voice was

61

not playful, not laughing. It issued from deep within his heart of hearts, and troubled the young girl.

"We came to play," she said reproachfully, as though scolding him for having arrived just to spoil their pleasure.

"I didn't come to play; I came because I had a dream."

"Were you ill?" the girl asked. This time her voice was filled with hidden tenderness.

"I was ill before I fell ill," answered Francis.

"I don't understand."

"May God grant that one day you shall."

"Once I heard you singing; it was at night," continued the girl, not knowing what to say any more, or how to find a pretext to prolong their chance encounter.

"You heard me every midnight, Clara. But you won't hear me again."

The girl tossed her head. Her long hair bounded against her shoulders and the ribbon which had secured it came undone.

"Why?" she asked, her eyes fixed on the ground.

"I don't know yet, Clara. Don't ask me. Perhaps I'll sing beneath some other window."

"Some other window? Which? Whose?"

Francis lowered his head. "God's . . ." he murmured, but so softly that the girl did not hear.

She came one step closer. "Whose?" she repeated. "Which window?"

But this time Francis did not reply.

"Come, Clara, let's go and play," said one of the girls. "Don't talk to him. Why are you talking to him?" They both began to pull her by the hand, anxious to leave.

But Clara stood her ground, toying with the green ribbon which had come undone from her hair. She was slender, lithe, and was dressed entirely in white, with no ornaments save a tiny golden cross, her baptismal cross, hanging from her neck, and, as a talisman, a silver lily between her slightly raised, still unripe breasts. What was astonishing about this girl was her eyebrows. Above the eyes they were slender, straight as arrows; but then they shot abruptly upward, and thus her black, almond-shaped eyes seemed constantly severe and angry.

Seizing her undone hair as though infuriated at it, she gave it a twist and tied it up tightly in the ribbon of green silk. Then she turned to her companions. "Come," she said spitefully. "We'll go further down to the other church, the Portiuncula, and let Sior Francis stay here to do what he likes. It seems he had a dream!"

Ermelinda picked up the basket, grumbling; Agnes, the younger sister, took the little basket that contained the fruit, and with Clara in the lead all three started off through the olive trees, headed for the plain below.

"We're saved . . ." murmured Francis, and he breathed in deeply, as though he had just escaped an immense danger.

He collapsed onto the doorsill and watched the three girls through the olive trees as they gleamed in the sunlight one moment, faded the next, and finally disappeared.

"We're saved . . ." he repeated, and he stood up.

It must have been almost noon. He looked at me. All signs of fear had vanished from his face.

"Brother Leo"—his voice had changed now, had become serious and resolute—"Brother Leo, didn't we say the two of us were an army and that we were setting out to deliver the Holy Sepulcher? Do not smile—I want you to believe! We're going to start with small, easy things; then, little by little we shall try our hand at the big things. And after that, after we finish the big things, we shall undertake the impossible. Do you understand what I'm saying to you, or do you believe I'm still bedridden in Bernardone's house, and that I'm delirious?"

"Undertake the impossible, Brother Francis?" I asked, terrified. "What do you mean? How far do you plan to go?"

"Brother Leo, didn't you yourself tell me how you once went to a famous ascetic who disciplined himself by living in the top of a tree? 'Give me some advice, Holy Father!' you called to him. And he answered you: 'Go as far as you can!' 'Give me some more advice, Holy Father!' you shouted a second time. 'Go further than you can!' was his answer. . . . You see, Brother Leo, we are going to go further than we can. Right now we are using the ruins of San Damiano's to give us momentum. Do you understand what I'm saying?"

"Don't ask me questions, Francis," I replied. "I understand nothing and I understand everything! Just command me!" My heart had caught fire; it could have consumed an entire forest.

"We'll gather stones. I still have some of Bernardone's money in my purse: we'll purchase cement and mason's tools and then the two of us will get down to the business of reinforcing the walls. We'll also buy tiles for the roof so that the water won't come in when it rains; and paint for the windows and doors; and oil for the saint's lamp. How many years has he gone without illumination? We shall illuminate him. Agreed?"

I rolled up my sleeves. His words had fired my blood.

"When do we start?"

"Now. San Damiano is exposed to the rain; he is falling in ruins, stumbling in the darkness; he cannot wait. But our souls, Brother Leo: do you think they can wait? They too are exposed to the rain; they too are falling in ruins, stumbling in the darkness. Forward, comrade! In God's name!"

He threw off his velvet coat and began to arrange the large corner-blocks that had fallen down and filled the yard. I lifted the hem of my robe to form a sizable pocket and then ran all about filling it with stones which I carried to one spot and deposited in a pile. While working, Francis began once more to sing the troubadour songs he had learned as a child. They were about love. Love for whom? The troubadours had embellished the virtue of the beloved lady; but this time as Francis sang, surely he was thinking of the Blessed Virgin Mary.

It was already evening when we returned home. The whole way we talked passionately about stones, cement, and trowels—like two masons; and it was just as though we had been talking about God and the salvation of the world which was about to fall into ruins. That evening I understood for the first time that all things are one and that even the humblest everyday deed is part of a man's destiny. Francis too was deeply roused; he too felt that there is no such thing as a small deed or a large deed, and that to chink a crumbling wall with a single pebble is the same as reinforcing the entire earth to keep it from falling, the same as reinforcing your soul to keep that too from falling.

As we came within sight of the house, Lady Pica was sitting at her window, searching the road anxiously. The darkness had not fallen yet; it was still light outside. Making us out in the distance, she went downstairs to open the door personally. She intended to scold her son for being late and for tiring himself while he was still sick, but when she stood in front of him and saw his face, she could not speak. She gazed at him in astonishment for a moment; finally she opened her mouth:

"Your face: why is it beaming like that, my son?"

"If you think it is beaming now, Mother, just wait!" replied Francis with a laugh. "This is only the beginning. We're on the first step, and all in all there are seventy-seven thousand."

He took his mother by the arm and leaned over to her ear.

"Tonight Brother Leo is going to eat with us—at the same table!"

The next morning we slipped out of the house at dawn like two thieves and went down to the market place. We bought tools—two hammers, two trowels—also paints and brushes, and we ordered tiles and cement. Then we set out hurriedly along the road to San Damiano's.

There were scattered clouds in the sky. The weather was cold; a nipping breeze came from the mountain. The cocks had begun to crow in the courtyards; men and beasts were awakening. The olive trees glistened. The oxen had already departed for their sacred daily toil.

"This is the way the soul awakens," said Francis, turning to me suddenly. "It too has oxen, five of them. It puts them under the yoke early in the morning and begins to plough and sow."

"To sow what?" I asked, unable to understand.

"The kingdom of heaven. The kingdom of heaven, or else the Inferno," answered Francis, and he stooped to pick a beautiful yellow daisy from the edge of the road.

But as he was putting out his hand, he suddenly restrained himself. He had changed his mind.

"The Lord sent it to adorn the road. We must not prevent God's creatures from fulfilling their duty." When he had said this he waved to the daisy with his hand as though saying goodbye to his own beloved sister.

When we finally reached the dilapidated chapel we found its curate seated on the threshold sunning himself. He was an old man bent over with the years, and ravaged, just like the tiny church of San Damiano, by poverty. When Francis was a short distance away from him, he halted for a moment, startled.

"Is it possible that you are San Damiano?" he mumbled.

But he set himself to rights immediately, and taking a few additional steps, came near the man and recognized him.

"It's old Father Antonio, the curate. I know him."

Relieved, he advanced and greeted the priest, kissing his hand.

"With your permission, Father, we are going to repair the church. The saint came to me in my dreams and I gave him my word."

All of a sudden the curate raised his head. Though his body was tottering, his eyes were still two flames.

"Why didn't he come to me in my dreams?" he asked angrily, reproachfully. "I've grown old in his service, haven't I? He's eaten me out of house and home with the oil I've needed to keep his lamp lit, the brooms to sweep the place out, incense to make him smell nice, wine to wash his effigy. And did he ever appear to me in my sleep to say anything pleasant to me? Never! And now—what next!—he's come to the likes of you. . . . Aren't you Sior Bernardone's debauched, prodigal son—the one who spends the whole night roaming the streets with his guitar?"

"Yes, Father, that's who I am: the debauched, prodigal son."

"Well then, what can God expect from you?"

"Nothing," Francis answered. "Nothing. But I expect everything from Him."

"What do you mean: 'everything'?"

"The salvation of my soul."

The priest lowered his head in shame and remained silent, his hand held over his eyes to keep the sun from burning them. Rolling up our sleeves, Francis and I got down to work and little by little, without consciously meaning to, we both began to sing. First we ran to and fro gathering stones; then the cement arrived and we took up our trowels. We were like a pair of birds building their nest.

"What do we resemble, Francis?" I suddenly asked my companion, and he answered laughingly: "Two birds who are building their nest in the springtime."

The priest had risen: he was gazing in our direction, saying nothing. Every so often he threw a furtive glance at Francis and crossed himself. Around noontime he left to go to his tiny house, which was next to the church, and in a little while he returned carrying a wooden platter with two barley rolls, two handfuls of black olives, an onion, and a small jug of wine on it.

" 'If a man work, let him eat,' commanded the Apostle Paul," he said to us with a smile.

It was then that we first became aware of our hunger. Sitting down cross-legged in the yard, we began our meal.

"Have you ever eaten olives as tasty as these, or such delicious bread?" asked Francis, chewing his barley roll with relish. "Have you ever drunk such exquisite wine?"

"Once and only once," I answered, "but that was in my dreams (hungry people obviously dream of bread). I had just entered heaven; along came an angel with a platter exactly like this one, and it was loaded with barley bread, olives, an onion, and a small jug of wine. 'You've come a long way; you must be famished,' the angel said to me. 'Sit down and eat and drink before you have your audience with God.' I stretched out on heaven's green turf and began to eat. Each mouthful went down inside me and instantaneously turned to soul. Bread, wine, onion: all turned to soul. Just like now."

We set to work again. Hewing stone, mixing cement, singing all the songs we knew, we calked the fissured walls. Night began to fall. For a moment I imagined San Damiano had emerged from the church and placed himself in the doorway, from where he was watching us with satisfaction. But then we saw it was the priest, and that he was smiling.

"Who knows, perhaps he's San Damiano after all," said Francis, glancing with respect at the tiny old man who stood on the threshold. "It's possible that after so many years of prayer and poverty the two of them have become one."

And truly, when darkness fell and we finally stopped work and went to bid him good night, his face was as radiant as a saint's.

I shall not relate here how many days and weeks we worked. How can I remember! The time raced by like a babbling brook and we babbled along with it, painting, chinking the tiles on the roof, wielding our hammers, trowels, and brushes. Each day the sun rose, mounted to the center of the heavens, set; the evening star appeared in the western sky, night fell, and we climbed up toward Assisi, happy, our hands spattered with cement. . . . The only thing I can say with certainty is that during each of those sacred days and weeks both of us experienced the sense of joy, urgency, and love possessed by the bird that is building its nest; we discovered, for the first time, the true meaning of "nest," "bird," and the exultation of realizing that your insides are filled with eggs! For the rest of our lives those days were to shine out, tender and lavish of grace, as though they had been a period of betrothal, the betrothal of our souls to God.

"What has happened, what has happened, Brother Leo?" Francis asked me one morning as we began work. "Did the world change or did we? I weep, I laugh, and weeping and laughing are the same thing. I believe I'm walking a man's height above the earth, suspended in the air! And what about you, Brother Leo?"

"Me? I believe I'm a caterpillar buried deep down under the ground. The entire earth is above me, crushing me, and I begin to bore through the soil, making a passage to the surface so that I can penetrate the crust and issue into the light. It's hard work boring through the entire earth, but I'm able to be patient because I have a strong premonition that as soon as I do issue into the light I shall become a butterfly."

"That's it! That's it!" shouted Francis joyfully. "Now I understand. God bless you, Brother Leo! We are two caterpillars and we want to become butterflies. So . . . to work! Mix cement, bring stones, hand me the trowel!"

Just as we were finally about to complete the rebuilding of San Damiano's, old Bernardone returned from his trip. He was taken aback when he did not find his son at the shop. Francis came no more to help with the business, but left at dawn, returned after dark, ate all by himself: Bernardone never saw him any more.

"Where does your darling go every morning instead of looking after the shop?" he asked his wife with irritation.

She lowered her gaze, not having the courage to face him directly.

"He had a dream," she answered. "San Damiano—great is his grace—came to him and ordered him to repair the church."

"And so . . . ?"

"He leaves every morning to go and build."

"By himself? With his own two hands?"

"With his own two hands."

"All alone?"

"No, with his friend the beggar."

Sior Bernardone frowned and clenched his fists.

"Your son is taking a bad road, Lady Pica," he said, "and you're the one to blame."

"Me?"

"You. Your blood! You have troubadours in your blood, and scatterbrains, and lunatics—and you know it."

The mother's eyes filled with tears. Bernardone took his walking stick.

"I'm going to go personally to retrieve him," he said. "He hasn't only your blood in him, he has mine also. There's hope for him yet."

He made his appearance at San Damiano's just before noon. His face was somber, his chest heaving from the exertion of the walk. Francis was perched on the church roof, chinking the tiles. This was the day we were to finish our work, and he was singing troubadour songs in his mother's native tongue with even more gusto than usual.

Bernardone raised his stick. "Hey there, master craftsman," he shouted, "come down, I need you."

"Welcome to Sior Bernardone," answered Francis from high up on the roof. "What do you want?"

"My shop is falling to pieces too. Come down and repair it."

"I'm sorry, Sior Bernardone, but I don't repair shops, I demolish them."

Bernardone let out a howl and banged his stick furiously on the cobblestones of the yard. He wanted to speak but was unable to find the words, and his lips just twisted and turned.

"Come down here at once," he bellowed at last. "I command you to come down! Don't you know who I am? I'm your father."

"Sorry, Sior Bernardone, but my father is God, God and no one else."

"And what about me, then?" called Bernardone, froth coating his lips. Standing in the sun as he was, it was as if smoke were rising from his hair.

"And what about me?" he shouted again. "What am I? Who am I?"

"You are Sior Bernardone, the one who has the big shop on the square in Assisi and who stores up gold in his coffers and strips the people around him naked instead of clothing them."

The priest heard the shouting from his small house and came out. As soon as he saw old Bernardone he understood. Terrified, he stepped forward, reached under his frock, and brought forth the sack of money which Francis had given him to use to buy oil for the saint's lamp.

"This money is yours, Sior Bernardone," he said. "Forgive me. Your son gave it to me, but I haven't touched it."

Without even turning to look at the priest, Bernardone grabbed the sack and thrust it into his ample pocket. Then, brandishing his stick again toward the roof:

"Damn you, come down and get the thrashing you deserve!"

"I'm coming," Francis answered him, and he began to descend.

I put down my trowel and waited to see what would happen. Shaking the dust and cement from his clothes, Francis started toward his father. Flames were darting from old Bernardone's eyes. He stood there glowering, ready to incinerate the rebellious boy. He did not move, did not speak, but, his stick raised in the air, simply waited for his son to come near him. Francis came, and as he bowed to greet his father, his hands crossed upon his breast, old Bernardone lifted his huge, weighty hand and gave him a strong slap on the right cheek; whereupon Francis turned the other.

"Strike the other cheek, Sior Bernardone," he said calmly. "Strike the other also; or else it might feel offended."

I started to run to my friend's defense, but he held out his hand. "Do not interfere with God's doings, Brother Leo," he said. "Sior Bernardone is helping his son find salvation. . . . Strike, Sior Bernardone!"

At this point old Bernardone became frantic. He raised his stick in order to baste his son squarely over the head, but his hand remained motionless in mid-air. Francis looked up in surprise. Fat grains of sweat had popped onto Bernardone's forehead, and his lips had turned blue. Fear deformed his face. You felt he was toiling to bring the stick down upon Francis' scalp. But his arm had turned to stone.

Francis saw how his father was staring into the air with protruding eyes, quaking from fright. Some infuriated angel must have swooped down upon the old man and restrained his arm. Francis did not see this angel and neither did I, but both of us heard wings beating angrily in the air.

"It's nothing, Father, nothing," said Francis. "Don't be afraid."

His heart pitied the man. He started to grasp him by the arm, but old Bernardone suddenly swayed and, with a single motion, crumpled onto the cobblestones.

When he came to, the sun was hanging at the zenith, the old priest still clasped the cup of water he had used to sprinkle the unconscious man's temples, and Francis, his head between his palms, was seated cross-legged next to his father and gazing at the sun-drenched flanks of Mount Subasio in the distance.

Old Bernardone sat up and retrieved his stick. I ran to help him rise to his feet, but he dismissed me with a wave of his hand. He got up, exhausted, and wiped away his sweat. Not breathing a word, not so much as glancing either at his son, who was still sitting on the ground, or at the tiny old priest with the cup of water, he shook out his clothes, leaned heavily upon his stick, and started slowly up the hill. Soon he had vanished behind a curve in the road.

That night Francis did not return home. I remained at his side. Searching in the vicinity of San Damiano's some days before, he had found a cave where every so often, abandoning his construction work, he would immure himself for hours on end. He must have spent the time praying, because when he emerged from the cave and returned to take up his work again there would be a nimbus of quivering light encircling his face, just like the halos we see on paintings of the saints: the flame of prayer had abided around his head.

We went to this cave and dragged ourselves inside. It was filled with the odor of damp soil. Placing two stones to serve as pillows, we lay down without eating, without exchanging a single word. I was exhausted and I slept immediately. It must have been already dawn when, waking up, I spied Francis seated at the mouth of the cave, his face wedged between his knees. I heard a persistent, muted murmuring; he seemed to be weeping softly, trying not to wake me up. I was destined many times in the succeeding years to hear Francis weep. But that morning his sobs were like those of an infant who desires to nurse and has no mother.

I crept to the entrance and knelt down next to him, riveting my eyes upon the sky. The stars had already begun to grow dim; several still hung in the milky heavens, and one, the biggest of all, was emitting flashes of green, rose, and blue light.

"Which star is that, Brother Francis?" I asked him to distract his thoughts. "Have you any idea?"

"It must be some archangel," he said, holding back his tears. "Who knows—perhaps the archangel Gabriel. It was such an archangel, gleaming with splendor, that came down one morning and pronounced the 'Hail, Mary.'"

He was quiet for a moment.

"And that star which is so bright—the one you see dancing there in the east and which is about to be smothered by the light of the sun—that is Lucifer!"

"Lucifer!" I exclaimed with surprise. "Why? Why? No, it's not right. He is more brilliant than the archangel Gabriel! Is that the way God punished him?"

"Exactly," answered Francis in a stifled voice. "There is no harsher means of punishment, Brother Leo, than to answer malice with kindness. . . .

"Why are you surprised?" he continued after a moment's silence. "Isn't that what God did with me—with me, vile, wretched, good-for-nothing Lucifer that I am? Instead of hurling down the thunderbolt to reduce me to ashes, one night when I was singing—gorged with food, drunk, debauched—what did He do? He sent San Damiano to me in my sleep and instructed me to place my back beneath the Church. 'It is in danger,' He said. 'Make it firm. I have faith in you.' I believed then that He was speaking about the ruined chapel, and I rebuilt it. But now—"

He sighed. Spreading out his arms, he took a deep breath.

"Now?" I asked, looking at him uneasily.

"Now my heart is still not calm. No, no, He wasn't speaking about the chapel—that is what has been on my mind all night. Brother

Leo, I am beginning to understand the terrible hidden meaning."

He was silent.

"Can't I hear it too, Brother Francis? Tell me so that I can rejoice along with you."

"You won't rejoice, poor Brother Leo. No, you won't rejoice; you'll be terrified. Patience—come with me, have faith. Little by little you shall understand, and then you shall begin to weep, and you may even want to turn back. The uphill road is indeed severe. But— who knows?—perhaps by then it will be too late for you to turn back."

I grasped his hand. I wanted to kiss it, but he would not let me.

"Wherever you go I go too, Brother Francis. And I won't ask any more questions either. . . . Lead on!"

We remained silent, watching the ever-increasing light. Little by little the mountainside had turned from purple to rose, then from rose to brilliant white. Olive trees, stones, and soil were laughing. The sun appeared, seated itself on a rocky ledge, and we, at the entrance to the black cave, lifted our arms to greet it.

I rose to go to San Damiano's so that I could gather together our tools, sweep out the church, and put everything in order.

"Give the tools to the old curate," said Francis, "but first kiss them one by one: they did their duty well. We have no further need of them, because the Church that we are going to strengthen now cannot be strengthened with trowels and cement."

I began to open my mouth to ask why, but closed it immediately. One day I shall understand, I said to myself. Let's try and be patient.

"Go, and God be with you," said Francis. "I plan to spend the day here in the cave. I want to implore God—I have so very much to tell Him—I want to implore Him to give me strength. Before me is the abyss. How can I leap across it? And if I do not leap, how shall I ever be able to reach God?"

I departed. It was many years later, when Francis already had one foot in the grave and was preparing to take leave of this life, that I learned what had happened inside the cave that day. He was lying on the bare ground outside the Portiuncula, I remember, and was plagued by the wood mice that came and wanted to devour the little flesh that still remained to him. Unable to sleep, he called me to sit down next to him in order to chase them away, and also to

73

keep him company. It was then, while I sat up with him that night, that he revealed to me what had happened inside the cave.

As soon as he had found himself alone he fell on his face and began to kiss the soil and call upon God. "I know Thou art everywhere," he called to Him. "Under whatever stone I lift, I shall find Thee; in whatever well I look, I shall see Thy face; on the back of every larva I gaze upon, at the spot where it is preparing to put forth its wings, I shall find Thy name engraved. Thou art therefore also in this cave and in the mouthful of earth which my lips are pressing against at this moment. Thou seest me and hearest me and takest pity on me.

"So, Father, listen to what I have to say. Last night in this cave I shouted joyfully: 'I did what Thou instructedst me to do. I rebuilt San Damiano's, made it firm!'

"And Thou answeredst me, 'Not enough!'

" 'Not enough? What more dost Thou wish me to do? Command me!'

"And then I heard Thy voice again: 'Francis, Francis—make Francis firm, rebuild the son of Bernardone!'

"How shall I make him firm, Lord? There are many roads. Which is my road? How shall I conquer the demons within me? They are many, and if Thou dost not come to my aid, I am lost! How can I push aside the flesh, Lord, so that it will not come between us and separate us? You saw for yourself, Lord, how troubled my heart was when I faced the young girl at San Damiano's, how troubled it was when I faced my father. How can I save myself from my mother and father, from women, friends, from comfortable living; and from pride, the yearning for glory, from happiness itself? The number of the mortal demons is seven, and all seven are sucking at my heart. How can I save myself, Lord, from Francis?"

He shouted and raved in this way the entire day, prostrate on the floor of the cave, throbbing convulsively. Toward evening, while I was still making the rounds of Assisi begging for alms, Francis heard a voice above him:

"Francis!"

"Here I am, Lord. Command me."

"Francis, can you go to Assisi—the place where you were born and where everyone knows you—can you go there, stand in front of

74

your father's house and begin to sing, dance, and clap your hands, crying out My name?"

Francis listened, shuddering. He did not reply. Once more he heard the voice above him, but nearer now—in his ear: "Can you trample this Francis underfoot; can you humiliate him? This Francis is preventing our union. Destroy him! The children will run behind you and pelt you with stones; the young ladies will come to their windows and burst out laughing; and you, exultant, dripping with blood from the stoning, will stand your ground and cry, 'Whoever throws one stone at me, may he be once blessed by God; whoever throws two stones at me, may he be twice blessed by God; whoever throws three stones at me, may he be thrice blessed by God.' Can you do that? Can you? Why don't you speak?"

Francis listened, trembling. I can't, I can't, he was saying to himself, but he was ashamed to reveal his thought. Finally he opened his mouth:

"Lord, if I must dance in the middle of the square and cry out Thy name, couldst Thou not send me to some other city?"

But the voice, severe and full of scorn, answered, "No! Assisi!"

Francis' eyes filled with tears. He bit into the soil his lips had been resting upon. "Mercy, Lord," he cried. "Give me time to prepare my soul, to prepare my body. I ask three days of Thee, three days and three nights, nothing more."

And the voice thundered again, no longer in Francis' ear now, but within his bowels: "No, now!"

"Why art Thou in such a hurry, Lord? Why dost Thou wish to punish me so?"

"Because I love you . . ." said God's voice. It was soft now, tender, and it came from within Francis' heart.

Suddenly all the bitterness fled his breast and a force entered him, not his own force, but an omnipotent one. He rose. His face had begun to shine; his knees were firm. He stood for a moment at the entrance to the cave. The sun was about to set.

"I'm going," he said, and he crossed himself.

Just then I returned from my begging, my sack full of stale bread. I saw him standing in the opening of the cave. His face was like the rising sun; it was dazzling, and I had to place my hand over my eyes to shade them. I had planned to say to him: I've brought

75

some bread, Francis; you must be hungry, you haven't had a thing all day, sit down and let's eat. But I was ashamed to say this, because the moment I beheld him I sensed that he had no need of bread.

As soon as he caught sight of me, he raised his hand.

"Let's go," he said.

"Where?"

"To leap!"

Once more I was too timid to ask him to explain. To leap? Over what—and why? I didn't understand. But he started out in front, striding hurriedly over stones and soil, and, together, we made our way to Assisi.

NIGHT WAS FALLING. The western sky was dark, the color of wild cherries; odd-looking, compassionate clouds began to rise and to cool the earth, which was still boiling from the great heat of the day. The fruitful plain of Umbria was resting. It had accomplished its duty, had given wheat, wine, and olive oil to men. Now, in repose, it gazed at the sky, waiting with confidence for rain so that the seeds beneath its soil could once more grow and form fruit.

The farmers were returning home, and in front of them, moving slowly, majestically, came the well-fed, guileless oxen. They kept turning and casting beneficent, unsurprised eyes upon us for a moment as though we were oxen of some other breed who were also returning to Assisi after our day's work, drawn on by the call of a stable full of hay and oats.

Francis marched in front, deep in thought. From time to time he stopped, looked at the sky, and listened intently as though expecting someone to speak to him. He heard nothing, however, except the soft rustling of the wind in the trees, and the sound of dogs barking far away in Assisi. Sighing each time, he would resume the ascent.

At one point he turned and waited for me to catch up.

"Do you know how to dance, Brother Leo?" he asked me softly, confidentially.

I laughed. "To dance? We're not going to a wedding, are we?"

"Yes, to a wedding, that's where we're going, Brother Leo—and do not laugh. The servant of God is being married."

"Which servant of God?"

77

"The soul. She is marrying her great Lover."

"Do you mean God, Brother Francis?"

"Yes, God, Brother Leo, and we must dance in front of Bernardone's house; in the middle of the square, Brother Leo: that's where the wedding will take place. And we must clap our hands and sing, Brother Leo; and the people will congregate, and instead of offering us almond cakes, their way of saying 'May they live happily ever after' will be to pelt us with stones and lemon rinds."

"What happened to the almond cakes and bay leaves and lemon flowers? Why stones and rinds, Brother Francis?"

"That is the way the Bridegroom wants it."

He resumed the climb and did not speak again. I watched his skinny calves and the naked, bloody feet that continually stumbled and tripped. He was running now, gazing constantly at Assisi: he had suddenly been invaded by a sense of urgency, of great longing. But when we reached the walls his knees gave way and he stopped.

"Brother Leo," he asked in a gasping, supplicating tone, catching hold of my arm, "do you remember how on that night on the Mount of Olives Christ lifted his arms to heaven and cried, 'Father, let this cup be taken from me'? The sweat was pouring from his forehead, Brother Leo. He was trembling. I saw him, Brother Leo; I was there and saw him! He was trembling."

"Calm down, calm down, Francis; do not shake so. Come, we'll go back to our cave. You'll spend your days praying, I'll spend mine begging, and in the evening we'll both sit in front of a piece of bread and we'll talk of God."

I spoke to him softly, sweetly, because I was afraid of his fiery eyes. But he was far, far away on the Mount of Olives, and did not hear.

"He was trembling," he murmured again, "He was trembling . . . but he seized the cup and drank it down in one gulp, right to the bottom!"

Releasing my arm, he passed resolutely through the city's gate, then turned and looked at me, raising his hand.

"Let's go," he said in a loud voice. And immediately after, in a whisper: "Christ, help me!"

I followed him at a run. I had divined his suffering and drew near so that I could share it with him. What does man's soul resemble? I kept asking myself as I contemplated Francis' pallor and the tremors that were passing through his body. What does man's soul resemble? A nest filled with eggs? The thirsty earth gazing at the heavens and waiting for rain? Man's soul is an "Oh!"—a groan that ascends to heaven.

Francis turned and glanced at me. "You can go back if you want, Brother Leo."

"I'm not going back," I answered. "Even if you leave, I'm staying."

"Oh, if only I could leave, if only I could escape! But I can't."

He lifted his eyes to heaven:

"Thy face is behind water, behind bread, behind every kiss; it is behind thirst, hunger, chastity. O Lord, how can I escape Thee?"

With a hop and a skip he turned into the first narrow lane and soon reached the Piazza San Giorgio, where he began to jump, clap his hands, and shout: "Come one, come all! Come to hear the new madness!"

It was the hour when the citizens were returning with laden donkeys from their vineyards and melon fields. The merchants and artisans were closing their shops and gathering in the cafés to drink a quarter-liter of wine and chat pleasantly with their friends. The old ladies sat on their doorsteps. Their sight had grown dim, but they did not mind, for they had long since lost interest in watching the streets, people, and donkeys of Assisi. On the other hand, the girls and young men, washed and in fresh clothes on this Saturday evening, were parading up and down the long, narrow city. The clouds had scattered, a cool breeze was blowing, the ribbons in the girls' hair were fluttering, and the young men grew excited and eyed the women with longing and desire. The first lutes already resounded within the taverns.

Suddenly: laughter, shouts, jeering. Everyone turned to look. Francis was visible at the edge of the square, hopping, dancing, his robe tucked up. "Come one, come all!" he was calling. "Come, brothers, come to hear the new madness!"

Behind him ran a hoard of laughing children, chasing him and throwing stones.

I raced in back, threatening them with my staff, but more appeared from every street, and soon they all joined together and charged Francis. He, calm and laughing, turned from time to time, held out his arms to the children, and shouted, "Whoever throws one stone at me, may he be once blessed by God; whoever throws two stones at me, may he be twiced blessed by God; whoever throws three stones at me, may he be thrice blessed by God"— whereupon a continuous stream of stones rained down upon him.

Blood was flowing now from his forehead and chin. The citizens rushed out from the taverns, guffawing. Even Assisi's dogs were roused; banding together, they started to bark at Francis. I had placed myself in front of him so that I could receive my share of the stones, but he pushed me aside. He was jumping and dancing rapturously, all covered with blood.

"Hear, brothers," he sang, "hear the new madness!"

Everyone was roaring with laughter. The young men began to whistle, meow, and bark to drown out his voice; the girls, crowded around the columns of the ancient temple, were screeching. Someone shouted from the tavern opposite:

"Say, aren't you Bernardone's son Francis, the *bon vivant?* All right, tell us about your new madness. Let's see what it is!"

"Tell us, tell us, tell us!" came from every side, accompanied by a chorus of guffaws.

Francis mounted the steps of the temple, opened his arms to the jeering crowd, and screamed: "Love! Love! Love!" Then he began to run from one end of the square to the other, jumping, dancing, shouting.

Leaning over the balcony of an imposing palazzo, a girl was watching—watching and crying.

"Clara!" came a voice from within. "Clara!"

But the girl did not move.

Suddenly my blood turned to ice. There was a roar, and the crowd made way, the booing ceased abruptly. A huge giant had rushed forward and grabbed Francis by the scruff of the neck. It was his father, Sior Bernardone.

"Come with me!" he roared, shaking his son furiously.

But Francis was able to catch hold of one of the columns of the temple.

"Where?" he shouted. "I'm not going anywhere!"

"Home!"

"My home is here—here in the square. And these men and women who are hooting me: they are my father and mother."

Old Bernardone went wild. Grasping his son around the waist with both his arms, he tried to wrench him away from the column.

"I'm not going!" screamed Francis, throwing his arms more firmly around the column. "I have no father, no mother; I have no home —only God!"

He was quiet for an instant, and then he began at once to shout again: "Only God! Only God!" The crowd roared with laughter.

"We haven't any buffoon to help us pass the time," said someone with a face like a mouse. (It was Sabbatino; I recognized him.) "Now, praise the Lord, we have Bernardone's son! Hello there, Francis, God's trained bear! Jump for us! Dance!"

Everyone roared with laughter.

At that moment the Bishop of Assisi happened to be walking across the square. He was a venerable old man, a good, simple soul with a gentle voice; a man who trembled when he thought of hell, trembled when he thought of heaven, and who was continually begging Satan to repent and return to Paradise quietly, supplicatingly, with no more thought of resistance.

This evening he had made his accustomed rounds of the poorer sections of the city. Behind him came the deacon with an empty hamper which the bishop had had filled with food to be distributed to the poor. As he was walking, his long ivory-hilted crosier in his hand, he heard the cries and stopped. Francis was still shouting, "I have no home—only God! Only God!" and the people were splitting their sides with laughter.

It seemed to the bishop that someone was in danger and desired aid from him, God's representative in Assisi. He quickened his pace as much as he could, and approached.

The darkness had not fallen; the last gleams of twilight still remained, and the bishop was able to see Francis and recognize him. And there on top of him was old Bernardone, struggling to drag him away. The bishop raised his crosier.

"Sior Bernardone," he said in a severe voice, "it is shameful for one of the leading men of the region to provide a theatrical show for everyone to see. If you have any differences with your son, let both of you come to our residence so that we may render judgment."

He turned to Francis. "My child, do not resist. You were calling God. I am God's representative in Assisi. Come with me!"

Francis released his grip on the column. He saw me next to him. "You come too, Brother Leo," he said. "The ascent is beginning."

The bishop led the way, followed by Francis and me, with old Bernardone behind us, grumbling. And still further behind, keeping a respectable distance, came the agitated populace, their eyes fixed abjectly on the ground.

Francis turned to me for a moment. "Brother Leo, are you afraid, are you ashamed?" he asked in a low voice. "I repeat to you: if you want to turn back, you can. Why should you become involved? Go!"

"As long as I'm with you, Brother Francis, I'm neither afraid nor ashamed. I'll never leave you as long as I live."

"You've still got time," he insisted. "I feel sorry for you. Go!"

At this I was no longer able to restrain myself, and I burst into tears.

Francis touched my shoulder tenderly.

"All right, all right, little lion of God. You can stay."

We reached the bishop's palace and entered the benighted courtyard. Behind us a large number of the townspeople squeezed their way inside, as did several notables who had raced to admire the state to which Bernardone's son had fallen.

The servants lit the chandelier, illuminating the great hall. Above the episcopal throne was a crucifix which showed Christ beautiful and well fed, with plump, rosy cheeks. Crossing himself, the bishop sat down on his throne. Sior Bernardone went and stood at his right, Francis at his left. Further back stood five or six notables, and further still, against the wall, the common people.

I remember everything that happened that night, remember it perfectly: the bishop's words, Francis' sweetness and resplendence, Bernardone's fury. But I am going to relate it hurriedly so that I can arrive at the essence—at the great moment when Francis stood naked before God and man.

As I was saying, the bishop mounted his throne and crossed himself.

"Sior Pietro Bernardone," he said, "I am listening in God's name. What complaint do you have against your son?"

"Lord Bishop," old Bernardone answered in a hoarse, exasperated voice, "this son of mine is no longer in his right mind. He has insane dreams, hears voices in the air, takes gold from my coffers and squanders it. He's ruining me! Until recently he spent it in having a good time and I said to myself that he was young and would get over it. But now I've finally lost all hope. He goes around with ragamuffins, sleeps in caves, weeps and laughs without rhyme or reason, and lately has been seized with a mania to rebuild ruined churches. But tonight this disease simply went too far. He came to Assisi and began to sing and dance in the middle of the square while everyone laughed. . . . He is a disgrace to my blood. I no longer want him!"

"And so . . . ?" asked the bishop, seeing Bernardone hesitate.

"And so," said old Bernardone, holding his arm over his son's head, "and so, before God and man I disown him, disinherit him. He is no longer my son."

There was muffled whispering among the notables and people, but the bishop restored silence with a wave of his hand. He turned to Francis, who had been listening with bowed head.

"What do you have to say in your defense, Francis, son of Christ?"

Francis raised his head.

"Nothing," he answered. "Only this—"

And, before any of us could prevent him, with a sudden movement he threw off the velvet clothes he was wearing, rolled them up into a bundle, and calmly, without uttering a word, stooped and placed them at Bernardone's feet.

Then, as naked as the day his mother brought him into the world, he went and stood before the bishop's throne.

"Bishop," he said, "even these clothes belonged to him. I am returning them. He no longer has a son; I no longer have a father. Our accounts are settled."

We all stood with gaping mouths; many eyes had filled with tears. Bernardone bent down, seized the bundle, and placed it beneath his arm.

The bishop descended from his throne. His eyes were wet. Removing his cloak, he wrapped it around Francis, covering his nakedness.

"Why did you do it, my child?" he asked in a melancholy, reproachful voice. "Weren't you ashamed before these people?"

"No, Bishop, only before God," Francis replied humbly. "I am ashamed only before God. Forgive me, Bishop."

He turned to the notables and the people:

"Brothers, hear what God has commanded me to do. Until now I called Sior Pietro Bernardone my father. Henceforth I shall say: 'Our Father who art in heaven.' I am breaking the links which bound me to earth; I am gaining momentum so that I may return to my home, to heaven. This, brothers—listen to it—this is the new madness."

Old Bernardone was unable to restrain himself any longer. Frothing at the mouth, he pounced on Francis, his fist raised. But the bishop managed to seize hold of him in time.

"You have no more power over him," he said. "Control your anger, Sior Bernardone!"

Benardone threw a ferocious glance around the room. Smoke was rising from his head. Biting his lips to keep himself from cursing, he squeezed the bundle under his arm and left, banging the door furiously behind him.

The bishop turned then to me. "Go and ask the gardener to give you one of his old garments to cover Francis' nakedness."

I ran out and returned in a few moments with an ancient coat that had been patched and repatched a thousand times. Francis traced a cross on the back with chalk and put the coat on.

He bowed, kissed the bishop's hand, then turned to the notables and the people. "Farewell my brothers," he said to them. "May God have mercy upon your souls!"

The bishop escorted Francis a short distance out into the courtyard. Bending over, he said to him in a hushed voice, "Careful, Francis. You're overdoing it."

"That's how one finds God, Bishop," Francis answered.

The bishop shook his head. "Even virtue needs moderation; otherwise it can become arrogance."

"Man stands within the bounds of moderation; God stands outside them. I am heading for God, Bishop," said Francis, and he proceeded hastily toward the street door. He had no time to lose.

The bishop clasped his hand compassionately. "Do not be in a hurry, my child. I see the air round about your head filled with struggle, anguish, and blood. Do not depart for the contest, my child, before you come to see me. I am old; I have experienced much that is unpleasant. What you are now going through, I have already gone through. I think I can help you."

"I shall come to ask for your blessing, Bishop," said Francis, and he strode across the threshold.

I ran behind, and we issued into the street. The moon had not yet risen; it was pitch dark outside. Clouds covered the sky. A damp wind was blowing: apparently rain had already fallen on the mountains.

The street was deserted. In the houses the lamps were being lit and people were sitting down for dinner. We both stood for some time in the middle of the road. Where should we go? In which direction—toward the plain or toward the mountain: the wilderness or the abode of men? God was to our left and to our right, both on the plain and on the mountain. Every route was a hallowed one.

Francis still had not chosen. He stood motionless in the middle of the street.

"And where are we going now, Brother Francis?" I asked him.

Francis laughed quietly, childishly. "To heaven," he replied. "Don't you understand? We've booted the earth goodbye; we've taken the leap. Forward, Brother Leo, in God's name!"

He turned to the right, the direction of Mount Subasio.

Leaving through the northern gate, we entered a wild, deserted area and began the ascent. Francis did not speak for a long time. He went ahead of me in the darkness and his slender body seemed to me like a sword splitting the road in two, while his oversize, tattered coat flapped in the wind like a pair of wings.

As for me, I was tired, hungry; I halted and looked down at Assisi. The lights were still burning. You could still hear the bustle of humans and the barking of dogs. A sliver of moon, crushed, full of affliction, appeared over the rim of the sky.

As soon as Francis did not hear my footsteps behind him, he turned. "Why are you hesitating, Brother Leo?" he called, seeing me with my eyes fixed on the benighted city in back of me. "Why are you looking behind you? Don't you remember Christ's instruction? Shake off the dust of Assisi from your feet; the dust of your father and mother, the dust of men!"

85

"Don't worry, Brother Francis, that's just what I'm doing: I'm shaking off the dust," I answered.

Alas! God had made me neither a hero nor a coward, and my soul flitted constantly between the two.

We started out again. Francis was happy, satisfied, and he had begun to sing softly, again in his mother's native tongue. Once more he had carried out God's command: he had sung and danced in the middle of Assisi, had abandoned his mother and father, broken the chains which were binding him to the earth, and saved himself. Had he not sung in the same way when he fulfilled God's first command by rebuilding San Damiano's? The second task had been more difficult, and for that reason the joy was greater.

We were in a forest of wild oaks now. The moon threw a pale, doleful light onto the branches and stones; from time to time an owl flew silently over our heads. Suddenly in the midst of Francis' singing we heard the heavy tread and breathing of human beings behind the trees. Francis cut short his song, and we stood motionless.

"Bandits have their hideaways here," I said. "We're lost!"

"How can you be lost when you have nothing to lose?" Francis replied. "Don't be afraid."

As we were speaking we heard the snapping of twigs: the footsteps were coming closer. All at once five or six ferocious men darted out in front of us with lifted daggers. Two of them grabbed me and threw me to the ground; the rest pounced on Francis.

"Who are you?" they shouted at him, grinding their teeth.

"I am the emissary of the Great King," Francis answered tranquilly.

"And what business do you have here?"

"I have come to invite my brothers the bandits to enter heaven. The Great King is holding a wedding. His son is being married, and the King asks you to take part in the festivities."

One of the bandits held a lighted torch near Francis and stared at his pale, hungry face, his bare, blood-stained feet, and his tattered coat. They all laughed.

"You the emissary of the Great King? You, a barefooted beggar, a ragamuffin!" they exclaimed sarcastically, and they began to search him to find his purse.

But they found nothing. Next, they examined the sack which I had on my back, and again found nothing—not even a crust of bread. They stared at Francis again in the light of the torch.

"He must be crazy," one of them said. "We're wasting our time."

"Let's give them a good beating and toss them in that ditch," said another. "By doing that at least we won't have wasted our time completely."

They lifted the oxtails they were holding and began to thrash us pitilessly. I howled with pain; but Francis, every time he received a blow from the lash, crossed himself and murmured, "Glory be to God!"

The bandits laughed.

"Good God, this fellow isn't a lunatic, he's a saint," said one of them.

"It's the same thing, isn't it?" replied another who appeared to be the leader. "We've settled their hash nicely. Lift them up now and toss them in the ditch."

They seized us by the feet and shoulders, threw us into the ditch, and then left, laughing and hurling insults at us.

Francis held out his hand and stroked my back.

"Does it hurt, Brother Leo?" he asked.

"And am I to suppose yours doesn't, Brother Francis?" I replied irritably. "My back is made of flesh, you know, and there comes a time when—"

"Do not blaspheme against the flesh, Brother Leo. Remember what we said one day: sooner or later it too can become spirit. And indeed it has already! I don't feel the slightest pain, Brother Leo, none at all—I swear to you."

The ditch was deep. We struggled to climb out of it, but kept slipping and rolling back down again to the bottom.

"This place is as good as any, Brother Leo," said Francis. "We were looking for a shelter to pass the night, weren't we? Well, here it is—the Lord sent it to us out of His abounding grace. So let's sleep here and in the morning God will dispatch the sun to show us the way."

Huddling against each other because of the cold, we closed our eyes. My back was still stinging me, but I was exhausted and I slept. Did Francis sleep also? I don't know. I rather doubt it, however, because from time to time in my sleep I heard a voice, a voice that was singing.

When morning came we scrambled out of the ditch on all fours and resumed our wanderings. Sometimes we remained silent for a considerable period, sometimes we exchanged a few words about God, or the weather, or the approaching winter. And each time we saw a village in the distance, Francis would pull my sleeve joyfully.

"Come, Brother Leo," he would say to me, "come, don't be slow. Inside those little houses there must be a soul longing to be saved. Let's go and find it!"

We would enter the village and Francis, as though he were the town crier, would shout:

"Halloo, villagers! Come and see! I bring new wares which I'm going to distribute to you free of cost. First come first served! Free! Free! Free!"

We had found a large ram's bell on the road. This Francis rang in the village streets while he shouted; and the inhabitants would hear and run—men, women, and children—to see what we were bringing and distributing free. Then Francis would step up onto a stone and begin to speak about love: we should love God and men, friends and enemies; we should love animals and birds and the very earth we step on. Carried away, he would speak about love, and when he could no longer find words to express himself, he would burst into tears. Many laughed when they heard him; some grew angry. The children bombarded him with stones. A few people came up to him in secret and kissed his hand. Afterwards, we would make a quick round of the doors with outstretched hands, begging. People gave us a few pieces of stale bread. Then, taking a drink from the village well, we would leave, headed for another village. It is impossible for me to remember how many days or weeks went by in this way. Time is round, and it rolls quickly.

In one small city—I forget its name—we encountered an old friend of Francis' who once upon a time used to accompany him on his revels. He had seen Francis stand himself in the middle of the square and begin to dance, sing, and hawk his new wares. Astonished, he ran up to him.

"Francis, my old friend," he shouted, "how did you come to this? Who brought you to such a state?"

"God," answered Francis with a smile.

"Your silk clothes and the red feather in your hat and your gold rings: where are they all?"

"Satan lent them to me. Now I have returned them to him."

The friend eyed him questioningly from top to toe, examined the coat that had been patched and repatched a thousand times, the bare feet, the uncovered head. But still he continued to be perplexed.

"Where are you coming from, Francis?" he asked finally, his voice full of compassion.

"From the next world," Francis replied.

"And where are you going?"

"To the next world."

"And why do you sing?"

"To keep from losing my way."

The friend shook his head in despair. He must have had a kind heart, this young man, because he took Francis by the hand and signaled me to follow. I ran behind them.

"If I understand correctly, Francis, my old friend, you want to save the world. But listen to me please: it's winter, come home with me and let me give you a warm coat. Otherwise you'll die of cold—and how will you save the world *then?*"

"I'm wearing God," said Francis. "I'm not cold."

The friend laughed. "You're wearing God," he said, "but that's not enough. You need a warm coat as well. You pity worms and try not to step on them; well, pity your body also. It too is a worm; wrap a coat around it. . . . And don't forget," he added, seeing Francis hesitate, "don't forget that your body is needed if you are going to save the world. Without the body—"

"You're right," said Francis. "That's the result of education: you're a sharp-witted fellow! Yes, the body is still needed. Lead on!"

We reached the house. It was obvious that the friend was rich. He went into one of the rooms and came out holding a long, thick woolen coat, a pair of sandals—the kind worn by shepherds— and a shepherd's crook.

"These are my shepherd's clothes," he said. "Put them on."

Francis looked at the woolen garment and held it up against him to judge its size. It came down to his feet. He tried on the hood, took it off. He was laughing like a child.

"I like it," he said finally. "I like it because it is the same color as the ploughed fields in autumn: it reminds one of the soil. Ruffino, in the name of Christ, give a similar one to my companion here, Brother Leo."

The friend was delighted to hear this.

"What a fine thing it will be," he said, "if I live in the memory of mankind because I gave you this coat which you've made into a monk's frock! Do you intend to found an order like Saint Benedict?"

"Do I intend to, or does God? He's the one you must ask—the one I ask."

He stepped aside and dressed himself in the new robe, using as a cincture a bit of rope which he found in the yard. In the meantime his friend brought me my clothes. I put them on, also tying a piece of rope around my waist. My back felt warm. The friend took my sack and went to the larder to fill it with provisions.

Francis extended his hand to his friend as soon as he had returned.

"Shake this hand of clay!" he said to him, and the friend laughed and squeezed Francis' hand.

"My dear, dear friend, Brother Ruffino, may God grant that this robe may one day secure your entrance to the kingdom of heaven. . . . Until we meet again!"

"Where—in the kingdom of heaven?" asked Ruffino, laughing.

"No, in the kingdom of this world. May God also grant that you too may one day start along the road of perfect joy."

We set out once more. It was cold; the sky was full of clouds.

"You see," said Francis with a laugh, "when you take no thought of what you're going to eat or wear, God thinks about it for you and sends you a Ruffino with a sack full of food and two changes of woolen clothes."

We proceeded eastward, admiring our new clothes like two children. You would have thought we had donned martial finery and were speeding to the wars.

"Brother Leo, the only joy in this world is to do God's will. Do you know why?"

"How should I know, Brother Francis? Enlighten me."

"Because what God wants, that, and only that, is also what we want—but we don't know it. God comes and awakens our souls, revealing to them their real, though unknown, desire. This is the secret, Brother Leo. To do the will of God means to do my own most deeply hidden will. Within even the most unworthy of men there is a servant of God, asleep."

"Is that the reason you repaired San Damiano's, then? Was it your own desire, but one which you didn't know about and which God revealed to you when He came in your sleep? Was that the reason you abandoned your mother and father?"

"Exactly. That's also the reason you gave up everything to follow me."

"But, Brother Francis, sometimes we want many things," I objected. "Which among all of them is the will of God?"

"The most difficult," Francis answered with a sigh.

There were claps of thunder in the distance. The air smelled of rain.

"And what do you want deep down within you now, Brother Francis? Can you find it before God tells you?"

Francis lowered his head as though listening for something.

"I can't," he said finally, sighing again. "I know what deep down within me I do not want, but I don't know what I do want."

"What is it that you don't want, Brother Francis? What is it that you hate and fear more than anything else? Forgive me for asking you."

Francis hesitated for a moment. He opened his mouth, but closed it again. Finally he made up his mind to speak.

"Lepers—that's what I hate. I can't bear the sight of them. Even when I'm far away from them, just hearing the bells they wear to warn passers-by to keep their distance is enough to make me faint. God, forgive me, but there is nothing in the whole world that disgusts me more than lepers."

He spat. Suddenly he felt nauseated and dizzy. He leaned against a tree to recover.

"The soul of man is evil, weak, wretched . . . evil, weak, wretched . . ." he murmured. "When wilt Thou take pity on it, Lord, and save it?"

It began to rain. Raising our hoods, we walked quickly in order to reach the nearest village. A young girl was proceeding in the opposite direction. "Give me your blessing, saints of God," she said, greeting us. Francis put his hand to his heart and returned the greeting, but he did not lift his eyes to look at her. She was pretty, well formed, sprightly.

"Why did you keep your eyes on the ground?" I asked him.

"How can I lift my eyes and face the bride of Christ?" he answered.

We walked and walked, but nowhere did we find even a trace of human habitation. The region was deserted. Soon the darkness came down upon us. The rain had grown continually stronger.

"Let's find some cave we can burrow into," I said. "God doesn't want us to go any further."

"You're right, Brother Leo, God doesn't want us to go any further. In other words, we don't want to either!"

Searching in the darkness all along the mountainside, we found a cave and entered. Francis lay down; he was content.

"God sends rain," he said, "but He also sends hoods; and when the rain grows heavier, He sends a cave."

"That's true wisdom," I said.

"No, true kindness," Francis corrected me.

I opened the sack and portioned out some of the abundant provisions that Francis' friend Ruffino had given us in parting. We ate and then, being as tired as we were, immediately closed our eyes to go to sleep. I dropped off at once, hayseed that I am. Alas, I had no cares great enough to keep me awake. But I don't think Francis slept at all. At dawn he uttered a cry and sprang to his feet.

"Wake up, Brother Leo," he called, prodding me with his toe. "Wake up, the day has begun."

"It's still dark out, Brother Francis," I answered sleepily. "What's your hurry?"

"I'm not in a hurry, Brother Leo, it's Him, it's God! Wake up!"

I rose. "Did you have a dream?"

"No. I couldn't sleep the whole night. When dawn came I closed my eyes and prayed to God: 'Father,' I said, 'let me go to sleep. I am a worker, a worker in Thy service. I did what Thou orderedst me to do—I repaired San Damiano's, I danced and became a laughingstock in Assisi, I abandoned my mother and father. Why dost Thou not let me sleep? What more dost Thou want from me? Wasn't that enough?'

"And then I heard a savage voice above me—no, not above me, inside me: 'It was not enough!'

"I swear to you I wasn't sleeping, Brother Leo. It wasn't a dream.

Perhaps everything else is a dream: you and I and this cave and the rain. That voice, however, was not a dream.

"'Not enough?' I shouted in terror. 'What more then dost Thou want from me?'

"'It is day now. Get up and start on your way. I shall stop the rain, just for your sake. Start on your way, and soon you shall hear some bells. It will be a leper sent to you by me. Run to him, embrace him, kiss him. . . . Do you hear? You act as though you didn't hear me. Why don't you answer?'

"I couldn't restrain myself any longer. 'Thou art not a Father,' I cried; 'Thou dost not love mankind. Thou art merciless and all-powerful and Thou playest with us. Just now Thou heardest me tell my companion while we were on the road that I could not bear to touch a leper, and immediately Thou wishest to throw me into leprosy's embrace. Does this mean there is no other road, no easier, more convenient road for poor, wretched man to take in order to come and find Thee?'

"Someone inside me laughed, tearing my entrails in two.

"'There is none,' said the voice after a moment, and then it was abruptly silent. . . .'"

Francis was standing unsteadily near the mouth of the cave, gazing out fearfully through the opening. His words had sent shudders through my body.

"And now?" I asked, looking at him with deep sympathy. He did not hear.

"And now?" I repeated.

This time he turned. "Stop talking about 'now,'" he said, frowning. "There is no such thing as 'now.' Get up so that we can go find him."

"Who?"

Francis lowered his voice. I sensed that his entire tormented body was trembling.

"The leper," he answered softly.

We emerged from the cave. It was growing bright outside; the rain had stopped. In the sky the clouds rolled along and fled as though pursued by the breath of God. On every leaf there hung a glistening drop of water, and displayed within the drop was the entire rainbow.

Setting out, we headed down toward the plain, which was still asleep, blanketed by the morning mist. Francis went in front, walking with giant strides. He was in a hurry.

The sun rose above the mountains; the earth grew warm and so did we. Far below, in back of the pine trees, we spied a large city.

"What city is that, Brother Leo?" Francis asked.

"I'm all confused, Brother Francis. I feel like I'm seeing everything for the first time. . . . It's Ravenna, I think."

Suddenly Francis stopped and grasped my arm. He was deathly pale.

"Do you hear?" he asked in a low voice.

"No. What?"

"Bells . . ."

And as he said this, I actually did hear the sound of bells coming from the plain, still far in the distance. We both stood still. Francis' lower jaw was quivering. The bells came continually closer.

"He's coming . . ." stammered Francis, leaning upon me for support. His whole body was quaking now.

"Let's get away, let's escape," I cried, and I clasped Francis around the waist in order to carry him to safety.

"Where can we go? Escape—escape from God? But how, my poor, unhappy Brother Leo, how?"

"We can take another road, Brother Francis."

"There will be a leper on every road we take. You'll see, the streets will become filled with them. They will not disappear until we have fallen into their arms. So, Brother Leo, put on a bold front —we're going forward!"

The bells could be heard near us now, just behind the trees.

"Courage, Francis, my brother," I said. "God will give you the strength to endure it."

But Francis had already darted forward. The leper had emerged from the clump of trees. In his hand he held a staff covered with bells which, as he shook the staff, warned passers-by to flee. As soon as he saw Francis running toward him with outspread arms, he uttered a shrill cry, apparently from fright, and halted, his knees giving way beneath him as though sudden exhaustion prevented him from continuing. I came close and gazed at him with horror. Half of his putrescent nose had fallen away; his hands were without fingers—just stumps; and his lips were an oozing wound.

Throwing himself upon the leper, Francis embraced him, then

94

lowered his head and kissed him upon the lips. Afterwards he lifted him in his arms and, covering him with his robe, began to advance slowly, with heavy steps, toward the city. Surely there would be some nearby lazaretto where he could deposit him.

He walked and walked. I followed behind, my eyes filled with tears. God is severe, I reflected, exceedingly severe; He has no pity for mankind. What was it that Francis had just finished telling me: that God's will was supposed to be our own deepest, unknown will? No, no! God asks us what we don't want and then says, "That's what I want!" He asks us what we hate and then says, "That's what I love. Do what displeases you, because that is what pleases me!" And you see, here was poor Francis carrying the leper in his arms, having first kissed him on the mouth!

The sun had risen nearly to the center of the sky when we felt the large, scattered drops of an autumn sun-shower. The city, which had grown larger now, suddenly loomed before us in the sunlight, its towers, churches, and houses glistening. We were drawing near.

Suddenly I saw Francis stop abruptly. He bent down and drew aside the robe in order to uncover the leper. But all at once he uttered a loud cry: the robe was empty!

Francis turned and looked at me, opening and closing his lips in a vain effort to speak. But his face was resplendent—ablaze! His mustache, whiskers, nose, mouth: everything had vanished in the conflagration.

The tears flowing from his eyes, he fell prostrate on the ground and began to kiss the soil. I remained standing above him, trembling. It wasn't a leper; it was Christ Himself who had come down to earth in the form of a leper in order to test Francis.

A villager came along. Seeing Francis sprawled out on the ground in the rain, weeping, he stopped.

"What happened to him?" he asked. "Why is he crying? Did brigands attack and give him a beating—is that it?"

"No," I answered. "A moment ago Christ came by here. He saw Him, and he is weeping from joy."

The villager shrugged his shoulders, laughed, and continued hastily past us.

Francis opened his eyes. He gazed at the cloudy sky, at the scattered sheets of rainfall that were bedimming the air. Looking down again, he saw me. He was still unable to speak. He smiled at me, and I fell immediately to the ground in the middle of the road, next to him, and began to kiss him and to stroke his face tenderly, trying to salve the effects of the divine thunderbolt which had fallen upon him. His body was still steaming.

I cannot say how long—how many hours—we remained there stretched out in the middle of the road, not speaking a word. But when we got up and looked around us, the sun was setting. The power of speech had returned to Francis.

"Did you see, Brother Leo? Did you understand?"

"I saw, Brother Francis, but the only thing I understood was that God is playing games with us."

"This, Brother Leo, is what I understood: all lepers, cripples, sinners: if you kiss them on the mouth—"

He stopped, afraid to complete his thought.

"Enlighten me, Brother Francis, enlighten me; do not leave me in the dark."

Finally, after a long silence, he murmured with a shudder:

"All these, if you kiss them on the mouth—O God, forgive me for saying this—they all . . . become Christ."

It was night when we finally reached the great city. We saw her tall, thickly branched pine trees, were able to make out her round towers in the half-light, and sensed everywhere around us the uncircumscribed breath of the sea. Smelling the salt air, we were refreshed. We had arrived in the celebrated city of Ravenna.

"I like it," said Francis. "It is a majestic city full of palaces, churches, and ancient glory."

"Let's pass the winter here," I said. "The rainy season is upon us; the rivers are swollen. Where can we go in such conditions? Here as well as elsewhere there must be souls awaiting you, Brother Francis."

We were tired. Unable to continue further, we stopped outside the city at the famous monastery of Saint Apollinarius. The doors were barred. Night had fallen and it was too late for anyone to go in. The rain began to come down in bucketfuls.

"We'll sleep here in front of the door, and in the morning, God willing, we shall enter to do worship."

Suddenly he realized he was hungry.

"Isn't there anything left in the sack, Brother Leo?" he asked.

"Nothing. Nothing but the ram's bell. We didn't pass a single village today. Are you hungry?"

"It doesn't matter. Tomorrow. This is a large city: somewhere, in some house, there will be a piece of bread the housewife baked just for us, and it will be waiting."

We crossed ourselves and lay down, glued to the gate like two leeches. Drenched and cold, we huddled close to one another again, our arms entwined.

"Brother Francis," I said, "all my life there's been something I've found perplexing. Enlighten me. Some people do not beg, and even if offered charity refuse to accept it. Others accept alms though they do not beg and still others beg actively. Which is right?"

"Holy humility requires that you hold out your hand to beg and that you accept what is given you, Brother Leo. The rest is arrogance. The rich have an obligation to the poor; let them fulfill their obligation. . . . But that's enough now. Don't ask anything else. Go to sleep; you're tired and so am I. Good night."

I realized that Francis was anxious to remain alone with God, so I stopped chattering, and closed my eyes. The whole night long it seemed to me in my sleep that I heard him talking, and sometimes laughing, sometimes weeping.

The next morning we both stood in front of the gate and waited for the doorkeeper to come and open up. Peering through the grating into the courtyard, which was light now, we saw the garden with its laurels and cypresses, the marble well in its center, the rows of vaulted cells on all sides; and in the background the celebrated church which had been constructed and ornamented by strange, masterful artisans from the Orient.

The sun came up; the doorkeeper appeared with his keys. He was gaunt and sullen, barefooted, had a small, curly white beard, and was munching something between his toothless gums. As soon as he saw us his expression grew savage.

"Beggars?" he asked angrily. "The monastery hasn't any bread for the likes of you, you loafers!"

"We aren't loafers, Father Major-domo," answered Francis pleasantly. "We work, just as you do. We also have keys, and we lock and unlock."

"Lock and unlock what, swindlers!"

97

"The Inferno."

"The Inferno?"

"Yes, the Inferno: our hearts."

The doorkeeper growled like a vicious dog, but said nothing. Taking the key, he twisted it in the lock, drew back the bolt, and allowed us to enter. The monks were not in their cells—matins had begun; we could hear the sweet psalmody. The daylight had descended now and fully invaded the cloister garden; the birds were awake; a young monk was drawing water, leaning over the well. Standing like archangels on either side of the church were two tall cypresses, as slender and straight as swords; and in the center of the courtyard, bathed in fragrance, was a luxuriant laurel.

Francis pulled off a leaf and kissed it. Holding it upright in his hand like a lighted candle, he pushed open the church door and entered. I was thirsty, and I paused long enough for the young monk to pull up the bucket so that I could take a drink. When I had refreshed myself I made the sign of the cross, gave thanks to God for sending us thirst and water, and strode across the threshold.

The monks were seated in their stalls, chanting. The air smelled of sweet incense. The sun, entering through the stained-glass windows, was tinted red, green, and blue. I spied Francis kneeling on the flagstones with his gaze fixed ecstatically on the vault above the altar.

I lifted my eyes too. What was this miracle I saw before me? Was it Paradise? I beheld a gigantic mosaic, green, white, and gold, with Saint Apollinarius in the middle wearing his golden stole, his arms raised in prayer. Flanking him were cypresses, angels, snowy-white sheep, and trees loaded with fruit. O God, what was this greenery, this freshness, sweetness? What untroubled immortal calm; what a verdant meadow for the soul to graze in until the end of time! Even I, peasant that I am, was unable to restrain my emotion. I knelt down next to Francis and began to sob.

"Quiet," Francis said softly. "Don't cry, don't laugh, don't talk. Just surrender yourself."

It seems to me that neither of us breathed a word that whole day. I don't remember how we left the church, or if the monks gave us a piece of bread, or when we entered the city. The only thing I remember is that we roamed up and down the streets looking at the people, towers, palaces and seeing nothing but a green meadow and in the middle a saint with white sheep running happily to greet him, and above, an immense cross spreading its arms and embracing the air.

Toward evening we halted at a large square, the one in whose center is the statue of Christ bearing a young sheep on his shoulders —the lost sheep which He is returning to the fold. The breadwinners were closing their workshops; the young boys and girls were arriving from their different neighborhoods to see and be seen. The rain had stopped; there was a scent of pine in the freshly bathed air. Francis grasped the ram's bell for a moment as though wanting to call the people to hear about the new madness, but he immediately changed his mind. His thoughts must have been elsewhere. He suspended the bell from the knotted cord which bound his waist and, sitting down on the ground, began to watch the inhabitants as they paraded by.

I squatted next to him. Suddenly he turned to me.

"Brother Leo, I've seen that meadow somewhere before, the green meadow where Saint Apollinarius and his herdsmen the angels graze their sheep. But where? When? I'm fighting to remember, but I can't. Was it in a dream?"

He fell silent; but suddenly he clapped his hands with delight.

"I've found it!" he exclaimed. "I've found it, praise the Lord! This worry about where and when has been bothering me for hours, but now I've found the answer." His face became suddenly radiant; his eyes filled with emeralds.

"Inside me!" he murmured happily.

Darkness was falling, and as the night advanced we heard Ravenna's many voices ever more clearly. The city was stretched out in the blackness like a myriad-headed, satiated beast, laughing, barking, neighing, singing with innumerable human, canine, and equestrian mouths, with innumerable mouths shaped like lutes and guitars. And as night overwhelmed us, for an instant it seemed to me that Christ was standing in the middle and that it was not a lamb He was carrying back to the fold: it was Ravenna.

"What are you thinking about?" asked Francis, seeing me with my eyes riveted on the stone statue of Jesus.

"I was thinking, Brother Francis, that it isn't a lamb He's holding, but Ravenna."

"It isn't Ravenna, Brother Leo; no, it isn't Ravenna. It's the world —the entire world."

We fell silent once more; and then an old man with a fierce expression came and stood before us. He was huge, with a clean-shaven upper lip and a long, tortuous white beard. In the gleam thrown out by the lanterns inside the taverns we were able to see that his sunburned face had been slashed by sword blows.

He sat down cross-legged next to us. He had overheard our last words.

"Pardon me," he said, "but I've seen you roaming, without talking, your sack empty, as though you're beggars and aren't beggars at the same time. A moment ago I finally heard you speak, and I liked what you said. For some time now I've been wondering what you might be: beggars, lazy idlers, invalids, saints? I can't seem to tell which."

Francis laughed. Raising his finger, he pointed to the statue of Christ above us.

"Look. We are the lost sheep, and we're bleating and searching everywhere for Christ. Christ is not looking for us, Father; we are looking for Him."

"And you came to find Him here in Ravenna?" the old man inquired sarcastically.

"Our Gracious Lord is everywhere," Francis replied, "but we never know where He will condescend to reveal Himself to us. Perhaps even in Ravenna."

The old man shook his white-haired head. "I was once looking for Him also," he said in a low voice, slowly stroking his white beard. "I found him far far away at the other end of the earth, amid the hubbub of war; but to reveal himself to me he had taken on the face of man—of a great king."

He sighed: it was as though his heart were being rent in two. Francis slid over and placed his hand on the old man's knee.

"Father," he said, "I implore you in the name of Christ who is above us: tell us how and when; help us to find Him also."

The old man lowered his head and for some time did not speak.

You could sense that he was silently choosing what to say and where to start, for he opened his mouth several times, but closed it again and continued his silence.

"It was in the East more than twenty years ago," he began finally; "in the holy city of Jerusalem, a strange Oriental world of perfumes and stenches. There are date palms like the ones we see on the paintings of the saints, and other trees even stranger, and a type of grapevine that grows to a man's height. The women are covered from head to foot like ghosts, and if their toenails ever happen to appear, you find that they are colored with red paint, as are their palms, and also the soles of their feet. I know because we captured a few of them alive in the war, and uncovered them and saw. . . . As for the men, the lawless Saracens: the moment they mount their horses they become one body with them and it's impossible to discover where the horse ends and the man begins. Two heads, six legs, one soul! And Sultan Saladin, their king, he's a stalwart if there ever was one. Dressed all in gold and pearls, he leaps on his horse while the animal is racing at a full gallop. His palace is full of women, fountains, yataghans, and he sits cross-legged upon the Holy Sepulcher twisting his mustache and threatening all Christendom."

Francis sighed.

"And we," he said, "my God, shame on us! We sit here idle in Ravenna, walking the streets and begging instead of rising up to deliver the Holy Sepulcher! Up, up, Brother Leo! Why are you sitting? Do you want to liberate your soul? Then liberate the Holy Sepulcher!"

"If you want to liberate the Holy Sepulcher," I objected, "then liberate your soul!"

The old man shook his head.

"That's youth for you. It thinks that if it rises up in arms it can conquer the world. I myself once did just that. I was an established citizen here in Ravenna, with children, fields, sheep, and a white horse which I loved like my own child. I abandoned everything except the horse—her I took with me. I cut two strips of red cloth, sewed them on my back to make a cross, and set out to deliver the Holy Sepulcher."

He stopped for a moment and made a gesture with his hand.

"Where to begin?" he said, unable to choose. "My head was full of seas, deserts, huge fortified towers with ravelins, and in the very center of my mind stood Holy Jerusalem. I journeyed on and on, sometimes by boat, sometimes on my horse, and I encountered swarms of wild savage men, men of all kinds speaking every conceivable language. My route took me through the celebrated city of Constantinople, which stretches over the world's two great land areas, Europe and Asia Minor. Seeing it, I went out of my mind. What are dreams in comparison? The mind of man is too small to contain such a miracle; sleep is too poor—where could it ever find such a dream to bring to us? I wandered throughout the city, gazing insatiably upon its palaces, churches, festivals, women. Forgive me, Lord, but I forgot completely about the Holy Sepulcher, and when I finally arrived in Jerusalem it had already fallen into the hands of the Christians, and the king of Jerusalem was—"

He grasped his beard and folded it up upon itself, covering his face. It was some time before he found his voice again:

"The king was a twenty-year-old boy. People called him Baudouin, but it did not take me long to realize that he was not simply a human being, but something else entirely. Was he, I asked myself (begging God's forgiveness for my audacity) was he the One I was seeking? When I first saw him, I shuddered. The Saracens were attacking once more on their horses and camels in an attempt to win back Jerusalem. The king uttered a cry, the trumpets blared, the labarum of war was hoisted into the air. We got into our armor and assembled on the plain outside Jerusalem, thousands of infantrymen and cavalry all awaiting the king's appearance.

"And then—oh, how can I recall it without my heart splitting in two?—then I saw him for the first time, then I realized that man's soul is omnipotent, that God, God in His entirety, sits inside man, and that it is unnecessary for us to run to the ends of the earth in His pursuit. All we have to do is gaze into our own hearts.

"They were carrying the king in a litter. His face had rotted away until only half was left; he had no fingers at all, no toes either. He couldn't walk—how could he possibly walk?—so they were carrying him. The leprosy had eaten away his eyes too and made him blind. I happened to be near him. I leaned forward to see him, but had to pinch my nostrils, the stench was so bad.

"This king was a shovelful of putrid flesh, but inside this shovelful of flesh his soul stood erect and immortal. How is it that God did not find it disgusting to be enthroned in such putrescence? The terrible sultan was besieging the impregnable fortress of Crac in the Moab desert, beyond the Dead Sea. The king went in the lead. He crossed the desert in the unbearable heat and we followed behind him, gasping for breath. Spurting out from within the litter was a force, a flame; the air crackled like a pine tree that has caught fire."

The old man stopped, not wishing—or perhaps unable—to speak further. I placed my palm on the aged warrior's knee and begged him to continue, but he clasped his hand around his throat, apparently trying to stifle the sobs which were rising there.

"When I recall that sight," he said finally, "my heart seethes, my mind grows fierce. Never have I seen the Mystery of God so clearly, so palpably. I was there in Jerusalem when the king died, aged twenty-four; I was there in the great palace where he gave up the ghost. Standing above him were his insatiable, demented mother and his sister Sybil—vain, beautiful, given over to the joys of the flesh. The rest of the room was filled with bloodthirsty noblemen— barons, counts, marquises all waiting breathlessly for the king to breathe his last so that they could throw themselves like so many famished, raving dogs upon the kingdom of Jerusalem and tear it to shreds, each taking away a piece in his teeth. And all the while the twenty-four-year-old king, that paragon of noble courtesy, was tranquilly, silently rendering up his soul to God, a crown of thorns on his putrescent head."

The aged warrior bit into his mustache. Huge teardrops were running down his sun-baked cheeks. Francis lowered his head to his knees and suddenly, in the darkness, he too broke out into lamentations.

Angrily, the old man wiped away his tears, ashamed at having wept. Then, pushing his hands against the ground for support, he rose, his aged bones creaking. Without nodding goodbye to us, without uttering a word, he disappeared.

Francis continued to weep.

"There you see what the soul really is," he said finally, raising his head, "and what God is, and what it really means to be a man. From now on this leper shall take the lead and show us the way. Get up, Brother Leo; let's be off!"

"Where to, in God's name?"

"Back to Assisi. That is where we shall gather momentum so that we can take our leap. Come, you lazybones of God, up with you!"

"Now, in the middle of the night?"

"Now! Do you think the Lord can wait till morning?"

THE ROYAL LEPER went in the lead and guided us for the entire return journey. It rained and rained; the rivers had overflowed, the roads had been flooded, and we sank up to our knees in mud. We were cold, we were hungry. In many of the villages we found ourselves greeted with a bombardment of stones and driven away. When Francis shouted, "Love! Love! Love!" the peasants turned their dogs on us, and we were bitten.

"What are these trifles we are undergoing for Christ's sake?" Francis would say to comfort me. "Games! Remember the leper-king!"

One night when we were drenched to the bone and nearly dropping from hunger and cold, we saw the lights of a monastery in the distance. We began to run. Perhaps the monks would be moved by compassion to bring us inside, give us a little bread to eat, and let us sit next to the hallowed fire to get warm. It was pitch dark outside and pouring. We ran, fell into the potholes, got up, began to run again. I cursed the rain, the darkness, the cold; but Francis, ahead of me, was composing lyrics in his head and singing them.

"What miracles we see here!" he sang. "Behold! Wings in the mud, God in the air! As soon as the caterpillars think of Thee, Lord, they are transformed into butterflies!"

Spreading his arms again and again, he joyfully embraced the rain and the air. "Sister Mud," he called, sloshing through the potholes. "Brother Wind!"

105

Suddenly he stopped and waited for me to catch up. I had fallen into a ditch again and was dragging myself along, limping.

"I've just finished composing a little song, Brother Leo," he said to me. "Do you want to hear it?"

"Is this the time for songs?" I replied with irritation.

"If we don't make up songs now, Brother Leo, when shall we ever do so? Listen: the very first animal to appear at the gates of heaven was the snail. Peter bent forward, patted it with his staff, and asked, 'What are you looking for here, my fine little snail?'

" 'Immortality,' the snail answered.

"Peter howled with laughter. 'Immortality! And what do you plan to do with immortality?'

" 'Don't laugh,' the snail countered. 'Aren't I one of God's creatures? Aren't I a son of God just like the Archangel Michael? Archangel Snail, that's who I am!'

" 'Where are your wings of gold, your scimitar, the scarlet sandals betokening your regality?'

" 'Inside me, asleep and waiting.'

" 'Waiting for what?'

" 'The Great Moment.'

" 'What Great Moment?'

" 'This one—now!'

"And before he had finished saying 'Now' he took a great leap, as though he had sprouted wings, and he entered Paradise. . . .

"Do you understand?" Francis asked me, laughing. "We, Brother Leo, are the snails; within us are the wings and the scimitar, and if we want to enter Paradise we must take the leap. . . . For the salvation of your soul, fellow athlete, jump!"

He grasped me by the hand, and we ran. Several minutes later he stopped, out of breath.

"Brother Leo, listen well to what I am going to say to you. Prick up your ears. Are you listening? I have the feeling you don't like the life we are leading very much. It seems oppressive to you, and you are fretting."

"No, Brother Francis, I'm not fretting. But we're all human. You forget this fact; I don't. It's as simple as that."

"Brother Leo, do you know what perfect joy is?"

I did not answer. I knew extremely well what perfect joy was: it was for us to reach this monastery, for the doorkeeper to take pity on us and open the gate, for a huge fire to be lighted for us in the fireplace, for the pot to be put on and heaps of warm food prepared for us, and for the monks to go down into the monastery cellar and bring up a large jug of vintage wine for us to drink! But how could I say such sensible things to Francis? His love of God had made him turn need inside out. For him hunger took the place of bread, thirst took the place of water and wine. How then could he understand those who were hungry and thirsty? I held my tongue.

"Even if we were the most saintly men on earth, the most beloved of God—remember well, Brother Leo, what I say to you: that would not be perfect joy."

We walked a little further. Then Francis stopped again.

"Brother Leo," he called, shouting because he was unable to make me out in the darkness, "Brother Leo, even if we gave sight to the blind, cast out devils from men, and raised the dead from their graves, remember well what I say to you: that would not be perfect joy."

I did not speak. How can you argue with a saint? You can with the devil, but not with a saint. Therefore I did not speak.

We proceeded, stumbling over the stones and branches which the rains had washed down onto the road. Francis stopped once more.

"Brother Leo, even if we spoke all the languages of men and angels, and even if, preaching the word of God, we should convert all infidels to the faith of Christ, remember well, Brother Leo, what I say to you: that would not be perfect joy."

My patience gave out. I was hungry and cold. My feet were killing me: I couldn't walk.

"All right, what is perfect joy?" I asked wearily.

"You shall see in a moment," replied Francis, and he quickened his pace.

We reached the monastery. It was closed, but lamps were still burning in the cells. Francis rang the little bell. I huddled in a corner next to the gate, frozen to death.

We cocked our ears and waited to see whether or not the doorkeeper would come to open the gate for us. I'm ashamed to say this, but since a sin once confessed is no longer considered a sin, I'll admit that I was silently cursing the fate which tied me to this terrifying wild beast of God, this Francis. Though he did not know it, he was like the leprous king of Jerusalem—a handful of flesh and bone, with God, God in His entirety, sitting inside. That was why he could endure, why he never felt hunger or thirst or cold, why the stones which people threw at him were like a sprinkling of lemon flowers. But I, I was a man, a reasonable man, and a wretched one. I felt hunger, and the stones, for me, were stones.

An inner door opened. Heavy footsteps resounded in the courtyard. It's the doorkeeper, I said to myself. He's taken pity on us. Glory be to God!

"Who's here at such an hour?" growled an angry voice.

"Open the gate, Brother Doorkeeper," Francis replied in a sweet, gentle tone. "We are two humble servants of Christ who are hungry and cold and who seek refuge tonight in this holy monastery."

"Go about your business!" bellowed the voice. "You—servants of God? And what are you doing roaming about the streets at such an hour? You're brigands and you waylay men and kill them and set monasteries on fire. Off with you!"

"Have you no pity, Brother Doorkeeper?" I cried. "Are you going to let us die of cold? If you believe in Christ, open the gate, grant us a corner where we can be sheltered from the rain, give us a piece of bread. We are Christians! Take pity on us!"

We heard the sound of a staff banging on the flagstones of the courtyard.

"Now you asked for it, you wretches! I'm coming out to give you both a thrashing," screamed the ferocious voice, and the lock of the street door began to grate.

Francis turned to me. "Bear it like a man, Brother Leo. Do not resist."

The door opened and out flew a gigantic monk holding a thick cudgel. He seized Francis around the neck.

"Villain, murderer, criminal," he shouted, "you've come to rob the monastery, have you? Take that! And that!"

The cudgel pounded Francis' weak, sickly body.

I darted forward to save him, but Francis held out his hand.

"Do not oppose God's will, Brother Leo! Strike, Brother Doorkeeper. You are my salvation."

The doorkeeper turned to me with a sardonic laugh and seized me by the nape of the neck.

"Your turn, you scoundrel!"

I lifted my own staff and got ready to swing, but Francis, with a look of desperation, cried, "Brother Leo, I implore you in Christ's name, do not resist!"

"I should let him kill me, in other words?" I shouted, full of indignation. "No, I'm going to resist, and I want you to know it!"

"Brother Leo, Brother Leo, if you love me, do not resist. Allow our brother the doorkeeper to do his duty. God commanded him to thrash us, so, we must be thrashed."

I threw my staff to the ground and crossed my hands upon my breast.

"Strike, Brother Doorkeeper," I said, my lips trembling with furor. "Strike, and may the wrath of God deal with you!"

The doorkeeper laughed at our words. His breath smelled of wine and garlic. He began to pound me with his cudgel and I heard my bones cracking. Francis, who was sitting on the ground now, in the mud, kept talking to me, giving me courage.

"Do not cry out, Brother Leo; do not curse, do not lift a hand in defense. Think of the royal leper, think of Christ when He was being crucified. Fortify your heart."

The doorkeeper finished his job. Giving each of us a final kick, he locked and barred the door.

I huddled in my corner, dying of pain. I was cursing to myself, but I did not dare open my mouth. Francis drew himself to where I had fallen, took hold of my hand tenderly, and stroked my painful shoulders. He nestled in the corner with me and we hugged each other to become warm.

"This, Brother Leo," he whispered in my ear as though not wanting anyone to hear, "this, Brother Leo, is perfect joy."

Now he had carried the thing too far! "Perfect joy?" I screamed, flying into a rage. "I beg your pardon, Brother Francis, but to me it sounds more like perfect impudence. The heart of man is impudent when it joyfully accepts nothing but what is unpleasant. God says to it, 'I brought you food to eat, wine to drink, fire to keep you warm,' and the heart of man answers, most insolently, 'Sorry, I don't want them!' When is it going to say Yes, the pretentious idiot!"

"As soon as God opens His arms, Brother Leo, and tells it to come. The heart shouts No! No! No! to the small, insignificant joys. And why do you think it does this? To save itself in order to reach the great Yes."

"Can't it arrive there any other way?"

"I cannot. The great Yes is formed only by these many No's."

"In that case why did God create the earth's riches? Why did He lay such a splendid banquet before us?"

"In order to test our stamina, Brother Leo."

"What's the use of arguing with you, Brother Francis? Let me go to sleep. Slumber is more merciful than God—maybe I'll dream about loaves of bread."

I rolled up into a ball, closed my eyes, and along came all-merciful sleep, God bless it! and enveloped me.

The next morning at dawn someone began to push me. It was Francis. I awoke.

"Listen, Brother Leo, he's coming!"

From inside the courtyard came the sound of the approaching doorkeeper, the keys clinking at his belt. The door opened.

"Glory be to God," I murmured. "Our troubles are over." I had already begun to lift my foot in order to cross the threshold.

Francis turned and looked at me, his twinkling eyes filled with saintly cunning.

"Shall we go in?" he asked me. "What do you think, little lion of God, shall we go in?"

I understood. He wanted to tease me because I was hungry and unable to resist the call of my stomach. My self-respect, however, got the best of my hunger.

"No," I answered, "let's not. I'm not going in!" I turned away.

Francis fell into my arms. "Bravo, Brother Leo. That's the way I want you: a true stalwart!"

He turned to the monastery. "Farewell, holy inhospitable monastery. Brother Leo has no need of you; he is not going in!"

Crossing ourselves, we set off once again on our journey. Francis was so happy, he flew.

The sun had come out; the rain had stopped. Trees and stones were laughing, the world glistening, newly washed. Two black-birds in front of us shook their drenched wings, looked at us, and whistled, as though taunting us. Yes, that's what they were doing: taunting us. But Francis waved his hand and greeted them.

"These are the monks of the bird kingdom," he said. "Look how they're dressed!"

I laughed. "You're right, Brother Francis. Really, in a monastery near Perugia I once saw a blackbird which had been trained to chant the Kyrie eleison! A true monk."

Francis sighed. "Oh, if only someone could teach the birds and oxen, the sheep, dogs, wolves, and wild boars to say just those two words: 'Kyrie eleison'! If only the whole of Creation could awake in this way each morning, so that from the depths of the forest, from every tree, every stable, every courtyard you would hear all the animals glorifying God, crying, 'Kyrie eleison'!"

"First let's teach men to say those two words," I said. "I don't see why the birds and animals need learn them. Birds and animals don't sin."

Francis stared at me with protruding eyes. "Yes, what you say is correct, Brother Leo. Of all living things man is the only one that sins."

"Yes, but on the other hand, Brother Francis, man is the only one who can surpass his nature and enter heaven. The animals and birds can't do that."

"Don't be too sure," protested Francis. "No one knows the full extent of God's mercy."

In this way, talking about God, birds, and man, we arrived one morning outside our beloved Assisi. Her towers, campaniles, citadel, olive groves, cypresses filled our eyes with bliss.

Tears blurred Francis' sight. "I am made from this soil," he said. "I am a clay lamp made from this soil."

Bending down, he scooped up some dirt in his hand and kissed it.

"I owe a handful of soil to Assisi; I shall return it to her. No matter where I die, Brother Leo, I want you to bring me here to be buried."

We had turned into a narrow, covered alleyway. It was Sunday today, and the bells were tolling the end of Mass. Francis had hardly finished what he was saying when he halted abruptly and leaned for support against the wall, breathing laboriously, as though suffocating. I had been running behind him, and all at once my breath was taken away also. Standing in front of us was Count Scifi's daughter. She was dressed completely in white except for a red rose on her bosom—but how pale she was now, how sad, how dark the rings around her eyes. All the time since we had last seen her that day at San Damiano's, how many nights she must have stayed awake and wept! The little girl had suddenly become a woman!

The nurse followed behind her, old and dignified. Seeing her mistress stop, she stopped too, and waited. The morning was bathed in sunlight and they had taken the longest possible route back from church so that they could reach the great house as late as possible and thus delay enclosing themselves within.

As soon as Clara saw Francis her knees gave way beneath her. She wanted to turn back, but was too ashamed. Forcing herself to be brave, she raised her eyes and gazed directly into his with a severe, melancholy look. Then she took a step toward him, stretched her head forward, and stared at his rags, his naked be-spattered feet, his starved face. She shook her head scornfully.

"Aren't you ashamed?" she asked him in a stifled, despairing voice.

"Ashamed? Ashamed in front of whom?"

"Your father, your mother, me. Why do you go to the places you do? Why do you shout what you shout? Why do you dance in the middle of the street like a carnival acrobat?"

Francis listened with bowed head, stooped, half-kneeling. He did not speak. Clara leaned over him, her eyes brimming with tears.

"I feel sorry for you," she said fervently. "When I think of you my heart breaks."

"Mine too . . ." said Francis, but so softly that only I, supporting him as I was to keep him from falling, managed to hear.

Clara gave a start. Her face became radiant. From the motion of Francis' lips she had divined his words.

"Francis . . . you think of me too?" she asked, her bosom swelling.

Francis raised his head.

"Never!" he cried, and he extended his arm as though to direct her to one side so that he could pass.

The girl uttered a shrill cry. The nurse ran to support her, but Clara pushed the old lady away. Her eyes flashing, she raised her hand:

"Accursed is he who acts contrary to the will of God," she said in a fierce voice. "Accursed is he who preaches that we should not marry, should not have children and build a home; who preaches that men should not be real men, loving war, wine, women, glory; that women should not be real women, loving love, fine clothes, all the comforts of life. . . . Forgive me for telling you this, my poor Francis, but that is what it means to be a true human being."

Yes, yes, that is what it means to be a true human being, my poor Brother Leo, and forgive me for telling you, I repeated in my turn (to myself) rejoicing in the girl's splendid words, and in her ferocity and beauty.

The nurse approached and put her arm around her mistress' waist.

"Come, my child," she said. "People will see you."

The girl laid her head on the old woman's breast and suddenly began to cry. God knows how many months she had been spinning those words in her heart and longing to see Francis and speak them out to him in order to relieve herself. And now, now that she had finally spoken, she had found no relief at all. Her heart was thumping, ready to burst.

The nurse drew her along calmly, gently, but the moment they were about to turn into the next lane, Clara halted. Unpinning the red rose from her bosom, she spun around, saw Francis still stooped over toward the ground, and threw it to him.

"Take it," she said. "Take it, poor, wretched Francis, as a remembrance of me—a remembrance of this world!"

The rose landed at Francis' feet.

"Come," the girl said to her nurse. "Everything is over now!"

Francis remained motionless, his gaze fixed on the pavement. Gradually he raised his head and looked around him fearfully. Then he squeezed my hand.

"Is she gone?" he asked softly.

"She's gone," I answered, and I picked up the rose.

"Don't touch it!" said Francis, terrified. "Put it at the edge of the street so that no one will step on it. Come, and don't look behind you!"

"Where? Still to Assisi? This meeting was a bad omen, Brother Francis. Let's change our plans."

"To Assisi!" he said, and he began to run. "Take the ram's bell,

113

ring it! Good God, to marry, have children, build a home—I spit on them all!"

"Alas the day, Brother Francis, I believe—forgive me, Lord, for thinking so—I believe the girl was right. A true human being—"

"A true human being is someone who has surpassed what is human—that's what I say! I implore you, Brother Leo, be quiet!"

I held my tongue. What could I reply? The longer I had been living with Francis the more clearly I sensed that there were two roads which led to God: the straight, level road, that of man, where you reached God married, with children, freshly shaved, full of food and smelling of wine; and the uphill road, that of the saint, where you reached Him a tattered rag, a handful of hair and bones, smelling of uncleanliness and incense. I was suited to the first of these, but who ever bothered to ask my opinion! So, I took the uphill road —and may God grant me the strength to endure!

We reached the center of the city. I went ahead of Francis and rang the bell, crying, "Come, come one and all to hear the new madness!" The people in the streets stopped. Now they'll pick up stones and start pelting us, I said to myself; now the children will emerge from every lane and begin to jeer at the top of their lungs. . . . But nothing happened. Silence. I became frightened. Was this the way we were going to be received now—without being hooted or booed?

No one lifting a hand to stop us, we continued on. Bernardone was standing outside his shop. His shoulders were rounded now, his skin had become yellow. When Francis saw him he turned coward for a moment and started to reverse his steps in order to find another route.

"Courage, Brother Francis," I said to him softly, taking hold of his arm. "This is where you are going to show us how brave you are."

Bernardone turned and saw us. At first a shudder ran through his body, but then he ran quickly inside, got his staff, and descended upon us, bellowing. Francis stepped forward and pointed to me.

"Here is my father, Sior Bernardone. He gives me his blessing; you give me your curse. He is my father!"

He took my hand and kissed it.

Bernardone's eyes filled with tears which he wiped away with the edge of his wide cuff. A considerable number of passers-by had

114

halted to stare hatefully at the rich merchant and his ragamuffin of a son. Father Silvester of the parish of San Niccolo was also passing by. He was about to intervene in an attempt to reconcile father and son, but he immediately changed his mind. "Let them settle their own affairs!" he murmured, and he went off toward his church.

Bernardone lowered his head and did not breathe a word. But his face had suddenly become covered with wrinkles. Feeling his knees begin to give way beneath him, he leaned on his staff for support and regarded his son for a considerable time, still not speaking. Finally, his voice full of complaint, he asked, "Have you no pity for your mother?"

Francis turned pale. He opened his mouth to reply, but his jaw began to tremble.

"Have you no pity for your mother?" Bernardone asked again. "She weeps all day and all night. Come home; let her see you."

"I must first ask God," Francis managed to answer.

"A God who can prevent you from seeing your mother: what kind of God is that?" said Bernardone, looking at his son imploringly.

"I don't know," Francis answered. "Let me ask Him."

He set off toward the upper part of the city, toward the citadel. I looked back for a moment and saw Bernardone still standing in the middle of the street, seemingly turned to stone. He was squeezing his throat with his left hand, as though attempting to stifle his curses or sobs.

Truly, what kind of God was that? I asked myself, remembering my poor, unfortunate mother, long since dead. What kind of God was capable of separating son from mother?

I gazed at Francis, who was in front of me striding hurriedly up the hill. He had already reached the fortress. I sensed that inside his feeble, half-dead body there was hidden a merciless and inhuman force which did not concern itself with mother and father, which perhaps even rejoiced at abandoning them. What kind of God was that—really! I did not understand! If it had only been possible for me to turn into some out-of-the-way lane and escape! Ah, to go into a tavern, sit down at a table, clap my hands and say: Waiter, bring me bread, wine, meat—I'm starved! On the double! I'm fed up with being hungry! And if Francis the son of Bernardone comes and asks if you've seen Brother Leo, tell him you haven't.

Francis knew of a deep cave in the mountainside. There he hid himself.

"Brother Leo," he said, bidding me goodbye, "I must remain here by myself for three days. Farewell. I have many things to ask God, and He and I must be alone. Farewell. In three days we shall come together again."

As he spoke he grew thinner and thinner, melted away, became one with the half-light of the cave—disappeared, air into air. Kneeling at the entranceway, he thrust his arms up toward heaven and uttered a heart-rending cry: he seemed to be summoning God to appear. I stood still for some time, looking at him and silently saying goodbye. Who could tell if he would ever issue from the prayer alive! I had a presentiment that the coming struggle was to be a terrible one, and that Francis' life was in danger.

For three days I wandered through Assisi, begging. Each evening I brought whatever alms the good Christians gave me and placed them on a stone outside the cave. Then I left quickly lest Francis see me and his meditations crash down to earth. But the following day I always found the food still on the stone, untouched.

On one of the days, I passed Bernardone's house. Lady Pica noticed me from the window, came downstairs, and brought me inside. She wanted to speak to me, to question me, but she was overcome with tears, and all she could do was gaze at me in silence.

How she had changed, aged! Her rosy cheeks had faded; the wrinkles around her mouth had deepened; her eyes were red.

"Where is he?" she managed to say, wiping away the tears with her tiny handkerchief. "What is he doing?"

"He's in a cave, Lady Pica—praying."

"And can't God allow him to come so that I may see him?"

"I don't know, ma'am. He's praying, asking Him. But he hasn't received an answer yet."

"Take a stool and sit down. Tell me everything. A mother's pain is large, as large—forgive me, Lord—as large as God Himself. Take pity on me and speak."

I related everything to her, starting with the day her son undressed himself in front of the bishop and continuing to the encounter on the road with the leper who was Christ, to Ravenna, where we had found the ancient warrior, to the monastery where we were thrashed, and last of all to the nobleman's daughter Clara and her sorrow.

Lady Pica listened, the tears streaming down her cheeks and onto her white collar. As soon as I had finished, she got up, went to the window, and inhaled deeply. A terrible question was on the tip of her tongue, but she dared not utter it. I understood, and felt sorry for her.

"Ma'am," I said, divining her question, "your son is mounting the stairs, one by one, with sure, firm steps. He is climbing toward God. Perhaps a volcano is erupting inside him and causing the world of the flesh to crumble in ruins, but his mind—I swear to you, Lady Pica, by the soul I shall render up to God—his mind remains clear and unshaken."

When Lady Pica heard these words she raised her head animatedly. Her lackluster eyes began once more to flash. She had become young again.

"Glory be to God," she murmured, crossing herself. "I seek no other gift from Thee, Lord."

She called the nurse.

"Take his sack and fill it."

Then she turned to me again. "Is he cold?" she asked. "If I give you some woolen clothes for him, will he wear them?"

"No, ma'am, he won't," I answered.

"Isn't he cold?"

"No. He says he wears God next to his skin. That keeps him warm."

"And what about you? Aren't you cold? Let me give you something warm to put on."

"Yes, I'm ashamed to admit it, ma'am, but I am cold. I'll also be ashamed, however, to wear the clothes you give me."

"Ashamed in front of whom?"

"How should I know, ma'am? Maybe Francis, maybe myself; maybe even God. Alas, the road I've taken doesn't tolerate any comforts."

I sighed. Oh, how much I should have liked to possess a warm flannel undershirt and thick woolen stockings and good sandals so that I would stop cutting my feet—and a coat that was heavier and had fewer holes!

The nurse came with the sack filled to the top.

"Go now, and may God be with you both," said Lady Pica, rising. "And tell my son that my great wish is for him to succeed in doing what I once tried and was unable to do. Tell him he has my blessing!"

The three days came to an end. On the fourth I climbed up to the cave early in the morning and stood outside, waiting. Thanks to Lady Pica's heart and larder, my sack was full of mouth-watering delicacies. I felt delighted, but above and beyond this I was trembling at the thought of seeing Francis. To talk three days with the Almighty was to expose yourself to immense danger. God might hurl you into a terrible chasm where He was able to survive but a man was not. Who could tell into what chasms this secret three-day conversation would throw even me! Courage, my soul! I repeated to myself. I'll cling to Francis' robe—and then who cares if I fall. . . .

And while I was mulling all this over in my mind, my body trembling, Francis suddenly emerged from the cave. He was radiant—a gleaming cinder. Prayer had eaten away his flesh again but what remained shone like pure soul. He held out his hand to me. A peculiar expression of joy was promenading over his face.

"Well, Brother Leo, are you ready?" he called. "Have you donned your warlike armor: your coat of mail, the iron *genouillères* and beaver, the bronze helmet with its blue feather?"

He seemed delirious. His eyes were inflamed and as he came closer I descried angels and phantoms within the pupils. I was terrified. Could he have taken leave of his senses?

He understood, and laughed. But his fire did not subside.

"People have enumerated many terms of praise for the Lord up to now," he said. "But I shall enumerate still more. Listen to what I shall call Him: the Bottomless Abyss, the Insatiable, the Merciless, the Indefatigable, the Unsatisfied. He who never once has said to poor, unfortunate mankind: 'Enough!' "

Coming still closer, he placed his lips next to my ear and cried in a thunderous voice:

" 'Not enough!' That is what He screamed at me. If you ask, Brother Leo, what God commands without respite, I can tell you, for I learned it these past three days and nights in the cave. Listen!

'Not enough! Not enough!' That's what He shouts each day, each hour to poor, miserable man. 'Not enough! Not enough!' 'I can't go further!' whines man. 'You can!' the Lord replies. 'I shall break in two!' man whines again. 'Break!' the Lord replies."

Francis' voice had begun to crack. A large tear rolled down his cheek.

I became angry: an injustice was being done. I felt overwhelming compassion for Francis.

"What more does He expect from you?" I asked. "Didn't you restore San Damiano's?"

"Not enough!"

"Didn't you abandon your mother and father?"

"Not enough!"

"Didn't you kiss the leper?"

"Not enough!"

"Well, what more does He expect?"

"I asked Him, Brother Leo. 'What else dost Thou want from me, Lord?' I said, and He answered: 'Go to My church the Portiuncula. I shall tell you there.' So, Brother Leo, let's go down and see what He wants. Cross yourself; tighten the rope around your waist. We're dealing with God, and from Him there is no escape!"

We descended the mountain at a run, traversed Assisi without stopping, reached the plain. It was February: biting cold, the trees still bare, the ground covered with morning hoarfrost, making one feel that snow had fallen.

We passed San Damiano's, left the olive groves behind us, and entered a small wood of pine trees and oaks charged with acorns. The sun's rays had struck the pine needles, embalming the air. Francis stopped and took in a deep breath.

"What solitude!" he murmured happily. "What perfume, what peace!"

And as he spoke, a tiny rabbit hopped out from the undergrowth, pricked up its ears, then turned and saw us. It did not become frightened, but looked at us calmly, erect on its hind legs as though it wanted to dance. Soon it vanished again into the bushes.

"Did you see it, Brother Leo?" asked Francis, extremely moved. "Our little brother rabbit was glad to see us. He shook his tiny legs and greeted us. A good sign! I have a premonition, Brother Leo, that we have arrived."

We advanced a little, and there between the oaks, isolated and charming, stood the tiny church of Santa Maria degli Angeli—the Portiuncula. It was built of aged marble; round about it were two or three crumbling cells which the ivy and woodbine had embraced. And then, suddenly rising before us—we hadn't seen it, it seemed to have stepped out of the church in order to receive us— was a young almond tree, covered everywhere with blossoms.

"This is Santa Maria degli Angeli," murmured Francis.

Our eyes filled with tears. We crossed ourselves.

"Sweet sister almond tree, our sweet little sister," said Francis, spreading his arms, "you dressed yourself, donned your finery. Now we have come. How nice to see you!"

Approaching the tree, he stroked its trunk.

"Blessed is the hand that planted you, blessed the almond that gave birth to you. You step fearlessly out in front, my little sister: you are the first to dare stand up against winter, the first to blossom. One day, God willing, the first brothers will come to sit here beneath your flowering branches."

We pushed open the door and entered. The church smelled of earth and mildew. The tiny window was hanging askew; bits of cement and wood had fallen from the roof; the spiders had spun a thick, delicately worked web around the statue of Santa Maria.

We pushed the cobwebs aside and approached the statue in order to do worship. Above us was a fresco on which we were able to perceive the Blessed Mother, dressed in blue, her bare feet resting on a slim half-moon. Swarms of chubby angels with strong arms and black fuzz on their cheeks were supporting her and drawing her up to heaven.

Lying open on the altar was the Holy Gospel—old, soiled everywhere by repeated fingering, eaten away by vermin, green with mildew.

Francis seized my arm. "Look, Brother Leo, there's God's sign to us! Go read the verses you find before you. God opened the Gospel as a way of revealing His will to us. Read loudly so that Santa Maria degli Angeli may resound again after so many years, resound and rejoice."

The sun's rays, entering through the shattered window, fell upon the Gospel. I leaned over and read in a loud voice: "Going forth, preach, saying, The kingdom of heaven is at hand. . . . Take no gold nor silver nor copper in your belts, no sack for your journey, nor two tunics, nor sandals, nor a staff. . . .' "

Suddenly I heard a loud screech behind me. Turning, I saw Francis kneeling on the dirt floor amid the bits of fallen plaster. He had begun to shout in a strident, hawklike voice:

"Nothing! Nothing! Nothing! We'll take nothing with us, Lord. Thy will be done! Nothing! Only our eyes, hands, feet, and mouths so that we can proclaim: 'The kingdom of heaven is at hand!' "

He dragged me forcefully outside. There he threw away his staff and sandals.

"Throw yours away too," he commanded me. "Didn't you hear: 'Nor sandals, nor a staff!' "

"This too?" I asked, anxiously hugging the full sack.

"The sack too! Didn't you hear: 'No sack!' "

"God expects a great deal from man," I murmured fretfully as I slowly removed the sack from my shoulder. "Why does He behave so inhumanly toward us?"

"Because He loves us," Francis answered. "Stop complaining."

"I'm not complaining, Brother Francis, I'm hungry. And just today our sack happens to be full of delicacies. At least let's eat first."

Francis looked at me sympathetically.

"You eat, Brother Leo," he said, smiling. "I can wait."

I knelt on both knees, opened the sack, and attacked the food. There was a small jug of wine inside too, and this I drank to the bottom. I ate and drank as much as I could—more than I could—like a camel preparing to cross the desert.

Francis, meanwhile, had knelt at my side and begun to talk to me.

"You realize, of course, Brother Leo, that God is right. Until now we have looked after only our own precious little selves, our own souls; all we've cared about is how *we* were to be saved. Not enough! We must fight to save everyone else as well, Brother Leo. If we do not save others, how can we be saved? 'In what way are we going to fight, Lord?' I cried to God, and He replied: 'Go to My church the Portiuncula and I shall tell you. There you shall hear My command.' Now I've heard it—you heard it too, Brother Leo, with your own ears: 'Going forth, preach, saying, The kingdom of heaven is at hand!' Here is our new duty, my brother and fellow warrior: to preach! To mobilize as many brothers as we can around us, as many more mouths to preach as possible, as many more hearts to love, feet to endure the long marches. To become the new crusaders, and to set off all together to deliver the Holy Sepulcher. What Holy Sepulcher, Brother Leo? The soul of man!"

He was silent for a moment, and then:

"This is the true Holy Sepulcher, Brother Leo. The crucified Christ lies inside man's body. We are departing to reach the soul, Brother Leo—not ours alone, but the soul of all mankind. Forward! You've eaten, you've quenched your thirst; let us go now to select our new companions. Two are no longer enough. We need thousands. . . . Forward, in God's name!"

He turned toward Assisi. The sun had risen above the citadel: the city gleamed like an open rose. Francis crossed himself and took me by the hand.

"Let's go," he said. "Who prevented me until now from joining with God? Francis! I pushed him aside. You do the same: push aside Brother Leo. A new struggle is beginning."

I held my tongue and followed. The abyss is beginning, I was thinking to myself, and I clung to Francis' robe. . . .

We climbed to Assisi and stood ourselves in the middle of the square. Francis unhooked the ram's bell from his waist and began to ring it to call the people to approach. A considerable number of passers-by stopped and formed a circle around him. They were joined by others who hurried out of the taverns where they had already begun (it was Sunday) to spend their morning leisurely sipping wine. Francis stretched out his arms to greet them.

"Peace be unto you!" he said to each person who approached. "Peace be unto you!"

When a great number had assembled and the square was full, he spread his arms.

"Peace," he shouted, "peace be unto your hearts, your houses, your enemies. Peace be to the world! The kingdom of heaven is at hand!"

His voice broke continually. He said the same things over and over again, and whenever he could no longer speak, he began to weep. "Peace, peace," he cried, exhorting his listeners to make peace with God, with men, with their hearts. How? There was but one way: by loving.

"Love! Love!" he shouted, and then he began to weep once again.

Women began to appear in their doorways or to climb up to the roofs of their houses in order to listen. The crowd did not laugh now, did not make fun of him, and each day Francis wandered through the streets of Assisi and preached the same words—always the same words, the same tears. I stood at his side and wept too, but did not speak. Early each morning I took the ram's bell and raced through the streets crying, "Come one, come all, Francis is going to speak!"

One evening as the preaching ended and we were about to climb to our cave to pass the night, a merchant named Bernard of Quintavalle came up to Francis. He dealt in cloth just as Sior Bernardone did, and was slightly older than Francis, with pensive features and blue, thoughtful eyes. He had never accompanied Francis on his all-night revels, but, as he subsequently confided to me, used to sit up long hours into the night studying the scriptures. The fierceness of Jehovah in the Old Testament frightened him, and when he reached Jesus, his heart filled with a mixture of sadness and joy.

He had heard about Francis, and had laughed at first, thinking that all this calking of churches, kissing of lepers, undressing in public and returning the clothes he was wearing to his father was but a new series of pranks on the part of Bernardone's pampered son. And now here he was holding a bell and making the rounds of the streets preaching, as he said, a new madness. Bernard was unable to understand exactly what the "new madness" was. Each day he saw Francis shouting and weeping in the square. He said he was fighting to save men from sin. How could *he* save men from sin, he who until now had spent his nights carousing? But this madness had endured beyond expectation. Could it be that God was truly giving him the strength to resist hunger, nakedness, and scorn? If I wasn't ashamed, Bernard said to himself, I would go up to him and speak to him. I haven't been able to sleep for many nights now. He comes again and again into my mind and gestures to me. What is he signaling me to do?

Finally, unable to restrain himself any longer, he had approached Francis.

"Do you remember me, Sior Francis? I am Bernard of Quintavalle. Would you deign to sleep in my house tonight?"

Francis looked at him; he perceived the affliction and great yearning that were in Bernard's eyes.

"What miracle is this, Brother Bernard? I was dreaming about you just last night! God has sent you, my brother—welcome! Your coming has some hidden meaning. All right, let's be off!"

He nodded to me. "Brother Leo, you come too. You and I don't part!"

We went to Bernard's mansion. The servants prepared a meal for us, and then, leaning against the door, listened while Francis spoke of God, love, the soul of man. The air had become filled with angels; gazing through the open window the servants saw heaven—verdant, brilliantly illuminated, the saints and angels chatting together as they promenaded hand in hand on the immortal grass, while above their heads the cherubim and seraphim glittered like stars.

But when Francis stopped speaking, everything returned to normal. The courtyard with its potted flowers surrounding the rim of the well was once more visible through the window. A servant girl burst into tears. For a moment she had entered Paradise, but now she had returned to earth again and had once more become a servant.

It was almost midnight. Bernard had listened with bowed head, enraptured by his visitor's words. Though Francis was no longer speaking, the host felt his guest's presence within him: barefooted, singing, dressed in tatters, he was marching in front and turning his head to signal. . . .

"Sior Francis," he said, looking up, "the whole time I heard you speak, this world vanished and nothing remained but the soul over the abyss, the abyss of God—singing. But I can't tell which part is true and which part is a dream. It is said, Sior Francis, that night is the most beloved of God's messengers. Let us see what message it will bring me tonight."

He got up. "Sior Francis, tonight you and I shall sleep in the same room."

Then, laughing in order to hide his emotion:

"People say that sainthood is a contagious disease. We shall see!"

But Bernard had his motives: he wished to test Francis. As soon as he had lain down he began to snore, pretending he had fallen asleep. The deception was successful. When Francis believed Bernard to be fast asleep, he slid out of bed, knelt on the floor, crossed his hands, and began to pray in a low voice. Bernard pricked up his ears, but heard nothing except these words:

"My God and my all! My God and my all!"

This lasted until dawn, at which time Francis crept into bed and pretended to sleep. Bernard, whose tears had flowed the entire night as he listened to Francis, rose and went out into the courtyard. I was already up and drawing water from the well. I turned and looked at him. His eyes were inflamed.

"What happened, Sior Bernard?" I asked. "Your eyes are all red."

"Francis did not sleep the whole night. He was praying, and a great flame licked his face."

"It wasn't a flame, Sior Bernard, it was God."

Francis appeared, and Bernard fell immediately at his feet.

"A thought has been tormenting me, Sior Francis," he said. "Take pity on me and soothe my heart."

Francis clasped Bernard's hand and made him stand up.

"I am listening, Brother Bernard. Not I, but God, will soothe your heart. Tell me your troubles."

"A great nobleman gave me a large treasure to keep for him. I have guarded it for many years, but now I plan to go on a long, dangerous journey. What should I do with his treasure?"

"You should return it to the man who entrusted it to you, Brother Bernard. Who is this great nobleman?"

"Christ. All my wealth I owe to Him: it is His. How then can I return it to Him?"

Francis fell deep into thought.

"This is an extremely grave question, Brother Bernard," he said finally. "By myself I cannot give you an answer. But let us go to church and ask Christ in person."

All three of us started for the street door. But at that moment someone knocked. Bernard ran to see who it was, and immediately uttered a happy cry.

"Is it really you, Sior Pietro? Why so early? You're as pale as a corpse."

Sior Pietro was a celebrated professor of law at the University of Bologna. A native of Assisi, he normally came home every so often to rest. This time, however, he had left Bologna because of the death of his most beloved student a few days before. He had been unable to restrain his sorrow, and had enclosed himself in his paternal home, refusing to see anyone.

"Are you alone, Bernard?" he asked.

"No. Sior Bernardone's son Francis is here too, and a friend of his."

"It doesn't matter; I'll speak in front of them," said Pietro, and he stepped into the courtyard.

He was a large-bodied, aristocratic man, with severe, grayish eyes and a short, curly beard. But studying long hours into the night had eaten away his cheeks, and his entire face was as dry and yellow as the expensive parchment used by monks to record Christ's Passion.

He collapsed onto a stool, breathing with difficulty. The three of us stood around him and leaned over in order to hear.

He took a deep breath.

"Forgive me," he said, "if I start from the beginning. I had a student named Guido whom I loved like my own son. He never lifted his head from his books. At the age of twenty he had the good sense and erudition of an old man. And mixed with this brilliant mind was something which is found very seldom: passion, flaming passion. That is why I loved him. . . . A few days ago he died."

He squeezed his lips together to hold back the rising sob, but two huge tears rolled down from his eyes. Bernard filled a cup with water and gave it to him. He drank.

"On the day of his final agonies I bent over his pillow and said to him, 'Guido, my child, if God decides to call you near Him, I have a favor to ask of you.'

"And he replied: 'What favor, my father? I'll do whatever you desire.'

" 'I want you to visit me one night in my dreams and tell me what goes on in the other world.'

" 'I shall come,' the youth murmured. He placed his hand in mine and then immediately gave up the ghost.

126

"I left Bologna at once and came here to be alone while I waited for him to visit me in my sleep."

Sior Pietro's voice broke and he was forced to stop again. Finally he managed to continue:

"He came. Today, at dawn . . ."

Bernard squatted next to him and clasped his hand.

"Courage, Pietro," he said. "Take a deep breath and tell us what he said to you."

Francis and I leaned further forward, anxious to hear.

"He was dressed in a strange kind of robe. No, it wasn't a robe, it was hundreds of strips of paper sewn together around his body—all the manuscripts he had written during the course of his studies, and on them were all the problems, questions, the philosophic and legal perplexities, the theological concerns: how to be saved, how to escape from the Inferno, to rise to Purgatory, and from Purgatory to Paradise. . . . He was so weighted down with papers, try as he might he could not walk. A wind was blowing; it fluttered the manuscripts, and as it did so the boy's skeleton became visible, covered everywhere with mud and grass. 'Guido, my child,' I shouted at him, 'what are these papers around you, these scraps that are preventing you from walking?'

" 'I've just come from the Inferno,' he answered me, 'and I am struggling to climb to Purgatory. But I can't. These scraps of paper are preventing me. . . .' When he had said this, one of his eyes turned into a tear and fell on me and burned my hand. Here, look!"

He held out his right hand. On it we saw a red wound, perfectly circular, like an eyeball. Bernard and I were overcome with terror—but Francis just smiled calmly.

Sior Pietro got up. "Everything is finished now," he said. "Before coming here I threw all my manuscripts into the fire and burned them—all my manuscripts, all my books. I am saved! Blessings upon my beloved student who brought me the message from the world below. A new life is beginning for me, glory be to God!"

"And what road are you going to follow now, dear Pietro?" asked Bernard. "What is this new life you are beginning?"

"I don't know yet, I don't know . . ." replied the savant pensively.

"I know!" Francis interrupted at this point. He reached out his hand and opened the street door. "I know! Come with me, both of you!"

127

Francis went in the lead. The two friends followed arm in arm, while I brought up the rear. These two souls are ready, I was thinking, ready to begin the ascent. . . .

We passed San Ruffino's. Mass was in progress, the church full: we did not stop. Instead, we turned the corner and reached the tiny church of San Niccolo, which was deserted. Francis pushed open the door and we entered. Above the altar hung the crucifix, illuminated by a tiny lamp. The story of San Niccolo was depicted on the wall in back, with the saint surrounded by fish, boats, and endless seas.

"Brother Bernard, you asked me a question," said Francis. "Kneel. Christ is going to give you the answer." He advanced to the altar, knelt, crossed himself, and took up the heavy Gospel, which was bound in silver.

"This is the mouth of Christ," he said.

He opened the Gospel, placed his finger on a verse, and read in a loud voice:

"If you would be perfect, go, sell what you possess and give to the poor, and you will have treasure in heaven."

He closed the Gospel, opened it once more, and read:

"If any man would come after me, let him deny himself and take up his cross and follow me."

Francis turned to Bernard, who had been listening on his knees, weeping.

"Do you have any further doubts, Brother Bernard?" he asked. "Do you want Christ to open His mouth once more?"

"No, no," shouted Bernard, carried away with emotion. He jumped to his feet. "I'm ready."

"So am I," said a voice behind him. It was Sior Pietro. He had been listening, fallen prone on the flagstones.

"Well then, let's go!" said Francis joyfully as he stepped between the two new converts and clasped each around the waist. "You, Sior Pietro, have already done what Christ instructed: you burned your wealth—manuscripts, books, pencils; you poured out all your ink and found relief. . . . Now it's your turn, Brother Bernard! Throw open your shop, call the poor, distribute the cottons you used to sell—clothe the naked! Smash your yardstick, open your coffers, distribute, distribute, find relief. Brother Bernard, it is necessary, absolutely necessary for us to restore to our poor brethren what we have borrowed from them. If a person withholds even a delicate gold chain, he will find it weighing down his soul, preventing it from rising and taking flight!"

He turned to the altar, to the Crucified.

"Christ, my Lord, how cheaply Thou sellest Thy goods to us! We give the contents of a tiny shop and with this we buy the kingdom of heaven. We burn a pile of old papers and receive everlasting life!"

"Come, let's not lose any time," said Bernard. Removing the store key from his belt, he began to run.

The faithful were emerging from Mass now; the churches were closing, the taverns opening. People flocked into the square.

The clouds had scattered; the sun shone brightly. Poor February with its scant twenty-eight days was as warm as June. The trees had already begun to unfold their first tiny curled-up leaves.

How many times in my life had I seen the arrival of spring! This, however, was the first time I realized its true meaning. This year, for the very first time, I knew (Francis had taught me) that all things are one, that the tree and the soul of man—all things—follow the same law of God. The soul has its springtime like the tree, and unfolds. . . .

As soon as we reached the Piazza San Giorgio, Bernard inserted his key and opened the shop. Standing on the threshold, he cried: "Whoever is poor, whoever is unclothed—come! In the name of Christ, I am distributing all my goods."

Francis placed himself to his right, Sior Pietro to his left, and I carried the rolls of cloth from the back of the store and made a pile in front of them.

How the people ran! Women, girls, old men, ragamuffins: how their eyes shone, how avidly they stretched forth their hands in the Sunday air! And Bernard, laughing, enjoying himself, joked happily with this one, teased that one, while with the large pair of shears he held in his hand he cut the cloth and distributed his wealth.

From time to time Francis turned to him. Bernard would sigh: "What joy this is, Brother Francis! What a relief!"

Father Silvester happened to pass by. The sight of Bernard pillaging and scattering his possessions made the priest's heart break in two.

"What a shame that such wealth should go to waste!" he murmured. "Without a doubt it's that lunatic Francis who's been putting ideas into his mind."

He stopped and watched, shaking his head. Francis divined what he was thinking.

"Father Silvester, you remember what Christ says, don't you? Forgive me if I remind you. 'If you want to be perfect, distribute your possessions to the poor, and you shall earn a great treasure in heaven.' So, why are you shaking your head?"

Father Silvester coughed, turned fiery red, and went on his way.

Francis felt distressed at having hurt him. "Father Silvester, Father Silvester!" he shouted.

The priest turned.

"I reminded you of Christ's words. Forgive me. You, the priest of God, know them better than I, the sinner."

If Francis had been closer, he would have been able to see two tears well up in the priest's eyes.

Evening came; the store was just four bare walls. Taking the yardstick, Bernard smashed it and tossed the pieces into the gutter. After he had thrown away the shears also, he crossed himself. "Glory be to God," he said. "I have found relief."

He placed his arm around Sior Pietro, and the two of them followed Francis.

All Assisi immediately buzzed with these strange doings on the part of a rich, sensible proprietor and a learned professor of law. We learned that the same night a large number of the older notables, all considerably shaken, gathered at the house of one of Bernard's uncles in order to determine how to exorcise this plague. The disease was obviously contagious, and most of all it attacked young people. Let's take care, they reasoned, lest it turn the heads of our sons as well and induce them to scatter among the ragged and barefooted the wealth that we and our forefathers amassed over so many years by the sweat of our brows. Here now is this new lunatic putting ideas into people's heads and undermining our houses. Let us expel him; let him depart the boundaries of our city—and go to the devil! Thus they decided to call upon the bishop and afterwards the council of village elders in order to request them to oust this scandal from Assisi.

In the modest home of the widow Giovanna, meanwhile, a solidly built, sunburned, jovial colossus was sitting by the fire warming himself. He watched his old aunt as she made the sign of the cross and blessed the name of the new saint—that was what people had recently begun to call Francis. As he himself confessed to us a few days later, he laughed at her and teased her, saying: "Bah, a playboy doesn't become a saint as easily as all that! I'll go and find this saint of yours, this Francis—yes, I'll find him, or my name isn't Giles. And I'll take a bottle of wine with me, and some tender roast pork to whet his appetite, and you'll see if I don't get him stinking drunk on you. Then I'll slip a noose around his neck and lead him to the square. As soon as I clap my hands he'll start dancing like a trained bear!"

Several days went by. Our group, now made up of four friars, left Assisi and found refuge in the deserted chapel, the Portiuncula. In front of the flowering almond tree we erected a hut made of branches coated with plaster—our first monastery.

For hours on end we knelt and raised our eyes to heaven, praying. Francis spoke to us of love, poverty, of peace—both the peace of each man's soul and the peace of the world. And I, who until now had done nothing but ask questions and investigate everything, now with the coming of the new friars, I learned to keep quiet. One day Sior Pietro said something which I shall never forget as long as I live: "The mind does nothing but talk, ask questions, search for meanings; the heart does not talk, does not ask questions, does not search for meanings. Silently, it moves toward God and surrenders itself to Him. The mind is Satan's lawyer; the heart is God's servant. It bows and says to the Lord, 'Thy will be done!' "

Francis listened to these words, and smiled.

"Sior Pietro"—he always addressed him in this way, out of respect—"Sior Pietro, you are right. When I was a young student a learned theologian came to Assisi at Christmastime. He mounted the pulpit of San Ruffino's and began an oration that lasted for hours and hours, all about the birth of Christ and the salvation of the world and the terrible mystery of the Incarnation. My mind grew muddy; my head began to reel. Unable to stand it any longer, I shouted, 'Master, be still so that we can hear Christ crying in His cradle!' When we got back home, my father spanked me, but my mother took me aside secretly and gave me her blessing."

Brother Bernard rarely opened his mouth to speak. Every day at the crack of dawn he would be kneeling beneath a tree, rapt in prayer, and it was evident from his lowered eyelids, his sunken cheeks, and the slight tremor of his lips that he was conversing with God. When from time to time he did chance to speak to us, the moment he pronounced Christ's name he would lick his lips as though they had been daubed with honey.

It was our practice to scatter as soon as the sun began to rise. One would go to fetch water, another wood, the third to beg, and Francis to make the rounds of the streets of Assisi and the nearby villages preaching love: the "new madness." Very often he also took along a broom in order to sweep out the village churches. "They are God's houses," he used to say, "and I am the custodian: it is my responsibility."

As we were kneeling and saying our prayers inside the hut one morning—it was the day of the great feast of San Giorgio—my eye caught sight of a huge man approaching very very slowly, obviously spying on us. Under his arm he had an immense bottle of wine and also an object wrapped in lemon leaves. The smell of roast meat hit my nostrils.

He was as tall as a steeple, sunburned, heavily built. Coming up to our hut with light, noiseless steps he pushed his face against the wall and commenced to pry at us through the branches. I watched him out of the corner of my eye.

Francis had begun to speak to us as he did every morning, revealing what he had said to God during the night, and what God had said to him.

The concealed giant pricked up his ears and listened, mouth agape. Suddenly he turned around, walked hurriedly to a clump of trees and in a moment returned with his hands empty. Then he glued his face to the hut once more and continued to listen.

"Lord," Francis was saying at this point, "if I love Thee because I want Thee to place me in Paradise, send Thine angel with his scimitar and have him close the gates against me. If I love Thee because I fear the Inferno, hurl me down into the everlasting flames. But if I love Thee for Thine own sake, for Thy sake alone, then open wide Thine arms and receive me."

The man who had been secretly listening took a long stride and halted at the doorway. His face had turned pale; two large tears were running down his cheeks. Falling at Francis' feet, he cried,

"Forgive me, Brother Francis. I am Giles, from Assisi, and I ridiculed you and made a wager that I could come and make you drunk, then slip a noose around your neck and bring you to the Piazza San Giorgio, where I would clap my hands and you would dance."

"And why not, Brother Giles," said Francis laughingly, "why not go and stand in the Piazza San Giorgio, where I'm sure everyone must be gathered today? You'll clap your hands and I'll dance. I don't want you to lose your wager."

He placed his hands under the other's arms and raised him up.

"Let's go," he said. "The people are waiting."

They left. Toward evening the three of us, Bernard, Pietro, and myself, were sitting outside the hut, waiting.

"Brother Francis is late," I said. "I wonder if he's still dancing."

"Yes, he's dancing," said Sior Pietro; and then, after a moment of silence: "Alas, I wouldn't have the courage to do such a thing. I'm still ashamed before men, and that means I still haven't learned to be ashamed before God."

As we were talking, Francis suddenly appeared; and behind him—huge, gay, stepping lightly as though he had wings—was Giles.

Francis took his companion by the hand and came up to us.

"He made me dance," he said with a laugh, "but I made him dance too! In the beginning I pranced all by myself before God, and he clapped his hands. But in a little while Brother Giles became jealous. He stopped clapping his hands, he grasped my shoulder, and the two of us began to dance together. It seemed that the whole of creation had taken hold of our shoulders and was dancing with us before God.

"And what a dance that was, my brothers! It is one thing for a person to dance by himself, and quite another when there are many —at first two, then three, then thirty-three, then a hundred thousand three, then all of mankind, and after that the animals and birds too, and then the trees and oceans and mountains: the whole of creation dancing before the Creator. Isn't it so, Brother Giles?"

"Don't give me any other job," he answered with a laugh. "Dancing is just fine! I shall place my hand on your shoulder, Brother Francis, and dance for all eternity."

"Let's welcome our new brother," said Francis, spreading his arms.

"Welcome! Welcome!" we all shouted, and we ran to embrace Giles.

The new friar blushed. There was something he wanted to say, but he hesitated to do so. Finally he worked up courage:

"Brother Francis, I've brought some food, and also a bottle of wine."

"We are celebrating your birthday today," said Francis, stroking Giles' broad shoulders. "Let's drink to your health. A little wine doesn't matter: God forgives us if we are unfaithful now and then to holy hunger and holy thirst. So, bring on the tools of sin!"

With a bound Giles went to the bushes and drew out the roast pig and bottle of wine.

"To Brother Giles!" said Francis, lifting the bottle. "Today he was born: may he thrive! Today he married. Today he sired a daughter—let us wish him all happiness. Her name is Poverty!"

Not many days had gone by before Father Silvester appeared at the doorway of the Portiuncula, just as we were leaving for our daily tasks. He came with lowered head, mortally ashamed, his eyes red from continued weeping, his hands trembling. Under his arm he carried a bundle.

Francis greeted him with open arms. "How splendid to see you, Father Silvester," he said. "What wind brings you to our shanty?"

"The wind of God," answered the priest. "The other day you upbraided me, Brother Francis, and your words were flames: they burned and cleansed my heart."

"They were not my words, Father Silvester, they were Christ's."

"Yes, they were Christ's words, but the way you said them, Brother Francis, made me feel as though I were hearing them for the first time, as though I had never read the Gospels. I've always read them every day, but the words of Christ have been just so many letters, so much noise—never fire. For the first time—thanks to you, Brother Francis—I understood the meaning of poverty, of love, and what God's will is. . . . And so, I came."

"What have you got in the bundle?"

"A change of clothes, my good sandals, and other things I'm particularly attached to."

Francis laughed.

"There was once an ascetic," he said, "who had been struggling for

134

years and years to see God, but without success. Something always loomed up before him and prevented him. The unfortunate man wept, shouted, implored—in vain! He just could not understand what it was that kept him from seeing God. One morning, however, he leapt out of bed, overjoyed. He had found it! It was a small, richly decorated pitcher which was the sole object he had retained from among all his possessions, so dearly did he love it. Now he seized it and with one blow smashed it into a thousand pieces. Then, lifting his eyes, he saw God for the first time. . . .

"Father Silvester, if you wish to see God, throw away your bundle."

Observing the priest hesitate, he took him tenderly by the hand and said, "Come with me. We shall walk along the road and you, out of love for Christ, will give your bundle to the first poor man we meet. People do not get into heaven with bundles, Father Silvester!"

"Can't I keep my sandals, just my sandals?" asked the priest, still balking.

"You have to be barefooted to enter Paradise," said Francis. "Stop trying to bargain, my brother, and come!"

Thus, as the wolf snatches up the lamb in its teeth, Francis snatched up Father Silvester in order to toss him into heaven.

Thy grace, Lord, is great, exceedingly great, and rich and many-eyed like the tail of a peacock. It overlays the world from end to end; spreads out, covers even the most humble souls, filling them with splendor. Witness the fact that before many days had passed, two good-for-nothings, the butt of all Assisi, came and kissed Francis' hand, asking to be accepted as brothers. One was Sabbatino, the other a man called Capella because he constantly, even when asleep, wore a tall hat of green velvet garnished with a red ribbon. I remembered Sabbatino immediately as the one who had sneered at Francis the night I arrived in Assisi looking for a decent Christian to give me alms. He was skinny and jaundiced, with a mousy expression and a hairy wart on his nose, whereas Capella was lanky, ungainly, and had long drooping mustaches, a monstrous pointed nose, and rabbit-like lips. He stuttered when he spoke, becoming all tangled up in his words.

"I can't sleep any more, Brother Francis," Sabbatino began. "I said bad things about you. I envied you because you were rich and

I poor, you were handsome and I ugly, you were well dressed and I had nothing but rags. Lately, every night I've lain down to go to sleep I knew it would be in vain. And if I did happen to fall asleep for a few moments you would come in my dreams and say to me, 'It doesn't matter, Brother Sabbatino, I hold no grudge against you, so go to sleep.' Your kindness tore my heart in two. I couldn't stand it any longer, and so I came. Do with me what you will. I shall follow your footsteps to the death!"

"I too," said Capella, "I too—with you to the death, Brother Francis. I'm sick of the world; the world is sick of me. What refuge is left me now except God? But I'll come with you only on one condition, Brother Francis: that you let me wear my hat. I don't want a hood. You'll say this is an eccentricity, but I'm used to this hat; in fact I feel it's just the same as my head. If you make me take it off I'll think you are decapitating me."

Francis laughed, but then his expression immediately grew severe.

"Take care, my brother," he said to him. "Could not the devil have become a hat and seated himself on your head? Take care he does not push you along the downhill road. From the hat the next step down may be the robe: you'll say, 'I don't want it!' And from the robe you may descend to the friars, saying, 'I don't want them!' And from the friars to love, saying, 'I don't want it!' And from love, to God, saying, 'I don't want Him!' "

Francis remained silent for a moment, plunged in thought.

"The uphill road," he continued, "has a summit: God; the downhill road has a bottom: the Inferno. This hat, my child, may hurl you down into hell."

He gazed deeply into Capella's eyes, and the new convert, unable to restrain himself, burst into sobs.

"If you don't give me the permission I ask of you," he said, "I'll leave you, and then I'm doomed."

Francis felt sorry for him. He placed his hand on the other's shoulder.

"Stay," he said. "I have hopes that God will win!"

How many souls in this world yearn for salvation and are ready to run headlong into the waiting arms of the Lord the moment they hear a voice inviting them! Whether they are respectable homeowners or disreputable tramps, one night they hear someone calling them in the silence. They jump to their feet with thumping hearts and all at once everything they have done up to that point seems vain, useless. They feel themselves ensnared in the Sly One's lime twig, and thus they fall at the feet of the person who called them and cry, "Take me, save me; you are the one I have been waiting for."

Not a day went by without someone emerging from the clump of trees around the Portiuncula and falling at Francis' feet.

"Take me, save me; you are the one I have been waiting for!" they said to him, and throwing off the clothes they were wearing, they donned the robe.

One day there came a simple, affable, somewhat corpulent peasant of about thirty years of age. He held a jug on which he had painted representations of the seven deadly sins, each with its name written beneath: Pride, Avarice, Envy, Lust, Gluttony, Wrath, Sloth.

"Brother, Father, listen to what I have to say," he cried, falling at Francis' feet. "I was calm and peaceful in my village. I cultivated and pruned my grapevines, harvested them: made a living. I had no wife, no children, no worries—or so I thought. But as soon as I heard your voice I realized that I was wretched. I looked into my heart, which I had thought innocent, and inside it I saw the seven deadly sins. I took this jug, therefore, and drew each of them on it, writing the names beneath. Now—look!—I am going to smash it at your feet—and I hope all seven go to the devil!"

He banged the jug against the stones and it broke into a hundred pieces.

"May my heart shatter in the same way and may the mortal sins spill out onto the stones!"

"What is your name, my brother?"

"Juniper."

"Juniper, so please it God that upon your branches thousands of souls shall build their nests!"

ΛΘΛM ΛNΘ ΘΔΘ sitting in Paradise, chatting:
    "If we could only open the gate and leave," says Eve.
"To go where, my dearest?"
"If we could only open the gate and leave!"
"Outside is sickness, pain, death!"
"If we could only open the gate and leave!"

Within me—forgive me, Lord—I was aware of both these voices.
As I listened to Francis my soul was in Paradise. I forgot my hunger,
my nakedness, the attractions of the world. And then suddenly
there would be a rebellious call: "Leave!"

One day Francis caught me weeping.

"Why are you weeping, Brother Leo?" he asked, bending over
and shaking my shoulder.

"I remembered, Brother Francis, I remembered."

"Remembered what?"

"A morning when I lifted my hand and picked a fig from my fig
tree."

"Anything else?"

"No, nothing else, Brother Francis—and that's why I'm weeping."

Francis sat down on the ground next to me and clasped my hand.

"Brother Leo, listen to what I'm going to say to you, but do not
repeat it to anyone."

"I'm listening, Brother Francis." I felt the warmth of his body as
he held my hand—no, not of his body, of his soul, and it was warming my soul.

138

"I'm listening, Brother Francis," I said once again, for he had remained silent.

He released my hand and got up. All of a sudden I heard a strangulated voice:

"Virtue, Brother Leo, sits completely alone on top of a desolate ledge. Through her mind pass all the forbidden pleasures which she has never tasted—and she weeps."

When he had said this he walked away with bowed head and disappeared behind the trees.

It is said that if a drop of honey falls somewhere the bees smell it in the air and speed from all directions to taste it. In the same way, the souls of men, smelling Francis' soul, the drop of honey, began to crowd around the Portiuncula—and who should arrive one day at the hour of sunset but the person who originally gave us the frocks we had on: our old friend Ruffino! "Winter is coming," he had said to us then with a chuckle. "God is not enough to keep you warm; warm clothes are needed too!" And he had given Francis and me the laborers' cloaks we wore, and also sandals and a staff.

As soon as Francis saw him now he laughed and called out:

"Well, well, from what I see, old friend, warm clothes are not enough; God is needed too!"

Ruffino lowered his gaze.

"Forgive me, Brother Francis, but then I was blind. By blind I mean I saw only the visible world, and nothing of what lies hidden behind. But after you visited my house and remained there for a moment, the air inside changed, became filled with enticing voices, invitations, and hands prodding me to leave. Finally the day came when I could resist no longer. I left my door wide open, tossed my keys into the river—and came!"

"Our life here is difficult, dearest friend, extremely difficult. How will you endure it? I pity the man who has grown accustomed to good food, soft clothing, and the warmth of women!"

"But I pity the man all the more, Brother Francis, who has been unable to wean himself away from good food, soft clothing, and the warmth of women. Do not spurn me, Brother Francis. Accept me!"

"There is something also as well, friend Ruffino: I believe you were among those who went to learned Bologna and had your mind

139

filled with questions. Here we do not ask questions; we have already reached the state of certainty. You will manage to bear the hunger, the nakedness, the celibacy—but will your intellect be able to endure our certainty without hoisting a rebel standard? This, friend Ruffino, is the great temptation for every unfortunate who has seated himself at the foot of the tree of knowledge and allowed the Serpent to lick his ears, eyes, and mouth."

Ruffino did not answer.

"Well, what do you think?" asked Francis, gazing compassionately at his friend.

"No, Brother Francis," Ruffino said softly, hopelessly, "I can't, I can't do it."

Francis sprang up and clasped his friend to his breast.

"You can, you can! You had the courage to say you couldn't, and that means you can! The heart is closer to God than the mind is, so abandon the mind and follow your heart: it and it alone knows the way to Paradise. And now undress yourself and don the robe. You remember the coats you gave us, don't you, the ones used by your shepherd? We modeled our frocks after them—they are the color of clay. Brother Ruffino, dress yourself in clay!"

On another occasion, as Francis was passing through a village he encountered a swashbuckler complete with sword, spurs, feathers in his hat, a suit of velvet, and curly, freshly washed hair which smelled of scented soap.

"Hello there, my stalwart!" cried Francis. "Aren't you tired of adorning yourself and twisting your mustache? It's time for you to tie the cord around your waist, place the hood over your head, and walk barefooted in the mud. Follow me, and I shall ordain you a chevalier of God."

The swashbuckler stroked his mustache, gazed at the tatterdemalion who was addressing him, and laughed.

"Wait till I take leave of my senses," he replied. "Then I'll follow you."

Three days later, there he was at the Portiuncula! As giddy as a bird being enticed by a snake, Angelo Tancredi came and fell into God's nest.

"I have come," he said, kneeling to kiss Francis' hand. "I grew weary of dressing, adorning myself, and twisting my mustache. Take me!"

But the one monstrous, snapping shark who fell into God's net did not appear until several days later. Francis and I were sitting on the doorstep of the Portiuncula. The sun still had not set, the friars had not returned from their begging. Of them, only Bernard had remained inside the Portiuncula, and soon he had left also, but not until he had fallen at Francis' feet to seek absolution. He did this each time he went to pray, because he never knew if he would issue from the prayer alive.

Francis sat gazing mutely at his hands and feet, rapt in contemplation. Finally, after a long silence, he sighed and said to me, "Brother Leo, when I think of Christ's Passion, my soles and palms ache to be pierced. But where are the nails, the blood; where is the cross? I remember going once to the courtyard of San Ruffino's on Good Friday when the traveling players who presented the Passion during the Easter season had come to Assisi. The man who portrayed Christ gasped as he carried his cross, and they pretended to crucify him, pouring red paint over his hands and feet to simulate flowing blood. When he uttered his heart-rending cry, 'Eli, Eli, lama sabachthani,' my tears began to flow. The men groaned, the women shrieked and wailed; the performance drew to a close. Then the actor came to our house, where my mother had prepared dinner for him. He began to laugh and joke, and some luke-warm water was brought him so that he could wash away the paint. I was small; I did not understand. 'But you were crucified, weren't you?' I asked him. He laughed. 'No, no, my boy. All that was a show—understand? —a game. I only pretended to be crucified.' I turned red with anger. 'In other words you're a liar!' I shouted at him. But my mother took me on her knee, saying, 'Quiet, my child, you're still too young to understand.' But now I've grown older, Brother Leo, I've grown older, and I *do* understand. Instead of being crucified, I simply think about the crucifixion. Is it possible, Brother Leo, that we too are actors?"

He sighed.

"Look at my hands, look at my feet. Where are the nails? In other words, is all this anguish just a game?"

At that moment a huge giant emerged from behind a tree. He

walked with heavy steps, was about thirty years old, hatless, solidly built, with high, arched forehead and a long, lion-like mane. Stopping in front of Francis, he placed his hand over his heart and saluted him.

"I'm looking for Francis of Assisi, the one who is gathering friars together to form an order. I am Elias Bombarone, from Cortona, a graduate of the University of Bologna. I find, however, that books constrict me too much; I want to engage in great deeds."

"I'm the one you're looking for, my friend," replied Francis. "I'm not gathering friars around me to found an order, but so that all of us may struggle together to save our souls. We are simple, illiterate people. What business do you have among us—you who are educated?"

"I want to save my soul also, Brother Francis, and it isn't going to be saved by means of education. I've learned a good deal about your life, and I like what I've learned. Sometimes the simple, illiterate man, by following his heart, finds what the mind will never be able to find. But the mind is needed too, Brother Francis. It too is a divine gift, and one which God presented to His most beloved creature, man. Who then is the perfect man? He who blends heart and mind harmoniously. What is the perfect order? That which has the heart for its foundation and allows the mind to build freely upon this foundation."

"You speak exquisitely, my unexpected friend; your mind spins out its arguments with incalculable skill. In short, I'm afraid of you! Please seek your salvation somewhere else."

"Brother Francis, you have no right to drive away a soul that wants to proceed along the road to salvation that you have laid out. For whom did you do this? Only for illiterates? The educated—have you not said so yourself?—have an even greater need to be saved. They are led astray by their minds, which want so many things, lay out so many roads, and do not know which to follow. Brother Francis, I have confidence in your road."

Francis said nothing. He was digging into the ground with his foot. Without asking permission, Elias sat down next to him on the doorstep.

"What solitude!" he murmured. "What peace!"

The sun was setting now. The treetrunks were rosy; the birds had begun to return to their nests, the brothers to come back from their begging. Juniper squatted before the hearth and lit a fire to begin the meal—he had been our cook ever since the day of his arrival. Bernard emerged in his turn from the clump of trees, having once more issued alive from his time of prayer. His eyes, though, were sunken and hollow, and he walked like a blind man. Looking at us, but not seeing us, he went inside.

"What solitude, what peace!" Elias murmured once more, watching the sun go down.

Francis turned and looked at the new visitor. I sensed that a great struggle was taking place inside him; he seemed to have some foreboding that this weighty giant would bring turmoil to the peaceful brotherhood.

There was a long silence. Suddenly Juniper rose to his feet and clapped his hands.

"The lentils are ready, brothers," he called. "Come and eat, in God's name!"

Francis stood up and extended his hand to the newcomer.

"We are glad to have you with us, Brother Elias," he said, and leading him by the hand, he brought him inside.

"Brothers, God has sent us new strength, a new brother, Elias Bombarone, from Cortona. Stand up and greet him."

We all went inside and knelt down on the ground, Francis placing himself next to the fireplace. Juniper brought the food and served it. We were hungry and we began eating with hearty appetites. All of a sudden Francis put down his spoon.

"My brothers," he said, "these lentils are too delicious, and the flesh is enjoying itself far too much: it is a great sin. I am going to add a handful of ashes."

As soon as he had said this he scooped up some ashes from the fireplace, threw them onto his plate, and began once more to eat.

"Forgive me, my brothers," he said. "It is not that I am better than you—no, no. But my flesh is more sinful, and I must not allow it to become rebellious."

"Why should we fear the flesh so much, Brother Francis?" asked Elias. "In other words, don't we have sufficient faith in our spiritual strength?"

"No, Brother Elias, we don't!" answered Francis, and he threw still another fistful of ashes over his lentils.

"The mouths that are preaching the word of God are multiply-ing," Francis said to me happily the next day.

"The mouths that want to eat are multiplying also, Brother Fran-cis," I answered him. "How are you going to feed them?"

Truthfully, the people of Assisi had begun to grumble: they were tired of feeding so many mendicant friars. One morning a messen-ger came to tell Francis that the bishop wished to speak with him and that he should come. "I'm at his service," Francis answered, crossing himself. Then, turning to me:

"I have a feeling he wants to scold me, Brother Leo. You come too."

We found the bishop seated in his armchair telling the black beads of his rosary. Piled on top of him were the cares of heaven and earth. It was his duty to divide his soul in two. First, he was a shepherd of men. It was necessary for him to keep sharp watch over the sheep that God had entrusted to him: scabies was contagious, and if one sheep should fall ill, he had to be careful that all the others did not catch the disease as well. But at the same time it was necessary for him to be concerned about his own soul. He, obvi-ously, was also one of God's sheep, and his duty was to follow the Great Shepherd.

When he saw Francis he tried to frown, but was unable to, for he greatly loved this saintly rebel who had abandoned what men most esteem in this world and had embraced what they most hate and fear: solitude and poverty. He had even conquered the scorn of his fellow men, and went about barefooted, preaching love.

He extended his plump episcopal hand. Francis knelt to kiss it, then rose and stood with crossed arms, waiting.

"I have reason to chide you, Francis, my son," said the bishop, fighting to make his voice sound severe. "I have heard a great deal about you, and all of it good; there is one thing, one thing only, that displeases me."

"Let me hear it, Your Excellency, and if it is God's wish that your will be done, it shall be done. Holy Obedience is a precious daugh-ter of God."

The bishop coughed, hesitating in order to work out beforehand what to say and how to say it so that Francis would not be infuri-ated.

"I've been told," he began finally, "that the faithful who are following in your train grow more numerous every day and that they have been pouring into this city and the nearby villages, knocking on doors to ask for alms. This is not as it should be! Everyone here is poor. How long do you expect such people to have extra bread to give to you and your followers?"

Francis lowered his head without answering. The bishop extended his hand and brought it down heavily on the Bible, which lay opened next to him.

"Besides, you forget what the Apostle says: *If any will not work, neither should he eat.*" His voice was angry now.

"We pray, we preach—that is work too," Francis murmured, but the bishop did not hear.

"Therefore, both as your bishop and as a father who loves you," he continued, "I have two requests to ask of you: first, that you put all your followers to work so that they shall no longer expect to live from the sweat of others; second, that you have something in reserve —a small property, a field, a vineyard or olive grove—and that you work it and lay up each year whatsoever God grants to the farmers. I am not saying you should work in order to become rich—God forbid!—but that you should do so in order not to be a burden on our brothers who have homes and children and who, even though they may desire to give alms to beggars, have no extra provisions with which to do so. Absolute poverty, my child, goes against both God and man. . . . That's what I wanted to say to you, and why I called you. Now consider well all that you have heard, and give me your answer."

Talking had fatigued him. He closed his eyes and leaned against the back of the armchair, his head drooping. The rosary slipped out of his fingers; I bent down and gave it to him. His hands were white and soft; they smelled of incense.

Francis raised his head. "With your permission, Bishop, I shall speak."

"I am listening, Francis, my child. Speak freely."

"One night when I was weeping, imploring God to enlighten my mind so that I could decide whether or not we should have something for the hour of need—a small field, a tiny house, a purse with an irreducible minimum of money, something to which we could say, 'You are mine!'—God answered me, 'Francis, Francis, he who has a house becomes a door, a window; he who has a field becomes soil, and he who has a delicate gold ring finds that the ring turns into a noose which seizes him around the neck and strangles him!' That, Bishop, is what God told me!"

The bishop blushed. He wanted to answer, but the words became tangled in his toothless mouth. The veins of his neck began to swell, and a young priest who was standing with crossed arms in the corner ran and brought him a glass of water. The bishop recovered his composure. He turned to Francis:

"Who can guarantee it was God who'spoke to you? Many times when we pray we hear our own voice and think it is the voice of God; many times, also, the Tempter assumes God's face and voice and then comes and leads our souls astray. Can you place your hand on the Gospel and tell me which of the words you hear when you pray are your own and which are God's?"

Francis turned pale. His lips began to tremble.

"No, I can't . . ." he murmured.

His knees gave way beneath him and he sank noiselessly to the floor.

"With your permission, Bishop, I shall begin to weep and wail. Your words are knives which have penetrated to my heart. How shall I ever be able to distinguish God from Francis now, or Francis from Satan?"

He hid his face in his palms and burst into lamentations.

Pitying him, the bishop bent forward in his armchair, took hold of him under the arms, and raised him up.

He turned to the young priest: "Bring a glass of wine for our visitor, my child. Bring three glasses so that we can all drink to his health."

Francis had collapsed onto a stool now and was wiping the tears from his cheeks and beard.

"Forgive me, Bishop. I have no resistance."

The young priest brought the three glasses of wine on a wooden tray. The bishop raised his glass.

"Wine is a sacred drink, my child," he said. "When consecrated by a priest it can become the blood of Christ. I drink to your health, Francis. Go now, and may God bless you. I do not want you to give me your answer right away. Think over what we have said, think it over well, and then come and tell us your decision. Poverty is good, but only up to a point; wealth is good, but only up to a point.

Moderation in all, my child, even in kindness, in piety, even in scorn for worldly possessions. The more immoderate these things become, the more danger of falling into Satan's grasp—so beware! Goodbye now, and good luck."

Francis was about to stoop to kiss the bishop's hand again and take his leave, but he restrained himself. A voice had risen within him: Do not go! it called. Do not be afraid of him. Give him an answer!

"Bishop," he said, "a voice is calling within me and preventing me from leaving."

"A voice, my child? Perhaps it is the voice of the rebel, of Lucifer. What does it say?"

"It says that the devil rejoices when he sees men afraid of poverty. . . . To have nothing, absolutely nothing: that is the road which leads to God. There is none other."

This made the bishop wild with rage. He banged his fist down on the Gospels.

"The devil rejoices, Francis, when he sees you oppose my will! Do not say a single word more, but go! And may God take pity on you and extend His hand over your head to cure you. You are sick."

Francis knelt, kissed the bishop's hand, and we departed.

We left Assisi, passed San Damiano's, and continued on toward the Portiuncula, not breathing a word the entire way. Finally Francis halted at a fork in the road. "The bishop's words were harsh," he said. "I want to be alone, Brother Leo. I'll go left to the riverbank and follow it until I reach the first hamlet, the one in the forest."

"The people there are wild and savage, Brother Francis. They will attack you. I'm afraid for your safety."

"But that's precisely why I'm going, lamb of God. I can't stand this easy life any more."

I returned alone to the Portiuncula. I had lost my zest for begging. The bishop's words seemed harsh to me also, harsh and—God forgive me—correct. Yes, I reflected, if anyone doesn't work, he shouldn't eat either. We ought to knuckle down to work like everyone else and earn our bread by the sweat of our brows—the way God commands.

I collapsed onto the threshold of the Portiuncula and began to wait for nightfall, when the brothers, and also Francis, would return.

147

I was worried; my heart felt uneasy. I knew I oughtn't to have left him alone, because wild brutes lived in the hamlet where he was going—men who denied Christ. They might strike him.

I jumped to my feet. The sun still had not gone down. I sped along the riverbank, reached the savage village, and entered it. The streets were deserted, but soon I heard dogs barking and also tumultuous laughter and shouting. I ran toward the noise, and what should I see but a crowd of men, women, and children. They had driven Francis to the brim of a well, where they were bombarding him furiously with stones. And he stood there with crossed arms, the blood flowing from his head. From time to time he spread his arms and whispered, "Thank you, children, God bless you all!" and then he crossed his hands once more over his breast.

Just as I was darting forward to place myself in front of Francis in order to defend him, a savage roar was heard behind him. Everyone turned. An immense giant had made his way through the mob and had lifted Francis up in his arms like a baby.

"Where do you want me to take you, poor miserable Francis?" he said, bending down over him.

"Who are you?"

"My name is Masseo, and I'm a carter. Everyone knows me. Where do you want me to take you?"

"To the Portiuncula," answered Francis. "I'm a carter too, Brother Masseo. I take men from earth and transport them to heaven."

Masseo set out, carrying Francis in his arms. I ran behind them. When we arrived at the Portiuncula the sun had gone down. Masseo deposited Francis on the threshold and squatted at his side. Bernard was praying in a corner; Capella and Angelo were just returning from their rounds of begging. One by one the other friars appeared—barefooted, famished, the knotted cord around their waists, their faces radiant with happiness. All was peaceful, gentle. The shadows fell gradually; the birds chirped their farewells to the light. Hesperus could be seen throbbing in the sky. Giles watched in silence while I brought water and began to wash Francis' wounds. Brother Juniper had commenced to arrange kindling between two stones in order to start a fire; Ruffino and Sior Pietro had gone to the riverbank to collect laurel leaves, and now they were inside the church, adorning the statue of Santa Maria degli Angeli.

"We are holding a wedding tonight," Francis exclaimed suddenly. "Masseo, do you want to be best man?"

Everyone turned in surprise. Capella jumped gleefully into the air. He had been holding his velvet hat in his hand, dusting it.

"A wedding, Brother Francis?" he asked. "Whose wedding?"

"I chanced upon a widow along the road," replied Francis with a smile. "For years now she has been going about barefooted, in rags, hungry, and no one has opened his door to give her alms. We, my brothers, shall open the door to her."

"For God's sake speak so we can understand, Brother Francis," shouted the friars. "Whose widow?"

"Christ's, my brothers. Do not stare at me like that, your eyes popping out of your heads. Christ's widow—Poverty. For her first husband's sake, I am going to take her as my bride."

He got up and looked at himself.

"I am dressed as a bridegroom," he said. "There is no need to change anything—the patched robe, the coarse knotted cord, the muddy feet, the empty stomach: I lack nothing. Nor does the bride. So why not begin? Come, best man—offer me in marriage!"

Francis went first, with Masseo second and the rest of us behind. We filled the church.

"Where is Father Silvester?" asked Francis, turning to see if he could find him. "Let him come to bless the wedding."

"And where's the bride?" I said. "I don't see her."

"You don't see her, Brother Leo, because your eyes are open. Close them and you shall see her."

He knelt in front of the altar and turned to his right.

"Sister Poverty," he said, his voice full of emotion, "Sister Poverty, precious, revered, most beloved companion of Christ, you who throughout His life remained faithful to Him, a courageous ally in the struggle; you who accompanied Him on His journey right to the foot of the Cross, right to the grave—I hold out my hand, I gather you up from the streets and take you as my bride. My lady, give me your hand!"

He stretched his arm out into the air, to his right.

Fallen on our knees in front of the altar, we all listened with astonishment to the strange bridegroom's words and watched him extend his hand to the invisible bride.

I closed my eyes, and when I did so I saw a pale woman next to Francis, at his right. She was downcast, dressed in black rags, but noble and lofty, like a widowed queen. And standing before them was Masseo, and he was placing two crowns of thorns upon their heads; and Father Silvester, holding a lighted candle, was intoning the triumphant marriage hymns.

When I opened my eyes I saw the brothers. Their faces were resplendent; sacred flames were leaping from their eyes. Suddenly we all jumped to our feet, joined hands, formed a circle, and began to sing and dance around Francis and the invisible bride. Brother Bernard had burst into tears, and Brother Capella had removed his celebrated hat and was waving it in the air, while Giles, next to him, clapped his hands. At this point Masseo grew bold, brought out from beneath his shirt the flute that he played at night when he traveled all alone, knelt down on both knees in front of Francis, and began to pipe merry pastoral airs. The humble chapel resounded like a sheepfold during a shepherd's wedding. And Santa Maria degli Angeli, astonished like the rest of us, looked down from her statue at the strange marriage and smiled at her Son, as though saying to him, my child, an excess of love has driven your friends insane. Just look at them: they get drunk without wine, they become bridegrooms without having a bride, hunger surfeits them, poverty enriches them. They are passing the bounds, my son, passing the bounds assigned to man; a little further and they will become angels. And the one in the middle—do you see him? That is our friend Francis, God's beloved buffoon.

When we left the church the sky was filled with stars. Francis continued on into the darkness; he wanted to be alone. The rest of us all lay down on the ground and listened to the night.

We did not speak. The strange marriage passed through our minds again and again. At first, several of the brothers were on the verge of laughter, but little by little we all began to perceive the secret meaning—little by little the laughter turned to tears, and then the tears to bliss. This is the way the souls in Paradise must weep, I thought to myself; this is the way they must laugh. Happiness, there above, must be just like this. . . . Our souls had been delivered for a moment from our minds and our flesh; they had no further need of lowly truths, the kind that can be seen and felt. Instead, each of our souls had become a young seagull poised on the

ocean of God, rising and falling in perfect accord with His merciful
will.

Francis did not return that night, nor the next day. Our hearts
were uneasy, but we said nothing. When evening came we all sat
down outside the Portiuncula to eat, each of us holding out what he
had collected during the day, to be shared by all. I put a piece of
bread into my mouth, but my throat was sealed tight. I got up.

"I'm going to find Brother Francis," I said. I set out toward Assisi
and started up Mount Subasio: something told me I would find him
praying in one of the caves he so loved. I could see that he was
passing through a difficult time again. A new anguish must have
been tearing apart his heart, and he had isolated himself with God
in order to seek His aid and mercy.

It was midnight when I arrived. I entered two or three caves, but
did not find him. Suddenly I heard a sound: tranquil, reproachful
weeping, like that of a tiny infant. Going close to the cave from
which the lamentations were coming, I peered into the darkness
and was able to see a pale face, and two upraised hands moving
back and forth in the air. I held my breath and listened. It seemed
to me that someone was speaking, that Francis was conversing with
someone.

"I want to do Thy will," he was crying; "I want to do Thy will,
but I am unable to!"

Afterwards: silence. I heard Francis' sobs and the sound of his
hands beating against his chest; then his voice again:

"How can I save others, I the sinner condemned to damnation?
No one realizes—no one but Thee, Lord—what hell, what darkness,
what mud exists in my bowels!"

Once again there was silence. Francis seemed to be listening to
the answer.

I was on the point of moving out of earshot: the two of them were
conversing together, and it was indeed a most boorish thing for
someone to spy on them and listen stealthily to their secrets. But I've
said it once and I say it again: I'm a boor! I stretched myself out
face down on the ground and strained to hear every word.

Soon Francis' voice was audible again, this time filled with anguish.

"Dost Thou forgive my sins? That is what I want to know: dost

Thou forgive my sins? If not, Lord, how can I begin? I have no faith in this mud which people call Francis."

For a considerable time I heard nothing—no voices, no weeping; nor could I any longer see the hands moving back and forth in the darkness.

But suddenly Francis uttered a heart-rending cry:

"When wilt Thou say 'Enough'? When? When?"

He jumped to his feet. Dawn was breaking; pale, uncertain glimmers crept forward and licked the rocky face of the cave. Francis took a step, but tripped and struck his head against the stone. I could see blood gushing from his forehead. Uttering a cry, I jumped up and ran to him.

"Don't be afraid, Brother Francis. It's me, Brother Leo!"

He lifted his eyes and stared at me for a long time without seeing me. At last he saw me, recognized me.

"I've been wrestling," he said in a whisper, gasping for breath; "wrestling, Brother Leo, and I am tired."

We left the cave. I kept hold of his arm so that he would not fall.

The light had struck the peak of the mountain now and had begun to descend. The world was awakening. Francis halted.

"Where are we going?" he asked. "Where are you leading me? I am fine here where I am. I'm tired, Brother Leo, tired."

He gazed at the summit. The light continually struck new slopes, waking stones, thorns, and soil. A partridge flushed noisily and passed in front of us, cackling. In the east the morning star danced and laughed.

"We are fine here where we are," he said again. "The night is finished, finished—praise the Lord!"

Sighing, he squatted down on a rock and extended his hands to the sun so that they could become warm. Lifting his head, he nodded to me to come sit next to him. Then he glanced around him, as though afraid there might be someone who could overhear us.

"Brother Leo," he said to me in an undertone, placing his hand on my knee, "the most dazzling of all the faces of Hope is God, but He is also the most dazzling of all the faces of Despair. Our souls sail and career between two precipices."

I said nothing. What could I say? I sensed that Francis had come from far far away, had descended from the most savage of peaks, and brought with him from those heights a message that was harsh and severe.

"Do you have sandals of iron, Brother Leo?" he asked me a moment later. "That is the kind you must put on, my faithful companion. Poor, unfortunate Brother Leo—we have a long, difficult road ahead of us."

"I have my feet," I answered. "They're tougher than iron: no matter where you lead, they will bring me there."

Francis smiled. "Do not boast, Brother Leo. I have come from far far away, and have seen and heard terrible things. Listen to me: If fear were being offered for sale at the market, Brother Leo, we should have to sell everything we possessed, in order to buy it."

"I don't understand," I murmured.

"So much the better," said Francis, and he fell silent once again.

The mountain was flooded with light now. Before us was a clump of wild broom covered with ambrosial blossoms. A tiny rose-colored cloud sailed tranquilly across the sky until little by little it too melted away under the sun's heat and vanished. A small bird with a red bonnet on its head came and perched on a rock opposite us. It waved its tail, turned its head anxiously in all directions, then glanced directly at us and as it did so (you couldn't help but feel that it knew who we were) it grew bold and began to whistle: softly, tauntingly at first; but soon it threw back its head, swelled its throat, and, gazing at the sky, the light, the sun, burst into song with drunken abandon. Everything vanished; nothing remained in the world save this bird and God—God, and a beak that was singing.

Francis listened, his eyes closed. A perturbed expression, but at the same time one of unutterable exultation, had poured over his face. His lower lip hung down, trembling.

Suddenly the bird stopped, spread its wings, and disappeared. Francis opened his eyes.

"Forgive me, Lord," he murmured. "For a moment I forgot myself."

He got up, troubled. "Come, Brother Leo!" he said, and we started the descent.

"Even though a man's heart is calm and decided," he murmured, "he need only hear a small bird singing, and he is lost!"

Taking a turn to avoid Assisi, we arrived at the Portiuncula. It was deserted. The friars had scattered and would not be coming back until evening.

"Bring the quill and inkwell," Francis said to me.

I brought the implements and knelt down on both knees, facing him.

"Write!" Francis commanded, stretching out his arm.

He was silent for a considerable time. I waited, quill in hand.

"Write: 'Enough is enough! I am tired of walking beneath blossoming trees, tired of having wild beasts come and lick me, of seeing rivers part to let me through, of passing through flames without being burned! If I remain here any longer I shall rot from security, laziness, and easy living. Open the door and let me go!'

"'Adam, Adam, you creature of clay: do not become insolent.'

"'I am not an angel, nor am I a monkey. I'm a man. To be a man means to be a warrior, worker, rebel. I have a strong feeling that outside there are beasts that bite, rivers that drown you, fires that burn. I shall go out to fight! Open the gate and let me!'"

Francis wiped the sweat from his forehead and glanced around to make sure there was no one who could overhear.

"Did you write it down?"

"Yes, Brother Francis. Forgive me, however, if I don't understand what you mean."

"It doesn't matter. Take another piece of paper and write:

"The bishop is correct. We too should earn our bread by the sweat of our brows. We should work—that is God's will. But we have wedded Poverty and with all due respect to you, Bishop, we are not going to abandon her.

"Write:

"Each friar who knows a trade must work at that trade, provided it is not dishonorable, nor a hindrance to the salvation of his soul. In payment for their work the friars shall receive the necessities of life, and never money. Money, for them, is just stones and chaff. And if their trade is not enough to feed them, they must not be ashamed to knock on doors and beg, for the giving of alms to the poor is a prescribed obligation for each of us; nor was Christ Himself ashamed to be poor, and a stranger, or to live on alms.

"Take care, my brothers, that we do not lose our share of heaven for things as transient and insignificant as earthly possessions. You

154

must be humble and of good heart, and must rejoice when you find yourselves among those who are humble and despised: among the poor, the ill, among lepers and beggars.

"Write, Brother Leo:

"Poverty, Obedience, Chastity, and above all, Love, are the great companions of our journey. And there is One who must march in front of us day and night, and upon Whom we must keep our eyes pinned—Christ. He hungered; let us hunger as well. He suffered; let us suffer as well. He was crucified; let us be crucified as well. He rose from the dead; we too, one day, shall rise from the dead."

I wrote and wrote, filling the paper. Then Francis took the quill and inscribed his name at the bottom in clumsily formed letters: Francis, God's little pauper.

"This is our Rule," he said. "Now write at the top of the paper: To Our Most Holy Father, Pope Innocent."

I gazed at Francis in astonishment. "We're going to send it to the pope?"

"No, Brother Leo. We are going to bring it to him personally—you and I. Your feet are of iron, aren't they? So are mine. We shall go on foot therefore to the Holy City, like impoverished pilgrims, and shall present it to the pope with our own hands. If he so desires, he will affix his seal at the bottom; and if he does not, then God will affix His seal—He has given me His word!"

"When do we leave?"

"Tonight."

"So soon, Brother Francis?"

"How many times do I have to tell you, Brother Leo—God cannot wait."

The friars began to arrive one by one as we were talking. They collapsed onto the ground, overcome with fatigue.

"We're wasting our time—in other words our souls—by going around all day long banging on doors," Brother Bernard whispered to his neighbor. "Instead, we should be motionless, on our knees, praying. . . . How long will this continue, Brother Pietro, how long?"

"As long as we have mouths, dear Bernard, so be patient."

At that moment everyone turned to look at Francis, who had risen and was about to speak. For some time he regarded each of the friars in turn, his eyes full of anxiety and sadness. He knew how exceedingly cunning the Tempter was, how credulous the heart of man, how sweet and all-powerful the flesh.

"My brethren," he said, "I have received a message from God, and I must go away for a short time. We have multiplied, have become an entire brotherhood, and now we must establish a Rule. I am departing in order to throw myself at the feet of Christ's shadow on earth, that he may give us his blessing. Do not be downcast. You will not remain alone; I shall be among you night and day, invisible. He who is invisible sees more clearly, hears more clearly, and is better able to read the thoughts of men. . . . But take care! Do not forget what we said during our holy vigils: Obedience, Chastity, Poverty, and above all, Love! And as one final command, my children, I leave you this: Cease begging. Each of you shall now take up some work—this one will serve in a hospital, that one will cut wood in the forest and sell it; or work as a porter, or weave baskets, or make sandals, or cultivate the earth, reap, vintage—whatever God sends him to do. Do not forget, however, that we have wedded Poverty. No one shall be unfaithful to her. You shall live from hand to mouth, each day's work supplying only what is needful for that day. Anything beyond belongs to Satan. Poverty, my children, Obedience, Chastity, Love! Those among you who have the gift of speaking to the people, cross yourselves and set out to do so. Go in pairs so that one may comfort the other; halt wherever you see your fellow men; halt, and then proclaim Love—full, complete love, for enemies as well as friends, for the poor as well as the rich, the wicked as well as the righteous: all are God's children, each one is our brother.

"I leave Father Silvester in my place during my absence. Obey him. He is a priest of God; he celebrates Mass before the holy altar, transforms the wine into Christ's blood, the bread into Christ's body. Of all of us, he stands the closest to God.

"Father Silvester, I deliver the friars into your hands. Watch over them. If a sheep falls ill, it is partly the shepherd's fault; if a sheep jumps over the fence and escapes from the fold, it is partly the shepherd's fault. Take care, Father Silvester!"

Spreading his arms, he embraced the friars one by one.

"Farewell, my brothers. This lamb of God, Brother Leo, shall accompany me. The moon is visible tonight and the road to Rome is gleaming, all white. We are leaving now. Cross yourself, Brother Leo. In God's name!"

Giles, Masseo, and Bernard burst into tears; the others kissed Francis' hand, without speaking. Ruffino approached and whispered something in his ear, but Francis shook his head.

"No, no, Brother Ruffino," he said. "We want neither staff, sandals, nor bread. God shall be our staff, our sandals, and our bread. Farewell, my children!"

He proceeded a few paces, then turned. His eyes had filled with tears.

"You—all of you—are my father and mother and brothers. Satan has hoisted his banner, and God shouts: 'All who are faithful, come!' Listen to His appeal, and shout in response, 'We are coming, Lord, we are coming!' Courage, my brothers. Good and evil are struggling, but the good shall win. Fear does not exist, my brothers, nor does hunger, thirst, sickness, death. The only thing that exists is God."

He took me by the arm.

"Come, let's go," he said. He was impatient to begin.

How many years have elapsed since that night when we crossed ourselves and set out on our journey! I sit in my cell now, close my eyes, and think: how many moons, how many summers and autumns, how many tears! Francis must be seated now at God's feet: he is probably leaning over and gazing at the earth, searching everywhere for the Portiuncula—but he will not find it. A gigantic church sits on top of it and crushes it with a profusion of towers, bells, statues, chandeliers, and gold! And the friars: they no longer march barefooted, but wear sandals and warm robes, and some—forgive me for saying so, Lord—have their knotted cords made of silk!

I remember that as we were walking beneath the moon Francis suddenly turned and stared behind him in terror. He seemed to hear bells and to see an immense basilica three stories high. He uttered a cry, crossed himself, and the edifice vanished into the moonlight.

"It wasn't real!" he murmured. "Glory be to God!"

Alas, Father Francis, it was all too real. But how can anyone put a bridle on man's vanity and arrogance? But how can Purity walk the earth without covering her feet with mud?

The journey lasted many days and nights. If we had not hymned God's praises along the way, if we had not conversed about the Lord, had not felt Christ traveling in front of us and turning from

157

time to time to smile at us, I doubt if we ever would have been able to endure such fatigue, such hunger, such cold during the nights!

When we entered a village we would knock hungrily on the doors to ask for alms, and sometimes the inhabitants gave us a mouthful of bread; sometimes they put a stone or a dead mouse into our hands and doubled up with laughter, whereupon we departed, blessing the home that had wronged us.

It was springtime, glorious weather. The trees began to blossom, the buds to swell on the grapevines. The fig trees were uncurling their first tender leaves.

"This is the way the Second Coming will be, Brother Leo," Francis kept saying to me. "It will be like springtime, and the dead will leap into the light like shoots."

One evening we reached a large market town just as the boys and girls were about to begin a great celebration: the burning of Father Winter. We went to the village square and saw the figure of Winter right in the middle, in front of the church. He was made of twigs and straw, and had a long beard of cotton. The unmarried boys and girls were holding lighted torches and dancing in a circle around him, singing the barefaced songs of spring. They were all fired up with excitement: they were young, unmarried; spring, plus the wine they had drunk, had swelled out their chests and loins, and their blood was boiling.

The married and the old watched and laughed, standing in a circle around them. Francis, leaning against one of the trees which bordered the square, watched also. I expected him to grow angry and leave, dragging me with him, but he continued to watch with wide-open, insatiable eyes.

"The human race is indestructible, Brother Leo," he said to me. "Look at those young men and girls. Look how their faces have ignited, how their eyes gleam, how they gaze at one another as though saying, 'Do not worry, even if the two of us were the sole people remaining on earth, we should soon replenish it with sons and daughters!' They too, Brother Leo, are following their road, a road which shall lead them to God. We go by way of poverty and chastity; they by way of food in abundance, and copulation."

As we were talking, the young man who was the lead dancer leapt forward and thrust his lighted torch into Winter's abdomen. All at once the old gaffer of straw caught fire. The flames shot straight up, rose, fell, and soon there was nothing left but ashes. The boys and girls threw away their torches with a wild shout and, groaning and shrieking, departed in order to pursue one another furiously in the darkness. The village became filled with laughter and panting.

Francis took my hand. We proceeded to the church on the opposite side of the square and squatted beneath its arched doorway.

"This was a fine day, Brother Leo," he said, and he settled himself against the doorpost, preparing to sleep. "Yes, this was a fine day: we saw the other face of the man who struggles. May it too be blessed!"

We departed again early in the morning.

"What freedom we have!" Francis exclaimed joyously. "We are the freest men in the world because we are the poorest. Poverty, simplicity, and freedom are identical."

We began to sing again in order to forget our hunger and fatigue.

Each day, however, Francis found his heart being filled with bitterness. In every village we entered, every city, Satan had set up camp. The people blasphemed, quarreled, stabbed one another, never set foot in church, never made the sign of the cross.

"The soul of man has revolted; it no longer fears God, Brother Leo," he kept saying to me. "Satan stands at the crossroads, assumes whatever face pleases him, and tempts mankind. Sometimes he appears as a monk, sometimes as a handsome young man, sometimes as a woman."

One day when we were finally nearing the Holy City, we halted —it must have been midday—and stretched out under a cypress to rest and catch our breath. Our feet were oozing blood, our shanks and scalps were covered with dust; we had been conversing since morning about Christ's Passion, and our eyes were swollen and inflamed with weeping. Just as we had closed our eyes halfway, in the hope that perhaps sleep would come and take pity on us, who should step out from behind the cypress trees but a fat, jovial monk with red sandals and a wide, red hat. He was clean-shaven, perfumed—a handsome specimen. Or could it have been that we actually did fall asleep and it only seemed to us that we saw him?

He came up to us, greeted us majestically, spread out a silk handkerchief on a rock, and sat down.

"Judging from your bare feet and from your robes, which are full of holes, you must be members of some new order, one that is extremely hard and strict. I take it you are making a pilgrimage to Rome."

"We are poor friars," replied Francis, "sinners, illiterates, the dregs of humanity, and we are journeying to Rome in order to fall at the pope's feet and ask him to grant us a privilege."

"What privilege?"

"The privilege of absolute Poverty, of possessing nothing, absolutely nothing."

The fat monk laughed. "I can see arrogance peeping through the holes in your robes," he said. "Nothing and everything are the same, and whoever seeks to have nothing also seeks to have everything—which you know well enough, you sly foxes, but you pretend to be poor, miserable devils just so you can dig your claws into everything without meeting any opposition and without anyone realizing what you are up to—not even God."

A quiver ran through Francis' body. He sat up beneath the cypress, terrified. "Everything?" he said, his lips trembling.

"Everything. And you possess everything already, hypocrite! You are the richest man on earth."

"Me?"

"Yes, you—for the simple reason that you have placed your hopes in God. What I want to see is this: for you to become so poor that you must renounce even the hope that one day you will see God. Can you do it? Can you? That is what perfect Poverty means; what it means to be a perfect ascetic. That is the highest form of sainthood. Can you do it?"

"Who are you?" cried Francis. "Get thee behind me, Satan!" He made the sign of the cross in the air, and all at once the monk melted into the sun and we heard nothing but a screeching, jeering laugh which faded away and then vanished behind the cypresses. The smell of tar and brimstone remained in the air.

Francis jumped to his feet. "Quickly, let's go," he said. "It's courting death to sit in the shade of a cypress. . . . Did you see, Brother Leo? Did you hear?"

"I saw, Brother Francis, I heard. Let's go."

We set out once again, but both our hearts remained in turmoil. Francis did not breathe a word the whole afternoon. He raced on ahead of me; I could hear him sighing frequently. Toward evening he turned and I saw him: his face was wasted away.

"Do you think he was right?" he asked in a whisper. "Do you think the thrice-damned monk was right? But without this hope, I'm doomed!"

I struggled to console him. "Words are diabolical," I said; "they are traps set by the Tempter. Don't let yourself be caught, Francis."

But he shook his head despairingly. "The words of the Tempter and the words of God are often identical, Brother Leo. When God wishes to inform us of His divine will, sometimes He sends the Tempter."

He was silent for a moment, but then he continued in a doleful voice:

"The monk was right. Our poverty is opulent—opulent, because it keeps heaven concealed deep down at the bottom of its coffer. True Poverty, Brother Leo, means that the coffer is entirely empty right down to the bottom; it contains nothing, not even heaven, not even immortality. Nothing, nothing, nothing!"

He reflected for a moment, and sighed. He wanted to say something further, but the terrible words were being smothered in his throat. Finally they managed to come forth:

"Lord," he whispered, "give me the strength to enable me one day to renounce hope, the hope, O Lord, of seeing Thee. Who knows: perhaps this, and only this, constitutes absolute Poverty."

His tears stifled his voice. He staggered, and I caught hold of him to keep him from falling.

"Don't say that, Brother Francis. It is asking to surpass the strength allotted to man."

"Yes, yes, poor Brother Leo, it is asking to surpass the strength allotted to man. But that is precisely why God expects this from us. Precisely! Haven't you been able to understand that yet, my poor, unfortunate fellow voyager?"

I hadn't nor would I ever. Didn't human nature have bounds, and weren't those bounds fixed by God Himself? Why then did the Almighty expect us to surpass them? Since He had not given us wings, why was he prodding us to fly? He should have given us wings!

We found a pine tree with long, thickly needled branches that inclined toward the ground, forming a natural shelter. The sun had beat down upon it all day long; fragrant sap was oozing from the trunk. We both collapsed to the ground, preparing to spend the night. Though a few dry crusts of bread remained in my sack, we did not have appetite even for a taste.

Neither of us spoke. I did not feel sleepy, but I closed my eyes, for I was unable to look at Francis' face any longer: never before had I seen such anguish there. Although he was biting his lips in an effort to suppress his emotion, I heard the groan of a wounded beast rising from his chest.

The stars came out; the earth's nocturnal voices rose from the soil; I felt the sweetness of night gradually penetrating me, wrapping itself cunningly around my bowels.

Suddenly there was a falling star in the sky. "Did you see that, Brother Leo? Francis called to me, pointing upwards. "A tear just rolled down God's cheek. . . . Is man then not the only one who weeps? Dost Thou weep also, Lord? Dost Thou suffer, Father, just as I do?"

He leaned back against the trunk of the pine tree, exhausted. I closed my eyes and was already feeling the tranquillity which heralds the approach of sleep when suddenly I heard Francis' voice. It was raucous, stifled, unrecognizable:

"I implore you, Brother Leo, do not go to sleep, do not leave me alone! A terrible thought is rising from the depths of my being, and I do not want to be left all alone with it!"

I opened my eyes. The heart-rending tone of his voice frightened me.

"What thought, Brother Francis? Could it be the Tempter again? Tell me and you'll feel better."

Francis came next to me and laid his palm on my knee. "You know, Brother Leo, man clings to a tiny blade of grass. Angels and devils tug at him and try to tear him away from this blade of grass. He is hungry, thirsty, the sweat gushes from his forehead, he is covered with blood, he weeps and curses—but does not let go. He is unwilling to release his grip on this tiny blade of grass, the earth. Brother Leo, heaven too is a blade of grass!"

He was quiet. I felt his whole body trembling.

"It's not Francis who is speaking," I cried with a shudder, "it's not Francis who is speaking, it's the Tempter."

"It is not Francis," he answered, "and not the Tempter, and not

God either. The voice speaking inside me, Brother Leo, belongs to a wounded beast."

I started to open my mouth, but Francis placed his hand over it. "Do not say anything else!" he bellowed. "Go to sleep!"

The sun had already risen when I awoke the next morning. Not finding Francis at my side, I circled the area, going from pine tree to pine tree, shouting his name. Suddenly I raised my eyes and saw him perched aloft on a high branch. He was peering between the needles, spying on two chirping swallows as they flew back and forth building their nest, transporting each time in their beaks a piece of straw, or a horsehair that had fallen on the road, or a lump of mud.

"Come down, Brother Francis," I shouted. "The sun has risen. Let's be on our way!"

"I'm fine up here," he replied. "Be on our way? Where? Rome is here, the pope is here. It is here that I shall receive permission to preach."

I held my tongue. Every so often I was overcome with the fear that perhaps my master had taken leave of his senses. I squatted on one of the roots of the pine tree, and waited.

"I'm not going anywhere," he continued. "I've received permission from the swallows, so there is no more need for us to go to the pope!"

Once more I said nothing. I was waiting for God's flame to subside within him. After a long silence I heard his voice for the third time, calm now, and full of compassion:

"Why don't you say anything, Brother Leo?"

"I'm waiting for God's flame to subside within you," I replied.

His laughter—happy, refreshing, childish—emerged from behind the branches and rang in my ears.

"There is little use in waiting, Brother Leo! As long as I have flesh and bones, this fire will not die down. First it will devour the flesh and bones; then it will devour the soul, and only after that will it subside. So, Brother Leo, there is little use in waiting! Anyway, I'm coming down!"

He pushed aside the branches and began to descend. His face was calm, resplendent. "This morning," he said, "I think I have begun to understand the language of the birds. Did you hear them? They talk about God's love, just as we do."

"Who do you mean, Brother Francis?"

"The swallows."

I wanted to laugh, but right away I reflected that all of us have nothing but outer ears and eyes, whereas Francis had inner eyes and ears in addition. When the birds sang, we heard only the melody; he heard the melody and also the words.

We knelt under the pine trees, said our prayers, and resumed our journey.

My heart was frisking like a newborn kid. For years I had longed to visit the Holy City, to make my pilgrimage to the tombs of the Apostles, to stand on the base of one of the columns of Saint Peter's and see the thrice-holy countenance of God's representative on earth. I had heard that no one could view it without lifting his hand to his eyes to shield them from the dazzling radiance.

At last we were coming near. The closer we came, the more clearly we heard the strong lowing of the Eternal City: it was like a cow giving birth, or like a wild beast racked by hunger. From time to time human voices flew into the air, trumpets blared, bells rang. Noble lords in armor and rich ladies mounted on black and white horses kept passing along the great street. Clouds of dust rose up; the heat was oppressive; the air reeked with the filth of horses, oxen, and men.

"We are entering the home of the Apostle Peter," Francis said to me. "Whatever you see and hear now has a secret meaning—so beware! Did you notice the noble ladies who passed us on their black and white horses? The vices and virtues promenade here in the same way: like great, noble ladies."

"Vices too, Brother Francis!" I exclaimed. "Here, in the home of the Apostle Peter?"

Francis laughed. "How simple and naïve you are, Brother Leo! How inexperienced! And how very much I like you! Where else do you expect the vices to be found? Here, of course, in the Holy City! This is where Satan is in danger and so this is where he concentrates all his troops. Cross yourself and enter. We're here!"

We turned into a wide street. Unaccustomed as we were to the sounds of a great city, we were deafened by the shouts, rumbles, barking, neighing. Merchants were hawking their wares at the top of their lungs; bishops passed us inside silk-lined litters, their escort running in front to clear the way. Prostitutes walked by, and the whole street smelled of musk and jasmine. . . . "These are the vices," I kept murmuring, and I lowered my gaze.

Suddenly both Francis and I cried out. A strange procession had appeared at the end of the road. In front came five or six heralds dressed in black and blowing long bronze trumpets. They stopped their horses every so often and a crier, mounted on a camel, thundered: "Christians, Christians, the Holy Sepulcher is passing! Gaze upon it, gaze upon it with shame! How long shall it be trampled and soiled by the Infidels? To arms, brothers, in Christ's name! Let us all join together to deliver the Holy Sepulcher!" Then he would be .silent, and the trumpets would sound again. Behind, advancing very slowly, came four oxen yoked to an oxcart, and upon the oxcart was a replica of the Holy Sepulcher, fashioned from wood, iron, and multicolored strips of cloth. This was crowned by a wooden horse with a hideous Saracen astride it, holding a standard—a half-moon on a green background—which he waved in the air, while the horse, its tail uplifted, defecated upon the sacred tomb. Following in back came a band of women dressed in weeds of mourning. They had let down their hair, and were beating their breasts and lamenting.

The pageant went by, turned a corner, and disappeared. It did not disappear from our eyes, however, but went by, went by, and seemed to have no end. Our tears flowed, the city grew indistinct, and we saw nothing now except the desecrated Holy Sepulcher: except our desecrated souls.

"We still have much work to do, Brother Leo," Francis said, wiping away his tears. "Life is short. Will we have time? What do you think, my brother?"

"There, you see, our earthly life does have some value," I replied. "So why desert it?"

Francis did not answer. He was thinking, and I rejoiced that I had made him reflect on this. You see, I loved life, that tiny blade of grass, and I did not want to release my grip.

It was growing dark. We were ready to drop, and as we went along the narrow streets, we stopped every moment to search for a place to sleep. A tiny, barefooted old man with a small, white, wedge-shaped beard had been following us for some time. Finally he came up to us.

"Excuse me," he said. "You appear to be strangers here, and poor, as I am myself. Like Christ, you have nowhere to lay your heads. Come with me."

"God has sent you," said Francis. "We shall go where you lead us."

We proceeded through filthy alleyways where the poor teemed like ants. Naked children were rolling in the mud, women doing laundry or cooking in the middle of the street, men squatting, throwing dice. Our guide went in the lead, walking hurriedly, and we followed in silence behind him.

Suddenly Francis leaned over to my ear.

"Who could he be?" he whispered. "Perhaps he's Christ, and he has taken pity on us."

"He might also be Satan," I answered. "We'd better be careful."

Our destination was a half-crumbling inn with a spacious court-yard and a well in the center. Looming black on all sides were dilapidated chambers, doorless, like caves.

The old man stopped, looked around, and took us into one of the rooms. He lit the lamp.

"You can spend the night safely here, brothers. This is a wicked city, and dangerous at night. God took pity on you."

"Who are you, my brother?" asked Francis, looking carefully at the old man.

"You'll find two stools and a jug of water here," the other continued. "Right now I'm going to get you some bread and olives, and then we can talk. You seem to be poor God-fearing men; I too am poor and God-fearing. In other words, we have much to talk about. I'll be back in a moment." He vanished into the darkness of the yard.

I looked at Francis. "I don't like that old fellow," I said. "There's some hidden motive behind his kindness."

"Judging from the look of his eyes, he seems trustworthy," said Francis. "Let's place our confidence in the man, Brother Leo."

Two mats had been unrolled on the floor. The glitter of several stars entered through a lofty skylight whose dividers formed a cross. It was completely dark now outside.

The old man returned with our bread and olives. He had also brought two pomegranates.

166

"Brothers," he said, "where I come from we have a saying: 'Few possessions and lots of love!' Welcome!"

We crossed ourselves and started to eat. Our host knelt in a corner and watched us. As soon as we had finished and given thanks to God, Francis began to speak, not giving the old man a chance to question him.

"We are two poor friars," he said. "We have other brothers as well, and we spend our lives glorifying God and begging. We do not want to own anything, and we've come here to the Holy City to ask the vicar of Jesus Christ to grant us a great privilege: the privilege of absolute Poverty. . . . Now you know everything. We've made our confession. Your turn next!"

The tiny old man coughed. For some time he remained quiet, fingering his beard. Finally he opened his mouth to speak.

"You have confided in me; I shall confide in you. God is my witness that I shall tell you the whole truth. I am from Provence and am one of the sect of true Christians, the Cathari—you must have heard of us. You love poverty, and so do we. But above all we love purity, chastity, cleanness, which is why we're called the Cathari. We hate pleasure, woman, everything material. We won't sit on a stool that a woman has sat on; we won't eat bread that a woman has kneaded. We don't get married, don't have children; and we don't eat meat, because a male and a female united to produce it. We don't drink wine, don't spill blood, don't kill, don't go to fight in wars. We have no use for the world: it is dishonest, a liar, fornicator, a trap set by the devil. Is it possible that God created it? No, the world is not God's work, it is the work of Satan. God created only the spiritual world; Satan created the material world into which our souls have fallen, and where they are now being drowned. To be saved, therefore, we must flee this world. How? Through the good offices of the Archangel of Salvation—Death."

The contours of the old man's face were sparkling; the air around his head vibrated with radiant heat. Francis had hidden his face behind his palms.

"What is Death?" continued the old man, swept away with emotion. "What is Death? The angelic gatekeeper! He opens the door, and we enter the life everlasting."

Francis lifted his head. For a moment his face grew dark, as though the wing of Death had passed over him.

"Forgive me, old man, but it seems to me that you scorn the world far too much. The world is an arena where we have come to wrestle in order to turn our flesh into spirit. Only after all the flesh has become spirit is the world no longer necessary for us. Let Death come then, not before. We must entreat God to give us enough time to obliterate the flesh."

"Only Death can do that," the old man objected stubbornly.

"If so, what worth does man have?" asked Francis. "We must do it, not Death."

Getting up, he unhooked the lamp from the wall and brought it close to the old man's face.

"Who are you?" he asked in an anguished voice. "Your words are seductive, dangerous. This is the way the Tempter speaks. I am going to leave."

He turned and nodded to me. "Get up, Brother Leo, we're going!"

I did not budge. Where could we have gone? Besides, I was too sleepy to move. "Running away doesn't seem to me a very manly way to act, Brother Francis," I said. "Why not stay? You have no reason to be afraid of him. Let him describe the road he has chosen to lead him to God. There are many roads."

Francis was standing in the doorway looking out into the night. The whir of the city had subsided; the stars hung over the earth, quivering. Within the ruins of the inn, an owl sighed gently.

Francis returned to his mat and sat down, leaning his back against the wall. "Yes, there are many roads," he murmured, "many roads . . ." Then he was silent.

The old man got up. "My words have entered your ears," he said. "Now, like it or not, they will travel inside you, slowly but surely, until they reach your hearts. I've had my say, I've sown my seed, and now the rest is up to God!"

Having declared this, he vanished into the darkness of the courtyard.

We remained alone. We blew out the lamp and sat in silence for a considerable time. I closed my eyes to go to sleep, but then Francis said to me in a voice that was tranquil, gentle, sad: "Brother Leo, I have confidence in your heart. Speak!"

"Don't listen to the old Tempter," I replied. "The earth is good. I, for one, would like to harness my body to a turtle so that my earthly passage could last as long as possible. Why? Because I like the earth! Forgive me, Lord: heaven is fine, as fine as one could wish, but oh, the scent of the almond tree in springtime!"

"Get thee behind me, Satan!" exclaimed Francis, shifting his position. "Tonight my soul has fallen between two temptations. Go to sleep!"

I could have asked for nothing better. I closed my eyes and dropped off immediately. When I woke in the morning I saw Francis kneeling on the threshold, listening in ecstasy to the awakening world.

€∪€N NO∪ after so many years, I grow dizzy
when I think of the Holy City. I can still see Francis
seated on a low stool in the pope's antechamber waiting to be
allowed to go in. From morning till night we waited, both of us
together: one day, two days, three. We were barefooted, tired,
hungry. Cardinals in brilliant robes paraded in and out, as did
great noble ladies; while Francis, seated on his humble stool,
prayed and waited.

"We'd find it easier to see Christ Himself," I said to him disgustedly on the third day.

"The pope's countenance stands high above us, far far away," he
replied. "We have been climbing for three days; tomorrow we shall
face him. I know because I had a dream. Patience, Brother Leo!"

And true enough, on the fourth day the young priest who served
as doorkeeper nodded to us, and the huge portals opened. Francis
crossed himself, but then hesitated a moment, his knees sagging.

"Courage, Brother Francis," I said to him softly. "Don't forget
that Christ is sending you. Stop shaking."

"I'm not shaking, Brother Leo," he murmured, and he strode
resolutely across the threshold.

We entered a long narrow chamber decorated everywhere in
gold, with Christ's Passion painted on the walls, and statues of the
twelve Apostles on either side. At the far end, seated on a high
throne, a bulky old man was meditating, his head resting on his
palm, his eyes closed. Apparently he had failed to hear us enter,
because he did not move. I remained near the door while Francis

went forward with trembling steps, approached the throne, knelt, and lowered his forehead to the floor.

For a long moment there was silence. We could hear the old man's heavy, fitful breaths—breaths which sounded just like sighs. Was he sleeping, praying, or observing us furtively with eyes that were only half-closed? I felt he was like a dangerous beast simulating sleep and ready to pounce upon us at any minute.

"Holy Father . . ."—Francis' voice was low, controlled, supplicating—"Holy Father . . ."

The pope raised his head slowly, then looked down and saw Francis. His nostrils were quivering.

"What a stench!" he exclaimed, his eyebrows vibrating with anger. "What are those rags, those bare feet! Who do you think you are?"

Francis replied with his face still against the floor: "I am a humble servant of God from Assisi, Holy Father."

"What pigsty did you come from? I suppose you think you're duplicating the aroma of Paradise—is that it? Couldn't you have washed and dressed yourself for your appearance before me? All right, what do you want?"

In the course of so many sleepless nights, Francis had memorized what he was going to say to the pope. He had pieced together the entire speech with extreme skill, giving it a beginning, a middle, and an end in order to prevent the pope from thinking he did not know what he was about. But now that he found himself before God's shadow, his mind failed him. He opened his mouth two or three times but was unable to utter human speech. Instead, he bleated like a lamb.

The pope frowned. "Can't you talk? Tell me what you want."

"I have come to fall at your feet, Holy Father, and to request a favor of you."

"What favor?"

"A privilege."

"You—a privilege? What privilege?"

"The privilege of absolute Poverty, Holy Father."

"You ask a good deal!"

"We are several friars who wish to marry Poverty. I have come to ask you to bless our marriage, Holy Father, and to grant us permission to preach."

"To preach what?"

171

"Perfect Poverty, perfect Obedience, perfect Love."

"We have no need of you, seeing that we preach all those things ourselves. Go, if you'll be so kind!"

Francis lifted his eyes from the floor and jumped to his feet. "Forgive me, Holy Father," he said, his voice steady now, "but I'm not going. God commanded me to make this journey to speak with you—and I have come. I beg you to hear me out. We are poor and illiterate; when we walk through the streets dressed in our rags we are battered with stones and lemon peels. People fly out of their homes and workshops to jeer at us. That—praise the Lord—is how our journey has begun. On this earth, doesn't every great Hope always start in the same way? All our trust is in our poverty, our ignorance, and in our hearts, which have caught fire. Before I left to come here and find you, Holy Father, I had drawn up clearly in my mind exactly what I intended to lay before you to make you say yes and affix your seal. But now I've forgotten everything. I look at you, and behind you I see Christ Crucified, and behind Christ Crucified, the Resurrection of our Lord, and behind the Resurrection of our Lord, the resurrection as well of the entire forsaken, totally forsaken world. What joy I see before me, Holy Father! How could it fail to bewilder a man's mind? It has bewildered mine; I am all confused, I don't know where to begin or what is the beginning, what the middle, what the end. Everything is the same now; everything is a sigh, Holy Father, a dance, a great cry that is hopeless and yet full of every hope. Oh, if you could only allow me to sing, Holy Father —then I would be able to convey what I wish to ask of you!"

I watched Francis from my corner and trembled as I heard his words. His feet began to shift impatiently, agitatedly, darting out one step to the right, one step to the left, sometimes slowly, sometimes hastily, like those of skilled dancers who establish their rhythm prior to throwing themselves heart and soul into the sacred intoxication of the dance. Without a doubt, the spirit of God was twirling him around. He would begin clapping his hands at any moment and dancing, whereupon the pope would have us both thrown out.

And in truth, while this thought was passing through my mind, Francis lifted his hands. "You mustn't take this in the wrong spirit, Holy Father," he said. "I simply have a great desire to let out a piercing shout, clap my hands, and begin to dance. God is blowing all around me—above, below, to the right, to the left—and spinning me about like a dry leaf."

I approached on tiptoe. "Francis, my brother," I whispered, "you are in front of the pope. Where is your sense of respect?"

"I am in front of God," he bellowed. "How else do you expect me to approach Him, if not dancing and singing? Make room—I'm going to dance!"

He bent his head to one side, stretched out his arms, advanced one foot, then the other, flexed his knees, leaped into the air, flexed his knees again, squatted down as far as the floor, and the moment he touched it lashed out with his legs and sprang into the air, his arms outstretched on either side—so that it seemed a crucified man was dancing before us.

I fell at the pope's feet. "Forgive him, Holy Father," I implored. "He is drunk with God and doesn't know where he is. He always dances when he prays."

The pope bounded off his throne, restraining his rage with difficulty. "That's enough!" he screamed at Francis, seizing him by the shoulder. "God isn't wine for you to use to make yourself drunk. Go to a tavern if you want to dance."

Francis stopped and leaned against the wall, panting. After a glance around the chamber, he came to himself.

"Leave!" the pope commanded, and he reached out to sound the bell for the doorkeeper.

But Francis drew himself away from the wall. He had regained his composure.

"Be patient, Holy Father. I want to leave, but I must not. I still have one more thing to tell you. Last night I had a dream."

"A dream? Look here, monk, I have immense concerns; I support the entire universe on my shoulders, and I have no time to listen to dreams."

"I fall and worship Your Holiness: this dream may be a message from heaven. Night is God's great messenger. You must deign to hear it."

"Yes, night is God's great messenger," said the pope. "Speak."

He seated himself once more upon his throne, a thoughtful expression on his face.

"It seemed that I was standing on a high, deserted rock and gazing at the Lateran Church, which is the mother of all churches. And as

I was gazing at it, suddenly I saw it totter. The campanile began to lean, the walls to crack, and I heard a voice in the air: 'Francis, help!' "

The pope clutched the arms of his throne and thrust the upper part of his body vehemently forward as though he wanted to pounce on Francis.

"And then, then? Don't stop!" His voice had become harsh; he was gasping.

"That was all, Holy Father. The dream fled and I awoke."

The pope jumped down from his throne and, leaning over, seized Francis by the nape of the neck.

"Don't hide your face!" he ordered. "Lift your head and let me see you."

"I'm ashamed, Holy Father. I am just a lowly worm."

"Take off your hood; lift up your face so that I can see you!" the pope ordered.

"Here, Holy Father," said Francis, and he lowered the hood, revealing his face.

A ray of sunlight came through the window and fell upon his features, illuminating the ravaged cheeks, the withered mouth, the large, tear-filled eyes.

The pope uttered a cry. "You!" he shouted. "You? No, no, I refuse to admit it! When did you have your dream?"

"This morning, at dawn."

"I too, I too," roared the pope; "this morning at dawn." He went to the window and opened it. He was suffocating. The hum of the city spurted inside. He closed the window again and returned to Francis with hurried steps.

"You—did you ever see God?" he asked angrily, scornfully, shaking him by the shoulder.

"Forgive me, Holy Father: yes, last night."

"Did He talk to you?"

"We stayed together the whole night without talking. Every so often, however, I said 'Father!' to Him, and He answered me: 'My child.' Nothing else. At dawn I had my dream."

The pope leaned over Francis, examining his face with great perturbation, insatiably. "The designs of the Most High are an abyss, an abyss. . . . Today at dawn when the dream left you, monk, it came and found me. I too saw the church lean and begin to collapse.

But I also saw something else, something which you did not see: a monk with an ugly face, dressed all in rags."

He paused; he was gasping for breath.

"No, no!" he roared after a moment, "it's too humiliating! Does this mean the pope is inadequate? Am I not the one who holds the two keys that open heaven and earth? Lord, why dost Thou wrong me like this? Was it not I who annihilated those unlawful, savage heretics, the Cathari, and buttressed the faith in Provence? Didn't I knock the bottom out of that cursed wasps' nest, the city of Constantine; and didn't I transport her indescribable riches—gold, dalmatics, icons, manuscripts, male and female slaves—to Thy court? Haven't I nailed the cross to all the citadels of Italy? Haven't I been fighting to rouse Christendom to deliver Thy Holy Sepulcher? Why then didst Thou not call me instead of having a ragged monk with an ugly face come to lean his back against the walls of the tottering Church to buttress them?"

He seized Francis again by the nape of the neck and dragged him to the window, into the light. Then he pushed back his head and leaned over him.

"Can you be the one?" he asked in a startled voice. "The face of the ragged monk was just like your face! Does this mean you are the one who is going to save the Church? No, no, it can't be possible! Lord, I am Thy shadow upon earth: do not humiliate me!"

He shook Francis' head violently, then extended his arm toward the door.

"Leave!"

"Holy Father," said Francis, "I hear a voice inside me saying 'Do not leave!' "

"It is the voice of Satan, rebel!"

"I recognized it as the voice of Christ, Holy Father. It is commanding me not to leave. 'Open your heart to My vicar on earth,' it says. 'His heart is filled with mercy; he will help you.' "

The pope bowed his massive head, returned with slow steps to his throne, and sat down. Gleaming on the back of the throne just above his head were two gigantic painted keys, one gold, the other silver.

"Speak," he said, his voice no longer harsh. "I have not been able to reach a decision yet. I am listening. Tell me what you want."

"I don't know where to begin, Holy Father, or what to say, or how to place my heart beneath the blessed soles of your feet. I am God's

175

buffoon; I hop, dance, and sing in order to bring laughter to His lips for a moment. That is all I am; that is all I am capable of doing. Holy Father, give me permission to sing and dance in cities and villages, and to be ragged and barefooted, and to possess nothing to eat."

"Why do you have such a great longing to preach?"

"Because I feel that we have reached the edge of the abyss. Give me permission to cry, 'We are hurling downward!' That is all I ask of you: to be allowed to cry, 'We are hurling downward!' "

"And you believe, monk, that with this shout you will save the Church?"

"God forbid! Who am I to save the Church? Doesn't it have the pope to defend it, and the cardinals and bishops, and Christ Himself? As for me, I ask only one thing, as you know, and that is to be allowed to cry, 'We are hurling downward!' "

He reached beneath his frock, brought out the Rule which I had written out from his dictation, and crept with it to the throne.

"At the foot of your throne, Holy Father, I place the Rule which will govern my brothers and myself. Please condescend to affix your sacred seal to it."

The pope riveted his eyes upon Francis. "Francis of Assisi," he said slowly in a grave, exhortatory tone, "Francis of Assisi, I discern flames around your face. Are they the flames of the Inferno or the flames of Paradise? I have no confidence in visionaries who seek the impossible: perfect love, perfect chastity, perfect poverty. Why do you wish to surpass human bounds? How dare you presume to attain the heights reached only by Christ, the pinnacle where He now stands alone, unrivaled? Insolence, that's what it is, unbounded insolence! Take care, Francis of Assisi: Satan's true face is arrogance. Who can assure you it is not the devil who is goading you to place yourself in front of everyone else in order to preach the impossible?"

Francis bowed his head humbly. "Holy Father," he said, "give me permission to speak by means of parables."

"More insolence!" roared the pope. "That is the way Christ spoke."

"Forgive me, Holy Father, but I cannot do otherwise. Without any conscious desire on my part, my thoughts, and not only my thoughts but also the greatest hope and the greatest despair, turn into tales when they remain for any period of time within me. If you rip open my heart, Holy Father, you will find there only dances and tales—nothing else."

He crossed his arms and was silent. The pope gazed at him mutely. Francis waited to hear his voice, but when the other did not speak he lifted his head and asked, "Shall I continue, Holy Father?"

"I am listening."

"When an almond tree became covered with blossoms in the heart of winter, all the trees around it began to jeer. 'What vanity,' they screamed, 'what insolence! Just think, it believes it can bring spring in this way!' The flowers of the almond tree blushed with shame. 'Forgive me, my sisters,' said the tree. 'I swear I did not want to blossom, but suddenly I felt a warm springtime breeze in my heart.'"

This time the pope was unable to restrain himself.

"Enough!" he cried, jumping to his feet. "Your arrogance knows no bounds, and neither does your humility. Inside you God and Satan are wrestling, and you know it."

"Yes, I know it, Holy Father, and that is why I have come to seek salvation from you. Extend you hand to me; help me! Aren't you the head of Christendom? And I, am I not a soul in danger? Help me!"

"I'll speak with God and come to a decision. Goodbye!"

Francis prostrated himself; then, walking backwards, he passed through the doorway, followed by myself.

We wandered through the streets, walking on air like two drunks. The alleyways opened and closed like accordions, the houses swayed, the bell towers tilted, the air filled with white wings. In order to make our way we had to stretch out our arms as though we were swimming. Frequently it seemed to us that we were being called by name, but when we turned to look we saw no one. Fine ladies sailed in front of us—frigates driven by a splendid following wind, all sails aloft; behind us we heard a sea of men, taverns, and neighing horses. Large clusters of black grapes hung around the windows of the houses, and the ancient Lateran Church was a thousand-year-old vine whose tentacles embraced doors, windows, balconies, the entire city, and then vanished into the sky, heavy with fruit.

When we reached the river we climbed down the bank, plunged

our heads into the water, and refreshed ourselves. Our minds became steady again; the world about us did also, and the grapes disappeared. Francis looked at me in surprise, as though seeing me for the first time.

"Who are you?" he asked in an anxious voice. But he came to himself immediately, and fell into my arms. "Forgive me, Brother Leo. I see everything as though for the first time. What is this whir that surrounds us on every side? Is it the city, is it Rome? And where are the Apostles, where is Christ? Come, let's go away!"

He glanced around him and lowered his voice. "Did you hear the pope? Yes, you were there, you heard him. How prudently he spoke, how staidly, with what confidence! Whoever follows him will never be damned to perdition, but neither will he ever leap above the mud which is man. As for us, Brother Leo, our purpose is to leap above the mud which is man!"

"But can we?" I dared ask. I regretted my words, however, the moment I uttered them.

"What did you say?" demanded Francis, halting.

I shrank back. "Nothing, Brother Francis. I didn't say anything; it was the Tempter speaking inside me."

Francis smiled bitterly. "And how long, Brother Leo, is the Tempter going to continue to speak inside you?"

"Until I die, Brother Francis. He'll die at the same time."

"Place your trust in man's soul, Brother Leo, and do not listen to the advice of prudence. The soul can achieve the impossible."

He proceeded quickly along the riverbank, his feet sloshing through the mud. Suddenly he halted and waited for me. He placed his hand heavily on my shoulder.

"Brother Leo, open your mind and engrave deeply there what I am about to tell you. The body of man is the bow, God is the archer, and the soul is the arrow. Understand?"

"Yes and no, Brother Francis. What are you trying to say? Bring your idea closer to the ground so that my brain can reach it."

"What I mean, Brother Leo, is this: There are three kinds of prayer.

"The first: 'Lord, bend me, or else I shall rot.'

"The second: 'Lord, do not bend me too much, for I shall break.'

"The third, Brother Leo, is our prayer: 'Lord, bend me too much, and who cares if I break!' Just as there are three kinds of prayer, so there are three kinds of men. Record it well in your mind, and do not tremble. . . . I don't know how many times I've told you this, but I say it again: Even now you have time to turn back, to escape—to keep yourself from breaking!"

I seized Francis' hand and kissed it.

"Bend me too much, Brother Francis," I said, "and who cares if I break!"

We continued on for some time in silence. I marched in Francis' tracks, jubilantly, but at the same time I trembled at the thought that unworthy as I was I should be following this pale dangerous man who prayed God to bend him too much, even though he break. . . . But what was I do do? I found myself voicing the same prayer, the only difference being that while Francis exulted, I trembled. He had told me to turn back—how could I? The angelic bread that he was feeding me was much too delicious. I remembered one night when the friars grumbled because they were hungry. Francis frowned and grew angry. "You are hungry," he said, "because you do not see the angelic loaf which lies in front of you as big as a millstone; you do not see it, and thus you do not reach out to cut and eat the slice which will satisfy your hunger for all eternity!"

Suddenly there was a familiar voice behind us: "Brother Francis! Brother Francis!"

We turned. A panting monk was racing to catch up with us.

"It's Father Silvester!" cried Francis, and he ran to greet him. "What are you doing here? Why did you abandon your flock?" he asked, squeezing him in his arms. Silvester, though breathless and weeping, began to speak immediately.

"Bad news, Brother Francis!" he said, gasping for air. "As long as you were with us the Tempter prowled outside our fold. He ground his teeth and howled, but dared not jump the fence and enter. He smelled your breath, Brother Francis, and this made him tremble. But now that you've left—"

"He jumped the fence and entered?"

"Yes, Brother Francis, he jumped the fence and entered. He bent over and whispered in the ears of Sabattino, Angelo, Ruffino; he fell upon the other brothers also, while they were asleep and their

179

souls unguarded, and spoke to them of soft beds, good food, women. The next morning they all awoke short of breath, scowling, and without rhyme or reason they spoke rude words to one another and began to quarrel. Many times after that they even came to blows. It was in vain that I stepped between them and shouted, 'Peace, brothers, let us live in harmony! Where is your fear of God? Aren't you ashamed to act this way in front of Francis? He is here among us and sees and hears us!' But there was little chance they would listen to me. 'We're starving,' shouted Sabattino. 'Tell Francis his trained bears won't dance unless he feeds them! We want to eat, to eat!' The Tempter had dug his talons into their bellies and was dragging them down into hell."

"Bernard too? Pietro?" asked Francis in anguish.

"Bernard and Pietro stayed off by themselves, always together, always praying."

"And Elias?"

"Elias wants to alter your Rule, Brother Francis. It seems too strict to him, too inhuman. He says absolute Poverty is oppressive, and that human nature is incapable of reaching perfect Love, or perfect Chastity either. He comes and goes, talks with the brothers both openly and in secret, and spends his nights writing the new Rule, with Antonio as his scribe. He has formidable goals in mind. He says he wants to build churches, monasteries, universities, to send missionaries far and wide to conquer the world. For he says that everyone—everyone in the world—must put on the hood and appear in this way before God."

Francis sighed. "What else is there to report, Father Silvester? Do not spare me anything. Speak."

"Capella is another who has raised his individual banner. He finds your Rule too soft and wants to follow you to Rome to receive papal sanction for a new order which he plans to establish personally. He says we should eat meat only once a year, on Easter day. The rest of the year nothing but bran and water, except on Sundays we can add a little salt. Also, since conversation is a luxury, we must not talk among ourselves, but only to God. He threw away his green hat with its red ribbon: kicked it, trampled it furiously, shouting, 'No hat! No hood either! We'll go about bareheaded, summer and winter!' "

"Do not stop, do not stop, Father Silvester," said Francis. "These are the deepest wounds. Strike!"

"New brothers have been arriving continually. They are educated and intelligent, are forever reading the thick manuscripts they carry round with them, or else writing or giving discourses in church; and they wear leather sandals, robes without patches, and laugh whenever they see us. How could we rebel against them, we who were your original brothers? With you absent, Brother Francis, we have no strength—how could we resist? Once two of the younger brothers spent the night in a house of pleasure. 'Where were you all night long?' I asked them the next morning when they returned exhausted and breathless. They didn't want to answer, but they gave off a strange, bitter smell, and Brother Bernard fainted."

Francis leaned against me to keep from falling.

"The original brothers scattered," continued Father Silvester. "I forced myself to be patient, saying you would return quickly to expel the Tempter and put everything in order again. But then a terrible thing happened, Brother Francis. It was Good Friday, and when the friars had assembled together in the evening, we found we had nothing to eat—the good people of Assisi had grown tired of feeding us. I began to speak to the brothers about Christ's Passion and to praise God for permitting us to spend this day, the day of His crucifixion, in prayer and complete abstinence. 'A full belly weighs down our prayers,' I said to them; 'it turns to lead and prevents them from ascending to heaven. The devil rejoices when he sees a man afraid of hunger.' But while I was speaking to them I was suddenly startled by the appearance of a black, well-nourished billy goat in the doorway. It had twisted horns, eyes which flashed bright green in the darkness, and a short pointed beard that was all aflame. Five or six of the brothers shouted with joy and leapt to their feet the moment they saw the goat. One of them had a long knife; the others undid their knotted cords and made nooses, then darted forward to lasso the animal around the neck. The buck rose on his hind legs, danced for a moment, and immediately shot off with a bound for the forest, the brothers in hot pursuit. I ran too, shouting at them, 'Stop, brothers, open your eyes! It's not a buck; it's Satan. You are committing a great sin!' But who could expect them to listen to me? Hunger had driven them frantic. They let fly their ropes and the brother with the dagger leaned forward, peering into the darkness and swinging his armed hand up and down into the buck—or so he thought; but he was only knifing the air. The goat continued to elude them. It kept turning around to look at them, and its eyes, in the darkness, were filled with flames. 'It's the devil,' I shouted. 'Don't you see the fires? I adjure you in the name of Christ Crucified—stop!' Several of the brothers became frightened and halted; but then the goat halted also—it seemed to be afraid the brothers might leave it—and without losing a second the brother with the knife jumped chest first on top of the animal. I watched them wrestle for a few moments, and then suddenly the knife entered the goat's belly and the black buck collapsed to the ground, bleating happily. Then the remaining brothers dashed forward, and in a flash the buck was torn limb from limb and in the mouth of each of the brothers there was a chunk of meat, dripping with blood. They chewed hurriedly, swallowed, grabbed a new mouthful; then, as though they had become drunk, they began to dance around the severed head and twisted horns, blood and fire dripping from their mouths. All this time I was beating my breast and weeping. There were thick fumes of sulphur weighing down the air; and suddenly—O Lord, Thou art indeed great—suddenly I saw the head move, saw it with my own two eyes. It rose into the air; the body came together and glued itself to the severed neck, the four hoofs rested squarely on the ground, I heard a short taunting bleat, and then, fully alive, the buck vanished into the night. But the brothers continued to dance and eat, unconcerned: the Tempter had bewitched their eyes, and they had seen nothing. I did not go back to the Portiuncula, but departed for Rome in order to fall at your feet, Brother Francis, and cry out to you: The brotherhood is in danger, our souls are in danger—come!"

"The task of shepherd is difficult, difficult indeed," murmured Francis, gazing at the thick, muddy water of the river as it flowed peacefully toward the sea. "It is my fault. I was overwhelmed with new cares on this pilgrimage; my soul forgot itself for a moment and ceased to watch over my flock. The brothers were left unattended; thus they scattered. It is my fault! I'm coming now, Father Silvester.

Gather them together again and adjure them to be patient: I am coming. Go, and God be with you!"

Father Silvester kissed Francis' hand. "Goodbye," he said, and he set out toward the north.

Francis turned to me. "It is my fault," he repeated. "I am the one who sinned, who craved women, food, a soft bed, and who filled his mouth with the goat's flesh!"

He began to beat his breast and sigh.

I placed my arm around his waist. We continued along the riverbank and both collapsed finally beneath a thickly foliaged poplar. Francis closed his eyes, completely exhausted. Evidently the friars had not left his mind, because he continued to sigh frequently. Finally he opened his eyes.

"Dreams," he said, "are the night birds of God: they bring messages. Before we left for this holy city, I dreamt of a black hen, so scraggy and with such small wings that no matter how far she stretched them she could not cover all her brood. It was raining, and many of the chicks, which were still without feathers, remained outside and got wet. . . . I should have understood the message and have decided not to go away."

While he was speaking an odd-looking monk saw us and stopped. He was dressed in a white robe secured by a leather belt; his feet were protected by thick sandals made of pigskin, and on his tonsured head he wore a black woolen hat. His face was rough, fierce, and his eyes two burning coals. When he saw Francis he halted and stared at him with surprise. At first he was troubled, then elated. Finally he opened wide his arms and cried, "My brother, who are you?"

"Why are you staring at me with such persistence?" Francis asked. "Have you seen me somewhere before?"

"Yes, yes—last night in my dreams. Christ appeared in my sleep. He was angry and had His hand raised, ready to smash the world. Suddenly the Blessed Virgin Mary came forward and cried, 'Have pity, my son. Look, here are two who are your faithful servants. Be patient; they shall buttress the world.' And one was me, unworthy that I am, and the other . . . the other: I think it was you, my brother. Your face, your bearing, the robe you have on, the hood —identical! Who are you? God has brought us together."

183

"My name is Francis of Assisi. I'm also called God's sweet little pauper, and also His buffoon," replied Francis, making room for the stranger to sit down next to him. "And yourself?"

"I am a monk from Spain. I've come from the ends of the earth to obtain the pope's permission to found an order which will make war against heretics and infidels. My name is Dominic."

"I too asked the pope for permission to found an order, and also to preach."

"To preach what, Brother Francis?"

"Perfect Poverty and perfect Love."

"And aren't you going to light fagots in the middle of every village to burn all heretics, sinners, and infidels?"

Francis shuddered. "No, no," he protested. "I am not going to kill sin by killing the sinners; I am not going to wage war against evildoers and infidels. I shall preach love, and I shall love; I shall preach concord, and shall practice brotherly love toward everyone in the world. Forgive me, but that, Brother Dominic, is the road I have chosen."

"Human nature is evil—evil, cunning, demonic," the wearer of the white robe exclaimed angrily. "The gentleness you talk about is not enough; what's needed is force. If the body gets in the way, you must obliterate it so that the soul may be saved. I shall burn fagots in Spain, and the souls there shall abandon their bodies below on earth in the form of ashes, and mount to heaven.

"*Ceniza y nada! Ceniza y nada!*" the monk began to shout, clenching his fist. "Ashes and nothing! War!"

"Love!"

"Force!"

"Mercy!"

"Brother Francis, life is not a promenade where couples walk arm in arm singing songs of love. Life is war, toil, violence! Is the sun risen? Well, get up then! Dig a well if you want a drink of water; strike evildoers squarely on the head if you expect to do away with evil; and when you die, take along a hatchet to break down the door of Paradise if you want to go inside. Paradise has no key, no master key, no doorkeeper. The only key to Paradise is the hatchet. . . . Do not look at me in terror, poor, sweet little monk. Scripture itself says the same: 'Men of violence have taken the Kingdom of heaven by force.'"

Francis sighed. "I didn't know that violence was also from God. You have broadened my mind; my heart, however, resists and cries, 'Love! Love!' But who knows: perhaps our antithetical roads may come together and we may suddenly meet each other in the course of our ascent to the Almighty."

"So please it God," the stranger replied. "But I am afraid you are a lamb fallen among men—among wolves. They shall eat you before you reach the goal of the ascent. Forgive me if I tell you in all frankness what is on my mind: You know all about love, but that is not enough. You must also learn that hate comes from God as well, that it too is in the Lord's service. And in times like these, with the world fallen to the state it has, hate serves God more than love."

"The only thing I hate is the devil, Brother Dominic," Francis replied. But immediately after he had said this, a quiver ran through his body, as though he were overcome with fright at having uttered such harsh words.

"No, no," he added at once, "I don't hate even him. Very often I fall prostrate on the ground and pray God to forgive our deluded brother."

"Whom do you mean?"

"Satan, Brother Dominic."

Brother Dominic laughed. "Lamb of God," he said, "if I had to choose, I would become God's lion. Lions and lambs don't mix— so farewell!"

He rose in order to leave.

"Farewell, Brother Dominic. Lions and lambs, love and force, light and fire, good and evil: all things, I want you to know, climb the same mountain, the mountain of God—only they do not know it. Hate does not know it, that's certain; love does know it, that's equally certain; and now that you are departing, my brother, I am revealing to you the happy secret: one day all shall join together at the summit where God stands with outstretched arms. May it so please our gracious Lord, lion of God, that we also may meet once more there above, and that when we do, you will not devour His little lamb!"

Now it was Francis' turn to laugh. Waving his hand, he bade the fiery monk goodbye.

We watched the white robe swell out in the wind and disappear around a bend in the river. Then Francis turned to me. Spread across his face was a smile which reached from ear to ear.

"Brother Dominic wants to eat us up," he said, "but he does not know—how could he know?—that the Day of Judgment is at hand, when lambs and lions shall merge and become one."

Bent over the parchment on which I write, I take a few moments' rest, the quill behind my aged ear. My eyes closed, I bring to mind all the days and nights we spent in the Holy City. I remember the churches, the prelates celebrating Mass, the small children warbling hymns to God, the sun poised in the center of the heavens, scorching us, and the violent squall which one day so refreshed the sun-roasted earth, and with it, our hearts. I remember Francis standing next to me beneath the portal of the Church of the Holy Apostles, staring in wide-eyed ecstasy at the rain, his quivering nostrils inhaling the smell of the earth, the special smell of wet soil, and happy tears running down his cheeks.

"Heaven is uniting with earth; God is joining with the soul of man," he said to me. "In your earthen bowels, Brother Leo, don't you sense the words of the Gospel being watered like seeds, don't you feel them sprouting? I feel that my heart inside me has been covered with a fresh layer of grass and that my mind has been filled with poppies."

The day when we finally received the Rule after so much anguish and the pope's huge seal with its two all-powerful keys hung from the edge of the parchment, affixed to it with a silk ribbon, I remember how we raced into the square in front of the papal cathedral, the Lateran Church, and began to hop, skip, and dance, arm in arm, like two drunkards. And Francis put his fingers to his mouth and whistled like a shepherd, calling his invisible flock.

What joy that was! What power man's heart has to create and re-create, modeling out of thin air! "This is Paradise!" I exclaimed to Francis. "Christ was right when he said the kingdom of heaven is inside us. Hunger, thirst, misfortune do not exist. The only thing that exists is the heart of man: it whirls nothingness around on its wheel and models it into bread, water, and happiness."

As we were dancing and whistling, an astonished young noble-woman came up to us.

"What happened to you?" she asked with a laugh. "Who fed you all that wine and made you drunk?"

186

"God!" replied Francis, clapping his hands. "The Lord Christ of the many casks. Come, join us yourself. Drink!"

"Where do you come from?"

"From nothingness, madam."

"Where are you going?"

"To God. On the way between nothingness and God, we dance and weep."

The young woman was not laughing now. Her dress was open at the collar. Placing her right hand over her exposed throat, she sighed, "Is this what we were born for?"

"Yes, madam: to dance, weep, and journey toward God."

"I am Jacopa, wife of the nobleman Gratiano Frangipani. My life has been exceptionally happy, and this makes me ashamed; it has been exceptionally lucky, and this makes me afraid. . . . I cannot talk to you here in front of everyone. Oblige me by coming to my home."

She led the way; we followed behind.

Who could have told us that this charming noblewoman was to become Francis' most faithful and precious woman companion, second only to Sister Clara? Who could have told us that inordinate happiness is able to push an honest soul into a state of contrition and tears?

"I am ashamed," Jacopa said to us when we had entered her palazzo, "I am ashamed to possess everything while countless women have nothing. It's unjust, unjust! If God is just He will send me some great calamity. Beseech Him to do so. If I were free I would go barefooted into the streets and beg from door to door. But I have a husband and children; I am in fetters."

Francis had been watching her admiringly. "You have a valiant, manly soul, madam, and a masculine mind. Permit me to call you Brother Jacopa instead of Sister. . . . Brother Jacopa, be patient. The day will come when you will be free and will go about barefooted in the streets, begging. The Lord is great. He feels compassion for women, and He will take pity on you. . . . Goodbye now, until we meet again!"

"When? Where?"

"Brother Jacopa, a voice inside me says: at the terrible hour of my death."

He raised his hand and blessed her. "Until then!"

187

"Why do you speak about death, Brother Francis?" I asked as soon as we had left Jacopa's mansion and had begun our journey homeward. "A plague on it! We still haven't finished our labor here on earth."

Francis shook his head.

"While we were dancing and whistling, Brother Leo, while we were at the highest summit of our exultation, I saw the black Archangel descending from heaven. 'Wait,' I nodded to him, 'wait a little longer, Brother Death!' And he smiled and halted in the air. Have no fears, Brother Leo: I shall die when the right time comes, not before, not after. When the right time comes . . ."

Heading north, traveling hurriedly, like horses returning to their manger, we shook the dust of Rome from our feet. From time to time, whenever we found water, we would halt, lower our faces, and drink; afterwards we would sit on a rock and gaze mutely into the distance, toward Assisi. As we came closer Francis' face grew somber and he found it harder and harder to part his lips to speak. Only when we encountered a child or a brilliant wild flower or a bird sitting on a branch and peeping did his expression brighten again.

Once he said to me, "As long as there are flowers and children and birds in the world, have no fears, Brother Leo: everything will be fine."

We marched and marched, our feet covered with bleeding wounds. We could no longer hold ourselves erect. On top of this we were constantly hungry, and at night we froze. Oh, for a platter of roast lamb and a jug of wine, I kept saying to myself, licking my chops. And after that a soft bed to sleep on. With what untold zest I would sing God's praises then. . . . It was in vain that I tossed my head and tried to drive away the temptation. The platter, jug, and bed invariably returned and hovered before me in the air.

Francis divined my thoughts. Overcome with sympathy for me, he placed his hand tenderly on my shoulder.

"Dear Brother Leo, I don't know why, but just now I thought of a great anchorite who once said something I have never been able to forget. Do you want to hear it?"

"I'm listening, Brother Francis," I said, and I lowered my eyes, afraid he might see the platter, jug, and bed in the pupils.

"One day a passer-by who had heard the holy man's sighs stopped and asked, 'Saint of God, what is it that you desire, what is it that makes you sigh so?'

" 'A glass of cold water, my child,' answered the ascetic.

" 'That's easy enough. Leave your jug outside at night, and you shall have cold water.'

" 'I did that once, my child. But that night I had a dream. It seemed I had arrived outside of heaven and was pounding on the gates. "Who's there?" came a voice from within. "It's me, Pachomius of Thebes." Then the voice resounded: "Go away. Heaven is for those who do not put their jugs outside at night in order to have a drink of cold water." ' "

I fell at Francis' feet. "Forgive me, Brother Francis. I still haven't succeeded in conquering the flesh. I continue to feel hungry, tired, cold. Wherever you go I go too; sometimes, however, my mind does not follow you—instead, it grows insolent and resists. I am before the gates of heaven, but they do not open."

"You must not lose heart, Brother Leo," he answered stroking my head. "Stand on your feet, and if the Tempter has straddled you, have no fears: the gates will open, and the two of you will enter together!"

"The Tempter too? He'll enter too? How do you know, Brother Francis?"

"I know because of my heart, which opens and receives everything. Surely Paradise must be the same."

We arrived at a tiny city perched on the flanks of a sharp, rocky mountain. At its foot were tumble-down houses, worn away by rain, sun, and time; at the summit the castle, fitted out with towers and long, swallow-tailed pennons. Here the lord lived with his falcons. The city was belted by vineyards and olive groves below on the plain.

"We'll stop here and rest for three days," said Francis, feeling sorry for me. "I see a tiny monastery there among the olive trees. God has taken pity on you, Brother Leo."

We entered the city. The farmers were returning from their labors: the sun was about to set. We seated ourselves in the garden of a ruined church. There were cypresses on all sides; the hedge was covered with sweet-smelling red flowers; in the center was a plane tree with tender, dark green foliage that had but just unfolded. An open, flowing spring was at its roots.

Francis looked around him and sighed deeply. "Paradise must be just like this," he said. "Do not seek anything more. This is enough for the soul of man, enough and more than enough."

Hearing much chirping above him, he looked up. A flock of sparrows was flying toward the plane tree: there they had their nests, and they were going home to spend the night. They perched on the branches, then scattered throughout the garden and began to peep happily before burrowing into their tiny houses to lay their heads upon their downy breasts and give themselves up to sleep.

Francis advanced slowly toward the flowing water, which was where the birds had gathered now. He held out his hands to greet them.

"Stay where you are, Brother Leo," he said to me. "Don't move; you might frighten them. Since I haven't any grain to throw them, I shall feed them with the word of God so that they may hear it and be able, like men, to go to heaven."

Turning to the birds, he leaned over them and began to preach, his arms spread wide.

"Sister Birds, God, the Father of birds and men, loves you greatly, and you are aware of this. That is why when you drink water you lift your tiny heads to heaven after each sip and give thanks to Him; why in the morning when the sun strikes your little breasts you fill yourselves with song and fly from branch to branch glorifying His name, the name of the Lord, who sends the sun, and green trees, and song. And you fly high up into the sky so that you can come close to Him and He can hear you. And when your nests are filled with eggs and you are mothers sitting on them to hatch them, God becomes a male bird, sits Himself down on the branch opposite, and sings to ease your labors."

A flock of doves passed overhead as Francis was speaking. They heard his sweet voice, descended, seated themselves round about his feet, and one small dove flew up and squatted on his right shoulder, cooing. Francis leaned further and further forward. He kept shaking his robe as though it were a pair of wings, and his voice chirruped, sweet as a nightingale's. It seemed he wanted to join the birds around him, and that he was struggling to become a bird, a large sparrow, in order to do so.

"Sister Sparrows, Sister Doves, consider what gifts God has bestowed upon you: He gave you wings so that you might travel through the air, and down to keep you warm in wintertime; He scattered many kinds of nourishment over the ground and in the trees so that you would not go hungry; He filled your breasts and throats with song."

Swallows arrived now and perched in rows along the hedge opposite us and also along the edge of the church roof. Folding their wings, they stretched their heads forward and listened intently. Francis turned to greet them.

"Welcome to our sisters the swallows, who carry spring to us each year on slender wings. Though it is still cold and rainy out, though the sun is shorn of its golden hair, you feel your hearts warm and full of summer. You sit on the snow-covered roof tiles, wing your way from bare branch to bare branch, and peck at winter with your sharp beaks to force it to depart. On the Day of Judgment you, my dear swallows, you before all other winged things, before even the angels with their trumpets, will fly to the cemeteries and begin to chirp above the tombstones, singing out the news of resurrection. The dead will hear you and will leap out of their graves onto the daisies to greet the eternal spring!"

The swallows beat their wings happily, the doves cooed, and the sparrows came close to Francis and began to peck tenderly at his robe. Holding his hand out over their heads, he made the sign of the cross and blessed the birds. Then he waved in all directions, bidding them farewell.

"Evening has come, Sister Sparrows, Doves, and Swallows; evening has come, go now and sleep. And if God has graced you with the ability to have dreams, may He grant that tonight in your sleep you will see Our Lady of the Swallows flying over your nests like a large swallow."

While Francis was speaking, a man had come by on horseback and halted, moved to laughter by the sight of a monk conversing with birds. He was middle-aged, an aristocrat, had a fat cudgel-like nose, voluptuous hanging lips, and was dressed in motley, with a crown of wide-leafed laurel in his hair and around his waist a gold chain with a tiny cloth monkey as a good-luck charm. A lute hung from his shoulder.

Following behind him was a troupe of young men and women, all with crowns of ivy and flowers. When they saw their leader stop, they stopped too and burst into peals of laughter. The rider's face was gleaming; the last rays of the evening sun had struck his head, igniting his blond hair.

I leaned over the hedge and beckoned to one of the young men, who came up to me. "Who is this lord, the one on horseback?" I asked him. "He is as handsome as a king."

"His name is Gulielmus Divini and he is truly a king. Haven't you heard of him? He has just been in Rome, where they crowned him with laurel at the Capitol and proclaimed him King of Song."

"What does he sing about?"

"Love, monk, love. I don't suppose you've ever heard of that, have you?"

He returned to his companions, laughing heartily.

The rider had reined in his horse, meanwhile, and had remained motionless, listening as the doves came, and after them, the swallows. Suddenly he turned to his laughing escort. "Be quiet!" he shouted at them angrily.

Francis was saying good night to the birds and preparing to cross the yard and leave when the King of Song jumped off his horse, ran to him, and fell at his feet.

"Holy Father," he cried, kissing Francis' bloody feet, "I was blind and now I have regained my sight; I was dead and now I have risen from the grave. Take me, bring me away from the world of men, save my soul! All my life I have sung the virtues of wine and women. I've grown weary of that. Take me so that I may sing the glories of God. I am Gulielmus Divini, and those idiots in Rome have just crowned me King of Song."

As soon as he had said this, he wrenched the crown off his head, pulled it apart, and strewed the laurel leaves over the ground.

"Now I feel pacified," he said. "I am going to throw away the motley too. Give me a frock, Holy Father. Here, I am removing this golden chain I have around my waist. Gird me with a knotted cord."

Francis leaned over, raised him up, and kissed him on the forehead.

"Rise, Brother Pacifico. I shall call you by this name, my brother, because you have just entered the peace of God. I kiss your forehead; it is still filled with song. You used to sing about the world; from now on you shall sing about the world's Creator. Keep your lute so that it too may enter God's service and be sanctified. And when the good time comes, Pacifico, my brother, I want you to know that you shall enter heaven with this lute hanging from your shoulder; and the angels will congregate round you and ask you to teach them new songs."

The young men and women ran to gather up the fallen laurel leaves. They gazed at the celebrated troubadour, unable to determine if this was just a new game he was playing, or if he had truly taken leave of his senses and decided to become a monk.

But Brother Pacifico turned to bid them farewell: "Goodbye, companions of my former life; now Gulielmus Divini is dead. Go bury him, and put this little monkey in his coffin—bury it too!"

He tossed them the gold chain with the cloth monkey. "Goodbye," he repeated. "Goodbye—we shall never meet again!"

The astonished young men and women dispersed, leaving the three of us alone. With Francis in the lead, we proceeded toward the small monastery in the middle of the olive grove. Brother Pacifico sang along the way.

"My heart is a bird, a nightingale, Brother Francis," he said. "It came along with the other birds to listen to you, and when it heard you, it lifted its beak toward heaven to begin a new song."

Francis laughed. "I am bringing a new madness to the world," he said, "and you a new song—the song of the new madness. Brother Pacifico, it's fine that we have joined forces. Welcome to our brotherhood."

We spent three days at the little monastery, recovering our strength. At the first sight of us, the monks frowned. Francis was laughing, Pacifico playing his lute, and I was accompanying the new brother in my raucous voice.

"Say, where do you think you are?" the Father Superior shouted at us. "This is a monastery: the house of the Lord."

"And how, Brother Superior, do you expect us to enter the house of the Lord—weeping?" answered Francis. "God shouts: 'I've had enough of weeping, I don't like sighs, I'm tired of seeing long faces. What I long for is the sound of laughter on earth!' Brother Pacifico, sound your lute, sing a song, gladden God's heart."

The monks got used to us gradually. Francis had them assemble in the courtyard each evening, where he spoke to them about love, poverty, and heaven.

"What do you think heaven is like?" he asked them. "Like some huge palace with a marble staircase, all filled with gold and wings? No! No! One night I saw it in a dream: it was a tiny tiny village completely surrounded by green meadows; and in the middle of the village, next to the well of the humblest, most abject hut, was the soul of man—identical with the Virgin Mary, and it was giving suck to God. . . ."

While Francis spoke, the night descended peacefully over us, the air filled with blue wings, and the monks closed their eyes happily and entered Paradise.

We resumed our journey northward as soon as the three days were over. Brother Pacifico's singing made the trip seem brief, and, before we knew it, one evening we saw the citadel and towers of our beloved Assisi.

"Welcome, dearest Assisi," said Francis, raising his hand and blessing the city. "Lord, help me face my friars calmly."

The sun had set by the time we appeared at the Portiuncula. We approached quietly, with Francis in the lead and Pacifico and myself following behind, exhausted. Francis wanted to surprise the friars so that he could see what they were doing and hear what they were saying. But as soon as we came closer, he stopped. We heard shouts and laughter. Smoke was ascending from the roof— the brothers must have been in the habit of making fires. Then the smell of roast meat struck our nostrils: they were cooking!

"They're celebrating," Francis whispered; "they're eating meat."

Just then an old beggar appeared. From far away he had smelled the aroma of meat being roasted and had run in the hope that he might receive a few mouthfuls as alms.

"Will you do me a favor, brother?" Francis asked him. "Let me have your cap, staff, and sack so that I can go and greet the friars. I'll give the things back to you right away. Do me this favor, and may the Lord repay you."

194

"Are you the one they call Francis of Assisi?"

"Yes, my brother."

"Then take them!"

Francis pulled the cap down over his ears, slung the sack across his shoulder, and, leaning on the staff, went and knocked on the door of the Portiuncula.

"In the name of Christ, my brothers," he whined, altering his voice, "take pity on a poor, sick old man who is hungry."

"Come in, old man," the brothers answered him. "Sit down by the fire and eat!"

Francis entered with his head bowed and his shoulders all hunched over so that it was impossible to see his face. He seated himself by the fire with his back turned toward the friars. A novice brought him a dish of soup and a slice of bread. Bending over, Francis filled his hand with ashes from the fire, threw them into the soup, and began to eat. The brothers recognized him at once, but none of them dared reveal this, so overcome with shame were they that Francis had caught them eating meat and celebrating. Lumps rose in their throats, and they were unable to continue their meal. They waited, bent over their dishes, sensing that the squall would be unleashed momentarily.

Francis ate two or three spoonfuls of soup and then, putting down his dish, turned to the friars.

"Forgive me, my brothers," he said, "but when I entered and saw you seated before such rich fare, I was unable to believe my eyes. Are these the poverty-stricken monks, I asked myself, the ones who go about knocking on doors and begging, and whom everyone takes for saints? If so, why shouldn't I enter their order and enjoy a comfortable life? So for the love of Christ, tell me please whether or not you are the humble friars of the pauper, Francis of Assisi."

The brothers were unable to restrain themselves any longer. Some burst into tears; some slipped away surreptitiously and ran off in terror; still others fell at Francis' feet and begged his forgiveness. Francis kept his arms crossed over his breast; he did not spread them to embrace the brothers, as was his custom. Elias approached; he, to be sure, did not weep, nor did he beg forgiveness.

"Don't you recognize the friars?" he demanded. "We've multiplied while you were gone. Raise your hand and bless them."

But Francis had allowed his head to fall upon his breast. He said nothing. The friars who had circled him stared in anguish.

Once more Elias spoke:

"Did you see the pope, Brother Francis? Did he affix his seal?"

Francis placed his palm over his breast. "The seal with its two keys is here, Brother Elias. Do not be impatient: tomorrow, God willing, I shall speak. As for now, come, let us all go inside the church and beseech the Lord to affix His seal as well."

The next day the friars assembled in a clearing in the forest. Elias went to and fro gathering them in circles around him and speaking in furtive undertones. His body was gigantic, the tallest of the whole brotherhood, and Francis, next to him, became even shorter than he was, even humbler—he simply disappeared. Forgive me, Lord, but I was never able to hold this man very dear to my heart. His glance was all pride and greediness; his soul found the Portiuncula too small, felt constricted by Poverty and Love. It wanted to spread itself out and conquer the world not only by means of kindness but also by force, and then to enter the kingdom of heaven as a knight on horseback. He should have been a follower of Dominic, the fierce Spanish missionary, and not of the sweet little pauper of Assisi. Why had God sent him to us? What was the Lord's hidden purpose? Was it possible that He wanted to pair together the unpairable?

One day I grew bold enough to tell Francis my feelings about Brother Elias. "Every brotherhood has its Judas," I said. "May God expose me as a liar, but all the same, I believe this man is our Judas."

"Even Judas is good, Brother Leo," Francis replied; "even he is a servant of Christ, and if God destined him to be a betrayer, it was precisely in betrayal that he did his duty."

He reflected for a moment, then lowered his voice:

"Do you remember the wolf of Gubbio? He used to enter the sheepfolds and kill the sheep; he was ruining the village. I felt sorry for the inhabitants and went into the forest to admonish the wolf in God's name not to eat any more sheep. I called him, he came— and do you know what his answer was? 'Francis, Francis,' he said, 'do not destroy God's prescribed order. The sheep feeds on grass, the wolf on sheep—that's the way God ordained it. Do not ask why; simply obey God's will and leave me free to enter the sheepfolds whenever I feel the pinch of hunger. I say my prayers just like Your Holiness. I say: "Our Father who reignest in the forests and hast commanded me to eat meat, Thy will be done. Give me this day my daily sheep so that my stomach may be filled, and I shall glorify Thy name. Great art Thou, Lord, who hast created mutton so delicious. And when the day cometh that I shall die, grant, Lord, that I may be resurrected, and that with me may be resurrected all the sheep I have eaten—so that I may eat them again!' ' That, Brother Leo, is what the wolf answered me. I bowed my head and left. Why did God decree that wolves should eat sheep? What insolence, Brother Leo, even to ask!"

But how could I have a heart like Francis', able to forbear and forgive everything! The sight of Elias Bombarone talking furtively with the brothers that day made me shake with anger and fear.

As soon as everyone was finally assembled, Francis rose, crossed his arms upon his breast according to his habit, and began to speak. His voice was tranquil, muted, sad; from time to time he extended his hand toward the brothers as though asking for alms. Using simple words, he related how he had entered the Eternal City, how he managed to see the Holy Father, what he said to the pope and what the pope replied, and how he knelt and laid the Rule at his feet. Three days later, surely on command from God, the pope had affixed his seal—look, here it was! Francis removed the hallowed parchment from his bosom and read it slowly, syllable by syllable, while the friars listened, fallen on their knees. And as soon as he had finished, he extended his arms above them and said something more—but now he was not speaking to them, he was praying:

"Holy Mistress Poverty, thou art our wealth. Do not leave us! Grant that we may be always hungry, always cold, and that we may have nowhere to lay our heads!

"Holy Mistress Chastity, purify our minds, purify our hearts, purify the air we breathe! Help us to conquer the Temptation that prowls around the Portiuncula—around our hearts—like a lion.

"Holy Mistress Love, adored first-born daughter of God, I lift my arms to Thee: hear me and grant my prayer. Widen our hearts that they may accept all men, good and bad; that they may accept all animals, wild and tame; all trees, fruitful and unfruitful; all stones, rivers, and seas. We are all brothers. We all have the same Father, and we all have taken the road which leads us back to our paternal home!"

He stopped. Perhaps he intended to say more, but Brother Elias jumped up, his gigantic body steaming, sweat flowing from his temples.

"Let the other friars speak too, Brother Francis," he called in a thunderous voice. "We are all equal before God, and each one has the right to speak his mind freely. . . . Brothers, you have heard the Rule which Brother Francis has brought us from the pope's hand. Do you like it or not? Let each of you rise and speak without constraint.'"

For a moment everyone remained silent. Some had objections to voice, but felt too much respect for Francis. Others had nothing to say; they had not understood very well what Francis had read, and thus they held their tongues—as did I, for although I agreed with the Rule I had no idea how to express my agreement.

Finally Father Silvester rose. "Brothers," he said, sighing, "I am the oldest here, and that is why I have been bold enough to rise and speak first. Listen to me, my brothers: the world is rotten, the end is near. Let us scatter to the four corners of the earth and proclaim the destruction of the world so that men may be frightened into repenting, and thus be saved. That is my opinion, but act as God enlightens you."

Sabattino leaped forward, his face yellow and embittered. "The world is not rotten," he shrieked; "only the lords are rotten. The first part of the fish to stink is the head! We should rise up, rouse the populace, and then attack our overlords—burn their castles, burn their silk clothes, burn the plumes they wear on their heads. This is the only true crusade, the only way we shall ever deliver the Holy Sepulcher. And what is the Holy Sepulcher: the wretched populace, which is being crucified. Resurrection of the people: that is the true meaning of the resurrection of Christ!"

"The people are hungry!" shouted Juniper, all aflame. "They haven't enough vigor even to stand on their feet, so let them eat first to regain their strength; they lack eyes to see how they are being oppressed, so let us open their eyes for them! Brother Francis, why don't we forget the kingdom of heaven for a minute and pay attention to the kingdom of this earth—that's where we must start! You've heard my opinion. We ought to have a scribe here to write everything down!"

Bernard was the next to rise. "Brothers," he said, his blue eyes brimming with tears, "let us depart the world of men. How can we expect to contend with the rulers of the age? Let us depart, take refuge in the wilderness, and dedicate our days and nights to prayer. Prayer is all-powerful, my brothers. A person prays at the top of a mountain, and the prayer rushes headlong down, enters the cities below, and rouses the hearts of all transgressors; at the same time it mounts to God's feet and bears witness to the suffering of mankind. My brothers, only with prayer—not with wealth, not with arms—shall we save the world."

At that point I myself got up to speak. I stammered out a few words but immediately became completely confused and burst into tears, hiding my face in my palms. Several of the brothers laughed, but Francis embraced me and had me sit down next to him, on his right side.

"No one else spoke with such skill, such strength," he said. "Brother Leo, you have my blessing."

He rose and spread his arms wide, as was his custom.

"Love! Love!" he said. "Not war, not force! Even prayer, Brother Bernard, is not enough; good works are needed too. It is difficult and dangerous to live among men, but necessary. To withdraw into the wilderness and pray is too easy, too convenient. Prayer is slow in producing its miracles; works are faster, surer, more difficult. Wherever you find men, you will also find suffering, illness, and sin. That is where our place is, my brother: with lepers, sinners, with those who are starving. Deep down in the bowels of every man, even the saintliest ascetic, there sleeps a horrible, unclean larva. Lean over and say to this larva: 'I love you!' and it shall sprout wings and become a butterfly. . . . Love, I bow and worship thine omnipotence. Come and kiss our friars; come and accomplish thy miracle!"

The whole time Francis spoke Brother Elias squirmed on the rock he was sitting on and nodded his head in breathless perturbation, signaling to his faction. Finally, unable to restrain himself any longer, he jumped to his feet.

"Don't listen to him, brothers! Love isn't enough; what's needed is war! Our order must be a militant one and the brothers fearless warriors with the cross in one hand and the battle-axe in the other. As the Gospel says, the axe must be laid to the root of the trees,

199

and every bad tree cut down and thrown into the fire. There is only one way to conquer the powerful of this world: by becoming more powerful than they are! Away with poverty, away with absolute poverty! Wherefore such arrogance, Brother Francis? Did not Christ Himself leave His Apostles free to possess sandals, staff, and scrip? Did not one of the Apostles have charge of the purse and struggle to keep it filled in order to feed the group? And you, Brother Francis, are you so audacious as to wish to surpass Christ? Wealth is an almighty sword; we cannot afford to remain disarmed in this ignominious cutthroat world! Our chief must be a lion, not a lamb; instead of holding an aspergillum in our hands, we must hold a whip. Or perhaps you forget, Brother Francis, that Christ took a whip and drove out all who sold and bought in God's Temple? I said it once, brothers, and I say it again: war!"

Five or six of the younger friars sprang to their feet with cries of joy and raised Elias up in their arms.

"You are the lion," they shouted. "Step in front; lead us!"

Pale and exhausted, Francis placed his hand on my shoulder and pulled himself to his feet.

"Peace, my brothers," he cried in a voice that was supplicating, afflicted. "How can we bring peace to the world if we do not have peace in our own hearts? One war begets another, and this still another, and thus there is no end to the shedding of human blood. Peace! Peace! Do you forget, Brother Elias, that Christ was a lamb and that He bore upon Himself the sins of the world?"

"Christ was a lion, Brother Francis," retorted Elias. "He says so Himself: *I have not come to bring peace, but a sword!*"

He turned to the friars. "Did you hear? Those were Christ's words; not mine, Christ's: *I have not come to bring peace, but a sword!*"

The friars rose with agitated hearts and separated into two groups. A few gathered around Francis and wept, but the majority surrounded Elias and broke into peals of laughter. Everyone began to talk at once and shout excitedly, until Father Silvester stepped into the middle. "Brothers," he said, "Satan, the black goat, has come once again among us. I see his green eyes in the air!"

Francis made his way through the friars who circled him, and going up to Elias put his arm around his waist.

"Brother Elias, all of you—listen," he said. "Our brotherhood is passing through a difficult moment. Allow the arguments and counterarguments you have heard during this meeting to settle down tranquilly within you. War? Peace? Prayer in absolute solitude? Time, God's faithful guide, will show us the correct road. Meanwhile, my brethren, do not forget your duty! The Holy Father had accorded us the privilege of preaching. The roads of the entire earth stretch before us; let us portion them out in a brotherly way and start our journeys. Our home here is too constricting. The Portiuncula is small: we live elbow to elbow, trip over each other, become irritated, angry—and then the Tempter comes. Go into the open air and set off along the main roads, traveling in pairs so that one can be a source of courage and comfort to the other. And wherever you see men gathered together, halt and strew before them the Word of God—immortal nourishment. I, with God's help, shall proceed to Africa. I shall find a boat, cross the sea, and, God willing, reach the faraway lands of the infidels where innumerable souls have never even heard the name of Christ. God willing, I shall bring it to them! Forward, brothers, in the name of the Lord. Let us scatter to the ends of the earth, and afterwards return here to the Portiuncula, the cradle where we were born, to relate to each other everything we have seen, suffered, and accomplished on this, our first apostolic campaign.

"Disperse now, my brothers, my children, disperse with my blessing to the four corners of the earth. The entire world is God's field. Plough it and then sow poverty, love, and peace. Strengthen the world that is tottering and about to fall: strengthen your souls. And elevate your hearts above wrath, ambition, and envy. Do not say: 'Me! Me!' Instead, make the self, that fierce insatiable beast, submit to God's love. This 'me' does not enter Paradise, but stands outside the gates and bellows. Listen now to the parable I shall tell you before we part. Remember it well, and let it be a remembrance of me, my children.

"Once there was an ascetic who struggled his whole life to reach perfection. He distributed all his goods to the poor, withdrew into the desert, and prayed to God night and day. Finally the day came when he died. He ascended to heaven and knocked on the gates. 'Who is there?' came a voice from within.

" 'It's me!' answered the ascetic.

" 'There isn't room for two here,' said the voice. 'Go away!'

"The ascetic went back down to earth and began his struggle all over again: poverty, fasting, uninterrupted prayer, weeping. His appointed hour came a second time, and he died. Once more he knocked at the gates of heaven. 'Who's there?' came the same voice.

" 'Me!'

" 'There isn't room for two here. Go away!'

"The ascetic plummeted down to earth and resumed his struggle to attain salvation even more ferociously than before. When he was an old man, a centenarian, he died and knocked once again on the gates of heaven. 'Who's there?' came the voice.

" 'Thou, Lord, Thou!'

"And straightway the gates of heaven opened, and he entered."

SUMMERTIME. Broiling sun, the sea sparkling, to our left the Greek islands; the boat filled with warriors in armor—adolescents, mature men, ancient graybeards all going like so many others to deliver the Holy Sepulcher. The crusaders had been besieging Damietta for months, but Sultan Melek-el-Kamil, a capable ruler and brave warrior, had not allowed the city to fall.

At Cape Malea we were caught in a fierce tempest. A myriad-headed, myriad-mouthed sea sprang up to devour us, and the stalwarts on board turned white, then green, and sighed as they gazed longingly at the coastline. Oh, if they could only jump, catch hold of a branch on dry land, and recover their manliness! The few women who were traveling with them began to scream. Francis went from man to man, woman to woman; he spoke to them of God, and they listened and were comforted. Night fell; a black, cloud-filled sky hung just above the sea, and between water and firmament the ship bounced, creaked, seemed ready to break apart. Francis had gone to the bow, where he had knelt down among the folded sails and begun to pray.

I approached him, but he neither saw nor heard me. His head extended toward the sea, he was chanting melismatically in a hushed, vibrato voice, as though casting a spell.

"O sea, sea, daughter of God, take pity on these men, thy brothers. They are not merchants or pirates; their aim is a noble one: they are proceeding to the Holy Sepulcher. Dost thou not see the red cross on their breasts? They are crusaders, soldiers of God. Take pity on them. Remember Christ, who one day called thee to be calm, and thou obeyedst. In Christ's name, I, His humble servant, adjure thee now to become calm!"

I had fallen face down on top of the sails. I heard the bellowing water, the wailing of the people inside the boat, and between people and frenzied sea, Francis interceding gently, supplicatingly, imploring the waters to grow calm. It was then I understood for the first time the man's true worth: at the height of desperation, at a time when the world was crumbling to pieces, he prayed. I was certain the sea heard Francis' words, that God heard them too, as did Death—they had all pricked up their ears to listen. And then— I swear it by the soul I shall render up to God—then the miracle took place; no, it was not a miracle, it was the simplest, most natural thing in the world: the sea became calm. At first it lowered its bellowing slightly, but still remained angry; it was balking before the yoke, trying to avoid subjection. But little by little it submitted, grew gentle, and by midnight it no longer beat maniacally against the ship, but stretched out peacefully around it, humble and becalmed. Unbelievers may deny that the soul can speak to the sea and command it, but as for me, thanks to Francis I know the secret: the soul is more powerful than the sea, more powerful than death; it is able to spring out of man's body and buttress the crumbling world. . . .

I crept to Francis and kissed his bloodstained feet. But he was unaware of me; his entire soul was out over the black waters, awake and vigilant lest the sea lift its head in rebellion once again.

The next morning water and sky were gleaming, laughing, and so were the people on board. Francis, yellow and exhausted from his ordeal, was still at the bow, squatting, his eyes closed. He had performed his work well, and now he allowed sleep to descend upon him.

The days and nights went by. The moon had been a thin sickle when we departed from Ancona; it grew larger and larger, became fully round, and then began once more to melt away and disappear. Everyone kept his eyes riveted southward, searching for a glimpse of the accursed Moslem coast. Little by little the water around us turned green. "The sea is mixing with the waters of the Nile," the captain explained; "we are nearly there." And indeed, the following morning we could clearly see the outline of the land at the center-point of the horizon. It was low, sandy, and colored rose by the first rays of the sun.

We anchored in an isolated cove. Francis fell prostrate on the beach, did worship, and traced a cross in the sand. The warriors set off to join the rest of Christ's troops, leaving Francis and me alone on the deserted shore. Far in the distance we were able to discern towers and minarets. Francis looked at me compassionately. "Brother Leo, lamb of God," he said, "we have entered the lion's mouth. Are you afraid?"

"Yes, I am afraid, Brother Francis," I replied. "But I pretend not to be, and wherever you go, I'll go too."

He laughed. "Even to Paradise, Brother Leo?"

"Even to Paradise, Brother Francis."

He raised his hand and pointed to the distant minarets. "Well then, let's go. This is the way to Paradise!"

He set out, walking in the lead. The sand burned our feet, but we began to sing, and thus forgot the pain. From time to time Francis halted and squeezed my arm to encourage me. Then he started out again at once, resuming his song.

"Ah, if only Brother Pacifico were here with his lute so that we could make our appearance before the Sultan like three intoxicated friars, three friars drunk with too much God!"

"I'm hungry, Brother Francis," I said, unable to contain myself any longer.

"Patience, Brother Leo. Look, the minarets are getting bigger and bigger. We're almost there. Don't worry, the moment the Sultan sees us he'll give orders for the pots to be put in the oven!"

As we were talking, we heard savage cries, and two Negroes leapt out in front of us, swords drawn.

"Sultan! Sultan!" cried Francis, pointing to the minarets.

They thrashed us soundly, then placed us between them and, doubled over with laughter, pushed us to the Sultan's palace and threw us down at his feet. By this time it was already evening.

The Sultan laughed as soon as he saw us. Poking us with his foot, he asked (he was accomplished in our language): "Well, and who are you, my wine-loving monks? Why have you entered the lion's den? What do you want?"

I raised my eyes and saw him. A beautiful person, he had a

curly black beard, slender hooked nose, and large, deep-black eyes. On his head was a wide turban, green, with a half-moon made of coral pinned on it. An immense Negro armed with a yataghan stood at his side: the executioner!

"Who are you and what do you want?" the Sultan asked again. "Get up!"

We rose. "We are Christians," said Francis, crossing himself. "Christ sent us because he took pity on you, illustrious Sultan. He wants to save your soul."

"To save my soul!" exclaimed the Sultan, struggling to hold back his laughter. "And how is it to be saved, monk?"

"By means of perfect Poverty, perfect Love, perfect Chastity, Sultan, my lord."

The Sultan stared at him with protruding eyes. "Are you in your right mind?" he shouted. "What is this nonsense you're talking about, monk? Do you mean to say I should abandon my wealth, palaces, wives, and become a ragamuffin like yourself to knock on doors and beg? Do you mean I should never touch a woman? But then what would be the use of living—can you tell me that? Why did God give us a key which opens women and lets us in? In other words I should become a eunuch—is that what you want?"

"Women are—" began Francis, but the Sultan extended his hand angrily.

"Shut your mouth, monk. Don't say anything bad about women, or I'll have your tongue cut out! Think of your mother, think of your sister if you have one; and above all, you who are a Christian, think of Mary the mother of Christ!"

Francis bowed his head and did not reply.

"And tell me, if you please, what you mean by perfect love," said the Sultan, nodding to the executioner to approach.

"To love your enemies, Sultan, my lord."

"Love my enemies!" exclaimed the Sultan, bursting into laughter. He addressed the executioner:

"Sheathe the yataghan. They're insane, poor wretches, completely insane. We won't kill them."

Then he turned again to Francis. This time he spoke more tenderly, as though addressing someone who was ill. "This heaven of yours: what is it like? Let's see if it's worth my while to go."

"Our heaven is full of angels and the spirits of the saints, and God sits at the very top."

"And what does one eat and drink up there? Who does one go to bed with?"

"Do not blaspheme. The inhabitants of Paradise do not eat, drink, or couple. They are spirits."

The Sultan laughed once more. "Spirits? In other words: air—is that what you're saying? Our heaven is a thousand times better. Mountains of rice, rivers of milk and honey, and beautiful girls who never fail to become virgins again the moment after you've slept with them. I'd have to be insane, monk, to go to your heaven. . . . Leave me in peace."

Francis grew angry. Forgetting where he was and that the Sultan, with a nod, could deprive him of his head, he began fearlessly to preach Christ's Passion, Resurrection, the Second Coming, and also the Inferno, where all Moslems will burn forever and ever. So carried away was he in preaching the word of God, that he became drunk and began to clap his hands and dance, laugh, sing, whistle. Without a doubt he had gone out of his senses for the moment. Chuckling, the Sultan watched him, and then he too began to clap, whistle, and shout in order to encourage the enkindled monk to continue.

Francis suddenly stopped. The sweat was gushing from his steaming body.

"Bless you, monk," said the Sultan. "I haven't laughed for ages. But now be still, because it's my turn to speak to you. Our Prophet loved perfumes, women, flowers; in his belt he kept a small mirror, and a comb for combing his hair. He also loved beautiful clothes very very much. Your prophet, so I'm told, walked barefooted, unwashed, uncombed, and his robe was made of thousands of patches. It's said that every poor man he encountered gave him one patch. Is that true?"

"True! True! He took upon Himself the suffering of every poor man in the entire world," cried Francis, carried away.

The Sultan stroked his beard. Presently he removed a tiny mirror from his waistband, twisted his mustache, and reached for his long amber-tipped chibouk. A small boy knelt and lit it for him. The Sultan took several soothing puffs and then tranquilly closed his eyes.

"This is an excellent time for us to be killed, Brother Leo," whispered Francis, turning to me. "Are you ready? I hear the gates of heaven opening."

"Why be killed so soon, Brother Francis?" I replied. "Wait awhile."

The Sultan opened his eyes. "Mohammed—great is his name!—was not only a prophet, he was also a man. He loved what men love, hated what men hate. That's why I bow down and worship him; that's why I struggle to resemble him. Your prophet was made of stone and air. I don't care for him at all."

He turned to me. "And what about you, monk: aren't you going to talk? Say something; let us hear your voice."

"I'm hungry!" I cried.

The Sultan laughed. He clapped his hands, and the two Negroes who had captured us came forward.

"Remove a pan from the oven and give them something to eat," he commanded. "Then take them away and let them go find their image-worshiping coreligionists. The poor wretches are insane, insane, and we ought to respect them."

The city was overrun by eastern troops. It reeked with the stench of the dead soldiers and disemboweled horses that lay unburied in the streets. Dervishes, dancing outside the mosques, slashed their heads with long knives until the blood ran down their white jelabs. In the cafés, chubby boys sang languorous Oriental songs, accompanying themselves on strange oblong instruments—tambouras. Women passed, veiled from head to toe, and for a moment the ill-smelling air was perfumed with musk.

Pinching our noses against the accursed stench, we followed the two Negroes rapidly through the narrow lanes until we came to the edge of the city. Here our guides halted and pointed toward a spot far in the distance, behind a low sand dune. "The Christians are there!" they growled, their brilliantly white teeth glistening in the sun. They gave us two strong punches in the back as a parting gesture and then retraced their steps at a run.

We set out, marching in silence. His lips bolted shut, Francis gazed at the ground, plunged in thought. As for me, I stared goggle-eyed all around me. The world seemed so unbelievably large! Here, thousands of miles from Assisi, countless souls lived in sin, never even having heard of the name of Christ. How were we going to be able to preach God's word to all these souls? Life was short; we would never have the time. With the world so limitless, where were we to begin?

The sand stretched out before us. Strange birds, red, with white bellies, passed overhead. At our backs was the tumult of the Moslem city, ahead of us, behind the sand dune, trumpets and the whinnying of horses. At last we were nearing the Christian host that for months and months had encircled the infidel city.

Suddenly Francis halted. "Brother Leo," he said to me, "when (and if) we return to our homeland, I am going to beg each poor man I meet to give me one patch to use for my robe. The Sultan was right."

"We had a narrow escape, Brother Francis."

"We lost one opportunity to enter Paradise," was his reply.

By this time we had climbed to the top of the dune. Stretched out beneath us, multicolored and tumultuous, were the myriad forces of Christ.

I prefer not to remember those days, those months. The din still haunts my mind, making me giddy. And the filth, the brazen songs, the cursing we heard when we reached the plain where the crusaders had pitched their tents! Poor Francis had to block his ears. Was this, then, what the soldiers of Christ were like? They spoke of nothing but the looting they were going to do, the women they were going to enslave, the Saracens they were going to slaughter. The name of Christ never crossed their lips. It is impossible for me to remember how many weeks we remained with them. Every day Francis stepped up onto a stone and preached about the Holy Sepulcher and God's mercy. The crusaders went by, some not even bothering to turn and look, while others stopped, but only to laugh or to throw a handful of sand at him.

The battle recommenced. The Christians charged the battlements and towers, scaled them, vaulted into the city—and the pillage and slaughter began! Francis ran among the soldiers of Christ and exhorted them with tearful eyes to be merciful, but they drove him away, jeered him, and continued to break down the doors of the houses. How can I ever forget the cries of the women and the groans of the men they slaughtered! The blood ran in rivers; wherever you turned you stumbled over a severed head. The air was thick with moans and wailing.

The face of the sky had filled with smoke from the houses and human bodies that were burning. The heat was stifling, the earth seething. Christ's labarum fluttered above the Sultan's palace, but the Sultan himself had leapt onto a fast horse and managed to escape, leaving behind him his women and possessions. Francis knelt in the palace doorway and implored God to avert His eyes from Damietta so that He would not see what His soldiers were doing below on earth.

"Lord," he shouted, the tears streaming down his cheeks, "man becomes a beast amid the blood of war, a bloodthirsty beast. He loses the faces Thou gavest him and becomes a wolf, a filthy pig. Take pity on him, Lord; restore to him the face of man—Thy face!"

The old and infirm had been crowded into a mosque. Francis remained among them, uttering words of comfort. Disease had blinded many of them; blood and pus oozed from their eyes. Bending down, Francis placed his hands over their eyelids and besought God to heal them. "They too are men, Thy children," he murmured. "Have pity on them!" He blew on their eyes and whispered words of comfort and love—until finally one day he caught the disease himself and his eyes became inflamed and started to burn. His sight grew dim; he could no longer see well enough to walk, and I had to hold his hand and lead him.

One day I said to him: "I told you the disease would attack you if you went near them, Brother Francis!"

"You are extraordinarily prudent, Brother Leo," he answered me. "What you say is sensible, but to a fault. In other words, you still cannot take the leap, can you? Are you going to continue to walk on the ground forever?"

"What leap, Brother Francis?"

"The leap above your own head, into the air!"

No, I was unable to take this leap, nor would I be able to ever. I had taken only one leap in my life, and that was when I had decided to follow Francis. Another was too much for me. . . . Every time I think of this leap I rejoice that I took it, and yet at the same time I constantly regret it. Alas, I never was the type for sainthood. . . .

"The world is terribly large, Brother Leo," Francis said to me on another occasion. "Behind the Saracens are the Negroes, behind the Negroes the savage cannibal tribes, and behind them a limitless ocean, one that you can walk on because it is frozen. How will we ever succeed, ever have time to preach the good news everywhere, the news that Christ came to the world?"

"Do not fret, Brother Francis: Time itself will succeed; Time will have time for all."

"Time . . . Time . . ." murmured Francis. "But we won't be here."

"You'll be watching from up in heaven, Brother Francis; you'll be working, seated astride Time."

Francis sighed. "Brother Leo," he said, "there was once an ascetic who died, mounted to heaven, and fell deep into God's embrace. He had found the perfect beatitude. Once day, however, he leaned out so that he could see the earth below him, and when he did this, he spied a green leaf. 'Lord,' he cried, 'Lord, let me leave, let me touch the green leaf once again!' Do you understand, Brother Leo?"

His words frightened me, and I did not answer. Alas! it was true: the power of the green leaf was as great as that!

Summer went by; autumn arrived.

"When are we going to leave, Brother Francis?" I asked. "It's autumn; I'm anxious to return to the cradle where we were born. This is another world; perhaps there is even another God here. Come, let's go away."

"Brother Leo," he answered me, "when two roads lie before you and you want to choose, do you know which is the best, which is the one that leads to God?"

"No, Brother Francis. Tell me."

"The most difficult, the steepest. Our life here is hard; therefore, let's stay."

He went about all day preaching, but no one bothered to listen. The mind and thoughts of all were on the prospect of looting Jerusalem.

"And Christ, don't you think of Christ, my brothers?" Francis shouted in desperation. "It was to deliver His tomb that you journeyed from the ends of the earth; it was for His tomb, the Holy Sepulcher!"

But they had long ago begun to treat him as a laughingstock. They would drag him by his robe, throw stones at him, die laughing

211

whenever he appeared on the streets ringing his ram's bell; and he in turn, overjoyed that he was being humiliated by men, would laugh along with them and commence to dance and preach in the middle of the streets.

"I am God's buffoon, men's buffoon. Come to laugh, my brothers, come to laugh!"

One day at noontime we lay down beneath the shelter of a doorway. The sun was out in full force; we were tired, and we quickly fell asleep. Suddenly, while I was sleeping, I heard Francis jump up and begin to shriek. When I opened my eyes I screamed as well, for two crusaders had laid a naked prostitute down at Francis' side in order to amuse themselves. The moment the brazen woman threw her arms around his neck he had sprung to his feet, quaking. Now the hussy was holding her arms out to him invitingly.

"Come, come," she cooed in a sweet voice. "Come, I am Paradise. Enter!"

Francis placed his hands over his eyes so that he would not see her. But suddenly his soul took pity on the woman.

"My sister," he said, "Sister Prostitute, why don't you want to save your soul? Do you feel no pity for it? And your body that has been surrendered to men for so many years: do you feel no pity for that? Allow me to place my hands upon your head and pray God to have mercy on you!"

"All right, place your hands on my head and start your incantation," she said amid paroxysms of laughter. "Call your God to come down and perform his miracle."

Francis placed his palms on the black unbraided hair, and raised his eyes to heaven. "Christ," he whispered, "Thou who descendest to the world for the poor, for sinners, for prostitutes, take pity on this woman, this naked woman. Her heart, deep within her, is good, but she has chosen the evil road. Extend Thy hand and guide her to the path of salvation."

The woman had shut her eyes. Little by little her face began to sweeten: surely she must have felt Francis' holiness descend from his hands into her brain, and thence to her heart, her bowels, her very heels. Suddenly, abruptly, she began to weep. Francis drew his hands away and traced the sign of the cross above her naked body.

"Do not weep, my sister," he said to her. "God is good; He forgives. Remember what He said to the prostitute when He was here on earth: 'Your sins are forgiven, for you have loved much.' "

The two soldiers had been standing off to one side all the while, guffawing. Now they began to whistle at the woman and taunt her. But she quickly gathered up her garment from the ground, wrapped it tightly around her body, and fell at Francis' feet.

"Forgive me, for I have sinned," she cried. "Don't you have a convent for me somewhere? Take me with you!"

"My sister, the whole world is a convent. You can live chastely in the world as well as out of it. Go, lock yourself in your house and have no fears. The Lord is with you!"

Winter bore down upon us. The army broke camp and departed for Jerusalem. Scattered clouds were visible in the sky. Flocks of crows followed God's host by day, packs of hyenas by night, and we ran behind as well. I held Francis by the hand: his eyes had grown smaller and smaller until they were but two narrow violently inflamed slits. A mist had settled over them, and the world had become dark.

On the morning of the third day he collapsed to the ground, gasping for breath.

"I can't continue, Brother Leo. I want to go right to the limit, but I can't. . . . Look!"

He showed me his feet. Blood was flowing from them, and also a yellow fluid.

He sighed. "And as though these wounds weren't enough, Brother Leo, new devils have entered me!"

I dared not question him. I had a premonition which these new devils might be, and I held my tongue.

We were surrounded by endless sand. The army had disappeared. At the edge of the desert the clouds had thickened and the sun grown dim. The sea was to our left, glittering in the distance. Bending down, I raised Francis onto my shoulders—he had fainted—and began to stagger with panting breaths toward the sea. It was midday when we finally reached the coast. A boat with a black cross painted on the stern had cast anchor, its becalmed sails hanging limp and useless. Two or three fishermen were drawing their nets onto the shore; there were a few huts built of cow dung or bricks and straw; and beyond, blue-green, the limitless sea. I laid Francis down on the beach and sprinkled him with sea water. He raised his eyelids.

"The sea?" he asked longingly. "The sea?"

"Yes, Brother Francis, the sea. We're going home."

He did not speak, did not object. Leaving him, I ran near the boat and called for the captain. As soon as he came I fell at his feet and implored him, hugging his knees:

"If you're returning to our country take us with you! We have nothing to pay our fare with, but God shall repay you."

"When?"

"In the next world, the real world."

"That will be the day!" the captain said with a laugh. "God is a bad risk. He owes me quite a lot already, and I've still to see Him open His purse."

"Take us with you!" I repeated. "Think of the Inferno, think of Paradise. The two roads lie before you. Choose!"

The captain scratched his beard nervously. "Listen, monk: I've been sitting here idle for three days and nights now waiting for a fair wind which doesn't come. You and your companion have constant dealings with God. Can you pray to Him to puff and swell out my sails? If you bring me a good wind I'll take you aboard, and you won't have to worry about any additional payment. Go back to your companion and start casting your spells!"

I ran to Francis. He, if he was willing to offer up this prayer, would surely be heard by God.

"Brother Francis, a boat from our land is anchored just in front of us. The captain says he'll take us aboard if we pray to God to send a favorable wind. Lift your arms to heaven and start praying!"

"The only miracles I believe in are those of the heart, Brother Leo," he replied. "I'm unable to accomplish anything beyond that, so do not ask me."

"Cry to heaven," I insisted. "God will hear you."

Francis lashed out: this man who was tottering on the brink of the grave lashed out, sprang to his feet, and seized me by the nape of the neck.

"Don't exasperate me, Brother Leo," he screamed. "Stop urging me every two minutes to shout, 'Give! Give! Give!' Do you think God has nothing better to do than to hand out loaves of bread, warm clothes, and favorable winds? He threw us down here in this desert, and if all our efforts have come to nothing, that's just

214

what He wanted. He unfolded a black wing above me and dimmed my sight: that's just what He wanted. He brought a boat, placed it directly in front of us, and now refuses to send a favorable wind: that's just what He wanted—or perhaps it's your opinion that He owes us an explanation for His actions! And now Your Lordship comes along and tells me to call upon Him to alter His will! Keep your mouth closed, Brother Leo; cross your arms and accept God. Let Him descend upon us in any guise that pleases Him—as hunger, or as a fine wind, or as the plague!"

Astonished to hear Francis speak so angrily, I bowed, kissed his hand, and said nothing. He realized then that his words had hurt me, and he regretted having uttered them.

"Forgive me, Brother Leo. The new devils inside me have poisoned my heart and tongue."

He continued to speak, but I was gazing tearfully at the sea and I don't remember what he said to me. Suddenly I saw the water begin ever so gradually to stir, to quiver. A warm breeze rose from the south. The ripples swelled slightly; then all at once, the moment Francis stopped talking, a fine wind blew and I saw the boat's sails flap and swell out.

"Hey, monks!" came the captain's happy voice.

I bent down and grabbed Francis under the arms. "A fair wind is blowing, Brother Francis. The captain is calling us. Let's go!"

"You ask Him for something," murmured Francis, "and He doesn't give it; you don't ask Him, and He gives it. . . . Well, whether He gives or not, praised be His name! Let's go."

After we had finally boarded the vessel, seated ourselves cross-legged at the stern, and begun to see the coast of Africa recede into the distance, Francis placed his hand on my knee. "Brother Leo," he said, "when we pray to God we must be seeking nothing—nothing. As time goes on, I begin to understand that He does not care at all for whining and begging. We have whined and begged far too much, I think, Brother Leo. A voice inside me—a voice which I heard today for the first time—calls out: 'You are not on the right road!' But which is the right road, Brother Leo? I still am unable to tell. We shall wait and see!"

The sea smelled sweet; the boat glided along with all sails set. The route home was a beautiful one and the days and nights passed like rapidly-alternating flashes of white and black. I sat in the stern with my back against the cables and gave myself up to thought. Yes, Francis was right: all our pains had gone for nothing. The Sultan had not become a Christian, and Francis' tearful words to the crusaders had been equally ineffective. Who could expect these armor-encased Christians to listen to him? They slaughtered, pillaged, looted shamelessly, forgetting why they had set out and where they were going. Was this God's will, in other words—and if so, why?

I asked myself this question, asked it in desperation, but could find no answer. Nor did I dare turn to ask Francis, who was at my side, because I remembered one night when we had heard a nightingale's song in the moonlight. We stopped and listened, holding our breath.

"God is inside the bird's throat and is singing, Brother Leo," Francis said to me in a whisper. And just as he said this, the bird tumbled out of the branches and fell to the ground. Francis bent down and picked the nightingale up in his hand. Its beak was all bloody. "It died from an excess of song," said Francis, kissing the tiny gullet, which was still warm.

But I became angry. "Why should it die, why should the tiny warm throat of the nightingale die?" I shouted. "Why should human eyes be turned to mud? Why? Why?"

Francis knit his brows. "And why," he shouted, "is man so impudent, always asking questions? Perhaps you require God to outline His reasons—is that it? Shut your brazen mouth!"

Now, in the boat, I remembered Francis' words and although my mind had revolted once more and begun to ask questions, I decided not to voice them.

One morning, when the coast of our country had finally become visible, Francis approached me, troubled. "I had a dream, Brother Leo, a bad dream. God grant that it does not come true!"

"Not all dreams are from God," I answered. "Don't be afraid, Brother Francis."

"I dreamt I was a hen, a brood hen, just like the other time. I had covered my chicks with my wings when suddenly a hawk darted out of the sky. I jumped up from fear and left my chicks uncovered. The hawk seized them in its talons and disappeared."

I did not utter a word. But I shuddered, and to myself I said: Elias! The hawk was Elias!

Francis sighed. "I shouldn't have gone away. It was wrong to abandon my children and leave them unprotected. . . . Who could the hawk be, Brother Leo?"

"We'll reach the Portiuncula in a few days, Brother Francis. Then we'll find out."

The coast was near at last. Leaning over the bow railing, we gazed longingly at the shore. Houses began to appear, as did olive trees, fig trees, vineyards. It was the beginning of spring. The meadows had turned green; the ground was fragrant—the savory and thyme must already have blossomed.

"I can't see our homeland very clearly," said Francis, "but I feel it in my arms as though it were my own daughter."

We jumped ashore. What joy it is to return to your homeland in the springtime when all the trees are blossoming! Francis stooped, as did I, and we kissed the soil. Then, crossing ourselves, we set out hastily, Francis clinging to my hand so that he would not stumble. We were both deeply engrossed in thought. From time to time Francis stopped, lifted his hand toward the north, toward the Portiuncula, and traced the sign of the cross in the air. He seemed to be blessing the tiny church, and also attempting to cast out the demons that inhabited it.

One day he woke me at the crack of dawn. We had spent the night in a hayloft.

"I had another dream, Brother Leo," he shouted in a frightened voice. "No, it wasn't a dream: I saw the Portiuncula between the trees, saw it with my eyes open. Three demons had attacked it. Their wings were like bats' wings, they had claws and horns, and their sinuous tails girdled our sweet little church and our cells. But I made the sign of the cross, cried, 'Begone, unclean spirits, in Christ's name!'—and they vanished."

"Your dream was a good omen, Brother Francis," I said to soothe him. "God was victorious."

Overjoyed, Francis sprang to his feet and began to dance in the hay. But all of a sudden terror spread over his features. He fell down on his face, palpitating; apparently he had seen some horrible vision in the half-darkness.

"What's the matter, Brother Francis?" I shouted, overcome with fright. "Did you see something in the air?"

Still trembling, he seized my hand. "Have pity on me, Brother Leo," he murmured. "Help me find my way out of the Inferno. Come, let us climb to the top of a high snow-capped mountain, to pray. Before I see the friars I must see God and be purified."

The thought terrified me. "But we'll freeze to death, Brother Francis," I said. "Winter isn't entirely finished yet, and the snow on top of the mountain will be up to our necks."

Francis shook his head. "If you have no faith, Brother Leo, yes, you will freeze, without a doubt. If you have faith, however, the sweat will flow from you, and the hair on your head will steam. It's daylight. Cross yourself and let's be on our way."

We began the ascent. As we rose higher the air grew icier and icier. I was shivering. Soon we reached the snow. Our bare legs sank in, at first up to the ankles, then to the shins. It was evening when we finally reached the summit.

"Are you cold, Brother Leo?" Francis asked me.

My lips were blue; I was frozen stiff, and could not speak. Francis stroked my shoulder compassionately.

"Think of God, poor wretched Brother Leo, think of God, and you'll feel warm."

I thought of Him, thought of Him—but there was little likelihood of my feeling warm: I was frozen solid! On top of this I was sleepy and hungry. Oh, I said to myself, if I could only lie down here in the snow and fall asleep and never wake up again—if I could only escape all this! I've had enough! I wasn't made out to be either a hero or a saint. How I deceived myself when I decided to follow this man who is both! I was suited to poking around lazily with ordinary men, knocking on doors, stopping awhile at the taverns: pursuing God, but leisurely. . . .

Francis had knelt down on the snow and begun to pray. Night fell; the sky filled with stars. I had never seen stars that were so huge, so sparkling, so near to man. Suddenly I heard Francis' voice:

"Where are you, Brother Leo? I don't see you."

"Here by your side, Brother Francis. I'm at your command."

"It's said that the saintly ascetics who live high up in the mountains take off all their clothes and then lower themselves into deep holes they dig in the snow. And when they do this, the sweat flows from their armpits."

218

"I'm no ascetic," I replied with irritation. "If you feel like getting undressed, no one is stopping you."

He took off his clothes and rolled in the snow, chanting in a strong voice the hymn sung by the three children in the fiery furnace. Then he wrapped himself in his robe, made a round pillow out of some snow, and lay down to go to sleep.

"Many new demons are tormenting me, Brother Leo. I roll in the snow in order to frighten them and make them leave."

I was about to reply: And by what rights should I have to freeze as well! but I restrained myself. Then, suddenly, Francis' eyes left their sockets. Quaking, he jumped to his feet, stretched out his arms as though trying to defend himself, and began to stagger backwards.

"There he is!" he whispered, horrified. "He's come again!"

I looked. No one was there. The air was empty.

"Who do you see, Brother Francis?" I cried.

"The beggar, the beggar with the hood, with the holes in his hands and feet. Look—the wound on his forehead, the cross: it's bleeding. . . . There he is! There he is!"

His entire body was shaking. I hugged him, spoke to him softly, sweetly, trying to quiet him.

"There he is! There he is!" he shouted again. "He's eying me scornfully and shaking his head. . . ."

He was trembling—not from the cold, but from fear. His still-protruding eyes were riveted upon the empty air in front of him. Suddenly he shuddered from head to toe.

"Help! He's coming!" he screamed, his teeth clattering.

I took him in my arms to prevent him from falling. "Call on God, Brother Francis, call on God to make him go away."

But Francis shook his head. "What if God is the one who sent him?" he murmured. Stooping, he grasped a fistful of snow to throw at the apparition, but then changed his mind. "Command me, my brother!" he said, taking a step forward. Then, after remaining silent for a moment, waiting in vain for a reply: "Why don't you speak? Who are you? Who sent you? Why are you shaking your head?"

He listened intently. Someone seemed to be talking to him.

"Go away and leave me alone," he cried a moment later. "Aren't I free to wrestle with devils if I want to? I like it! I'm not an archangel, I'm a man; every demon is inside me, and I wrestle. God is on my side, so I have no need of you. Go away! There's no use your showing me your pierced hands! Go away, I tell you! I'm not an angel and have no desire to be an angel. I want to win with my own strength, unaided."

He lifted his arm and flung the snowball he was holding, then burst into frenzied laughter. "I hit him square in the face. He's gone, destroyed!"

He collapsed to the ground and, grasping my arm, pulled me down next to him. For some time he did not speak. Taking a handful of snow, he rubbed his fiery temples. At last he turned and looked at me. "Brother Leo, I want to say something to you, to ask you something. I implore you not to be frightened: I'm not the one who is speaking; it's the demons inside me."

"I'm listening, Brother Francis." My jaws were clacking.

"Can you tell me why God created woman, why He detached a rib from man and created her, why every man spends his entire life seeking to become reunited with this detached rib? Is this God's voice speaking through me, or the devil's? What do you think, Brother Leo: marriage, childbirth, the begetting of sons—are they holy sacraments or not?"

His words made me shudder. He trembled as he spoke, and I actually saw the sweat flowing from his forehead. Who could ever have believed that such demons would be in him, tormenting his loins?

"Speak, Brother Leo," he continued in an anguished voice. "Do not remain silent. Is it possible that we have taken an evil road, a road which opposes God's will? Wasn't it the Lord Himself who said, 'Increase and multiply and be like the sand of the sea'?"

"Brother Francis," I replied, "I fall at your feet and ask forgiveness for saying this to you—but it is the devil, the devil of the flesh, who is talking at this moment through your mouth: the devil with the huge breasts!"

He uttered a heart-rending cry and sprawled out on top of the snow. Then he undid the cord which was around his waist. The whole night long I heard him groaning and beating his loins and thighs maniacally. At the break of dawn he jumped up, naked, his flesh blue with cold and discolored by the welts he had inflicted upon himself. He began to shape the snow into balls which he placed in piles arranged in a line in front of him.

"What are you doing that for, Brother Francis?" I cried, trembling with the fear that he had gone out of his mind.

"You'll see in a moment," he answered as he toiled with his hands and feet to give human shape to each of the seven mounds of snow that he had now packed in front of him. "You'll see in a moment, Brother Leo, in a moment!"

And indeed, in a moment I clearly saw seven snow-statues lined up one next to the other: a fat woman with huge pendulous breasts, on her right two boys, on her left two girls, and behind her a man and woman with bowed heads.

Francis gazed at them and was suddenly overcome with laughter. "Look, Sior Francis, son of Bernardone," he cried, "that is your wife, those your children, and behind them are your two servants. The whole family had gone out for a stroll, and you—husband, father, master—are walking in the lead."

But suddenly his laughter gave way to ferocity. He lifted his hand toward heaven. At the instant he did so the sun appeared, the mountain began to gleam; below, far in the distance, Assisi hovered weightlessly in the air, uncertainly, as though composed of fancy and morning frost.

"Lord, Lord," Francis cried in a heart-rending voice, "command the sun to beat down upon my family and melt them! I want to escape!"

He sank to the ground and began to weep. I went to him, wrapped his robe around him, then picked up the knotted cord, which was all covered with blood, and tied it about his waist.

"Come, Brother Francis," I said, taking him by the hand and lifting him up, "we'll go to the Portiuncula and let the brothers light a fire to warm you—to warm both of us. If we stay here we'll die of cold. Besides, as you undoubtedly see for yourself, we still are not ready to appear before God."

Francis stumbled forward, his knees constantly giving way beneath him, his hand trembling in my grasp. We did not talk. The sun grew continually stronger; it embraced us, warmed us compassionately, as though it were God's eye and had seen us and decided to take pity upon us. As I gazed at it I forgot myself for a moment and allowed Francis' hand to slip out of my own. He took two steps, three, then stumbled and fell on his face. I ran to lift him up.

Blood was flowing from his head. Two sharp stones had incised a deep wound on his forehead—in the shape of a cross. Raising his hand to investigate the wound, he suddenly quivered with fright.

"What's the matter, Brother Francis? Why are you shaking?"

"What shape is the mark on my forehead?"

"A cross."

"A cross!"

His whole body was trembling. Suddenly he parted his lips, was about to speak. But I had already understood.

"Quiet, Brother Francis," I shouted. "Quiet! I understand."

I was shaking too. I took him by the hand again, and we resumed our descent in silence.

Good Lord, drooping as we were from cold, hunger, and despondency, how were we ever able to go down the mountain and traverse the plain without collapsing to the ground! Where did we find the strength? Assisi stood at the center of the horizon and grew continually more stable, continually larger. We felt that it was no longer made of dreams and fancy, but of stones and cement, and we were able to distinguish the citadel, and the various towers and churches. I believe it was this view of Assisi coming ever closer that gave us the strength to continue. Francis himself was not able to see it—his eyes pained him and gave off a never-ceasing discharge. But I stopped every few moments and explained what was happening:

"It's coming closer. Now the towers are clearly visible, and I can see the dome of San Ruffino's. . . ."

Francis would listen and be encouraged to quicken his pace.

"I'm afraid, afraid," he said over and over again. "Remember the dream, Brother Leo. . . . In what condition will we find the brothers? How many of them will the hawk have snatched away from us? I'm racing because I want to reach them quickly, but at the same time I say to myself: Oh, if I could only never arrive!"

When we got to the Portiuncula the sun was about to set. Our hearts were beating wildly: we felt as though we had been away for countless years and that the Portiuncula was a living thing: our mother. . . . Advancing quietly, without speaking, we pushed aside the branches noiselessly, and approached. The door was open, the yard deserted. Not hearing any voices, we became frightened. What had happened to the friars? It was dark now and they should have been back. We went inside. A lamp was burning in the corner, and we were able to make out Brother Masseo crouching in front of the hearth, blowing on the fire. The wood he had used was wet, and the smoke made Francis choke and begin to cough. Masseo turned, saw him, and fell into his arms.

"Brother Francis! Welcome, welcome!" he cried, kissing his knees, hands, shoulders. "We were told you died far away in Africa. The brothers began to quarrel. They grew tired of living together, and decided to disperse. Most of them—all the young ones—went with Elias; they're combing the villages now, collecting gold for the huge church they say they intend to build. Bernard and Pietro are living in solitude in the forest, praying. Father Silvester took the original brothers with him and is preaching in the nearby villages. They return here from time to time, then leave again. I was the only one who stayed. I've been sitting here, lighting the fire every night, and waiting for you. . . . Welcome, a thousand times welcome, Brother Francis!"

He covered him once again with kisses and endearments.

Without uttering a word, Francis sank down in front of the fire. He watched the flames devour the wood, and held out his palms to become warm. From time to time he parted his lips and murmured, "Sister Fire, Sister Fire." Then he resumed his silence.

"Aren't you going to say anything, Brother Francis?" asked Masseo, who yearned to hear him speak. "Would you like me to go and gather together all the brothers and bring them to you? I've grown tired of staying here doing nothing. Command me!"

"What can I say, Brother Masseo? What can I command? I shall simply sit here in front of the fire and wait. That's what a voice inside me tells me to do."

Squatting before the fire in my turn, I heated some water and washed Francis' feet. Then I dipped a fresh cloth into lukewarm water and cleaned his eyes, which had been sealed by their discharge.

None of us spoke. Masseo and I felt a profound calm in our hearts, a sense of security now that Francis was together with us in our house. Outside, a strong wind had risen. The trees knocked against each other and groaned. Far in the distance dogs were barking.

Masseo had put the pot on the fire to cook us a hearty dinner. During our absence he had sold baskets woven from cane and osier which he cut along the riverbank; thus he had maintained himself by working. Francis kept his hands continually extended toward the fire, as though praying. You could tell from his face that he was plunged in a state of inexpressible sweetness: he had forgotten earthly things, and it seemed to me for a moment that he was hovering in the air above the hearth. (I had always heard that when saints think of God they conquer the weight of the body and hang suspended in mid-air.) Then I saw him descend ever so slowly and resume his position, leaning tranquilly forward toward the flames. . . . None of us spoke. We were happy, and we sat in silence while the night advanced.

Suddenly Masseo and I turned our heads toward the door. Someone had knocked.

"It must be one of the brothers," said Masseo. "I'll let him in." He rose, his immense body coming within a hair's breadth of touching the cane-lathed ceiling. He opened the door, and right away we heard a loud cry: "Oh!" followed by, "What do you want? No woman is allowed near here. These are sacred precincts, my lady."

I got up, astonished. A woman was standing on the threshold, her head so completely muffled that I saw nothing but her eyes.

"Let me come in, my brother," she said in her sweet voice. "I want to see Brother Francis—it's absolutely necessary for me to see him."

The sound of this voice threw Francis into turmoil. He buried his face in his hands as though trying to hide. I had recognized the voice too, and I went up to him and said softly, "It's Clara, Brother Francis."

He seized my arm. "I don't want to see her!" he groaned in terror. "Have pity on me, Brother Leo: I don't want to see her! Melt her, Sister Flame," he murmured, turning his face toward the fire. "She's made of snow—melt her! Let her become water and go away, let her flow into God's ocean."

But the young woman had already stepped across the threshold and had knelt at Francis' feet. She removed her wimple, exposing her features, but Francis kept his face hidden behind his palms and did not turn to see her.

"Have pity on me, Father Francis," said the girl, her voice a blend of sweetness and complaint. "Lift your head and look at me."

"If you are truly Clara, the noble daughter of Count Scifi, and if you love God, if you fear God—go away!"

Lowering his hands, he revealed his face. It was gouged, wasted away, covered with stains from the blood which was running from his eyes.

"Look at me if it does not disgust you," he said. "As for me, I am blind and cannot see you—glory be to God!"

"Father Francis," answered the girl, pressing her face against his feet, "have no fears: I am not going to raise my eyes to look at you; nor do I want you to look at me. All I want is for you to listen. Please!"

Francis crossed himself. "In the name of Christ Crucified, I'm listening."

"Father Francis," the girl began, her voice deep and assured, "do you remember the day I encountered you as you were walking barefooted and in rags through one of the lanes of Assisi? Ever since then my soul has found my body too narrow, too constricting: it wants to escape. I've melted away like a candle. If you look down at me, Father Francis, you will be frightened. But if you could see my soul you would rejoice, because it too is wearing a robe with cowl and knotted cord, just like your robe; it too is barefooted. My life with my parents and girl friends no longer gives me any pleasure. I want to leave the world of men: it has grown too narrow, too small for me! Cut off my hair, Father Francis, and throw it into the fire. Wrap me in your robe, tie the knotted cord about my waist. Let me go to the wilderness to roost on a rocky ledge like a martin. I want to flee, to flee the soil!"

She had begun to chirp, truly like a martin. Masseo and I had lowered our eyes; we were weeping, overwhelmed by the magnitude of the soul's yearning to become one with God! Francis, his face immobile, hard as stone, listened as the girl continued to speak. She lay prostrate at his feet, her hair covered with ashes from the fireplace, and she stopped frequently, waiting for him to reply. She waited, waited, but he remained mute, and his features grew continually harder.

"Do not turn away your face, Father Francis," she cried; "do not become angry. Don't you walk barefooted through the streets and dance and sing and call all souls to come? Don't you say, 'I am the road that leads to God. Follow me'? I heard your voice, abandoned my parents, home, fortune, my youth, my beauty, the hope of having children—and came. You are responsible, and therefore you

225

shall hear me out whether you like it or not. Listen: today I bade farewell to the world. I dressed in my most expensive clothes, combed my blond hair for the last time, put on my golden earrings and bracelets, my string of huge pearls, and went to church. I wanted the fashionable world to see me, to see my beauty and bid it farewell; for my part, I wanted to see this world's ugliness for the last time. Next, I visited my girl friends, also for the last time. I jumped with joy, laughed, and my astonished friends asked me, 'What has happened to make you so happy, Clara? Are you going to be married?' 'Yes, I'm going to be married,' I answered them, 'and my bridegroom is more beautiful than the sun, more powerful than a king.' 'And when in God's name is the wedding?' 'Tonight,' I said with a laugh. 'Tonight!' Then I returned home and gazed in silence at my father, mother, and sisters, gazed at them for a long time, bidding them an unspoken farewell. I could already hear the wailing and lamentations that would come from the house in a few hours' time when I would be gone and they would be looking for me and unable to find me. How could they possibly find me, since I would be in God's bosom! As soon as it was dark outside I came down quietly from my room, set out along the road, flew through the olive grove, past San Damiano's, and reached your sacred retreat. You called me and I came."

"I? I called you?"

"Yes, Father Francis, it was you—last night while I was sleeping. You know very well that when we go to bed only the body sleeps: the soul lies awake. Last night I heard you calling me by name. It was you, Father Francis. You were standing beneath my window once more and calling me. 'Come! Come! Come!' you said. So, I came."

Francis uttered a cry and started to rise in an effort to escape. But he immediately sat down again. Groping with his hand, he found a log, which he threw into the fire. Then he buried his face once more in his palms and remained this way for a considerable time, without speaking.

The girl waited and waited, but when his voice did not come, she grew angry. With a brusque movement she sat up on her haunches, her torso erect, her fists clenched.

"I spoke, Father Francis," she said; "I poured out my heart at your feet. Why don't you answer? It is your duty to answer!"

Silence. Outside, a fierce wind rattled the door. Francis extended his arms, glanced around him, managed to see us. "Brother Leo, Brother Masseo, come near me!" he shouted as though he were in danger and calling for help.

Filling his hand with ashes, he rubbed them furiously into his hair and against his face. They entered his eyes.

"Don't you feel sorry for her, Brother Francis?" I pleaded. "Take pity on the girl."

"No!" he cried, and it was the first time I had ever detected such rigidity, such bitterness in his voice.

He wrenched his hand away from my shoulder. "No! No!" he cried again. "No!"

Clara sprang to her feet, frowning. Her expression had grown harsh. Deep within her the proud lineage of her father had been wounded.

"I'm not going to implore you," she said; "I'm not going to grovel at your feet. Lift your eyes and listen to me! I am an immortal soul, just as you are, and I'm in danger. You go the rounds of cities and villages proclaiming you shall save the world. Well then, save *me!* You have an obligation to do so. If you don't—if you refuse—my soul shall hang itself around your neck and drag you down into hell. Stand up, I tell you, give me the robe which I ask of you, cut off my hair and throw it like so much kindling into the fire. Then lay your hand on my shaven head, bless it, and address me as Sister Clara!"

Jumping up, Francis threw a glance at the door and started toward it, apparently attempting to flee. Masseo and I rose to block his path. He stopped. His entire body was trembling, as it always did when he was forced to make some great decision against his will. Bowing his head, he staggered back to the hearth and leaned against the jamb. The reflections of the flames danced upon his body; his face seemed to be ablaze. Suddenly we heard a taunting, heart-rending voice:

"Can you, the young countess, the daughter of the great lord Favorino Scifi, can you walk with bare feet?"

"I can," the girl answered in a firm, proud tone.

"Can you endure hunger, and can you knock on doors and beg for your food?"

"I can."

"Can you bathe lepers, and rinse them, and kiss them on the mouth?"

"I can."

"Can you who are so lovely agree to become ugly? And when the children of the street run behind you shouting, 'Humpback! Bow-legged hag!' can you rejoice that you who used to be so beautiful have fallen now to the state of being a humpbacked, bowlegged harridan—all for Christ's sake?"

"I can, I can," repeated the girl, and she raised her hand as though taking an oath.

"You cannot!"

"I can! The daughter of Count Scifi is able to bear not only the rigors of affluence, but also those of poverty, nakedness, and ridicule. She can do whatever the others do."

"I don't trust you women. Eve's serpent has been licking your ears and lips for too many centuries. Do not lead me into tempta-tion. Other ladies will gather round you, and you'll all climb up to the convent roof to ogle the brothers, who in turn will climb up to the roof of their monastery to gaze at the sisters—and presently a robust, well-nourished devil of the flesh will shuttle back and forth between the two cloisters. No, get up and return home. We don't want women!"

"Women are God's creatures just as men are, and have souls, and want them to be saved."

"Women must take a different road if they wish to reach God. They must marry and have children, allow their virtue to flower and bear fruit not in desert solitude, but in the very midst of the world of men."

"It's in vain that you try to assign boundaries to virtue. Virtue is capable of flowering and bearing fruit wherever it wants to—and its great preference is for solitude."

"Intelligence, in women, is an impertinence! Who taught you how to find a retort for everything that is said?"

"My heart."

Suddenly Francis abandoned the wall he was leaning against and began to pace back and forth, stumbling every few steps. I ran to take his hand.

"Leave me alone," he shouted. "Don't touch me!"

He turned abruptly, and with one stride was in front of the fire-

place. Stooping, he clutched a handful of ashes and then brought
them down heavily over the girl's head. He rubbed the ashes against
her hair, her face, her neck, and thrust a mouthful between her lips.
He was murmuring something—we could see his lips moving, but
neither of us could distinguish a full word. He growled, lowed,
bleated like a lamb, howled like a wolf. Gradually, after much toil,
his voice regained its human characteristics, and we were able to
hear two words in the fierce silence, two human words, and only
two:

"Sister Clara . . . Sister Clara . . ."

The fire flared up; the reflections of the flames danced upon the
faces of Francis and Clara, both smeared with ashes.

The lamp began to sputter and die, but no one rose to add more
oil: we had all turned to stone. And when the lamp went out and
we remained alone with only the gleam of the fire, Francis'
voice was heard again, calm and peaceful now, gentle, completely
human:

"Sister Clara, welcome to our order!"

In no time the news spread from mouth to mouth throughout
Assisi and the surrounding villages that Francis had returned from
Egypt. He had done signs and wonders there, it was said. The
Sultan had been converted, baptized, and had accordingly turned
the city of Damietta over to the crusaders. Among those who heard
the good news were the dispersed friars. Mortally ashamed, they
converged upon their former sheepfold from every direction, and
were received by Francis with open arms.

They all came. Soon the Portiuncula was full, and branches had to
be brought and new shelters set up everywhere around it. Bernard
and Pietro arrived still rapt in contemplation, their eyes half-closed;
Capella silent and bareheaded; Pacifico with his lute slung over his
shoulder. Last of all came Elias, severe, fierce, with his robust body,
his brambly eyebrows, his clean-shaven upper lip. He was accompanied by his followers, and in his hand he held a thick book.

"God's love for you is indeed great, Brother Francis," he said. "He
preserved you, let you remain upon earth so that you might have
time to reach your lofty goal. I imagine your feet still have a considerable amount of climbing ahead of them."

"It's time you learned, Brother Elias, that man's goal is God and that the only way we can reach this summit is by dying."

"Excuse me," objected Elias, "but I'm of the opinion that the only way we can reach our goal is by living."

The air changed, became turbulent. Everyone waited in silence for the squall to break out.

For three days Francis went among the friars, questioning them, talking to them, struggling to discover which roads they had taken during his absence in Egypt. Several had gone to renowned Bologna to preach. But the learned theologians there had quickly exposed their ignorance and, completely humiliated, the brothers had been forced to hold their peace. Stubbornly refusing to be discouraged, however, they opened a school in the arrogant city, a school where numerous new friars came to study Holy Scripture. They purchased enormous tomes and studied far into the night: they did not preach, did not pray or work—they studied.

Francis listened to this, his heart seething with grief and indignation.

"We are lost, Brother Leo, we are lost," he kept saying to me. "We sowed wheat, and behold, our field is now covered with brazen poppies and nettles. What are these scholars, these wolves that have entered our fold? I have no use for education or knowledge. Satan inhabits our minds, God our hearts. The heart is illiterate; it has never even opened a book. What is going to become of us, Brother Leo? Where are we headed? For the abyss!"

The following day he came across a novice who was unknown to him. This novice was exceptionally pale, with shriveled cheeks and enormous eyes. He was bent forward, poring avidly over a book which he held in his hands. God, for him, had disappeared, the friars had disappeared, the entire population of the world had disappeared. Nothing remained between heaven and earth except this young man and his book.

Francis went up to him and tapped him on the shoulder. The youth gave a start.

"What's your name?"

"Antonio."

"Where are you from?"

"Portugal."

"Who gave you permission to have a book?"

"Brother Elias," answered the novice, squeezing the volume against his breast.

But Francis reached out and seized the book. "You don't have my permission!" he shouted angrily, and crying "Ashes! Ashes!" he hurled the book into the fire.

But when he saw the novice gazing at the flames with tearful eyes, he took pity on him. "Listen, my child," he said, "each year at Easter I used to watch Christ's Resurrection. All the faithful would gather around His tomb and weep, weep inconsolably, beating on the ground to make it open. And behold! In the midst of our lamentations the tombstone crumbled to pieces and Christ sprang from the earth and ascended to heaven, smiling at us and waving a white banner. There was only one year I did not see Him resurrected. That year a theologian of consequence, a graduate of the University of Bologna, came to us. He mounted the pulpit in church and began to elucidate the Resurrection for hours on end. He explained and explained until our heads began to swim; and that year the tombstone did not crumble, and, I swear to you, no one saw the Resurrection."

The novice grew bold and replied, "I, on the other hand, Brother Francis, never see the Resurrection unless I am entirely clear in my mind how and why Christ rose from the dead. I place my faith in nothing but man's mind."

Francis began to foam at the mouth. "That's precisely why you shall be damned," he cried, "precisely why as long as you live you shall never view the Resurrection. How and why! What impudence! The mind of man is accursed."

Brother Giles had stopped to listen. He had enjoyed Francis' words, and had been forced to put his hand over his mouth to hide his laughter. As soon as I took Francis' hand and began to lead him away, Giles ran up behind us.

"God speaks through your mouth, Brother Francis," he said. "You talk, and in me your words are immediately transformed into action. One Sunday while you were away this same novice, Antonio, came to me with a bundle of smudged papers under his arm and asked permission to go to San Ruffino's in Assisi to preach a sermon. 'I'll give you permission with pleasure,' I answered him, 'but on one condition: you must mount the pulpit and start crying "Baa! Baa!" like a sheep. Nothing else—just "Baa! Baa!"' The novice thought I was teasing him. He turned red with anger, took the sermon he had written, and thrust it beneath his robe. 'I am not a sheep, Brother Giles,' he said to me haughtily, 'I am a man. I don't bleat, I talk. God gave man a great privilege: the ability to talk.'"

"And how did you answer him, Brother Giles?" asked Francis, seeing the other hesitant to continue.

"To tell you the truth, Brother Francis, I was completely confused. All I could do was cough: I hadn't the slightest idea what to say. Luckily I saw Brother Juniper returning from the forest with an armful of wood. I ran to help him unload, and thus I escaped."

"There is a better answer than that, Brother Giles," said Francis, laughing. "You shall see presently! Come, Brother Leo."

"Where are we going this time?" I asked, trembling lest he bring me again to the top of some snow-covered mountain.

"To Satan's wet nurse: Bologna."

He was silent for a moment, and then: "Our boat is shipping water, Brother Leo. I'm afraid it might sink. O Bologna, Bologna, it is you who are going to devour our Portiuncula!"

We walked—no, we did not walk, we ran. The weather was warm, delightful. The apple and pear trees had blossomed; the first poppies beamed in the fields; small white and yellow daisies covered the ground. A warm breeze was blowing, the kind that induces buds to open. It reached right down to my heart and made it open too. I don't know why, but during all those spring days I kept thinking of Sister Clara, rejoicing that Francis had interceded with the bishop in her behalf and induced him to grant her San Damiano's as a hermitage.

One morning we reached Bologna, a large majestic city with streets teeming with people, red streamers waving in front of the taverns, fruits and vegetables piled high in the market place, beautiful women passing on horseback, with multicolored feathers in their hair. Turning into a narrow lane, we arrived at a tree-lined square away from the center of the city. Francis glanced around him, then proceeded to the School of Theology which had been established by Elias with several of the new brothers. He knocked on the door, entered at a run, and found himself in a vast chamber with a long, narrow table round which sat five or six brothers, reading. The walls were covered with maps, and with shelves packed with books.

"Apostates!" shrieked Francis. "Apostate friars, what are you doing here among these tools of the devil? For shame!"

The startled friars jumped to their feet. Francis strode back and forth closing the books they were reading, and shouting, "Woe unto you, apostate brothers! You forget Christ's words: 'Blessed are the poor in spirit.' God commanded me to be simple and ignorant. He took me by the hand and said to me, 'Come, I shall guide you to heaven by the shortest path. You, in turn, take your brothers by the hand and guide them along the path which I am about to show you!' I took you all by the hand, but you slipped out of my grasp and started to follow the wide road which leads to Satan. Get up now, remove all these volumes from the shelves, and pile them in the yard. You, Brother Leo, run to find a torch! The rest of you: leave at once, return as quickly as you can to your mother, the Portiuncula. In the name of holy Obedience, go!"

He heaped the books, maps, and ancient manuscripts in the middle of the yard. I ran to him carrying a torch.

"Here, give me Sister Fire," said Francis.

He took the torch, crouched down, and wedged it into the bottom of the pile. "In Christ's name, and in the names of holy Humility and holy Poverty!" he said, crossing himself.

Then he turned to the brothers who had come to the school to study. "How many of you are there?"

"Seven."

"I see only six. Where's the other?"

"In his cell. He's ill."

"Make him get up. Take him on your shoulders and leave. I'll find the keys and lock up."

When everything had taken place as he wished and the six had set out, carrying their ailing comrade, and nothing remained of all the parchments and papers but a tiny pile of ashes in the middle of the yard, Francis bent down, took some of the ashes in his hand, and spread them over both palms.

"Look, Brother Leo. Read. What does this book say?"

"It says that man's knowledge is nothing but ashes, Brother Francis. '*Ceniza y nada! Ceniza y nada!*' as that strange white-robed monk shouted at us, the one we met in Rome."

"Is that all? Doesn't it say something else? Look—here, at the bottom of the second page. What do you see?"

I bent over his hand and pretended to read: "God looked down, saw the earth, and shouted for his daughter Fire. 'Fire, my daughter,' He said to her, 'the earth is rotten; her stench has risen up to heaven. Descend and reduce her to ashes!'"

"No, no," protested Francis, startled. "It doesn't say 'Reduce her to ashes'; it says 'Descend and purify her.'"

Francis was impatient to return to the Portiuncula. He had grown nervous and taciturn; it was apparent that he was struggling to make some great decision. When I awoke the following morning—we had spent the night in a grotto not far from the Portiuncula—I saw him jump to his feet, terrified.

"I had a dream, Brother Leo, a horrible dream. Get up quickly."

"What did you dream about, Brother Francis?"

"There is a different shepherd now. The sheep go down to the plain, to the rich pastures; their loins are growing heavy and fat."

"I don't understand, Brother Francis."

"The sheep go down to the plain; but we, Brother Leo, do not want to become fat. We shall remain in the mountains and graze on stones."

"I beg your pardon, Brother Francis, but I don't understand, I tell you."

"And we shall dance and clap our hands, and God shall while away His time by watching us from on high. Agreed, Brother Leo?"

He began to walk at a rapid pace, anxious to arrive. I ran behind him, panting.

It was lamp-lighting time when we reached the Portiuncula. The brothers were all assembled, listening to Elias talk to them. Holding our breath, we hid behind the trees and pricked up our ears to catch his final words.

"My brothers," he was saying, "I have told you once and I tell you again: our order is no longer a baby. It has grown up. The tiny infant-clothes are too small for it now; it needs new and larger garments, the clothes of a man. Absolute Poverty was fine when two or three brothers set out and opened the way for us. They went about barefooted; a chunk of bread given them as alms was sufficient to gratify their appetites; a dilapidated shack was large enough to shelter them. But now, praise the Lord, we have become

234

an army, and absolute Poverty stands as an obstacle in our way: we do not want it. We have to build churches and monasteries, to send missionaries to the ends of the earth, to feed, clothe, and shelter thousands of brothers. How can we do all that with absolute Poverty?"

I clasped Francis' hand. It was trembling. "Did you hear, did you hear, Brother Leo?" he whispered to me. "They want to evict Poverty from her home." His eyes had filled with tears. He was ready to dart forward and begin shouting, but I restrained him.

"Quiet, Brother Francis, quiet. Let's hear the rest. Patience!"

Elias' voice grew continually more thunderous:

"And perfect Love is an obstacle as well. The first brothers sang and danced in the streets. The children pelted them with stones and lemon rinds, the men thrashed them mercilessly, and they kissed the hand that was tormenting them. This is what they termed perfect Love. A child can be thrashed, but an army—never! Our version of perfect Love does not carry a handkerchief to wipe away her tears, she wields a sword to defend the just and kill the wicked. Our Love is armed to the teeth! We live among wolves and therefore we must become lions, not lambs. Christ Himself was a lion.

"So much, my friends, for perfect Love. Perfect Simplicity no longer suits us either. The mind is God's great gift to mankind; it is the mind that sets man apart from the animals. Therefore we have an obligation to enrich our minds, to establish schools where the brothers may study, to cease being a laughingstock for all and sundry. The heart is fine; it too is a great gift from God. But it is mute—mute, or else disdainful of speaking. The mind holds the Word as its sword, and the Word, my brothers, is the Son of God. We must be Christian soldiers, not Christian buffoons; and our choicest, surest weapon is the Word. We bow and kiss the hand of Brother Francis. He did his duty splendidly up to now. He suckled our order while it was an infant, but now it has grown: it bows, kisses its parent's hand, and sets out on its journey, leaving him behind. Farewell, Brother Francis, we are departing!"

Francis had been hopping up and down during the entire speech; he wanted to rush forward, but I held him tightly by the arm. "Be patient, Brother Francis," I kept saying to him. "Let him finish so that we can see how far he's going to go."

235

"The dream . . . the dream . . ." Francis murmured. "If only God will come to our aid!"

We heard the friars clapping their hands and shouting ecstatically. Many were doubtlessly embracing Elias, others kissing his hand. At this point Francis could contain himself no longer, and with one impulsive movement he was at the door. I followed behind him.

The moment the brothers saw him they became petrified and shrank back from Elias, leaving him alone in the center. He was holding a hooked shepherd's staff which reached above his head. Francis stumbled toward him.

"Where did you find that staff, Brother Elias?" he asked in a trembling voice.

But Elias changed the subject. "I was just talking with the brothers," he said.

"I heard, I heard everything. But I was asking you about the staff. Where did you find it?"

"I don't know. Should I say it was a miracle? While I was dozing this morning, my head resting on a stone, a friar whom I had never seen before but who bore a remarkable resemblance to you, Brother Francis, came and drove this crook into the ground next to me, then vanished immediately. Was it you by any chance, Brother Francis?"

"Yes, it was me, and may my hand be cursed! I was dozing, just like you," Francis growled, clenching his fists. "It was me, Brother Elias!"

But he corrected himself immediately: "No, no, it wasn't me; it was someone else—and may His hand be blessed!"

Elias watched Francis babbling away, and smiled sympathetically. Many of the friars were laughing in secret. I overheard two of them behind me:

"He's taken leave of his senses," one was saying.

"Quiet," the other answered. "You ought to pity the poor fellow."

Bernard, Pietro, and Father Silvester went up to Francis; the rest of the original brothers ran to kiss his hand. Elias and his faction held their ground, while behind them the novices stood silent and uneasy as Francis, biting his lips, obviously to keep himself from weeping, approached them one by one with raised hand, blessing them, his pale face coated with bitterness. As soon as he had blessed everyone he asked that a stool be brought so that he could sit down, for he was tired and wished to say a few words to the brothers. Masseo hurried off and returned with the stool. Francis sank down upon it, then bent over and covered his face with his hands, remaining this way for a long period, without speaking. Next to him as I was, I could see that the veins in his temples had begun to swell. I signaled to Juniper, who brought him a cup of water. Francis drank two sips. "God bless Brother Water," he murmured, taking a deep breath. Then, exerting all his strength, he rose and opened his arms wide.

"My brethren," he said in a gasping voice which we could scarcely hear, "my brethren, God entrusted me with a handful of seed, and I went out to sow. I lifted my arms to heaven and prayed the Lord to send rain, and it rained; I prayed Him to send the sun so that my sprouts might grow, and He sent the sun, the sprouts grew, the field became covered with green grain. I leaned over to see which seed it was that God had entrusted to me, and I saw: hallowed wheat, but also vain, arrogant poppies. Such is God's will, I reflected. Who knows—corn poppies are red, beautiful, they have a black cross over their hearts—perhaps beauty is just as nourishing for men as wheat is. So, blessed be the poppies! My brothers—those who are wheat, and those who are poppies—listen to me: I have something grave to say to you tonight.

"I believe that Brother Elias is correct. Yes, I have done my duty. It was to sow, and I have sown. Now let others come to water, mow, and harvest the crop. I was not born to reap, to enjoy the profits, but to plough the soil, sow, and then depart. I swear to you that I do not want to leave. I love you exceedingly, my brothers, I adore our brotherhood—how can I leave it? But last night it seemed to me that God came in my sleep. I did not see Him, I only heard His voice: 'Francis,' He said, 'you did what you could; you can do no more. Go now to the Portiuncula. One of the brothers holds a staff which reaches above his head—' "

Francis' voice broke. We all waited with gaping mouths. Elias took a step forward, but Francis threw a biting glance at him, and he stood still.

"I swear to you," he continued, "the thought it would be Elias never entered my head. Forgive me for saying this, Lord, but he is dangerous: his virtues are the opposite of those with which our order was founded and solidified. Perfect Poverty, perfect Love, perfect Simplicity are not for him! He was born a conqueror, and these virtues are unsuitable for a conqueror. . . . I had in mind Bernard, the lover of solitude, or Sior Pietro, or Father Silvester. They would have guided Christ's flock to the pastures which suited it—to arid land, hallowed stones, to the bush which burns yet is not consumed. These are the ones I had selected, but He chose another—His will be done! Do not approach, Captain Elias. I shall call you when my grief is assuaged, my heart relieved; when the hands I shall place upon your head will no longer quiver and burn with indignation, but be cool, like love itself."

He crossed his arms over his breast and raised his head. The discharge from his eyes began to run down his cheeks again, covering his mustache and beard with blood. He was in pain, but he bit his lips and did not reveal his suffering.

"Though I do not understand, Lord," he murmured, "I do not ask questions—who am I to ask questions? I do not resist—who am I to resist? Thy designs are a bottomless pit. How can I descend into this pit to examine it? Thou lookest thousands of years into the future and then Thou judgest. What today seems an injustice to man's minute brain becomes, thousands of years hence, the mother of man's salvation. If what today we term injustice did not exist, perhaps true justice would never come to mankind."

Francis' face grew continually brighter as he spoke. This thought had come to him in all its freshness, as though it had never occurred to him before, and his heart began to grow calm. Turning smilingly to Elias, he nodded for him to approach. Elias came forward, the shepherd's staff held tightly in his hand.

"Bow your head, Brother Elias," he said in a gentle voice. "I shall give you my blessing. Look, my hands are cool; they aren't trembling."

He laid both hands on Elias' head. "Brother Elias," he exclaimed in a deep voice, "God is intricate, unfathomable. He apportions his divine grace among men in whatever way He likes; He uses a standard of measure which is not the same as ours; His thought is such that the mind of man cannot even approach it without being turned to ashes. Give me the staff!"

Elias hesitated for an instant and then drew the staff back, squeezing it tightly in his hand. But Francis reached out and repeated in a commanding tone: "Give me the staff!"

Bowing his head, Elias surrendered the staff to him. Francis continued in the same deep, calm voice:

"God issued a command, Brother Elias, and I am obeying Him. Lord, if I have interpreted Thy voice incorrectly, give me some sign. Let me hear thunder now while the sky is clear; or bang against the door and smash it to pieces; or cut off my hand before I place it on this man's head to give him my blessing."

He waited in silence. Nothing. Then he raised his arm with a violent motion and cried: "Brother Elias, I lay my hand upon your head; bow down. My brother, I turn my flock over to your care. Lead it where God shows you; pasture it as God counsels you. It is no longer to me that you must render account, but to God. There is only one thing that remains in my power to do, and that is to give you my blessing. . . . I bless you, Brother Elias. Take the staff, step out in front, guide the flock!"

Tears gushed from his eyes and mixed with the blood. He gazed around him at the friars, one by one, as though taking leave of them.

"Forgive me for weeping, my brothers," he said, wiping his eyes with the cuff of his robe. "I did not realize that parting was so sorrowful. Farewell! Do not be sad: I am not going to leave your sides, but shall remain with you always, mute and unseen. You shall see me only at night in your dreams. . . . And you, O you three charming, inseparable sisters—saintly, thrice-noble Dame Poverty, my wife, all ragged, barefooted, and hungry; and saintly thrice-noble Love, O Maria, you who carry no handkerchief to wipe away your tears, nor sword to kill, but instead the infant God, whom you suckle; and you, saintly, thrice-noble Simplicity, whose reply to all questions is 'I don't know, I don't know,' followed by your all-knowing smile: I implore all of you not to abandon the brothers, but to remain with them through their difficulties. Run around the flock like ever-vigilant greyhounds, and do not allow a single sheep to go astray."

He fell silent, but then looked at us all once again, and smiled. His heart still had not been emptied.

"If we were to select a bird to engrave on the seal of our order, which would it be, my children? Not the eagle—Brother Elias; nor the peacock—Brother Capella; nor the nightingale—Brother Pacifico; nor the wild dove that is such a lover of solitude—Brother Bernard; nor even the golden oriole—Brother Leo; but the hooded skylark!"

Smiling, he began to compose the skylark's panegyric:

"Brother Skylark has a hood just like we do; his feathers are colored the same as our robes, the color of soil, and are equally simple and poor. He wings from street to street, branch to branch in search of a grain of wheat to eat. And in the morning, every morning without fail, he ascends high into the heavens—singing, intoxicated with the light. He disappears, soars out of sight, then suddenly falls back to earth again like a tiny lump of clay. . . . Brother Skylark has said his morning prayers: he climbed up to God and returned again to the soil."

Elias raised his hand, indicating that he was about to speak.

"He who sows, Brother Francis, also reaps in the very process, because in his mind he has a foretaste of the future harvest. You are blessed, Brother Francis, because you accomplished to perfection the task entrusted to you by God, the task of sowing. Now, with tranquil heart and clear conscience, you relinquish the high staff to other hands. When you appear before God, Brother Francis, your arms will be filled with ears of grain. I raise this staff and vow to you that I shall transform the road you laid out from a footpath wide enough only for three or four brothers to a boulevard which shall accommodate thousands. I shall broaden the virtues on which you built our order so that they may be enjoyed no longer by only three or four brothers, but by thousands. And this humble Portiuncula I shall transform—I give you my oath—into a mighty fortress and palace of God."

When he had said this, he commanded that two stools be placed before the fire. Taking Francis by the hand, he had him sit down on one, while he himself sat down next to him on the other. Then, one by one, the brothers filed by, followed by the novices; everyone kissed first Francis' hand, then Elias'. Francis' face was calm and sorrowful; Elias' beamed triumphantly, and authority promenaded over his lips, eyebrows, and imposing lower jaw.

THE NEXT DAY Francis bent down and kissed the threshold of the Portiuncula. Then, groping in the air, he found my hand. "Come, poor Brother Leo. We are being driven out of our home."

He started along the path through the woods, stumbling every few steps. I had to keep a tight grip on his hand to prevent him from bumping into the trees. As soon as we finally reached the hut of branches which he had built in the forest with his own hands, he sat down on the ground and swept his gaze around him.

"Has the world grown dark, Brother Leo," he cried, "or have I become completely blind? I don't see anything, Brother Leo, I don't see anything!"

"Father Silvester knows many secret cures," I replied. "Among other things he can heal eye diseases, or so I've heard. I'll go call him."

"No, no, Brother Leo, let me be. I'm fine here in the darkness. True, I don't see the world about me, but I'm able all the better to see its Creator."

He fell silent. His pains had grown continually more acute, and in order to forget them for an instant he directed his thoughts elsewhere. "How is Sister Clara?" he inquired, asking me to come close to him because he was unable to raise his voice. "How is she? I almost forgot her, it's been such a long time now. But God, I'm sure, did not forget her. Tell me, what has become of her?"

"She followed your instructions, Brother Francis, and went to San Damiano's to lead the life of an ascetic. As soon as the ladies of Assisi heard about it they started coming to ask questions, and many were reluctant to return home, for Clara's life seemed extraordinarily sweet to them. They all revere her. The very first who ran to remain at her side was her sister Agnes: she too entered the convent, cut off her hair, and donned the robe. And there were also others who looked with favor upon the Bridegroom—unmarried girls, and even two or three married women. Clara is like a drop of honey. The bees arrive from all directions, distribute their possessions to the poor, bid farewell to the tumult of the world, and come to find the peace of God at San Damiano's."

"May God assist them," said Francis. "Women are wild, savage beasts. Only God Almighty is capable of subduing them. Only He!"

"You may rest assured, Brother Francis, that Clara is following in your footsteps—one by one. Like you, she visits the lepers, and washes and feeds them; like you, she throws ashes onto her dish to prevent her food from being tasty and giving pleasure to the flesh. All night long she lies awake, praying. Her body has grown old already, her cheeks have withered, her eyes are dimmed with tears. In this way she is preparing to appear before God. Father Silvester is the only one among all the friars who goes from time to time to learn what is happening at her convent. And if any of the sisters wishes to receive Holy Communion, he hears her confession."

I hesitated for a moment, but finally decided to go on.

"Brother Francis, with your permission I am going to say something else to you: The life at San Damiano's is holier than the life at the Portiuncula. Why? Because Sister Clara keeps a firm grip on the reins, while you surrendered them—and to whom: to Elias!"

"Not I," Francis protested, "not I, but God. I heard His voice. He commanded me to do it."

I shook my head. "You know very well, Brother Francis, that Satan is able to counterfeit God's voice in order to ensnare mankind."

A shudder passed through Francis' body. "Be still!" he cried. "You're tearing my heart in two. If it wasn't God's voice, I'm doomed!"

The discharge from his eyes began to flow again; the excruciating pains recommenced. Moved by pity for him, I approached and threw my arms around him.

"Forgive me, Brother Francis. Yes, yes, it was God's voice. Do not cry."

He said nothing. He had covered his eyes with his palms and was groaning with pain.

That night he could not sleep. He kept stepping outside so that his moans would not wake me—but how could I even close my eyes! It broke my heart to hear him. As soon as daylight came I went to find Father Silvester.

"Go back and light a fire," he instructed me. "I'll follow presently with the cautery—and may God come to our aid!"

I found Francis seated in front of the doorway with his head wedged between his knees, as was his custom, and his arms and legs squeezed into a ball. He was sleeping. Walking on tiptoe, I entered the hut and lighted a fire. Then I sat down next to him to wait for Father Silvester. Francis sighed from time to time: he must have been dreaming. His knees were quivering; his head kept falling lower and lower. A little more and it would have touched the ground.

The sound of Father Silvester's footsteps behind the trees disturbed him, and he awoke. Stretching out his hand, he found me.

"Is that you, Brother Leo?"

"Yes, Brother Francis. Set your mind at ease. Why are you trembling so?"

"Kneel down, Brother Leo, kneel down and join me in calling Brother Death to come. I can't go on."

As he was talking, Father Silvester appeared before us holding a long piece of iron in his hand.

"Who are you?" asked Francis, apprehensively.

"It's me, Father Silvester. I've come to heal your eyes. With God's help, I'm going to make your pain go away so that you can devote yourself to prayer again."

"Pain is prayer too, Father Silvester; it too is prayer. . . ." Sighing, he lay down supine on the ground.

Father Silvester crossed himself and thrust the iron into the fire, leaving it there until it became red-hot. Then he removed it and approached. Francis was able to discern the priest's shadow above him, and also the red-hot iron he had in his hand. He stretched forth his arms.

243

"Brother Red-hot Iron," he said imploringly, "do not force me to suffer too much, I beg of you. I am made of flesh, not of iron like you, and my endurance is not very great."

"Call upon God to give you courage, Brother Francis," said Father Silvester. "Clench your teeth and cling to your soul for dear life. This is going to be painful."

But before Francis had time to call upon God, Father Silvester had already applied the red-hot iron to the sick man's temples. Francis uttered a heart-rending cry and fainted. We threw some water over his face, then lifted him up, brought him inside the hut, and laid him down on his mat. He began to twist and turn, to writhe convulsively, screaming for Brother Death to come and release him.

Father Silvester remained at his side, praying. I sank to the ground and began to weep.

When Francis recovered from his fit and raised his head, I shuddered. His temples were two deep wounds, his eyes two fountains of blood. He stretched out his hand to find my arm, and clung to it desperately.

"Brother Leo, Brother Leo," he gasped, "tell me that God is infinitely merciful; otherwise my mind shall sink into chaos. Tell me He is infinitely merciful: give me the strength to go on!"

"Think of Christ on the cross," I replied. "Think of the nails in His hands and feet, the blood that ran from His side."

Francis shook his head. "He was God; I am only clay!"

He sat up on the mat, thrust his head between his knees as before, and did not utter another word that entire day.

Toward nightfall I ran to the Portiuncula to beg a few pieces of bread from the brothers. It was a turbulent evening. The object plummeting down behind the trees was not the sun, it was a huge fiery cannonball that ignited the forest as it passed—the forest, stones, and, in the distance, the high citadel of Assisi: all were encased in flame. I ran, suddenly overwhelmed by a strange fear. This sun, the flaming trees, and, inside me, my heart: everything seemed to have caught fire, and I was running lest the conflagration engulf me as well. The moment I stood in front of the Portiuncula, however, I felt calm. The sight of our order's beloved, orphaned cradle made me recall the hours we had spent there, hours sweet beyond description: the holy prayers, the holy conversations, the holy dinners where one dry crust of bread satisfied our hunger; and Francis beaming among us like a kindly sun. . . . I stood still for a few minutes to catch my breath. Inside I could hear the friars laughing heartily. One of them was mimicking Francis' voice while the others split their sides. But as soon as I entered and they saw me, they fell silent. The original brothers were absent, the new ones busy eating their dinner, which was spread before them on the ground.

"What's become of the sweet little pauper?" one of them asked. "Doesn't he sing and dance any more?"

"We could hear his screams even here," replied another. "Father Silvester went to extract his eyes, I think."

I did not answer them. My heart had risen up threateningly and begun to hiss inside me like a viper, full of venom. I knew that insults and curses would come out of my mouth if I opened it, and since I feared God, I held my peace. Taking the scrap of bread they threw me, I left.

Because of Francis' illness, we could no longer think of going away. Father Silvester came daily, and one morning he brought Francis a message from San Damiano's.

"Sister Clara kisses your hand, Brother Francis, and begs you to visit her. She says you still have not been to her convent to bless the sisters; that they still have not had a chance to see you and to hear a comforting word from your lips. They are women after all, and though they are safe in God's bosom, they still have need of comforting. . . . Sister Clara sends the following message through my mouth: 'Bestow upon us the gift of your presence at San Damiano's, Brother Francis, so that we may see you, listen to you, and be comforted.' "

Francis shook his head. "What do you think, Father Silvester? Should I go?"

"Yes, Brother Francis. They're women. Take pity on them."

"Father Silvester, once more I am going to speak by means of parables. Brother Leo, you listen too. Oh, if only all the friars were here to listen!

"One day, the father superior of a monastery expelled one of the monks for having touched a woman's hand. 'But she was a devout woman and her hand was pure,' protested the monk. The father

245

superior replied: 'The rain is pure also, and so is the earth, but when they join they become mud. It is the same when a man's hand touches the hand of a woman.'"

"Those are hard words, Brother Francis," said Father Silvester, "hard for women to hear."

"They're even harder for men," I said, fearfully recalling all the young ladies I had seen in my life: all the hands I had desired to touch. Thousands!

"Think of the Blessed Virgin," suggested Father Silvester.

"No one touched her hand, not even Joseph," Francis replied, crossing himself repeatedly. "You seem to have forgotten Eve!"

"Well, in any case, what answer should I give Sister Clara? She'll be standing at the door of San Damiano's waiting for me. What shall I tell her?"

"Tell her I'll come when the road from the Portiuncula to San Damiano's is covered with white flowers."

"In other words, never—is that what you mean?"

"*Never* and *always*, Father Silvester, are two words which only God may utter. It's possible that right now, now while we are talking, God has paved the road with white flowers. Brother Leo, go and look!"

Father Silvester shook his head skeptically, but I got up and rushed outside, my heart thumping. I started along the path through the woods. It was still morning, and so cold out that you would have thought the ground covered with snow. My heartbeats seemed to ascend to my throat. I was certain of the miracle: I smelled it in the air. Francis' bloodstained face had beamed when he turned and said to me, "Brother Leo, go and look!"—for in his mind the road had already blossomed.

I ran, reached the highway, and immediately let forth a shout: the entire road—hedges, stones, dirt—was blanketed everywhere with white flowers, as far as the eye could see! Falling to my knees, I gave thanks to the Invisible. Then I pulled up a handful of flowers, rushed back to the hut, and entered, breathing heavily from exertion and joy.

"Brother Francis," I shrieked, "the road is covered with white flowers. Look, I've brought you a handful."

Father Silvester fell at Francis' feet and kissed them. "Forgive me, Brother Francis. I shook my head; I did not have faith."

246

Taking the flowers, Francis placed them over his bloody eyelids and upon the wounds at his temples. "Father . . . Father . . ." he murmured, kissing the petals again and again, and weeping.

"Why are you surprised?" he asked, turning to us. "Everything is a miracle. What is the water we drink, the earth we tread, the night which descends upon us each evening with its stars; what are the sun, the moon? Miracles, all of them! Just look at the humblest leaf of a tree, just look at it in the light—what a miracle! The Crucifixion is painted on one side; you turn the leaf over on the other and what do you see: the Resurrection! It is not a leaf, my brothers, it is our hearts!"

Father Silvester kissed Francis' hand. "Brother Francis, you asked for a sign from God and it came: the Lord strewed the road with flowers. Shall I go tell Sister Clara to expect you?"

"Yes, tell her I am coming. Tell her it is not because I wanted to, but because God commanded me. And bring her these flowers which fell from heaven. When they touched the earth they became all covered with blood."

With these words, he gave Father Silvester the bloodstained flowers which he had been holding in his hand.

After Father Silvester's departure I knelt down to light a fire. I heated water and then washed Francis' face, cleaned his feet and hands, and tidied his hair, using my fingers as a comb. He, his arms spread wide, allowed me to tend to him as though he were a small child. When I had finished I took hold of both his hands and lifted him up. But his knees gave way beneath him; he was unable to stand erect.

"How are we going to go, Brother Francis?" I asked in despair. "Your knees won't support you."

"Forget my knees, Brother Leo, and worry about my soul. That will support me. . . . Start walking!"

Biting his lips, exerting all his strength, he left the hut. We started along the path.

"Brother Leo," he said as soon as we were outdoors, "how many times must I tell you that the soul of man is a divine spark—in other words, that it is all-powerful. But we do not know this, and we squash it under our flesh, under our fat. Ah, if we could only let it go free!"

He hesitated for a moment, and then:

"You believe I'm unable to walk, do you? You believe my soul is unable to support my body? Now you shall see!"

He began to stride along the path, his knees firm and unsagging. When we reached the wide road we looked for the flowers, but they had vanished—it was as though they had been a layer of winter hoarfrost melted by the rising sun. Francis crossed himself.

"This is a miracle too," he said. "The flowers came down from heaven, delivered their message, and then returned. They did not want human feet to step on them."

Falling silent, he set out in the direction of San Damiano's, proceeding gingerly along the very edge of the road. Sister Clara, followed by two of the nuns, had already left the convent in order to receive Francis. When she caught sight of him she halted, crossed her arms, and waited with downcast eyes; but as soon as she was able to hear the sound of his footsteps she raised her head and blushed to the roots of her hair.

"God be with you, Sister Clara; God be with you all, my sisters," said Francis in greeting, and he held out his hand to bless them.

"Welcome to our home, Father Francis," Clara replied. "We've been expecting you for thousands of years."

She fell prostrate before him and kissed his feet.

"Do not complain, Sister Clara," answered Francis. "I sent you messages regularly through Father Silvester."

Clara prostrated herself once more, requesting permission to speak.

"Messages do not satisfy us, Father Francis. Words which come from far away are nothing but wind, air—and they scatter. We are women. To be calmed we must see the movement of the lips that are addressing us, we must feel upon our heads the hand that is held over us in benediction. We are women, I tell you. If you refuse to come here to comfort us with your words, Father Francis, we are lost."

The two of them walked ahead, still conversing, while we others followed behind. When Francis reached the convent door he halted, swept away by the sight before him. What a lovely little garden—it was Paradise! How sweet the flowers smelled!

"What did you plant in the courtyard, Sister Clara? I can't see clearly."

"Lilies and roses, Brother Francis. And in autumn we have violets. That's all."

Francis extended his hand and blessed the yard. "Sister Yard, Sisters Lilies and Roses, I am delighted to be here with you! May it please our gracious Lord that on the Day of Judgment you too shall rise from the earth and enter heaven together with Sister Clara."

He stepped inside. The walls were whitewashed with lime; the statue of the Blessed Virgin showed Our Lady smiling as she clasped her Son tightly to her breast. The sisters prostrated themselves, kissing Francis' feet, and he in turn placed his hand on each of their heads and blessed them. They were all tightly wrapped in white wimples, and when they walked, they resembled doves.

A stool was brought for Francis. Clara knelt on the floor next to him, while the sisters remained standing behind, their arms crossed. For a long time no one spoke. Every eye was fixed upon the saintly visitor. How sweet that silence was, how secure we all felt! I was certain that throngs of angels had come down to San Damiano's and were now standing unseen in the air, waiting like the rest of us for Francis to speak. He, however, was in no hurry. You could sense from the expression on his face that he was rapt in unspeakable exultation.

"How clean, how fragrant that air was," he said to me later; "how long it's been since I enjoyed the odor of freshly washed clothes, and of trunks which fill the room with the fragrance of mint and laurel the moment you open them!"

"Take pity on us, Father Francis; let us hear your voice," said Sister Clara finally, kissing the hem of his robe.

Francis raised his head with a start and stretched his arms, as though awakening. "I am glad to be here, my sisters. What more do you expect me to say? When I was in the world and used to hold banquets for my friends, I would throw back my head and sing:

> *A thousand greetings, my friends,*
> *Ten thousand greetings to you!*
> *The valley is covered with flowers,*
> *The fields with verdure and dew.*

My sisters, the same song rises now from my heart: a thousand and ten thousand greetings

He was extremely moved. I had not seen him so happy for ages. This was the atmosphere he loved: the purity, cleanliness, and ardor which now surrounded him—also those white wimples! He spoke again:

"Listen to me, my sisters, and forgive me if I tell you about a caterpillar that just came again to my mind. This is not a story, it's true—truer than truth itself. . . . Well, once there was a caterpillar which crawled and crawled, until finally in its extreme old age it arrived before the gates of heaven. It knocked and a voice came from within: 'No caterpillars allowed here! You're in much too much of a hurry, it seems to me.'

" 'What shall I do, Lord? Command me,' answered the caterpillar, and it curled up into a ball, it was so afraid.

" 'Suffer some more, struggle some more, transform yourself into a butterfly!'

"The caterpillar returned to earth accordingly, my sisters, and began its journey all over again from the beginning."

"Tell us who this caterpillar is, Father Francis," Clara begged. "We are simple uneducated women. Enlighten us."

"The caterpillar is me, Sister Clara, and you, and also all the sisters listening to me, and every person who crawls upon earth. Good God, what feats this poor wretched caterpillar must accomplish before being transformed into a butterfly! Struggle and more struggle, my sisters, ascent along the uphill road, extreme suffering; and purity, love, poverty, hunger, nakedness, tears—all these are required! Satan has laid his snares everywhere; they are just waiting for us to fall in. If you bend down to smell a flower, my sisters, you will find him there; if you lift a stone he will be hidden beneath and waiting; if you see a blossoming almond tree he will be crouching in the branches, ready to pounce upon you. He is in the water we drink, the bread we eat, the bed on which we lie down to go to sleep: Satan is hidden everywhere, my sisters, everywhere—hidden and waiting. What is he waiting for? For our souls to become momentarily fatigued and drowsy, for the instant when they cease to stand as our ever-vigilant sentinels, and thus enable him to leap on us and drag us down into hell. My sisters, you are the ones I am thinking of, the ones I pity—much more than the men; because you are women, and your hearts do not steel themselves easily against the beauties of the world. You look upon them and they please you. Flowers, children, men, earrings, silk garments, stunning plumes: my God, what snares! How many women can possibly escape?

"Morning and evening, my sisters, you pray for all those women on earth who adorn themselves with cosmetics and jewelry, for all those women who laugh. In heaven, the Blessed Virgin echoes your prayer. Don't you hear a deep, divine silence above your heads at night, and in the midst of this silence a sound like the rustling of the leaves of the poplar: the sound of invisible lips praying and beseeching? It is the Virgin Mary, and she is praying for all women everywhere.

"But you must be on your guard, my sisters. Do not say to yourselves: 'We have entered the convent, we have escaped the world and are now promenading in heaven.' This thought is a trap, my sisters, a trap laid by Satan. Listen to what I am going to tell you. We are all one—I swear it to you. If a single woman somewhere at the ends of the earth paints her lips, the shameful color spreads over your lips as well! What is the definition of heaven? Complete happiness. But how can anyone be completely happy when he looks out from heaven and sees his brothers and sisters being punished in hell? How can Paradise exist if the Inferno exists also? That is why I say—and let this sink deep down into your minds, my sisters—that either we shall all be saved, all of us together, or else we shall all be damned. If a person is killed at the other end of the earth, we are killed; if a person is saved, we are saved."

Francis' words made my heart pound with astonishment, for this was the first time I had ever heard him embrace the world with such overabundant love. His heart had blossomed luxuriantly in this feminine air; as he looked at the sisters, his compassion sprouted wings which covered the entire earth.

The nuns had all fallen to their knees. Creeping slowly forward until they encircled Francis, they gazed at him in ecstasy, their faces beaming as though being struck by the sun.

Francis felt their warm exhalation upon him. He parted his lips once more:

"The awareness of your presence around me makes my heart expand, my sisters, makes it desire everyone to enter it—everyone, the wicked as well as the virtuous, so that there may be an end to lamentation and wailing both in this world and the next. O God, a rebellious thought is mounting from my heart to my lips. Permit me to reveal it to these women, for they are my sisters. Their hearts are feminine, full of love and compassion—they will understand. Listen, my sisters: Now, at this moment—O God, forgive me!—I feel sorry even for Satan. There is no creature more unfortunate, more wretched than he, because once he was with God, but now he has left Him, denied Him, and he roams the air, inconsolable. Why is he inconsolable? Because God allowed him to retain his memory. Recalling the sweetness of Paradise as he does, how can he ever be consoled? We must pray for Satan too, my sisters; we must pray that our gracious Lord will take pity on him, forgive him, permit him to return and take up his place among the archangels.

"Love: that—God bless it!—is woman's destined role. Satan is an ugly bloodthirsty beast, but if he is kissed on the mouth he becomes an archangel once more. That, my sisters, is Perfect Love. In the same way, let Perfect Love kiss Satan so that his original, radiant face may be restored to him.

"Love . . . Love!" Francis cried until his voice was stifled by sobs. Then he lowered his face into his palms and gave himself up to weeping.

Tears began to fall from Clara's eyes as well. Soon she was joined by all the sisters, and lamentations echoed throughout the convent. When Francis heard this, he raised his head, extended his arms, and said in a troubled voice: "I did not intend to make you weep, my sisters. Forgive me. I came to talk to you about heaven, not about hell, and I wanted you to talk to me about heaven also, so that we all could be comforted. Life is oppressive; if Brother Death did not exist to open the door and let us depart—my God! What an unbearable prison this earth would be, what an unbearable prison our bodies would be! But now (what joy, what an ineffable hope—no, not a hope, a certainty), now the soul has crowned itself with lemonflowers and begun to advance over the stones and precipices of the earth, crying, 'O my beloved husband, my beloved husband—Thou, Lord!' "

One of the nuns felt faint. Sister Clara had the window which overlooked the courtyard opened, and the scent of lilies and roses invaded the air. Then, growing bold, she touched Francis' knee and said in a soft voice, "Father Francis, when I look at you I feel that Adam never sinned."

Francis allowed his hand to rest lightly on her white wimple. "And I, when I look at you, Sister Clara," he replied, "feel that Eve never sinned."

For a long time there was silence, a silence overflowing with sweetness and compassion, as though Francis had never stopped speaking. All the sisters, without ceasing their laments, continued to listen to the unspoken words. It seemed to them that Francis was still discoursing about woman's destiny, about love, about the kiss which transforms Satan into an archangel. It was the first time they had felt what an infinitely divine gift it was to be a woman, and also what a responsibility.

Suddenly in the midst of this hallowed silence we heard violent banging on the street door. It flew open, and in rushed the friars from the Portiuncula. They were quivering with fright.

Clara jumped to her feet. "What's wrong, my brothers? Why did you force our door?"

Juniper wiped the sweat from his brow and replied, "Forgive us, Sister Clara, but while we were at the Portiuncula we saw flames leaping toward the sky. Your convent is on fire!"

"Fire! Fire!" screamed all the brothers. "Fire, Sister Clara!"

But Clara smiled. "You did not see flames, my brothers; it wasn't a fire you saw, it was simply Father Francis talking."

The sun was about to set. Francis rose and said goodbye to Clara and the sisters. Once more he blessed them, placing his hand on the head of each.

"You did a wonderful thing for us, Father Francis," said Clara. "You consoled woman's inconsolable heart. Now what can we do for you?"

"I actually do have something to ask of you, my sister. A very great favor."

"Command us, Father Francis," cried all the nuns.

"I would like you to beg a patch from each poor man you meet, and with the patches you collect, to sew me a robe. This is the favor I ask of you."

Clara kissed his hand. "Why don't you ask me to give you my very life, Father Francis? Next Sunday, God willing, we shall deliver the robe you desire to Father Silvester, and he will bring it to you."

We left, Francis walking in the lead with firm knees while the rest of us followed, conversing jubilantly about the miracle. Behind us, Clara and the sisters stood at the street door of the convent to watch us depart, and many were the tears they were forced to wipe from their eyes.

Francis did not speak the whole of the next day. He curled up in front of the hut at dawn and remained there, sunning himself. The air was warm, a gentle breeze was blowing; from time to time one of the friars appeared on his way to bring water, cut wood, or pick some wild chicory. A blackbird kept passing overhead; it would whistle two or three times and then vanish. Since Francis could not see well, he pricked up his ears and listened avidly to the world about him. His features were so rapt in ecstasy that I dared not approach him the entire day, but when, toward evening, the flame subsided, I went to him and sat down on the threshold, at his side.

Stretching out his hand, he "saw" me. "What a miracle this is, Brother Leo!" he exclaimed. "Ever since the day my sight decreased, the sounds I hear have been indescribably sweet. Oh, the rustling in the trees, the swarms of birds in the air!"

He was quiet for a moment, and then:

"Since the day my sight decreased, Brother Leo, I have been able to see the invisible. My inner eye is open now. Today, all day long, its circle of vision grew continually larger. In the beginning I was able to see from here—from this doorway where I am sitting—to the Portiuncula. I had a clear view of the brothers there as they argued with each other, or prayed, and I could see Father Silvester standing apart from the rest and weeping with bowed head. After that, the circle widened and I saw Assisi with its towers, campaniles, and houses, its lanes crowded with people, the young girls sitting in their doorways embroidering; and my own mother on her knees behind the window, tears flowing down her cheeks. Afterwards, the illuminated arena grew still wider and I saw Rome: its wide streets, perfumed lords and rouged ladies, the pope reflecting on the state of Christendom, his venerable head resting on his palm; and by the riverbank the savage white-robed monk lighting fagots in his imagination in order to burn heretics and infidels. . . . After that I saw still further—blue sea, white islands, fierce Crete, then Egypt with the Sultan: he was galloping away on his horse, and is galloping still, trying to escape the Cross which is pursuing him. . . . Finally, Brother Leo: great brightness, huge stars, and the seven heavenly spheres with saints, archangels, angels, cherubim, seraphim—and then all at once my sight grew dim, I became blind, and it seemed to me that I fainted. I had obviously gone closer to God than He permits."

I said nothing, happy that his soul could travel across heaven and earth by means of visions and enable him in this way to forget his afflictions. For although his wounds had run the entire day, the blood dripping from his beard until it transformed the ground below into a quagmire, he had been far far away from his body, and had not felt the slightest pain.

He remained silent for several minutes, but then, weighing his words carefully, he said, "Brother Leo, man's body is the ark of the Old Testament, and God travels inside it."

It was growing dark. Chirping came from every tree; grasshoppers and crickets, the first voices of the night, began their song. Two low-flying bats darted silently back and forth in front of us, and at one point one of them came within a hair's breadth of becoming tangled in Francis' hair.

"What was that?" he asked me, shaking his head violently. "A wing just touched my head."

"A damned bat, Brother Francis. A plague on it!"

"All living things have their history, Brother Leo; you must never speak ill of any of them. The moment you know the history of a man, a wild animal, or a bird, your ill feelings will turn to love. Do you know the bat's history?"

"No. But you are going to tell me, Brother Francis."

"All right, listen. At first the bat was a mouse living in the basement of a church. One night it emerged from its hole, climbed onto the altar, and began to nibble at a consecrated wafer. As it ate, wings sprouted on its back and it became our sister the bat."

The bat passed in front of us again, hunting for mosquitoes.

"I beg your pardon, Sister Bat," I said, lifting my hand. "I wasn't aware that your wings were made of consecrated wafer."

Francis, meanwhile, had cupped his hand over his ear. He was listening to the flow of the river below us.

"Listen, Brother Leo, listen to the river singing down in the gorge, listen to how impatient it is, how it races to flow into the sea. Our souls are impatient in the same way, Brother Leo: they race to flow into heaven. O Lord, when will they arrive?"

"Take your time, take your time, Brother Francis. You're still needed on earth. Didn't you see how much good you did the sisters at San Damiano's yesterday? They couldn't keep themselves from wailing, the joy you gave them was so intense."

Francis sighed. "What did I say there? I was drunk! O Lord, forgive me!"

"Why? Because you felt sorry for Satan, Brother Francis? Because you yearned to implore God to pardon him?"

"No, no!" replied Francis, his voice full of affliction. "Because the presence of women threw my heart into turmoil. O Lord, why must the flesh be so powerful, so completely indestructible? It is useless to starve it, whip it, not allow it to sleep; useless to plunge it into the snow to freeze it to death, useless to make it a shovelful of mud. Through all this it remains untamed, unyielding; it continues to hold the red banner aloft, it continues to shout!"

Francis had suddenly caught fire. He rose.

"Get up, Brother Leo! In the name of holy Obedience I command you to repeat whatever I say, to repeat it exactly, without altering a single word. Will you do it?"

"I took a vow never to disobey you, Brother Francis. Command me."

"Very well then, let's begin. I'll say, 'Woe is you, Francis! You committed so many sins in your life that you won't be saved, but shall go to the very bottom of hell!' And you will answer, 'True, true, you committed so many sins in your life, Francis, that you won't be saved, but shall go to the very bottom of hell!' Are you ready?"

"Ready, Brother Francis."

"Well, why don't you speak!"

"Joy unto you, Brother Francis. You committed so many good deeds in your life that you shall go and sit at the very summit of Paradise!"

Francis gazed at me in amazement.

"Why don't you obey me, Brother Leo? You heard what I said, didn't you? What are these words I hear? I command you in the name of holy Obedience to repeat the words exactly as I instruct you."

"With pleasure, Brother Francis. Speak. I shall obey."

"All right then, I'll say, 'Wicked Francis, do you have the impudence to expect mercy after all the sins you have committed in your life? No, no, you accursed sinner, God will throw you into hell!' Now it's your turn, Brother Leo. Listen well to what you're going to say to me: 'Yes, yes, God will throw you into hell!' Speak!"

"No, no, blessed Francis, God's mercy is infinitely greater than your sins. Everything will be forgiven you and you will enter Paradise."

This time Francis became angry. Seizing me by the shoulder, he shook me violently.

"How dare you oppose my will! Why do you insist on answering the opposite of what I tell you? For the last time, in the name of holy Obedience I command you to obey."

"With pleasure, Brother Francis. I swear I'll repeat what you say exactly, without changing a word."

Francis began to beat his breast. Fear gushed from his eyes. He was chastising himself, weeping, and talking all at the same time.

"Wicked, accursed Francis, there is no salvation for you! There is no mercy for you! The Inferno has opened its mouth and is swallowing you."

"Brother Francis," I cried—I too was weeping now—"O saint and great martyr, God is infinitely merciful; Poverty, Love, and Chastity, the three great saints, are standing on the golden threshold of Paradise waiting to receive you; and holy Chastity has a crown of thorns in her hand."

Francis sank to my feet. Frightened, I fell down next to him.

"Brother Francis, why are you hugging my knees?"

"Why must you torment me so, Brother Leo? Why must you continually oppose my will?" he cried amidst his tears.

"Brother Francis, I kiss your hands and beg you to forgive me. It's not my fault, however. I swear to you that the moment I open my mouth to repeat what you command me to say, my tongue—without my knowing how, or wanting it to—simply goes out of control. I hear a voice inside me which is more powerful than your voice, and whatever it says to me, I say to you. This voice must be God's, my bro——"

"It must be Satan's, you mean!" Francis interrupted me. "The devil wants to lull my soul to sleep; he wants me to be left unguarded so that he can enter me. But I won't let him!"

Rising, he undid his knotted cord and tossed it to me. "Take this cord, Brother Leo, take it and beat me. Do you hear: beat me until I bleed."

As soon as he had said this he bared the upper part of his body. The sight of it filled me with pity. What was there to strike? Nothing but bones wrapped in a skin that was discolored from repeated floggings and covered everywhere with welts and scars.

"Have you no mercy for me, Brother Francis?" I cried. "How can I lift my hand against you?"

This was too much for Francis. "I warn you, Brother Leo," he cried in a rage, "I warn you that unless you do what I tell you, I'll leave! We shall part, Brother Leo! Yes, by the heaven that is above us, we shall part!"

He turned his back to me. "Goodbye!"

I was terror-stricken, for I realized that he had made up his mind and was actually going to do it. "Brother Francis," I replied, baring my own back, "for every blow I give you I am going to give myself two. I beg you not to deny me this favor!"

He leaned forward without answering, and I began to flog him with the knotted cord; also to flog myself. In the beginning I hit him lightly, but this only served to anger him. "Harder, harder," he shouted. "How can you feel pity for this flesh, this whore!" I began to strike harder, one blow for Francis, two for myself; and as I swung, my rage increased. It was something quite involuntary: I was carried away, carried away by a strange intoxication, and though the pain was intense, the more I suffered, the more someone inside me rejoiced. I kept uttering wild, happy cries; I felt as though I were finally taking my revenge on a beast that had harmed me and had now fallen into my hands. The knotted cord was red with both Francis' blood and my own, but I, far from bringing the thrashing to an end, continued to strike mercilessly.

"That's enough, Brother Leo," said Francis. He had grown perfectly calm.

I pretended not to hear. I had worked up momentum, and I kept beating my chest and back, ever avid for more. The pain made me writhe and twist: I was dancing. I had done many bad things in my life, and now it seemed to me that I had begun to pay for them and unburden myself. . . . Remember the woman you chased through the osiers, the one who got away from you? Remember the bread you stole from a certain oven? There, take that! Liar, coward, glutton, fornicator, drunkard: take that! And that! Thus I continued to beat myself, rejoicing and finding relief.

"Enough!" Francis commanded once more, and, wrenching the bloody cord out of my grip, he tied it around his waist. "Enough, enough, Brother Leo. We must retain a little strength so that we can begin again tomorrow morning."

"I had a very good time, Brother Francis," I said as I collapsed to the ground from exhaustion.

"You did not have a good time; you suffered. It's exactly the same thing."

We went inside. I lit a fire, squatted down next to the hearth, and in a few moments was asleep. In my dreams I saw myself holding a small roast pig in my arms, sucking in its juice.

Bernard and Sior Pietro came to visit us early one morning. Kissing Francis' hand, they sat down, one on either side of him. It was still cold out, the fire was going, and all three kept their faces turned toward the hearth. No one spoke, but from time to time Francis reached out to touch Bernard on his right and Pietro on his left, as though wishing to make certain they were still near him. Then he would join his hands together again in an attitude of prayer, his face beaming with joy. . . . I stood in the back corner, watching them. They resembled three veteran warriors who had met once more on a cold day after years of separation, and had lit a fire to warm themselves. I had pricked up my ears in order to overhear what they said, but none of them opened his mouth. You felt that the air between them was vibrating, however, and that a string of unspoken words was being unwound from mouth to mouth. Without the slightest doubt, this was how the angels spoke in heaven. How long did their silence last—how many hours? It seemed to me that time had come to a standstill, that one hour and one century were of the same length. Eternity must be the same, I reflected: stationary and mute.

The fire had gone out; the sun had mounted a spear's-length above the horizon. Bernard and Pietro rose. Stooping, they kissed Francis' knees, then his hand and shoulders. Francis began to weep, and the other two joined him. All three fell into each other's arms and remained motionless, prolonging their embrace as long as possible. Then, slowly, without uttering a word, they separated. The two friars walked to the door, crossed the threshold, and disappeared behind the trees.

As soon as I remained alone with Francis, I sat down next to him. My tongue was itching me: I wanted to speak.

"Why didn't any of you talk, Brother Francis?" I asked. "You hadn't seen each other for ages. It's strange that none of you had anything to say."

"But we did, Brother Leo," replied Francis with surprise. "We spoke; we were speaking the whole time. We told each other everything, and when we had nothing more to say, we parted."

"I didn't hear a word, Brother Francis."

He smiled. "Which ears were you listening with? You should have listened not with those two clay ones that stick out so far on either side of your head; not with those, but with the others, the inner ears."

He stroked my shoulder. "You know, of course, that we have inner ears and eyes and an inner tongue made not of clay, but of flame. It is with these, Brother Leo, that you must hear, see, and talk!"

Early Sunday morning Father Silvester brought the robe which the nuns had sewn for Francis out of the scores of patches they had begged from the poor, each pauper contributing one patch as a gift to Poverty's bridegroom. Francis clasped the robe to his bosom, kissed the mud-bespattered patches one by one, then blessed holy Poverty, his wife.

"Whoever does not crave riches is rich; whoever is rich but craves further riches is poor. I, praise the Lord, am the richest king on earth, Brother Leo, and this frock is my royal robe."

"Enjoy it in good health, Brother Francis. It is the wedding gift sent you by your wife Poverty."

He put on the new robe and began joyfully to admire himself.

There were black patches, blue patches, green patches—patches of every conceivable color—and as Francis walked with the robe swelling out around him in the breeze, he resembled some strange piebald bird that had borrowed a feather from each of its brothers in the airy kingdom.

"Brother Leo," he said to me, "I long to see the friars, I long for them to see me. They might still be at church. Come, let's go hear Mass with them."

His eyes had improved during the last few days, his knees had grown somewhat firm. He led the way, pushing aside the branches, and I followed behind, entirely happy. Francis is like a child, I was thinking, like a child—that's why I love him. Now he's going to the brothers to show off his new robe!

The skies were threatening; a warm raindrop struck my lips. Francis raised his head, gazed upward, and stretched out his hand as though begging the heavens to give him a drop too. "What is this great joy I feel, Brother Leo?" he asked, turning to me. "It's as though I had put on the whole world's poverty, as though I had lifted the whole world's poor onto my shoulders and begun to march with them. To go where? To take them where? God grant that it may be to heaven! Yes, poverty really suits us, Brother Leo —it suits us like a red silk ribbon in the hair of a sweet little girl!"

Suddenly we heard Elias' thunderous voice behind the trees. He was preaching a sermon. Francis stopped, hesitated. He seemed to want to turn back.

"Brother Elias is talking," he whispered. "Mass is over; he must be explaining the Gospel."

"No doubt he's interpreting Christ's message to make it fit his own needs," I replied with malice. I just could not stomach this brother. In my thoughts—forgive me, Lord—instead of calling him Elias I called him Judas.

Francis gave me a severe look. "Brother Leo, the earth has seven levels, heaven has seven spheres, and yet the total is still too small for God. But man's heart is not too small—the Lord can fit within it. Take care, therefore, that you do not wound man's heart, for in doing so you may be wounding God."

As soon as he had said this, he continued on toward the Portiuncula, his head bowed.

The tiny church was buzzing like a beehive. Elias, the high staff in his hand, stood on a stool in the middle; he was addressing the brothers, who thronged everywhere around him. Never had I known a man so willful as this Elias, so insatiably avid, so capable of projecting power from his entire body—except perhaps Francis' father, Sior Bernardone.

When Francis entered, several of the friars turned and noticed him, but no one budged. A few laughed when they saw his robe. Though Elias had caught sight of the visitor, he made no attempt to step down from his stool to welcome him. Francis inched his way along the wall until he found a corner he could squeeze into. Bowing his head, he began to listen. Elias was speaking about the new Rule which the brothers were henceforth to follow. I learned subsequently from Father Silvester that he had been working on it day and night for the past week, for the old one did not please him. He regarded it as too naïve, too narrow: it constricted him.

"Times have changed," he was shouting, "times have changed, people have changed, and so has the countenance of heaven and earth. The old truths have become falsehoods; the old virtues are the swaddling bands in which our order was protected when it was an infant, but now that we have grown it is imperative that these old bands be unwrapped and that we be allowed to breathe freely. The new Rule, my brothers, brings you these new truths and new virtues."

He raised the shepherd's crook and cast a swift, flashing glance at Francis.

"Whoever does not agree," he cried, "let him rise and leave. Discipline is the most rigid of our new virtues. There is no room in our brotherhood for more than one opinion. We are not irregulars, but soldiers in a standing army which is waging war. This Rule is our general."

As soon as he had said this he unrolled a huge scroll covered with red and black letters.

"I have explained each of the new commandments to you and what Poverty, Love, Chastity, and Obedience shall mean to us from this moment on. Raise your hands and shout 'Aye!' "

All the brothers raised their hands and shouted "Aye! Aye!"—all except Francis and me, who were the only ones to remain with crossed arms. Elias' thunderous voice resounded once again:

"Happy is the brother, happy the brotherhood, that keeps pace with the rhythm of the times. Alas for him"—he threw a second flashing glance at Francis—"alas for him who lags behind!"

He turned in triumph to the humble friar who had been listening in silence, huddled in his corner.

"Welcome, Brother Francis! Why are you shaking your head? Don't you agree? Do you have any objection you'd care to raise?"

"My brothers," Francis replied, stretching forth his arms, "my children, Brother Elias: forgive me, but I do have one thing, one tiny thing to say, and I shall say it. Today there are so many, so very many people who pursue wealth, power, and learning that I say, Blessed is the man who remains poor, humble, and illiterate!"

"Now it's my turn to tell you something, Brother Francis," answered Elias with a scornful laugh. "The duty of the man who is truly alive is to conform to the times in which he lives."

"To oppose the times in which you live," retorted Francis, "is the duty of the *free* man! God took me by the hand and said to me, 'Francis, step out in front, illiterate, stupid, barefooted as you are; step out in front, guide the flock I have entrusted to you, take this path and you shall find me.' The path in question, Brother Elias, is called Humility."

"Since you insist on speaking in parables, Brother Francis, very well, God took me by the hand also. He showed me a wide road and said, 'Take this road and you shall find me!' The road in question, Brother Francis, is called Combat."

But Francis shook his head violently. Refusing to give in, he addressed Elias in a loud, despairing voice: "Brother Elias, I fear that you are leading Christ's sheep astray. The road you speak of is not called Combat, but Easy Living. No wide road leads to God; only narrow pathways lead to His house, to Paradise, Brother Elias. The wide road is the road of Satan. I see now why God sent me to this assembly of yours today. It was to cry, 'Stop! Go no further, my brothers. Turn back! Return to the old, narrow path!'"

"The sun does not turn back, Brother Francis," shrieked Elias; "the river does not turn back; man's soul does not turn back, but follows the impetus maintained by God. Do not listen to him, my brothers. We bow and kiss your hands, Brother Francis, and then we advance beyond you. Goodbye!"

Cries came from every direction: "Goodbye, Brother Francis, goodbye!"

Francis lifted his sleeve to wipe away his tears.

"Is there anything else you'd care to say, Brother Francis?"

"Nothing, nothing," replied Francis. He burst into a wailing lament and slowly, noiselessly, sank to the ground. I bent down to help him to his feet.

"Let me be, Brother Leo," he whined. "Don't you see: *it is finished!*"

Several of the friars—Sabattino, Juniper, Pacifico, Ruffino—crowded around him to express their sympathy, the remainder of our original allies having departed with Father Silvester to avoid hearing Elias. All those who remained faithful to the law had now become rebels.

Elias came up to Francis and unrolled the scroll before his eyes. Antonio, the young novice, stood behind with inkwell and quill.

"Here is our new charter, Brother Francis," he said, leaning over him. "Affix your seal; do not oppose us. Several rebellious brothers have already deserted. Discord is making its way into our order. Affix your seal so that we may all live together in harmony!"

"Dead men have no seals, Brother Elias," replied Francis in a gasping voice full of despair, and he pushed away the charter which Elias was waving in front of his eyes. "Goodbye!"

I raised him up. Placing my arm round his waist, I led him outside and started along the path. But he did not have enough strength left to walk now, and despite my support he kept sinking to his knees and falling. Eventually I had to lift him up in my arms. He was light—just a bale of rags. When we reached the hut I found him unconscious. Laying him down on his mat, I sprinkled him with water until finally, after a considerable time, he came to. He gazed at me then with inexpressible sadness, closed his eyes, and—it seemed to me—fainted once again.

For four days and nights he did not open his mouth either to eat or speak. He was failing, melting away like a candle. When I awoke on the fifth morning and looked at him, I became terrified. His head was a fleshless skull: his cheeks, lips, temples had sunk away; and each of his hands was nothing more than five bones.

"Brother Francis," I called to him, placing my mouth against his ear, "Brother Francis!"

But he did not hear.

"Dearest Francis," I called again. "Father!"

He remained immobile. I clasped him in my arms. His robe was an empty sack; his feet stuck out at the bottom like two pieces of wood. Leaving him, I ran to the Portiuncula.

"Help!" I cried. "Brother Francis is dying. For the love of God: help!"

Elias lifted his head from the parchment on which he was writing. "You say he's dying?" he asked.

"He hasn't eaten anything for four days and nights, not even bread or water. And today he doesn't have enough strength left to breathe. Come—all of you. We must save him!"

"We, how can we save him?" asked Elias, putting down his quill. "If God has decided to take him, we must not stand in the way—nor can we."

"You can, you can," I cried in desperation. "He's deliberately advancing toward the grave; he wants to die, Brother Elias, because you wrote a new Rule which departs from the route he first laid out. Since that time a knife has been in his heart: he wants to die, and if he does, Brother Elias—I say this in front of all the brothers— you will have to answer for it."

Elias rose.

"Well, what do you want me to do?" he demanded with irritation. "Speak!"

"Take the charter you've written, go to Francis, and tear it up in front of his eyes. That's what he's waiting for, that's what is needed to bring him back to life. If you don't do it—and I say this in front of all the brothers also—if you don't do it, Brother Elias, Francis, our father, will die, and you will be his murderer!"

Five or six of the brothers gathered around me and fixed their eyes upon Elias, waiting. The feeling that they were on my side made me begin to shout even louder than before.

"All right, all right, stop your screaming!" cried Elias, squeezing the scroll tightly in his palm. He put on his sandals and got his staff. "Let's go," he said to me in a disgusted tone of voice. Then, turning to the brothers: "Make sure no one touches my desk. Antonio, keep watch."

The young novice went up to him and spoke in an undertone in order not to be heard. I was able to catch his words, however. "Brother Elias," he whispered, "what are you doing! You're not going to tear up our Rule, are you?"

Elias smiled, and gazed at him lovingly.

"Don't worry, my child, I know what I'm doing."

We arrived at the hut. When we bent over the mat on which Francis was lying, and lifted up his robe, we both started with fear. It was not a human body that we saw before us, but a string of bones surmounted by a skull. The eyes had already retracted into their sockets. Nothing remained on the face except mustache, beard, and eyebrows, all three covered with blood.

Tying my heart into a knot, I placed my mouth against Francis' ear and cried, "Brother Francis, Elias has come—do you hear? He's come to tear up the charter, the new Rule. Open your eyes, Brother Francis, open your eyes to see!"

He moved slightly, uttered a short, shrill cry, but kept his eyelids shut. Next, Brother Elias leaned over him.

"It's me, Brother Francis, me, Elias. Open your eyes. Do you hear? I'm going to tear up the charter in order to soothe your heart!"

Finally, after much labor, Francis managed to open his eyes. It was just as though the lids had been sewn permanently shut. He glanced at Elias without saying a word, and waited.

Elias removed the scroll from beneath his frock. Unrolling it, he began to tear it slowly into tiny tiny pieces. A little color rose to Francis' cheeks and lips.

"Throw the pieces in the fire, Brother Leo," he said.

He turned to Elias. "Brother Elias, give me your hand."

He grasped Elias' hand and held it for a few moments in his own. Then he burst into tears.

"Brother Leo," he called to me afterwards, "if there is any milk, give me some to drink."

Francis returned to life slowly, with great difficulty. Each day he became more animated. He began to open his mouth in order to eat, to move his lips in order to talk; he would draw himself to the threshold of the hut to sun himself, and in stormy weather he squatted next to the hearth and listened in exultation to the downpour as though he had never heard rain before, as though he had become entirely arid, had wrung his body dry, so to speak, and now felt the rain falling upon it to irrigate him—and not only his body, but also his soul.

"Brother Leo," he said to me one day, "the soil and man's soul are exactly the same. Both thirst, and both wait for the heavens to open so that their thirst may be quenched."

One day Francis' beloved Brother Giles arrived after returning from a circuit of the distant villages. Francis fell into his arms and kissed him again and again. He loved him exceedingly because, as he said, Giles kept his eyes constantly pinned on heaven. Kneeling on the ground, the visitor laughingly related all he had seen and everything that had happened to him as he went from town to town. Some of the villagers, taking him for a madman, had greeted him with jeers; others, taking him for a saint, had prostrated themselves at his feet. And he had cried, "I am neither a madman nor a saint, but a sinner. Father Francis showed me the road to salvation, so I threw off my sandals and started along it."

"I entered every village holding a basket of figs or walnuts," Giles explained, "or at least some wild flowers if I could find nothing else. Then I cried, 'Whoever gives me a slap, I shall give a fig; whoever gives me two slaps, I shall give two figs.' The whole village ran to slap me, punch me, beat me until I was half-dead. As soon as the basket was empty I would depart contentedly to refill it, and then proceed to the next village."

"Brother Giles, I like you! Receive my blessing," said Francis.

"I also came across the saintly Bonaventura, Brother Francis. He took a different road: he believes that learning is an aid to salvation. So I went and asked him, 'Father, can both the illiterate and the literate be saved?'

" 'Why of course, my brother,' he replied.

" 'And are the uneducated and the educated equally capable of loving God?' What do you think his answer was? Listen, Brother Francis: it will warm your heart! 'An old ignorant illiterate crone,' he said, 'is far more capable of loving God than a learned theologian is.' The moment I heard those words, Brother Francis, I began to race through the streets shrieking like a town crier, 'Hear!

Hear! The learned Bonaventura says an ignorant crone is far more capable of loving God than learned Bonaventura is!' "

"Receive my blessing, Brother Giles," Francis repeated, smiling with satisfaction. "If anyone opens your heart, he will find the true Rule written upon it in large red letters—all of them capitals."

His former companions in the struggle came to visit him from time to time in this way and he was comforted, for their love nourished him more than bread and milk.

On another occasion Brother Masseo appeared holding a sheaf of beautifully ripe grain which he planned to sear over the fire and give Francis to eat.

"Where did you find those ears of grain, Brother Masseo?" Francis asked uneasily. "I know it's not beyond you to do something bad in order to do something good. I wonder whose field you climbed into to pick those ears for me."

Masseo laughed. "Don't be an old grouch, Brother Francis. No, I didn't steal them. On my way here I met a peasant woman loaded down with a bundle of wheat. 'Where are you going, monk?' she asked me. 'Are you one of *them?*'

" 'What do you mean?' I asked.

" 'I mean are you a follower of the sweet little pauper?'

" 'You hit the nail on the head, my lady. How did you know?'

" 'Because your frock has thousands of holes in it and you walk barefooted and never stop laughing, just as though someone were tickling you.'

" 'God is tickling me,' I answered. 'That's why I laugh. . . . Why not come closer to God yourself: then you'll begin to laugh too.'

" 'No time,' she answered. 'I have a husband and children, and I can't walk barefooted on the stones, so leave me alone. But there is one thing I'd like you to do for me.' She lowered the bundle from her back, drew out a handful of ears, and gave them to me. 'I've heard that he's hungry,' she continued. 'I am poor; give him this grain—a greeting from poverty.' "

Francis pressed the ears to his heart. "This bread of beggary is the true bread of the angels, Brother Masseo. So please it God that your peasant woman may enter Paradise crowned with ears of grain!"

Masseo went to the fire and began to singe the ears, then to rub them and collect the seeds.

"I have something else to tell you also, Brother Francis," he said. "You must not take it in the wrong spirit, however. Shall I speak?"

"Speak freely, Brother Masseo."

"But I think I did something foolish, mad. It will make you angry."

"Madness, Brother Masseo, is the salt which prevents good sense from rotting. I myself, don't forget, used to go through the streets crying, 'Hear! Hear the new madness.' So, speak."

"No matter where I go, Brother Francis, I find your name on everyone's lips. Many people want to journey here on foot so that they can kiss your hand. 'How is this possible?' a haughty count asked me one day. 'I once saw this celebrated Francis. He is not learned, carries no sword, cannot trace his descent from a great family. On top of this he is undersized, puny, and has an ugly face all covered with hair. How is it, therefore, that everybody desires to see him? I don't understand!'"

"And what was your answer?" inquired Francis with a chuckle.

"This is where the madness starts, Brother Francis. 'You know why everyone wants to see him?' I said to the count. 'It's because he exudes an odor like the beasts of the forest: a strange odor which makes you dizzy the moment you smell it.' 'What is this odor?' the count asked me. 'The odor of sainthood,' I replied. . . . Did I speak well, Brother Francis?"

"No, no!" cried Francis. "Don't ever say that again, Brother Masseo. Do you want to have me hurled into hell?"

"What should I say then? Everyone asks me."

"What you should say is this: 'Do you want to learn why everyone runs behind him, why every eye wants to see him? It is because these eyes have never seen, nor will they ever see in the whole wide world a man so ugly in appearance, so weighted down with sins, so unworthy. And it was precisely because of this that God chose him: in order to put beauty, wisdom, and noble lineages to shame!' That is what you must tell them, Brother Masseo, if you wish to have my blessing."

Masseo scratched his head and glanced at me out of the corner of his eye as though to ask: "Should I say it or shouldn't I?"

"Tell them whatever is at the tip of your tongue," I advised him. "And stop scratching your head!"

"Oh, yes, there was one more thing I wanted to mention to you, Brother Francis; only one more and then I'll go. I really do smell an odor about you, an odor like musk, or rose incense—I'm not sure which. I can smell you a mile away. That's how I found you just now at this hut—by your smell."

At long last we were preparing to leave the vicinity of the Portiuncula. Francis had grown tired of wrestling with men, and was anxious to bury himself again in some mountain cave where he could speak to God in complete solitude.

"I was made to live alone and isolated like a wild animal," he always used to say. "It was precisely because of this that God commanded me to come forth and preach to mankind. Good Lord, what can I say to them? God knows I cannot speak. I was born to sing and weep."

Father Silvester appeared at the door of our hut a few days before our departure, together with five of the old, faithful brothers: Bernard, Pietro, Sabattino, Ruffino, and Pacifico. An aged peasant who had loaded down his donkey with grapes and was on his way to Assisi to sell them had just presented a cluster to Francis, and he had taken them in his hands and begun to gaze at them in amazement, ecstatically, as though he had never seen a grape before.

"What a miracle this is, Brother Leo!" he exclaimed. "How insensible, how blind men are not to see everyday miracles! A bunch of grapes: what a great mystery! You eat them and you feel refreshed. You crush them and they give you wine. You drink the wine and you immediately lose your reason: sometimes God expands inside you and you open your arms and embrace all of mankind; sometimes you fly into a rage, draw your knife, and kill!"

At that moment Father Silvester and the other brothers appeared on the threshold. They all knelt to kiss Francis' hand.

"We have come to receive your blessing," said Father Silvester. "We are going out to preach the word of Christ as you have revealed it to us."

"And where, God willing, do you plan to go?"

"Wherever the road leads us, Brother Francis. Wherever God leads us. The entire earth is Christ's field, isn't it? We shall go out to sow."

Francis placed his hand on each of their heads. "Go, my brothers, go with my blessing. Preach using words if you are able. But above all preach with your lives and deeds. What is it that stands higher than words? Action. What is it that stands higher than action? Silence. My brothers, mount the entire ladder that leads to God. Preach with words, preach with action, and afterwards, when you are alone, enter the holy silence which encompasses the Lord."

Falling silent, he gazed lovingly at each of the brothers for a long time. It was as though they were going to the wars and he did not know if he should ever see them again.

"Men's hearts are hard, they are stones," he said with a sigh. "But God is with you, so do not be afraid. Each time you are persecuted you shall say: 'We came to this world to suffer, to be killed, and to conquer!' What do you have to fear? Nothing. Whom do you have to fear? No one. Why? Because whoever has joined forces with God obtains three great privileges: omnipotence without power, intoxication without wine, and life without death."

The brothers stood motionless and looked at him. They were saying goodbye without opening their mouths.

"I too am departing, my brothers," continued Francis. "I am going out to preach salvation to rocks, wild flowers, and mountain thyme. The Day of Judgment is coming near, my brothers, so let us hurry. When it arrives it must find all men, animals, birds, plants, and stones prepared. Everything you see about you—the entire earth —must be prepared, ready to mount to heaven. What is heaven, my brothers, if not the entire earth, the same that we see about us—but virtuous!"

"So please it God that our order may always follow the strait and narrow road," said Bernard. "Your road, Brother Francis."

Sior Pietro prostrated himself, then touched Francis' knee. "A question has been bothering me for a long time, Brother Francis, and I didn't want to part with you before receiving an answer directly from your lips. How long, Brother Francis, is our order going to continue along this strait and narrow road?"

"As long as the friars walk with bare feet," replied Francis. Then he fell silent, as did all of us.

"The sun is already a full span above the horizon," said Father Silvester presently. He rose, and the others rose with him. "You are right, Brother Francis: we must hurry. . . . Farewell!"

"God be with you!" replied Francis, and he traced the sign of the cross in the air above their heads.

AFTER HE HAD SAID farewell to the brothers, Francis bent down and kissed the threshold of the Portiuncula; then he glanced all round him with his dimmed sight and took leave of the birds, the trees, and the thorns, savory, thyme, and wild herbs along the ground—the humble plants which burgeoned each year round our aged mother, the Portiuncula.

"In God's name, Brother Leo," he said, crossing himself, and we started on our journey.

"Have you any idea where we're going?" I asked.

"Why should I? The Lord knows, and that's enough. Haven't you ever seen a heliotrope, that yellow, radial plant which looks so much like the sun? It stares Brother Sun straight in the eye and obediently turns its face to follow his journey. Let us do the same, Brother Leo: let us keep our eyes fixed on God."

The summer was nearly over; the earth reclined with an air of satisfaction, like a woman after childbirth. The fields had been reaped, the graves vintaged; dark green, still-diminutive fruit already glistened between the leaves of the orange trees. The swallows were waiting for the cranes to come and take them away on their wings. A layer of thin, tender clouds blanketed the sky—rain had begun to approach from the mountain, and the soil was fragrant.

Francis breathed in deeply. It was a long time since I had seen his face so relaxed. Climbing to the top of a knoll, we leaned for a moment against the crumbling wall of some ancient tower. I looked out at the plain below me. What serenity, what sweetness! You felt that the soil had performed its function and was now lying back, fully content.

"It reminds me of a sacred icon I once saw in Ravenna," said

Francis, turning to me; "part of the booty brought by the crusaders from Anatolia. They had set out to deliver the Holy Sepulcher, but as soon as they discovered Constantinople, flabbergasted by its riches and beauty they forgot all about Christ and fell upon the city. They burned it, slaughtered its inhabitants, pillaged its wealth, and then returned home with their spoils. This extraordinary icon, the Assumption of the Blessed Virgin Mary, was brought to Ravenna. And what a miracle it is, Brother Leo! The Mother of God reclining on her bed with crossed arms, her whole face smiling contentedly, and she has a purple wimple over her head, her aged hands are lined from household chores, her cheeks withered, her feet worn away by the stones and thorns of the ground. But you can see the smile of a hidden inner joy bubbling up out of her mouth and pouring over her chin, temples, and eyelids. She has done her duty and is tranquil. What duty? To give birth to the Savior of the world. . . . And now as I gaze upon this productive, tranquil plain, Brother Leo, I say to myself: In autumn the soil—the Virgin Earth—sleeps in exactly the same way."

We journeyed for many days, many weeks. Where were we going? Wherever God decided, for Francis refused to determine time or place: like the heliotrope, he was content to follow the face of God.

"What happiness it is," he kept saying to me, "what joy not to have any will, not to say 'I,' but to forget who you are, what your name is, and to give yourself up with confidence to the puffs of God's wind! That is true freedom! If someone asks you who is free, Brother Leo, what will you reply? The man who is God's slave! All other freedom is bondage."

One day we stopped in a tiny village. Francis tolled the ram's bell, and the men and women of the village assembled to hear him. They knew who this barefooted stranger was, for the knowledge of his miracles and his love for the noble Lady Poverty had reached this far. They too were poor; they too, without consciously willing it, were his disciples.

Francis stepped up onto a rock. "What need is there for me to preach to you, my brothers," he said to them; "what need to show you the road which leads to Paradise? You have already taken this road, because you are poor and humble and illiterate, and you are hard workers, as it pleases God you should be."

273

He fell silent. A crowd of restless swallows had gathered round him, perched on all the rooftops and upon a ruined tower. They must have been ready to depart, and were only waiting now for a suitable wind. Francis started to speak again, but the swallows began to flit here and there, descending a whole flock at a time on top of him and drowning out his voice with their chirping.

"My brothers," he cried, struggling to be heard above the twittering all around him and above his head, "my brothers, our life here on earth is a deceptive dream. The true life, which is eternal, awaits us above in heaven. Do not regard the soil beneath your feet, but lift your eyes high, my brothers, open the cage where the soul thrashes itself, covers its bill with blood—and fly away!"

Francis shouted himself hoarse, but the swallows had not the slightest intention of leaving him! Instead, new flocks gathered round him continually, warbling, peeping, refusing to go away. At last Francis turned to them. His voice was all sweetness and supplication:

"My little brother swallows, I beg of you, let me have a turn to speak! You who carry spring to the world—O tiny, graceful carters of God—fold your wings for a moment, gather quietly on all sides, along the rooftops, and listen. We are talking here about God, the creator of swallows and men—about our common Father. If you love Him, if you love me, your brother, then be still! I see you are ready for the great journey to Africa—may the Lord be with you! But before you begin, it is fitting that you should listen to God's word."

As soon as the swallows heard this speech they folded their wings and lined up in silence around Francis. Some perched on his shoulders; all directed their tiny round eyes toward God's crier and remained motionless, except that their intense joy made them flap their wings from time to time, as though they longed to dart into the sky an hour before the appointed moment. At the sight of this miracle the peasants, men and women alike, fell at Francis' feet.

"Take us with you," cried the women. "We have no further use for our homes or husbands; we want the kingdom of heaven! We shall throw off our sandals, don the robe, and follow you to the death!"

And the men, kissing Francis' feet and beating their breasts, cried, "We have no further use for our wives or fields; we too want the kingdom of heaven. Take us, Brother Francis, take us with you!"

Francis was terror-stricken. What could he do with them, where could he take them, how feed them? And what would become of the population of the world if everyone became a monk or nun?

"Wait, my brothers," he cried. "You misunderstood me. There isn't just a single road leading to heaven. The monk—without wife, bread, home, or hearth—takes one road; the simple, pious believer another. He marries, has children, assures the continuance of the race. It isn't right—nor is it God's will—for the soil to be left unploughed and unsown by you, or for women to cease bearing children. For you, you who live in the world, God made sweet conversation, bread, the hearth, and honest cohabitation. I swear to you that by continuing in the way you are now living, you shall be able to reach the gates of heaven!"

Many of the ploughmen grew angry.

"First you light a fire for us and then you try your best to put it out. Either what you first told us is correct and we must renounce the world if we want to be saved—or it isn't. If this is the case, friend, leave us in peace. Go somewhere else!"

"What you've done is dishonest—dishonest, monk!" shrieked the women, who were even more outraged than their husbands. "Like it or not we're coming with you! Women get into heaven as well as men, don't they? How did the Blessed Virgin manage? Well, you're not going to keep us out!"

Francis clapped his hands in desperation. "Wait," he implored them, "wait, I shall come back. First distribute all your belongings to the poor; married couples, observe chastity; do not curse, do not let yourselves become angry; thrice daily fall on your knees all together and pray. A long preparation is required, my children. Make yourselves ready; I shall come!"

"I shall come, I shall come," he continued to shout as he departed from the village with immense strides. I raced behind him. In back of me were a dozen or so women, and they had already begun to curse:

"Impostor! Liar! Parasite! Swindler!"

The first stones began to fly, but by this time we had succeeded in getting far enough away from the village. When it was no longer in sight we halted to recover our strength.

"I think we were wrong, Brother Francis," I was bold enough to say. "You must tell each one only what he can support. Anything beyond is temptation."

Francis sat down on a stone. He was lost in thought, and did not answer. I knew his mind was laboring, because I saw the veins swell at his temples and on his forehead. Sitting down opposite him, I waited. The village had bequeathed us several pieces of stale bread, some olives, and two bunches of grapes. I was famished.

"Cross yourself and let's eat, Brother Francis," I implored. "Aren't you hungry?"

But he, plunged deep in meditation, did not hear.

"Brother Leo," he said after a long silence, "I pity the village where no one is a saint, but I also pity the village where everyone is a saint!"

I had begun meanwhile to eat by myself, and to reflect at the same time upon all I had seen and heard in the village. The Tempter must have entered me, because I soon commenced to talk to myself, wearily, disgustedly. Since you say so yourself, Brother Francis, I reasoned, since it's possible to find God by taking the easy, level road, why then bother with the ascent and all its torments? The married man with his children, cottage, fields, his ample food: can he find God? You say Yes. So, let's get married, set up a household like everyone else, and live like men. We have only one purpose: to reach God. Why not reach Him strong and well nourished instead of worn-out and decrepit? In the awful state you're in, Brother Francis, how can you expect to present yourself before God the day after tomorrow? You remember what the pope said, don't you: 'What a stink! What pigsty did you come from?' Well, God will say the same! This was how I talked to myself, devouring huge mouthfuls in the process. I finished the first bunch of grapes, then pinched a good portion of the second. I swear to God if it hadn't been for the presence of Francis—how annoying!—I would have gone straight back to this village and gotten married on the spot. I had already seen a girl who struck my fancy. And it goes without saying I would have been a God-fearing husband and would have knelt in prayer three times a day—thirty times a day! But at the same time I would have advanced toward God at a reasonable pace, leisurely; and behind me I would have brought along my wife and children so that we could all enter Paradise together!

Francis shifted his position. Lifting my eyes, I saw him and cringed. I felt I had committed a sin.

But Francis smiled at me. "You are right, Brother Leo," he said. "The monk's life is oppressive. Not all men are able to support it, nor should they, because if they did the world would fall in ruins. Listen to how God enlightened me while I was sitting on this blessed stone. We are going to organize another order by the side of our strict one. This new order shall be softer, tractable enough so that no devout Christian who chooses to live in the world need be excluded. The brothers in this docile order will be able to marry, work their domains, eat and drink in moderation; they will not have to walk barefooted or wear a frock, but will be required simply to live virtuously, make friends with their enemies, give alms to the poor, and keep lifting their eyes from earth to heaven. . . . What do you say, Brother Leo? Are we of one mind?"

I wanted to ask him why we could not enter this order ourselves, but I was too ashamed, too afraid.

"It's a very good idea," I answered, at a loss what else to say.

What *could* I say? I had made my bed; now I had to lie on it. I was hunting for God before I met Francis, but this had never taken away my delight in food. Since I joined him I'd had no further worries about finding God: I simply followed in Francis' footsteps, calm in the knowledge that he knew the way perfectly. But the problem of food, wine, and all the other comforts continued to torment me—yes, and though I am ashamed to admit it, I do: also the problem of women.

"What is on your mind, Brother Leo?" Francis asked, seeing me thoughtful.

"I'm thinking about God," I replied in an effort to change the subject.

"Do you remember the years you pursued Him all over the earth? You never found Him, Brother Leo, for the simple reason that He was inside your heart. You were like the person who looks everywhere for his gold ring, looks everywhere day and night and cannot find it because he is wearing it on his finger."

One evening at dusk, we arrived at the famous castle of Monte-feltro. Multicolored banners were flying from the top of the tower;

277

trumpets blared from the loopholes around its circumference; expensive red tapestries hung from the castle windows; the great fortified entranceway was adorned with myrtles and laurel. Noble lords and ladies were passing over the drawbridge, charming pages running to help the ladies dismount in front of the doors. Behind, all along the steep road which ascended from the plain below, other resplendently bejeweled ladies were visible, and also lords encased in golden armor. Servant boys and girls in brand-new checkered livery ran up and down carrying silver trays loaded with drinks and delicacies.

"Paradise must be exactly like this," I gasped, dazzled by the wealth and beauty.

"Much simpler, Brother Leo," Francis replied. . . . "They must be having some celebration," he continued, glancing at the lords, ladies, and flags. "Let's go celebrate with them. What do you say, Brother Leo?"

"With pleasure, Brother Francis." What more could I possibly have wanted!

Francis advanced over the drawbridge, calm and assured, as though he had been sent an invitation. I, however, grew timid.

"But we weren't invited, Brother Francis. They'll chase us away."

"Have no fears, lamb of God. This celebration is taking place for us—haven't you realized that yet? It is taking place to enable us to enter this savage fortress and begin to fish."

"To fish?" I asked, surprised. "But I don't see any lake here, or any river or ocean. Only stones!"

Francis laughed. "So you forget we are fishers, do you? Instead of catching fish, we catch souls. God's ways are many. Perhaps—who can tell?—there will be some soul here that is suffocating inside its silk clothes and beautiful body, some soul that wants to escape and be saved. Perhaps it was for this soul's precious sake that God had the noble lord of the castle hold this celebration: to entice us to enter—which, as you see, is just what we are doing!"

With these words, he strode over the threshold and past the ironbound gates.

The great courtyard was filled with horses. In the kitchens all fires were blazing. Meat was boiling in huge caldrons or sizzling away, spread out on grates, and the aroma perfumed the air. My nostrils began to vibrate; I could find little enthusiasm for advancing any further.

One of the cooks happened to pass us. "What's going on, brother?" I asked him. "What are they celebrating?"

"The master's son is being invested with knighthood," he replied. "They're all in the chapel right now, and the bishop is blessing the new armor."

He looked me over from head to toe and saw that I was barefooted and that my robe was full of holes—which did not seem to please him very much.

"Now just to make things clear," he said with a frown, "tell me: were you invited?"

"But of course," I answered. "What did you think?"

"By whom?"

"By God!"

The cook laughed. "Go on, you're hungry and you came to eat, poor wretch. . . . None of this business about God," he called, continuing on in the direction of the kitchens.

Francis, meanwhile, had been admiring the majestic coat-of-arms above the lintel: a lion rampant, holding a heart, and above the heart the words "I fear no one."

Francis pointed the bearings out to me. "Apparently this noble lord fears no one, perhaps not even God. The heart of man is a pretentious idiot, Brother Leo; pay no attention to what it says, but forgive and pass on. If we were to have a coat-of-arms, what device would you suggest?"

"A lamb—a lamb eating a lion," I replied with a laugh.

"No, lamb of God. The trouble is you're hungry and are prepared to eat even a lion. The day will come, however, when lions and lambs shall live together in peace; therefore, do not make yourself so ferocious. If you asked me, I would have a tiny bird emblazoned on our scutcheon, a tiny, humble bird which mounts to heaven each morning—singing."

"The skylark," I said, recalling Francis' words to the brothers at the Portiuncula. "The bird with the hood."

"Exactly! Bless you, Brother Leo. . . . But I hear anthems in the chapel. Come, let's attend the service."

We entered the chapel, which was at the base of the tower. Good

Lord, how beautiful it was! All bathed in light, it bristled with swords, iron armor, spurs of gold, with noble ironclad knights who had come to salute the new chevalier. And the great ladies with their long robes: what costly, multicolored veils, what towering, gold-studded hats, what feathers, what strings of pearls around their throats, what golden bracelets, and—my God!—what smells: all the perfumes of Arabia! No, Francis say what he will, I still imagine Paradise with its male and female saints to be like this, exactly like this. Such raiment, only better, is what God will give to the blessed. Aren't they knights also—knights of God? Isn't heaven the Round Table where all the heroes sit? And Christ, isn't he King Arthur?

It was too much for me. Completely bewildered, I huddled behind a column and stared in goggle-eyed wonderment. Suddenly, what did I see but Francis pushing his way through the noblemen until he reached the sanctuary, where the bishop was in the process of blessing the new knight, a blond, deathly-pale youngster. Francis waited for the blessing to end; then he knelt in front of the prelate and said, "Your Excellency, give me permission to speak, in Christ's name."

Several of the lords had recognized him. I heard them whispering among themselves: "It's Francis of Assisi! The new anchorite!"

The bishop gave him a disdainful look. "What do you plan to say?" he asked.

"I don't know, Bishop. Whatever God puts into my mouth. Have faith."

"Who are you?"

The elderly castellan took a step forward and addressed the bishop. "Deign to give him permission; he's Francis of Assisi."

The bishop lifted his arms. "Be brief," he commanded. "The banquet is ready."

"The banquet is ready in heaven!" began Francis, seizing upon the bishop's words. "The banquet is ready, my brethren; the Day of Judgment approaches. There is little time left, but even now we can still be saved, we can mount to heaven and take our seats at God's immortal tables. But with iron armor, with spurs of gold, with silk veils, with parties and laughter and a life filled with comforts one does not mount to heaven. The ascent is rigorous, my brethren; it exacts sweat, and struggle, and abundant blood."

The lords and ladies wrinkled their faces. The bishop shook his ivory crozier nervously. Comprehending, Francis continued in a gentler voice:

"Forgive me. I am addressing knights, and it is my duty therefore to speak their own language. Listen, I pray you, to what I came to say. If a knight desires to win the love of his lady, what feats he must accomplish, what struggles undergo, what visible and invisible forces—seas, wild beasts, men, demons—he must wrestle with and conquer if he is to make his lady open her arms! He will set out to deliver the Holy Sepulcher, or he will ride his horse over the Hair Bridge, or climb to the top of ruined towers at midnight and drive away ghosts at sword's point. And he never turns coward. If you open the heart of the lord of this castle, you will see engraved there the words: 'I fear no one.' Why? Because never absent from his mind are a pair of open, sweet-smelling arms.

"All this, dear lords and ladies, you know better than I. But there is something you do not know, or which you know but forget: the existence of another Lady, not an earthly lady, but a celestial one; and of another order of Knighthood, and another struggle. Who is this Lady? The kingdom of heaven! What is this struggle? To renounce temporal goods and embrace instead Poverty, Chastity, Prayer, perfect Love—which are everlasting. If we defy danger, fear, and death in order to win a transient body, what trials must we then undergo to win the eternal Lady?"

The lords began to grow indignant and to grumble over the bare-footed monk's unbounded impertinence. Divining this, Francis climbed down the sanctuary stairs and stood amidst the assembled noblemen.

"Do not grow angry, ironclad lords," he said. "I speak as one knight to another. It does not matter that you are noblemen; I am the slave of no one except God, and this patched and repatched robe I have on is my knightly armor. I too have entered the contest: I go hungry, freeze, torment myself, struggle—all for the sake of my Lady's beauty. And *my* Lady is a thousand times better than yours. This is the Lady I am speaking to you about: this is the Lady whose existence makes me exhort you to begin the struggle while you still have time. . . . And you, my young knight, my blond well-bred lad: hear what God, through my mouth, commands you to do. The lord your father boasts, 'I fear no one.' You, the son, must engrave in your heart the words, 'I fear no one but God.' Perhaps it was for this very reason that the Almighty sent me to your tower tonight just as you were taking the pledge of knighthood—to bring you this message, my son!"

Francis kissed the bishop's hand, then nodded to me, and we made our exit. Night had fallen; the sky was filled with stars. Together with the horses and servant girls, we stood in the yard while the lords and ladies left the chapel and proceeded in silence to the huge hall where the laden tables awaited them. The footboys and maidservants began scurrying back and forth between hall and kitchen carrying the meat and wine, and whenever they opened the door to the banqueting chamber, a great uproar could be heard, and laughter, and violins being tuned.

Francis had settled himself comfortably on the ground in one corner of the courtyard. His eyes closed, he leaned peacefully against the wall, but I—I was hungry. I insinuated myself into the kitchen, where I successfully begged bread, meat, and a pitcher of wine. Taking these, I ran happily to Francis.

"Wake up, wake up!" I shouted. "Let's eat."

"You go ahead," he replied. "Go ahead, feed your donkey."

I downed a sizable sip of wine and began to feel merry.

"Your donkey needs to be fed also, Brother Francis. Do you know what happened to the peasant who tried to accustom his donkey to going without food? Just as the poor thing was about to learn, it died!"

Francis laughed. "Take care of your own donkey, Brother Leo. Give him another sip of wine so he'll begin to bray; and don't worry about other people's donkeys." As soon as he had said this, he closed his eyes again.

I began my meal, and while I was eating, and giving thanks to God for having made meat so delicious, a young lord with feathers in his hat came up to us. Bending over, he recognized Francis.

"Is he asleep?" he asked me.

"No. He never sleeps. Call him by name."

"Father Francis! Father Francis!" cried the youth.

Francis opened his eyes, saw the splendidly dressed figure in front of him, and smiled.

"Hello, my young lord," he said. "What induced you to abandon the banquet and the beautiful ladies in order to come here? Surely God sent you."

"Your words just now in chapel penetrated to my heart, Father Francis," replied the youth, his voice full of emotion. "All my life I have listened to what the priest says in church, but I have never really heard anything. Tonight, for the first time, I heard. I've come to ask a favor of you, Father Francis. I am Count Orlando dei Cattani, lord of the castle of Chiusi in Casentino."

"What favor, my child?" asked Francis. "I will do all I can for the salvation of your soul."

"I own a desolate mountain in Tuscany called Monte Alvernia. It is isolated, peaceful, without trails or human footsteps. Its sole inhabitants are hawks and partridges. I present it to you, Father Francis, for the salvation of my soul."

"That's just exactly what I was looking for!" exclaimed Francis, clapping his hands with joy. "Now I see why I left the Portiuncula: it was to go to this mountain. From its wild uninhabited summit my prayers, despite their burden of sin, will surely rise to the feet of the Almighty. In Christ's name I thank you, my young lord, and accept your offer."

"Pray for my soul," said the count, kissing Francis' hand. "And now with your leave I shall go back to the others and enjoy myself with the beautiful ladies!"

"God be with you," said Francis, blessing him. "Enjoy yourself until you hear the trumpets sound."

"What trumpets?"

"Those of the Day of Judgment."

"That won't be for a long long time!" said the count, laughing, and he departed at a run, anxious to return to the banquet.

Francis saw that I was still eating. "Feed your donkey well, Brother Leo," he said. "We have the ascent of a rough, inaccessible mountain ahead of us. You've asked me over and over again where we're going. To Monte Alvernia, my fellow athlete, to Monte Alvernia. I have a premonition that there, in the snows of its lofty peak, the Lord will be waiting for us."

"In the cold, the rain, the snow!" I exclaimed, horrified. "Why didn't he send word for us to go find Him on the plain?"

"God is always found amid cold, rain, and snow, Brother Leo, so stop fretting. On the plain you'll discover rich lords and beautiful, amorous ladies; also Death, which is the lord castellan of that world; also your poor old donkey, Brother Leo. But the true Brother Leo climbs the mountain."

I said nothing. Ah, if it were only really possible, I was thinking, if it were only really possible for a person to leave his donkey on the plain to graze in rich pastures, while his soul, weightless and insensible to hunger and cold, climbed the mountain!

They allowed us to sleep in one of the stables. The air smelled of manure and the sweat of horses. Raising his arm, Francis blessed his equestrian brothers. "We are going to spend the night together, Brother Horses," he said. "Do not kick or whinny, if you please. We're tired; let us sleep. Good night."

We spread out some straw and lay down. We were truly tired, and slumber overcame us at once. From time to time I heard singing in my sleep, accompanied by guitars, and the laughter of women. It was as though the sky had parted above my head and Paradise had begun to descend together with the angels. But I always sank immediately back into oblivion, and the angels with their guitars and laughter were swallowed up into the sky.

Francis awoke full of enthusiasm. "Did you put on your iron sandals?" he asked me. "We have a long ascent ahead of us."

"Why, of course. Here they are!"

I showed him my naked feet, all covered with wounds. "May God take pity on us at long last!" I murmured, crossing myself; and with this, we began the journey to our newly converted mountain.

Francis was thoughtful, silent. We had left the castle behind us. Not a leaf was stirring, and the banners drooped limply from their poles like so many varicolored rags. The sky was overcast; to our right a gray, hairless sun began to mount behind the clouds, imparting a dull luster to the leaves. Only the quivering raindrops at their edges glittered brightly. The sound of the cocks crowing at the castle could still be heard in the damp air.

"We're going to have a change in the weather, Brother Francis. Listen to the cocks. More rain, I'm afraid."

But Francis' mind was elsewhere. "Brother Leo," he said to me, "the circle is about to close at last; the end is approaching—glory be to God. In the beginning I prayed the Almighty to let me remain all alone in the wilderness, to let me address Him from there. He granted my request; but then He quickly seized me by the scruff of the neck and tossed me among men. 'Abandon your solitude,' He shouted at me. 'You have settled down too comfortably all by yourself, and this displeases me. Go, go the rounds of cities and villages; preach, choose companions, form an order, and then set out all together to deliver the Holy Sepulcher: the heart of man!' I gave up my solitude accordingly (but not without a sigh, Brother Leo); I chose the brothers, and we set out. What saintly poverty we enjoyed in those early days! What love, harmony, chastity! Do you remember how our unbounded joy used to make us all burst suddenly into tears? Trees, birds, stones, streams, and men all seemed to have just issued fresh from God's hands. And Christ was with us; we did not see Him, but we felt His sacred breath in the air, His palms resting on our heads. We saw Him only at night, when our flesh was asleep and the soul had opened its eyes. But after that . . . after that—"

Francis' voice failed him. He glanced at me. Large tears were hanging from his eyes.

"After that," I said, "wolves entered the sheepfold and we dispersed."

"They threw me out," said Francis, sighing. "They threw me out, Brother Leo. . . . The circle is closing, I tell you; I am returning again to solitude. Once at the top of this lonely mountain I shall howl in seclusion, howl like a wild beast. There are many demons still inside me, pounds of flesh still round my soul. Ah! If only God gives me time to do away with the flesh, to obliterate it so that my soul may be left free to escape! To escape, Brother Leo, to escape!"

He jerked his arms vehemently toward the sky, and for a moment I thought he had sprouted wings and begun to fly away—so great was his anticipated joy. Afraid of being abandoned, I seized hold of his frock and clung to it.

Just then a peasant appeared along the road; he was pulling a tiny donkey at the end of a rope, and upon the donkey was a woman nursing an infant, her breast exposed. Francis halted and stared at her with protruding eyes.

"Give us your blessing, Father," said the peasant, placing his hand over his heart. "This is my wife, and the baby is my son. Bless us."

"God be with you," Francis replied. "Happy voyage, Joseph!"

The amazed peasant began to laugh. But he was in a hurry, and did not have time to stop.

"Joseph, Brother Francis?" I said. "How did you know his name?"

"But didn't you understand, lamb of God? The man was Joseph, and his wife was the Virgin Mary suckling God. They were on their way to Egypt.

"How many times must I tell you, Brother Leo," he continued after a moment, "to use your inner sight as well as your outer? Your eyes of clay show you a peasant with his wife and child. But the others, the eyes of the soul—what a miracle they see! The Blessed Mother of God astride a donkey; Joseph; Christ nursing: all pass before us once again, and they shall continue to pass, Brother Leo, for all eternity."

I sighed. Alas! My hide was thick, my heart smothered beneath layers of fat. When would I too be able to push aside this world and see the other world behind it, the eternal one?

The first drops began to fall, slapping to the ground the few leaves which still remained on the fig trees. It was almost evening. Ahead of us atop a rocky ledge we saw a small deserted church, its white walls glistening in the rain.

"God loves us," I said. "Look, He sent a church where we can spend the night."

We pushed open the door and entered. As the evening light came in behind us, we were able to see that the walls were covered from the floor right up to the dome with colorful, densely populated frescoes representing the temptation of Saint Anthony. We saw the holy anchorite struggling in desperation against an entire battalion of devils. Some were dragging him by the beard, some by the armpits; others had caught hold of his cowl, cincture, feet. . . . Further up, two devils were turning a lamb on a spit while the ascetic gazed at it, pale, fainting from hunger, his nostrils flared, and the laughing devils beckoned him to approach. On the opposite wall: a blond, naked woman with greedy eyes, pressing her huge breasts against the ascetic's knees. He was ogling her desirously, and from his mouth a red ribbon unrolled straight up toward heaven, and upon the ribbon, written in black letters, were the words: "Lord, Lord, help!"

I became extremely upset. Suddenly I had a satanic yearning to reach out and touch the woman's accursed body. So great was this yearning that I began to tremble all over, and Francis turned and looked at me questioningly. Calling up all my strength, I checked my hand in mid-air. But my arm was numb and painful.

Francis took a candle from the candelabrum, lighted it at the lamp which hung before the icon of Christ, and went from painting to painting. He did not speak, but his hand was shaking.

I stood at his side and joined him in gazing at the paintings by the light of the flickering candle. Suddenly I heard him murmur: "Lord, O Lord, why didst Thou make temptation so beautiful? Hast Thou no pity for man's soul? I am but a lowly worm, yet I pity it."

We still had some bread and meat left over from what I had begged at the castle. Sitting down on the stone floor, I spread out our fare. Francis knelt opposite me and leaned forward to blow out the candle.

"It will be better if we don't see," he said.

He blew, but his hand was trembling and the still-burning candle fell onto his robe, igniting it. I darted forward to extinguish the fire, but Francis resisted.

"Don't put it out! Don't put it out!" he screamed at me.

But I, not being able to discern the invisible world behind the visible one, saw the fire already touching his skin, and immediately threw the edge of my robe over the flames, smothering them.

"You shouldn't have done that; no, you shouldn't have murdered Sister Flame," he complained to me. "What did she want? To eat, to devour my flesh. But that is exactly what *I* wanted, Brother Leo! To be released!"

Without taking a single bite, he lay down and closed his eyes. But I ate heartily and then, sated and drowsy, stretched out next to him and fell asleep at once. Toward midnight, however, I was awakened by the sound of Francis screaming. I opened my eyes and was able, in the light of the sanctuary lamp, to see him waving his arms in the air as though struggling with something.

"Brother Francis!" I called. "Brother Francis!"

But there was little chance of his hearing me. He must have been in the middle of a horrible nightmare, for he was beating his hands and feet against the floor, and bellowing.

Leaning over him, I touched his forehead. The sweat was run-

287

ning in torrents; his hair was sodden and dripping. I grasped his shoulders, shook him. He opened his eyes.

"Don't be afraid, Brother Francis," I said, caressing his quivering hands. "Don't be afraid, it was only a dream—a plague on it!"

He sat up and tried to talk, but could only stammer unintelligibly.

"Calm yourself, Brother Francis. It's almost morning. Day will come and dispel the phantoms of the night."

"They weren't phantoms, Brother Leo, they weren't phantoms. All those paintings are alive! As soon as they saw I had closed my eyes, they climbed down from the walls. At the same time all the demons inside me came forth and, together, both began to attack me. O God, it was unbearable!"

With the sleeve of his frock he sponged his bleeding eyes. He was panting, his teeth chattering. Outside, a strong wind whistled through the pines which surrounded the little church. From time to time lightning flashes entered through the tiny window of the sanctuary and fell like saber blows across Francis' livid bloodstained features. He quickly covered his face each time with the sleeve of his frock. I remember he once told me that thunderbolts were the glances of the Almighty, and now he was ashamed to let the Lord see him—for the vapor of the temptations was still rising from his flesh.

We both waited anxiously for the dawn, neither of us uttering a word. I too had begun to be afraid. The little church now seemed haunted to me also, full of dangerous unseen presences; and when the lightning illuminated the storied walls I covered my face with my robe so that I would not see the paintings and the paintings would not see me and pounce upon me. Next to Francis as I was, my mind as well as his had begun to totter—or was it perhaps that my inner eyes were opening and enabling me to see the invisible?

Francis recovered his composure little by little. Soon he had placed his hand in mine; apparently he wished to comfort me.

"Do not be distressed, Brother Leo. Even fear is an aid to salvation. It too is holy; it too is man's friend."

The thunderclaps had come nearer now. All of a sudden the squall broke out. We heard the rain beating with happy, cackling laughter against the church roof. It's just as well, I said to myself. Francis is exhausted from his struggle last night with the demons.

He may as well remain lying down a little while longer to recover his strength.

The first feeble, bemired light entered through the tiny window; on the walls long white beards and pale ascetic faces began to shine, as did the horns, tails, and guffawing mouths around them. But it was day now; God's light had come and I was not afraid. We could hear a bird peeping. The earth was awakening amidst all the rain and mud. Francis had closed his eyes again and was listening exultantly to the sound of the male waters falling from heaven.

"Brother Leo, don't you feel intense joy, just as the earth does, whenever the floodgates of heaven open? Oh, if I could only be a clod of soil and could dissolve into the celestial waters! But the soul, not being made of earth, keeps a firm grip on the body and prevents it from dissolving."

"Why does it hold on like that, Brother Francis? It should let go, the way you want it to, and allow the body to be lost—and saved!"

Francis shook his head. "It is trying to go somewhere, Brother Leo; yes, without a doubt it is trying to go somewhere and it possesses no other donkey to carry it. Thus it feeds and waters this donkey until it reaches its destination; then it dismounts joyfully, gives the beast a kick, and abandons it in the earth, to return to dust."

Two or three birds were chirping now. The rain had grown more gentle.

"Let's go," said Francis. "It stopped raining. . . . In God's name!"

He tried to get up, but his knees gave way beneath him, and he collapsed to the floor.

"Your donkey is tired, Brother Francis. Let the poor thing rest a little so that it will be able to carry you some more."

"We mustn't allow our donkeys to do as they please, Brother Leo. If I had listened to mine I would still be living in Sior Bernardone's house; I would still be singing serenades beneath windows. Come, help me. Let's make the beast get up."

I grasped Francis under the arms, drew him to his feet, and then followed behind as he proceeded to the door with faltering steps.

The world outside was drenched. The stones glistened; the soil had turned to mud; the sky above loomed pitch black. The pine trees had been pummeled by the torrents, and they exuded a balm like honey.

"It's going to rain again, Brother Francis."

"Let it. The soul won't allow its body to be dissolved just yet, so have no fears, Brother Leo. Come!"

We began our march, wading through mud which reached up to our ankles. Our feet were soon as heavy as lead, and we could hardly lift them.

One hour, two hours had passed in this way when suddenly I saw Francis plunge headlong to the ground, his face burrowing into the mire. In desperate haste I sped to lift him up before he suffocated. Placing him across my shoulders, I commenced to run. I felt like cursing his obstinacy, also my own imbecile desire to do things contrary to my nature. It had begun to rain again. I continued to walk with my burden for a half-hour more and then—praise the Lord!—I saw some houses among the pine trees. Though I was ready to drop, this gave me the strength to keep going, and I finally arrived, covered head to toe with mud. Francis was still unconscious. Finding one of the street doors open, I entered. An old peasant rushed out into the yard, followed by his wife, a gaunt creature all shriveled up like a raisin.

"Eh, good Christians," I said, "my companion fainted from exhaustion. In Christ's name, let me lay him down for a while in your cottage—until he comes to."

The man scowled; he did not like to be annoyed. But the old woman took pity on us. Grasping Francis' feet while I held him under the arms, she helped bring him inside. We laid him down on the bed, and she brought rose vinegar which she applied to his temples. She also held some under his nose for him to smell. Francis opened his eyes.

"Peace be to this house, my brothers," he said to the two peasants, who were leaning over him.

The man took me by the arm. "Who is this monk? I've seen him somewhere."

"It's Father Francis, Francis of Assisi."

"The saint?"

"Yes, the saint."

The peasant clasped Francis' hand. "If you are really Francis of Assisi and the saint everyone says you are, then I have a word to tell you for your own benefit: Be sure to live up to your reputation for honesty and goodness, because many souls who believe you to be honest and good have placed themselves in your hands."

Tears welled up to Francis' eyes.

"My brother, I shall never forget what you have said. I shall struggle as hard as I possibly can to be honest and good, so that those souls who have entrusted themselves to my care will not be ashamed of me. Bless you, my brother, for reminding me."

As soon as he had spoken he attempted to kiss the man's hand, but the other, anticipating him, kissed the mud on Francis' feet.

When I saw the old peasant's devotion, I was encouraged to say to him: "My brother, we still have a long journey ahead of us. We're going to Monte Alvernia, and my companion is unable to walk. For the love of Christ, wouldn't you like to give us your donkey so that Father Francis can ride?"

"With pleasure, monk, with pleasure. If I didn't have a donkey to give you I would carry him on my own back, for the salvation of my soul. I have committed many sins in my life, as you can well imagine, and now the time has come for me to redeem myself." He turned to the old woman. "Kill a hen, wife, and give some broth to the sick friar so that he'll be able to hold his head up. We'll eat first and then we'll start our journey. I'm going to come with you, monk."

I was delighted, since I've always been a great lover of chicken. And a little while later when I sipped the warm, fragrant soup and, stretching out my hand, took a huge piece of lean white meat together with the bird's small liver—oh, how can I describe it? Forgive me, Lord, but even now when I recall that meal my mouth waters. God grant that what Francis says is true and that hens are eligible for Paradise. If so we'll kill one each Sunday—for the greater glory of the Lord.

We lifted Francis up, placed him on the donkey's back, and started on our way.

"Is Alvernia far?" I asked our guide.

"Further than the devil's mother! What business do the likes of the two of you have around that wild mountain? I'm glad I'm not in your shoes! They say Captain Wolf, the bandit chief, has his hideaway at the summit. Aren't you afraid?"

"Why should we be afraid, my brother? We don't own anything. We belong to the order of holy Poverty."

"Poor devils, you chose the wrong order! If you think you've gone hungry up to now, just wait—the worst is yet to come. As for me," he said with a laugh, "I belong to the holy order of comfortable living."

"Yes, but we, hungry and barefooted as we are, have a chance of entering the kingdom of heaven."

"It's possible, monk; I don't say it isn't. But I have a chance of entering the kingdom of heaven just like you if I'm lucky enough to receive the sacrament at the last minute. Since both of us suck on this consoling 'chance' for the whole of our lives, isn't it more in a man's best interests to eat, drink, and kiss in order to make sure he doesn't lose his earthly life *as well* as the life eternal? Why look at me like that? If I don't get into heaven I have only one life to lose, while Your Holiness has two. My calculations are correct, I presume."

I coughed. There was nothing I could say in reply, for I had often—oh, how many times—made the same calculations to myself. Poor Brother Leo, what could you do? Francis went in the lead and it was your job to follow!

We walked along road after road until nightfall, when we entered a cave. Our guide collected an armful of wild grass and fed his donkey; next, he opened his sack, brought out the leftover chicken, and fed us. Producing a small jug of wine as well, he threw back his head and drank, then passed the jug to me. I could hear it cackling like a partridge above my lips.

"You'll have to excuse me, monks," he said. "I chose the order of comfortable living—remember?"

Having reminded us of this, he lifted the flask to his lips once again and emptied it. Immediately afterwards, he placed a stone beneath his head to serve as a pillow, crossed himself with amazing rapidity, and fell asleep.

The next morning the weather was divine: sky absolutely clear, trees and stones glistening, the sun outfitted with a crop of long blond hair. We set Francis on the donkey and departed.

Soon we reached a large village whose name escapes me. Francis wanted to stop and preach, but the peasant was in a hurry.

"If you start to preach, expecting to convince these lubbers that they should know and follow God's commandments, expecting to drum some sense into their thick skulls, we won't reach Alvernia this year or the year after either. You'll have to forgive me, but I'm in a hurry to get back to my village. Unlike you monks, I have work to do. I struggle to put enough sense into the soil to make it nurture some grain and enable me to produce bread so that we can eat. I struggle to put enough sense into the vines to make them produce grapes for me to tread and turn into wine, so that we can drink, become merry, and then glorify the Almighty Lord."

"Just for a few moments . . ." Francis begged. "Just enough time to say two words, only two . . ."

"Words about God have no end. Don't think you can fool me! You talk and talk, get drunk on your own eloquence, then open the Gospel, and after that there's no stopping you!"

He raised his stick and whacked the donkey on the rump. The animal gave a start, then lowered its head and bolted, coming within a hair's breadth of catapulting its rider to the ground. The peasant glanced at me.

"Well, what do you think: wasn't I right?" he asked, laughing behind his gray mustachios. "Forgive me for saying so, but if you keep on the way you are, telling first this one, then that one, to be saved, you won't have time to save yourselves. . . . I've got a neighbor in the village—Caroline, God bless her! She's nicely built, with a good-sized rump and a pile of children. Do you know what she said to me one day? Here, bend over and let me whisper it in your ear so the saint won't hear me."

I liked this portly, succulent old man; I liked him because he was comfortable and prosperous, and because the sap still flowed in his veins.

"What did she say?" I asked, leaning over. "Speak softly."

" 'Marino'—oh, yes, I forgot to tell you my name is Marino— 'Marino, by doing first this one's pleasure then that one's, I never found time to have any children by my husband.' "

He burst into peals of laughter.

"The same thing will happen to you, poor devils," he concluded.

Thus, conversing together, we made the time go by. Thanks to the grace of God, it did not rain. The pine trees were fragrant, the sun cool, and the old man still had some food in his sack. This we soon did away with, however.

"That's the end of our comfortable living, monk," he said as he turned the bag inside-out. "By the way, what's your name, just to make things clear?"

"Brother Leo."

"Yes, it's the end of our comfortable living, poor old Leo. Before long I'll leave you at the foot of the mountain and then you'll rejoin the order of Poverty. You called it 'holy' if I'm not mistaken."

"Yes, holy Poverty."

"A plague on it! Don't mention that word to me: it makes my hair stand on end."

The sun had finally begun to set. At a turn in the road a huge, forbidding mountain suddenly came into view.

"There—that's Alvernia," said old Marino, pointing toward the mountain. "I hope you enjoy it!"

Francis crossed himself; then, raising his hand, he blessed the mountain. "Sister Alvernia, I'm glad to see you," he said. "I greet the stones and wild beasts that inhabit you; I greet the birds and angels in the air round about you! Look, my soul: it's Sister Alvernia. Do not be afraid."

I, not breathing a word, stared in terror at the savage uninhabited mountain. It was bare rock except for a few clumps of pine trees here and there, and a few oaks. Two hawks that had been roosting on a ledge soared upward and began to plait wreaths in the air above our heads.

"It's a good thing we're not hens," said the old man. "They would eat us; and then goodbye to the kingdom of heaven!"

Suddenly a peasant darted past us, but Marino whistled at him and he stopped. Our guide went up to the man and they spoke together in undertones for a long time, standing in the middle of the road. When Marino returned to us, he was wearing a long face.

"This is as far as I go," he said. "Not a step further!"

"What's the matter, Marino? Here, at the beginning of the ascent, is just when we need your help the most. What news did your friend bring you?"

"He said that Captain Wolf the bandit chief came down from his hideaway and is roaming around the foot of the mountain. He must be dying of hunger."

He lifted Francis off the donkey and sat him down upon a stone beneath one of the pine trees.

"Farewell, saint of God," he said. "You have no possessions, no children, and you're not afraid of robbers. With me it's different."

He turned and winked at me. "Well, what do you say?" he hissed into my ear, indicating the road back with his thumb.

I threw a glance at Francis.

"No, Marino, I'm not leaving my post. You go, and may God be with you!"

He shrugged his shoulders, mounted his donkey with a leap, and was gone.

I sat down next to Francis. It wasn't cold out, but I was shivering. And as I sat there, all at once I heard chirping and the rustling of wings. I lifted my eyes, and what did I see but swarms of birds of all kinds—sparrows, larks, orioles, chaffinches, blackbirds, plus a lone partridge—all flitting about our heads, as though welcoming us to their lairs. Growing continually more bold, they came closer and closer until finally they squatted proudly round Francis' legs.

"Sister Birds, Sister Birds," Francis murmured with emotion, "yes, yes, it's me, your brother, returned from his sojourn in strange, faraway lands. I've come, I've come, and now, on this holy mountain, we shall live together at last; and if there is anything you need, you must tell me, and I shall intercede with God, our Father, in your behalf."

The partridge gazed at him tenderly from its position at his feet and listened with its head inclined to one side, like a human being.

And just as we were all completely transported by the miracle, two shrieking peasants ran up to us. "Why are you sitting there, you poor fools?" they cried. "Wolf is coming!"

"Which way?"

"There! There!"

I jumped to my feet, my heart in my mouth.

"Let's get away, Brother Francis, let's get away!"

"Stay here, man of little faith, while I go find Captain Wolf. Have no fears: God is omnipotent, and it is quite possible that He will transform this Wolf into a lamb."

He rose and set out in the direction indicated by the two peasants. I hid my head behind the sleeve of my frock and waited, completely alone. I knew that God was omnipotent, and yet I still had no confidence. How many times had He allowed His faithful to be eaten by wild beasts or to be killed by infidels! The safest thing would be for us to take to our heels. As the proverb had it: God helps those who help themselves!

But a cup of milk given me by a passing shepherd boy was enough to send my heart back to its place. I was actually ashamed, and I decided to go find Francis in order not to desert him in time of peril. Just as I was about to get up, however, I changed my mind. It's safer here, I said to myself.

I cupped my ear on the chance that I might hear Francis calling me. But everything around me was silent, serene. The darkness had begun to rise from the plain, covering the olive groves and vineyards below. It mounted without respite, headed for the mountain; layer by layer, the world was vanishing.

Suddenly a huge, savage voice resounded from behind the rocks above me. It grew constantly louder: it was approaching. But then I was able to distinguish that it was not one voice, but two: the first hoarse, wild; the other tender and weak. Recognizing Francis' singing, I jumped to my feet.

As the voices came still closer I was able to make out the words of the song. It was the anthem "Christ Is Risen from the Dead, Trampling Death by Means of Death." They met, I said to myself; they met, became friends, and now they're both returning to God's fold. And truly, I spied Francis in the dim light approaching with a ferocious-looking man, all beard, mustache, and long shaggy mop of hair. They were walking arm in arm, nodding to me.

"Here is your famous Captain Wolf," cried Francis merrily. "He isn't a wolf any more, he's a lamb."

"A lamb, brother, but one that eats wolves," growled the bandit chief. "I mustn't forget my profession."

"Yes, at first. But later you will come closer to God, and then you'll even stop eating wolves."

Francis suddenly fell silent. He had discovered a silver amulet on Captain Wolf's broad hairy chest. There were some words engraved on the amulet, but with his impaired sight he was unable to read them.

"What do you have there, my brother? What are these words you carry about with you?"

The bandit chief blushed from shame. With a yank he removed the amulet from his neck. "Old sins. Don't read it!" he said, about to throw it into the bushes.

"No, no, I want to, Brother Lamb. All your sins have already been forgiven. The wolf is dead. Long live the lamb!"

He brought the amulet close to his eyes, and read: "Enemy of God and man."

Captain Wolf took it from Francis' hands, crushed it, and threw it away. "Friend of God and man!" he exclaimed. "I'm going to order another amulet and have 'Friend of God and man' written upon it. And now, until tomorrow! Climb up the mountain the count gave you. I'll come first thing in the morning and build you two shelters of branches and mud. Then I'll go back down to stand watch—and heaven help the man who tries to pass without my permission."

He reflected for a moment.

"Wait—I'd better go along with you now. I'll guide you. There aren't any trails on the mountain, and you might get lost."

He clasped Francis in his meaty arms and lifted him up like an infant.

"Let's go," he said. "You don't need a donkey, Father Francis."

An hour later we reached a flat exposed area. Towering in the center was an imposing oak densely covered with leaves. Francis addressed our guide:

"Brother Lamb—that's what I'm going to call you from now on—Brother Lamb, when you build my hut tomorrow, please build it beneath this oak; and set Brother Leo's a little further off, far enough so that we won't be able to see each other and so that if I call him, he won't hear. I must be completely alone on this mountain, my brother."

"With pleasure, Father Francis. And tomorrow I'll bring you bread, olives, and whatever else I find. I don't want either of you to die of hunger, because I've never heard anyone claim that dead men are able to pray. Every so often, therefore, I'm going to bring you all you need to keep you from kicking the bucket. I'll steal from the rich to feed the poor. And why not? Isn't that just? Why shake your head, Father Francis? Without a doubt it wasn't God who portioned out the goods of this world, but Satan—which explains why the distribution is so illegitimate. I am simply going to restore things to their proper places."

Having said this, he kissed Francis' hand and vanished into the night.

IT IS WITH BOTH terror and unspeakable joy that I bring to mind the days we lived on Monte Alvernia —days, months, or was it years. Time hovered above us like a falcon and beat its wings with such rapidity that it seemed not to be moving at all. The moon rose and set, sometimes like a sickle, sometimes like a silver disk. At times the snow began to melt and the water ran down the slopes of Alvernia just as Francis' prayers did, fructifying the plain; at other times it fell and accumulated, rose-colored in the morning, flashy-white at midday, bluish in the evening. It came without noise, tightly girdling our two huts. Each morning Francis stepped onto the white blanket and scattered crumbs from the bread which Brother Lamb (God bless him!) regularly brought to keep us from dying of hunger. The birds had come to take this for granted. They surrounded Francis' hut at the break of dawn, urging him to appear. One sparrow hawk had grown particularly bold: each morning it circled the hut and screeched loudly in order to wake him.

The cold was frightful. Our robes had long since been reduced to shreds, and the wind swished through them, turning our skin blue. It was indeed a wonder I was able to survive such an ordeal without joining the choir invisible! Perhaps Francis was right when he said that whoever thinks of God keeps warm in winter and cool in summer. I must say that I had God in my thoughts with extraordinary frequency on that inhuman mountain, but on the other hand I also thought quite often about a pot boiling away over a roaring fire, and heated wine with a generous spoonful of pepper thrown in to warm one's bones, and the table set, and the whole world filled with the aroma of roast pig. Who would care then if the snow was packed over your head outside? The door would be bolted and neither snow, cold, nor hunger able to enter. Security! Security! And God would not be forgotten either, for after you had eaten and drunk your fill you would lift your arms to the ceiling, safely inside your house, and thank the Almighty for having made fire, pigs, and doors. . . .

If anyone is wondering about Francis, there was no danger of his suffering from either cold or hunger, because God, an unquenchable fire, burned within him day and night, and because the bread of the angels stood constantly before his lips, warm, white, and fragrant. Despite this, my concern for him tormented me on occasion and made me leave my shelter to see what was happening. I used to observe him go each morning, noon, and evening to the black cave which was his accustomed place of prayer. And what a miracle I saw! When he set out to speak with God both his stature and way of walking were entirely different from when he had finished and was returning to his hut. When he departed he was stunted, humpbacked, exhausted, and he stumbled through the snow, constantly falling and dragging himself again to his feet. But when he had completed his prayer and begun to return: What presence he had! What a giant emerged from the black cave! With towering, erect body, he strode gallantly through the snow, and above his head was a fiery column of air ten times his own height.

Forgive me, Lord, if I felt envious when I saw him like this. What was he made of—pure steel? pure spirit?—to enable him never to be hungry or cold, and never to say "enough"? As for me, I shivered day and night, and was starving, and had neither the inclination nor the strength for prayer—nor the impertinence, for even if I had raised my eyes and arms to heaven, my thoughts would have remained down below on earth, far down indeed, and the words which I would have said to God would have been nothing but iridescent bubbles, full of air.

It was three or four days since I had last lifted my hands to heaven. Brother Lamb came as usual to leave me our alms: bread, olives, goat's cheese, and whatever else he found.

"Do you want me to light a fire?" he asked.

"No," I answered with a sigh. "Brother Francis doesn't permit fires."

"Why?"

"Because it's cold out, he says."

"But that's exactly when you need a fire, you idiot."

"That's exactly why we don't want one."

"Well then, what do you use to keep warm?"

"God."

Captain Wolf shrugged his shoulders.

"Turn everything upside down if you want; it's your own affair. As for me, I'm going back to my cave, where I've got a pile of thick logs blazing away on the hearth. The pot is on, Brother Leo. Yesterday I killed two partridges and I'm preparing them with rice. Are you coming to have a bite, Brother Leo—to grease your innards, warm your bones, poor devil?"

My mouth began to water.

"Oh, gladly, gladly, my brother, if I only wasn't afraid of Brother Francis."

"He doesn't have to find out."

"But it's my duty to tell him."

"Supposing you do. What will he do to you?"

"Nothing. He'll sigh, that's all—and a knife will pierce my heart."

"As you like, Brother Leo. All the same, keep the partridges in mind—partridges, steaming rice, abundant wine, and a roaring fire. Repeat it over and over again to yourself like a charm—partridges, steaming rice, abundant wine, roaring fire—and perhaps you'll come. Until then . . ."

He rubbed his hands together and stamped his feet on the ground to thaw them out.

"Aren't you afraid of God, my brother?" I asked.

"I'm not afraid of men, so how can you expect me to be afraid of God?"

He began the descent, and the mountain echoed with his laughter.

I was left alone. Never had the wilderness and my own utter solitude seemed so unbearable. Partridges, steaming rice, abundant wine, roaring fire . . . I got up and went as far as the door, where I stopped. "Shame on you, disgraceful Leo! When Brother Francis finds out, how will you endure his sigh? Stay in your hut. Dry bread is good too, and so is the cold. Others have the right to eat their fill and to keep themselves warm; you don't! You have other rights, much greater ones." "Such as . . . ?" "Need you ask? By means of your life you will show others the road to salvation." "And what if I die?" "So much the better. In that case you'll show others the road to salvation by means of your death. You have put on the angelic vestment, the frock. You are not a man any more, but neither are you an angel: you stand in the middle. Did I say 'stand'? No, you aren't standing, you are progressing toward the angelic—progressing little by little, with each of your good deeds." "I'm still a man; in fact I seem to be growing continually more human. Give me your permission just this once, and afterwards I'll become an angel, a real angel, I swear to you!" "Do as you like. You are free. Depart freely for the Inferno if you like—I won't stand in your way. Have a nice trip!"

My head whirling, I went back inside the hut and sank down onto the floor. I was on the point of bursting into tears. All of a sudden, however, I felt myself carried away by rage. An angel, he said, an angel! "It's easy enough to be an angel when you have no stomach, but just try when you do! Just try! I want to see if you can keep your mouth from watering when two boiled partridges are steaming in front of you right under your nose. Inexperience loves to preach! I'm a man; Captain Wolf has invited me to eat, and I'm going!"

I darted outside. The snow had stopped. The clouds were breaking up; the sky gleamed between them like patches of tarnished copper. I kept my eyes on Captain Wolf's huge, deep footprints and stepped in each, following them. I wasn't walking, I was flying. I went as fast as I could, and owing to my haste fell two or three times, covering my beard with snow. Finally I arrived in front of our new convert's grotto. I bent down, gasping for breath. The fire was blazing; the aroma of roast partridge saturated the air. I could see Captain Wolf kneeling before the coals, stirring the contents of the pot.

"Hello!" I called from the entrance.

He turned. "Welcome to the monk!" he said with a laugh. "Come in, come in. Dinner is served. Loosen your belt!"

I entered, undid my knotted cord, and squatted next to the fire. O Lord God Almighty, what joy! Never in my life had I felt such gratitude toward God, such love, such a delightful need to pray and to address Him as Father! Truly, who is more a father: he who tosses his children out without giving them a mouthful of food or a garment to throw over their backs, or he who lights a fire for them and puts the pot on to boil and portions out food for them to eat?

We washed our hands with snow, spread a sheepskin over the ground in front of the hearth, and placed the pot in the middle; then, cutting ourselves huge slices of bread, we sat down cross-legged opposite each other—the repentant bandit chief and the so-called lion of God. We stretched forth our paws. Captain Wolf took one of the partridges, I the other, and for a considerable time you heard nothing in the cave but the working of our jaws and the gurgling of wooden wine mugs.

What bliss! What Paradise! God forgive me, but this was how I pictured heaven, let Francis say what he would. Yes, the Sultan was right. . . .

The day began to grow dim. Opposite me I saw the large-boned face of our beloved bandit chief glowing bright red in the firelight. I had imbibed more than enough wine and at intervals—forgive me, Lord—I saw two horns on his forehead, two twisted, glossy horns butting the air. For a moment the thought crossed my mind, making me shudder, that perhaps the Tempter had dressed himself in Captain Wolf's body. Perhaps this man opposite me was the devil; perhaps he had lured me with a partridge, and here I was—caught in his net! When we had done away with the two birds and had emptied the divine flask, we threw fresh logs on the fire. I was in seventh heaven, and I began to sing the anthem "Christ Is Risen" while Captain Wolf kept time for me by clapping his hands. And now and then he too cried out in a wild, booming voice which reverberated throughout the cave.

"My brother, my brother!" he shouted, embracing me in an outpouring of love. "I'm going to say something to you, but I don't want you to take it ill. I swear by the partridge I've just eaten that wine is better able to bring men together and make them into brothers than the Gospel is. Forgive me for thinking so. But look, just now I had a sip of wine and my eyes opened and I saw—saw that you were my brother."

This was followed by a profusion of hugs and kisses.

"What I want, Brother Wolf, is for you to be able to see, without the aid of wine, that *all* men are your brothers. Because as soon as you're sober, what happens? Everyone becomes your enemy again, and the feeling of brotherhood vanishes."

"In that case, would that we were able to stay drunk our entire lives!" exclaimed Captain Wolf, sucking a final drop from the flask.

"Agreed, Brother Wolf-Lamb! Ah, if only I had the power, I would perform my own miracle: I would establish a Rule whereby each morning the brothers would drink a huge bottle of wine and would then dash out furiously to the villages and cities to preach. Just imagine how they would hug and kiss the people they met, how they would defy every danger, how they would sing and dance in praise of the Lord! Their ascent would be simple as can be, and thoroughly delightful into the bargain. From the warmth of emotions proceeding from wine they would advance to those proceeding from God, and from there straight to heavenly bliss!"

"Enroll me in your order, Father Leo!" laughed Captain Wolf, letting me in his enthusiasm have a staggering punch on the back. "What do you say: I'll take along an immense string of sausages and a jug of wine, and we'll go find Francis and tell him about the new Rule."

Suddenly I felt afraid. Turning, I gazed toward the entrance of the cave. It seemed to me that Francis' shadow was flitting all about and that I had heard a deep sigh in the air. I got up.

"It's time for me to be going. What if Francis visits my hut and doesn't find me there?"

"Tell him you were praying, Brother Leo. And really, in accordance with the new order what else was all this—the partridges, rice, warmth—but prayer offered up to the Lord? Tell the truth: did you ever feel so close to God as you did tonight? That is the meaning of prayer!"

How could I sit down to explain to the bandit that prayer was something else, since I myself had never discovered what it was?

Captain Wolf accompanied me for a good part of the way. He was in a fine mood, and did not stop chattering.

"Once, when I was a bandit (I still am, but don't tell Francis: it might disturb him—he's a bit naïve, you know); as I was saying, once when I was a bandit, some poor devil of a priest wanted to confess me. 'Do you pray?' he asked. 'Of course! But in my own manner,' I told him. 'That is to say . . .' 'By stealing.' 'And you have no intention of repenting, miserable wretch?' 'There's plenty of time. I'm only thirty-five years old. When I become a decrepit old graybeard unable to stand on my legs any more, then I'll repent. Everything in its due time, my friend. When you're young: steal. When you're old: repent.' The priest flew into a rage. 'Take it easy, old man,' I said to him. 'Don't you realize I'm closer to Christ than Your Holiness is?' 'You?' 'Me. I'm the thief who was crucified next to Christ, on his right side.'

"That, my dear Brother Leo, is the whole trick, and don't you forget it. At the last instant, when death is approaching, you have to find a way to get on Christ's right side, not on the left. On the right, poor miserable Brother Leo, or else you're done for!"

I was in a hurry to flee as far as possible from this bandit chief. Some demon inside me was enjoying everything he said. God, the devil, Francis, the life of ease—these were all in a flutter within me. Oh, when would I be by myself so that I could put everything back in order!

"Farewell, my brother. May God repay you for the good you have done me, and forgive you for the bad."

He squeezed my hand, nearly breaking it. "Don't forget to write the new Rule," he called after me. "Don't forget now—remember, it's for your own good!"

I talked and gesticulated to myself the whole way back. It was nighttime when I reached my hut. How cold I found it inside, good God, how lonely! I had fled from heaven and returned to hell. Wrapping myself tightly in my robe, I lay down. The wind was whistling through the trees outside; wolves were howling in the distance. I found it impossible to close my eyes; nor did I feel my heart pure enough to allow me to pray. Finally, shortly before daybreak, a heavy sleep full of nightmares overwhelmed me. The moment my sight filled with darkness I dreamed that I was in Egypt, at Thebes, where the great desert hermits had set up their huts. I was a hermit also—Arsenius by name—and while I was kneeling in prayer and thinking of my father Nilus, a centenarian anchorite whose hermitage was five miles away, a monk ran up to me. "Hurry, Brother Arsenius," he cried, "your father is asking for you. He's dying, and he says you should come quickly so that he can give you his blessing." I jumped to my feet and set out as fast as I could,

305

weeping as I ran. The sun was frightful. A camel caravan was proceeding along the main road in the distance, and I could hear the sad, monotonous song of the drivers. Finally, about noontime, I reached my father's retreat. I saw him laid out on the sand surrounded by five or six monks who were undressing him and washing the body while chanting continually. One of them turned to me. "He rendered up his soul to God just a moment ago," he said. "He never stopped pronouncing your name and calling you, but you came too late," said another. As they spoke, however, the dead man seemed to hear, for he moved. The monks took to their heels, terror-stricken. My father's lips stirred; he opened his eyes and gazed at me. "Bend down, my son," he murmured. "Can anyone hear us?" His eyes were laden with fear; his beard, ears, lips, hair were all covered with earth.

"No one, Father. We're alone."

"Bend down. I have a terrible secret to confide to you. Bend down further." I did, and he placed his mouth against my ear. His voice was weak, faltering, as though it were coming from far far away or rising from a deep, empty well: "Arsenius, my son, we have been duped. We have been duped, and now it's too late! There is no heaven, and no hell either!"

"What is there then—chaos?"

"No, not even chaos."

"But what, then?"

"Nothing!"

Raising himself up, he clawed my neck, nearly strangling me. Then, all at once, he rolled onto the sand. . . .

I uttered a piercing cry and awoke, grasping my head between my hands for fear it would split. The ascetic's lips were still against my ear, his words were still bounding from organ to organ: from my heart to my kidneys, kidneys to lungs, lungs to throat—strangling me. "We've been duped. . . ." If it was true, what then? "Brother Francis," I cried, "Brother Francis. Help! Help!"

Getting up, I went to the door and stood there, gazing outside. Snow everywhere. The dawn had begun to mount from the horizon; it groped its way along the snow, sometimes disappeared, fell like a man, but then lifted itself back up again: it was holding the daylight in a dim lantern and struggling to illumine the world. I could not bear to look; it made me sick at heart. Sinking to the ground, I curled up into a shivering ball and began to bang my head against the rocky floor. Blood ran over my face, but instead of suffering, I felt somewhat calmed. I got up. A sign will appear to me, I said to myself, a sign which will make me understand; some signal from God: a bird, a thunderclap, a voice—who could tell? God's tongue was rich and varied. He would speak to me and give some explanation of my suffering.

It had been days since I'd seen Francis, so I set off toward his shelter. I began to climb, plunging into the snow with my bare feet. I had to exert all my strength to keep from cursing. Do you call this living? I cried out to myself. Even the wild beasts have something, they have fur to wear—while we, we're just two slugs, two snails without shells. . . . I grumbled in this way until I finally reached the ridge from where Francis' hut could be seen. I glanced in every direction. Suddenly I saw Francis at the top of a high ledge with his arms stretched out on either side so that it seemed, amid all the snow, that a black cross was nailed to the rock. Fearing that he might freeze to death up there, I rushed forward as fast as I could in order to climb the rock, take him in my arms, bring him back to his hut and then—whether he agreed or not— light a fire and revive him. But before I had scrambled even half-way up the rock, I uttered a loud cry. Francis was suspended a full arm's span above the top of the ledge, hovering tranquilly, delicately in the air, his arms constantly outstretched to form a cross. Terrified at the thought that he might fly away, I exerted all my strength, climbed to the summit, and reached out to catch hold of him by the hem of his frock. But he, calmly, delicately as before, came down and sat upon the rock.

He glanced at me as though not knowing who I was, as though astonished at the sight of a human being. I took him in my arms and stumbled down the ledge, falling and pulling myself up again until I was completely exhausted. But I managed to reach his shelter. I made a fire, brought Francis next to the hearth, and began to massage him vigorously in order to thaw out his blood. Little by little he came back to life. Opening his eyes, he recognized me.

"Why did you bring me down, Brother Leo?" he murmured. "It was better for me up there."

"Forgive me, Brother Francis, but you would have died."

"But didn't you see how I was rising into the air? I had begun to die. Why did you bring me down?"

He looked at his palms and at his swollen, bloody feet.

"They hurt!" he murmured breathlessly, clasping me in his arms. "They hurt, Brother Leo! My hands and feet feel as though someone had driven nails through them. At night I can't close my eyes, they hurt so much."

He was silent for a moment, and then:

"Forgive me, O my faithful donkey. Your torments have still not come to an end. We have not arrived yet, but we are coming close. Follow me—and do not lose heart!"

He placed his hand on my head.

"Bless you, little lion of God. Go now to your hut. I want to be alone."

I returned to my shelter, not knowing what to think. Could this be the sign I had been seeking from God, I wondered. This—Francis rising in the air? Yes, God's tongue was exceedingly rich, and He had answered me with this vision. At night God had sent the dream to jar me; the next day He had dispatched the vision to steady me again. He plays with us as a father with his small children when he wishes to teach them to suffer, love, and endure. When I entered my desolate, icy hut at last, my mind had grown calm.

One sin, however, was still weighing upon my heart: the partridges, the warmth, the rice. I crossed myself and resolved to go to Francis in the morning and confess so that this burden could also be lifted from me. In a short time winter was going to be over and I would embark on the new spring free of cares—pure, my heart filled with swallows.

The next day found me at Francis' feet. I confessed my transgression to him; then I lowered my forehead to the ground in front of his feet, and waited. Francis did not speak, did not sigh. I was aware of nothing except a tremor in the big toe of each of his feet. I waited and waited. Finally I could not endure so much silence any longer.

"Well, Brother Francis?" I asked. "What penance are you going to give me?"

308

"Your sin is a grave one, my child. For three days and nights I shall put neither bread nor water into my mouth."

"But it wasn't you who sinned," I cried, "it was me. I'm the one you must punish!"

"What difference does it make, Brother Leo? Aren't we all one? I sinned with you; you fasted with me. We've lived together such a long time: how is it possible you still have not understood this? Go now, with God's blessing!"

He stooped to raise me up. I kissed his hand, and was suddenly overcome with tears.

"Never again," I cried, sobbing. "I swear it, Brother Francis, never again."

"I told you once before, didn't I, that 'never' and 'always' are words which belong to God. Only He may pronounce them. . . . Go. But take care, lamb of God: you just came within a hair's breadth of being gobbled up by a wolf!"

The snows had begun to melt. The sky cleared; beneath the snow, the brooks commenced to flow along the ground, descending toward the plain. Bushes lifted their heads and issued into the light; each time a breeze blew, the flakes that were still sitting on the trees crumbled noiselessly and fell to earth. The first cuckoos could be heard whistling in the forest, ejecting winter with their cries. And man's heart heard its brother the cuckoo and replied joyfully from its very depths. It was evident that both belonged to the same order, the order of Spring.

Heaven and earth alike became gentle, no longer afflicting mankind so severely; and sometimes when I went and placed the daily ration of bread outside Francis' shelter I would see an imperceptible smile on his withered lips.

"Spring is coming, Brother Leo," he kept saying to me in a joyous voice, "Spring, the earth's Blessed Lady Full of Grace. Behold, wherever she places her foot, the snow melts."

"The almond trees must already have begun to blossom on the plain," I answered him one day.

"If you want my blessing, Brother Leo, do not think about blossoming almond trees, for the Tempter crouches in their branches, nodding to us. Instead, turn your eyes inward and gaze at the almond tree within you—your soul—as it blossoms."

I used to sit for hours in the doorway of my hut, watching spring come; I felt that this very act was an unspoken prayer, a prayer full of gratitude rendered up to God. With the turn in the weather I had begun to go down to the foot of the mountain to cut cane and osier in order to weave baskets. During the day I would weave for hours on end, and in the course of my work I found my thoughts turning to God—much more rapidly, more surely, than when I knelt down with the express purpose of praying. I rejoiced that I was able in this way to blend manual work with prayer.

One day as I was sitting outside my hut weaving my baskets, I heard someone stamping over the rocks, breathing heavily. I knew it could not be Brother Wolf, since he never panted and always approached with inaudible footsteps. I got up, ran toward the sound—and who should I see but Father Silvester!

"Welcome, welcome!" I cried.

My heart leapt with joy to behold one of the friars after so many months. I embraced him and sat him down next to me.

"I haven't a thing to offer you, my brother. Only bread and water."

But Father Silvester's mind was not on food. "How is Brother Francis?" he asked in an anguished voice.

"Alive and suffering. You won't recognize him, he's so eaten away by fasting and prayer. Every morning before daybreak, just at the hour he falls asleep for a few moments, a hawk comes and wakes him up. You would think God had ordered even the birds to torture him."

"His father is dying, Brother Leo; he sent me to tell Francis to come quickly so that he can see him before it is too late. He seems to be sorry for everything he did. Perhaps he wants to ask his son's forgiveness."

I thought of those first high-spirited days when we shook the dust of the world from our feet and stepped into God's fire. How many years, Lord, how many centuries had passed since then!

"Where is his shelter, Brother Leo?"

"I'll come with you," I said. "It's there, between the rocks. Let's hope he's not praying; otherwise he won't be able to speak to us."

We climbed up to the hut and found it empty.

"He must be praying in his cave," I said. "Let's go there, but very quietly. We mustn't disturb him."

310

We halted at the cave's entrance. At first we saw nothing in the darkness, but we were able to hear a sighing, imploring voice: "O my poor crucified Hope, my poor crucified Love! O Christ!" After a pause, the voice resumed in a tone that was even more suppliant, more despairing: "O my poor crucified Hope, my poor crucified Love! O Christ!"

Father Silvester started to enter, but I seized hold of his frock. "For God's sake, don't go near him," I whispered in his ear. "He gave me strict orders not to call him or touch him while he was praying. 'If you touch me,' he said, 'I shall crumble into a thousand pieces.' "

We remained outside the cave, one to the right of the entrance, the other to the left, waiting for him to finish his prayer and emerge so that we could speak to him. The sun reached the zenith, declined, was about to set, but Francis, kneeling and motionless, his arms spread wide, continued his imploration, repeating the same words over and over again. Finally, at dusk, we heard a deep, despairing sigh. Francis rose and came out, staggering as though drunk, his eyes red from blood and the flow of tears. We extended our hands to him, but he did not see us—his eyeballs had rolled inward: they were gazing at his bowels. He advanced several paces, tripping because he was unable to see. Then he halted; he seemed to be struggling to remember which direction he had to take to find his hut. He raised his hands to his temples: he felt suddenly dizzy. But he soon came round and began to walk again.

We followed behind on tiptoe in order not to startle him. As he was finally nearing his shelter, however, he heard the sound of a stone which had stirred beneath our feet. He turned. At first he did not recognize us, but as we came closer his face began to beam, his lips quivered, and he smiled. He held out his arms; Father Silvester fell into them.

"Brother Francis, Brother Francis, I've missed you so very much, I'm so glad to see you!"

Francis said nothing. He began to sway. Supporting him under the armpits, we helped him into the shelter and sat him down on the sheepskin which Brother Wolf had brought for him.

He turned to Father Silvester. "What has happened to the brothers?" he asked anxiously.

Father Silvester lowered his head and did not reply.

"What has happened to the brothers?" Francis repeated in an anguished voice, clasping the priest's hand. "Have no pity on me, Father Silvester. I want the truth!"

"They've changed route, Brother Francis. They've gone down to the plain to graze your flock in rich pastures."

"And what about holy Poverty?"

"They want to clothe and feed her, fatten her up, put sandals on her feet. And the Portiuncula seems too abject and despicable for them to deign to live there. They've gone through all the towns and villages collecting gold, and Brother Elias has just laid the foundations of an immense church three stories high and has sent for celebrated artisans and painters to decorate it. He says absolute Poverty must dwell in a palace, which is exactly what they are building for her."

"And holy Love?"

"The brothers have dispersed, some this way, some that. The old ones, our first brothers, refuse to obey the new shepherds; and when the new ones meet them on the road they laugh at their torn frocks and bare feet, and instead of addressing them as brothers they call them 'the barefooted ones.'"

"And holy Simplicity?"

"She's dead as well, Brother Francis. They've opened new schools. Some of them run to Bologna, others to Paris, and they study until they're so horribly clever they can shoe a flea. They collect thick tomes and mount the pulpit and give discourses, toiling and moiling to prove that Christ is God, that He was crucified, and that on the third day He rose from the dead. And they mix everything up so much that your mind turns upside down and your heart to ice. The day the wise men began to speak was the last day Christ was ever resurrected."

Suddenly—before we had time to prevent him—Francis fell face down on the ground. He remained there for a long time without speaking, except that every so often we heard a reproachful murmur: "God, O God, why? Why? It's my fault!" Then he would relapse into silence and begin to beat his forehead against the ground. We raised him up by force. He looked around.

"Brother Leo!"

"Here, Brother Francis, at your command."

"Open the Gospel, let your finger fall on a verse, and read."

I took the Gospel, opened it, and let my finger come down in the middle of the page. Then I went to the doorway, where there was more light.

"Read!"

Leaning over, I read: *The hour is coming, indeed it has come, when you will be scattered, every man to his home, and will leave me alone.*"

"More!" ordered Francis in an anguished voice. "What else does it say?"

"*Yet I am not alone, because the Father is with me.*"

"Enough!"

He took Father Silvester's hand.

"You heard Christ's voice, my brother. Though the friars have scattered, you must not feel sad. I myself allowed the pain to overwhelm me for an instant; but, as you see, we are not alone. The Father is with us, so why should we be afraid? He shall lead the sheep back along the uphill road; He shall nurture His flock with hunger once again."

A long silence followed. Francis was plunged in despair, but also in hope. We could sense that he was extremely far from us, far away in the future. Now and then strange sounds passed from his mouth into the deep silence, sounds like barking from a remote corner of the earth. It was as though he were a sheep dog barking at the flock to make them reassemble and return to the fold. Presently he fell asleep for an instant, but opened his eyes immediately and looked at us, smiling.

"I just had a very odd dream, my brothers. Listen: The friars were gathered in the Portiuncula and Elias was portioning out the world among them. A ragged, barefooted monk came by. Seeing them, he stopped and shook his head. One of the brothers was moved to anger. 'What are you doing, staring at us like that and shaking your head?' he shouted. 'Why do you go about barefooted, with a frock full of holes, your hair uncut, your unwashed body splattered with mud? Don't you know that our new general has expelled Poverty from the order? Go to your monastery and take a bath and get yourself some sandals and a clean frock so that you won't put the rest of us to shame.' 'I refuse!' 'You refuse, do you?' shrieked Elias, jumping to his feet. 'I'll have you lashed—forty strokes!' 'Go ahead.' 'What is your name?' 'First let me have the forty strokes.'

313

When the ragged monk had been whipped, and the blood was flowing, Elias repeated: 'Now tell us your name.' 'Francis,' the other replied, 'Francis of Assisi.'"

He looked at us. The smile had disappeared from his face.

"They thrash me, they expel me even in my sleep," he murmured. And then: "Glory be to God."

He closed his eyes. We realized that he had already departed and was far far away from us.

Father Silvester glanced in my direction, as though hoping I would give him the courage to speak to Francis.

"Brother Francis," I said, "come back from wherever you are, and listen. Father Silvester has a sad message for you. Command him to speak."

Francis pricked up his ears; he was struggling to hear me.

"What did you say, Brother Leo? A message? What message?"

"Ask Father Silvester. He's the one who will deliver it to you."

"Silvester, my brother," he said, clasping the priest's hand, "my heart can bear whatever message you bring. What is this message? Who is it from?"

"From your father, Brother Francis; from Sior Bernardone."

Francis crossed his arms and lowered his head, saying nothing.

"From your father," repeated Father Silvester. "He sent me to tell you to come so that he can see you and speak to you before he delivers up his soul to God."

Francis remained motionless.

"Your mother is inconsolable. She lies fallen on his pillow, weeping and lamenting. She is waiting for you, only for you, Brother Francis; she is waiting for you to come so that she may see you and be comforted. . . . Come!"

Francis neither spoke nor moved.

"Didn't you hear? What answer shall I give?"

Suddenly Francis rose, stretched his arm out toward Assisi, and traced the sign of the cross in the air.

"Farewell, Father," he whispered. "Forgive me!"

He turned to Silvester. "If you reach him in time, my brother, tell him I cannot leave this mountain. You know how a lion seizes a hare and bangs him playfully against the ground, don't you? Well, God has seized me in the same way. I cannot escape; I am writhing in God's claws and cannot escape. . . . Say to my father: 'Till we meet again!' "

"And to your mother?"

"The same: 'Till we meet again!' "

"Have you no pity for them?" Father Silvester asked hesitatingly. "They're your parents! Request God's permission. His goodness is infinite; He'll grant your request."

"I already asked Him once."

"And what was His reply?"

" 'I am your mother and father': that was His reply."

Father Silvester bowed and kissed Brother Francis' hand.

"Farewell, Brother Francis. Act as God guides you."

"Until we meet again, my brother," answered Francis, and he closed his eyes.

He wished to remain alone. We both left and went to my hut, where Father Silvester stopped for a moment to look around him. Stones, huge rocks, a few desiccated brambles were all that he saw on the ground; in the sky, two circling hawks.

"God wears a different expression below on the plain," he murmured. "Jehovah inhabits this peak; Christ lives below and promenades over the fields. How can you bear it here, Brother Leo?"

"I can't, but Francis bears it for both of us," I replied. Then I went into my hut to fetch him some bread.

"For your trip. You'll be hungry."

We embraced.

"Watch carefully over Francis," he admonished me in parting. "God is tearing him to shreds and will eat him. Don't you see: only his two wounded eyes are still alive—nothing else. If they are extinguished as well, Brother Leo, the light will go out of the world."

Once again the moon rose, set, rose, set. First spring, then summer came and went. From our elevation we watched the change in the earth's face. The green wheat on the plain turned yellow and was reaped; vines that had been mere black stumps gave forth leaves and buds, then hanging grapes, and were vintaged. All this time our mountain remained as it was: flowerless and desolate. September arrived, autumn: Francis' favorite feast day was drawing near. He now ate nothing but a single mouthful of bread, drank only a single sip of water, abstaining for the sake of the True Cross. This adoration had begun years earlier, and he had written in the Rule, with his own hand: "We worship Thee, Lord, we sing Thy praises, because with Thy Holy Cross Thou didst deign to redeem the sins of the world." And now as the fourteenth of September, the date of the Feast of the Exaltation of the Cross, drew nearer, Francis was like a rapidly-melting candle in front of a crucifix. He was unable to sleep any more. Night and day he kept his eyes fixed on heaven, as though expecting the thrice-hallowed symbol to appear amidst lightning flashes and angelic wings. Once he took me by the hand and pointed to the sky.

"You look too, Brother Leo. Maybe you'll see it. Scripture says that the Cross will loom in the heavens when the Lord comes to judge. Brother Leo, I have a premonition that the Lord is coming to judge—now!"

He glanced at his hands and feet.

"Man's body is a cross, Brother Leo. Spread your arms and you'll see. And upon this cross God is crucified."

He raised his arms toward heaven.

"Christ, my beloved," he murmured, "one favor I ask of Thee, one favor before I die. Let me feel Thy sufferings and holy Passion in my body and soul, let me feel them as intensely as is possible for a sinful mortal. . . . Thy sufferings and holy Passion, Lord . . ." he kept repeating over and over again, as though delirious.

He wrapped his hands and feet in his frock.

"They hurt!" he whispered. "Go, Brother Leo. Leave me alone with my pain. You have my blessing."

I departed, feeling extremely uneasy. Lord, how was his flame ever going to subside and avoid reducing him to ashes! As the feast of the Cross approached I saw the extent to which Francis was being daily wasted away by his joy, anguish, and pain. He tried to conceal his torments, but I sensed that the pains in his hands and feet were unbearable. He was struggling with his feeble, exhausted body to relive Christ's Passion, to endure its superhuman suffering. Would human flesh be able to withstand such affliction?

My anxiety made me creep stealthily each day to a place behind a rock which stood opposite his shelter. In this way I was able to watch him unobserved. He did not go to his cave any more, but instead climbed the ledge outside his hut, where he remained the entire day with his arms uplifted in prayer, mute and immobile, as though he were petrified. Toward evening a splendor began to lick his features, and the hair of his head caught fire.

On the vigil of the Feast of the Exaltation of the Cross I was unable to sleep. I knelt down shortly before midnight to pray, but I could not get Francis out of my mind. The air in the vicinity smelled as though it were burning, as though a terrible thunderbolt had fallen on Francis' head. I rose and went outside. The sky above me had caught fire. Stars were jumping like sparks and plunging toward the earth. The Milky Way shone brightly; the night was transparent, the rocks luminous. Goatsuckers flew from tree to tree uttering piercing cries; a warm, gentle breeze was blowing, a springtime breeze, the sort that induces buds to open. Unable to comprehend where such sweetness and calm were coming from, I stood motionless and looked around me. The sky was filled with swords, while the earth below was all kindness and obedience, like a compliant wife.

The closer I came to Francis' hut, the more my heart trembled: it was on such nights, when the heavens were infuriated and the earth submissive, when a springtime breeze like this one was blowing—it was on such nights that miracles took place. I entrenched myself behind my rock, and looked. Francis was kneeling in front of his hut, given over to prayer. A quivering disk of fire licked his face and palms. I could clearly see his hands and feet beaming in the glare from the lightning flashes—no, not beaming: burning!

I watched him for a long time, crouching motionless behind my rock. The breeze had subsided; not a leaf stirred. The eastern sky began to shine bluish white. The largest of the stars were still flashing and dancing in the sky. The first songbird chirped in a distant tree. The night was collecting its stars and darkness, preparing to leave, when suddenly there was a vehement, brilliantly-red flash in the heavens. I lifted my eyes. A seraph with six wings of fire was descending, and in the midst of the fire, wrapped in the plumes, was Christ Crucified. Two of the wings embraced His head, two others His body, and the last two, one on each side, enwrapped His arms. Alvernia was encircled by a ring of flames whose glow descended, irradiating the plain below. The winged figure of the Crucified rushed down upon Francis with a hiss and touched him for the space of a lightning flash. Francis uttered a heart-rending cry as though nails were being driven into him, and, spreading his arms, stood crucified in the air. Then I heard the six-winged seraph utter several words, rapidly, melodiously, as though it were a bird. I was unable to make out what these words were, but I distinctly heard Francis shout, "More! More! I want more!" and after that the divine voice replying, "Do not ask to go further. Here, at the Crucifixion, man's ascent comes to an end." Then Francis cried again, desperately: "I want more, more—the Resurrection!" And the voice of Christ replied from amid the seraph's wings, "Beloved Francis, open your eyes and look! Crucifixion and Resurrection are identical." "And Paradise?" cried Francis. "Crucifixion, Resurrection, and Paradise are identical," said the voice, and as it pronounced these final words there was a clap of thunder in the heavens, as though another voice were commanding the vision to return to God's bosom; and all at once the six-winged conflagration rose like a red and green lightning flash and mounted with a hiss into the sky.

Francis lay stretched on the ground now, face down, writhing convulsively. I bolted out from behind my rock and ran to him. His hands and feet were bleeding profusely. Lifting him up and opening his frock, I saw that blood was also flowing from a deep open wound in his side, a wound which seemed to have been made by a lance.

"Father Francis, dearest Father Francis . . ." I murmured, sprinkling him with water to bring him to. I was no longer able to address him as "Brother." I didn't dare, for he stood now far above the heads of the brothers, far above the heads of all mankind.

He could not hear me, so submerged was he in complete unconsciousness. Only his face continued to move, twisting and turning from terror.

I washed his wounds, but they immediately opened again and the flow of blood recommenced. I began to weep. His body will be drained dry, I was thinking; he'll lose all his blood and will die. God fell upon him too heavily. The divine grace was excessive. He will die. . . .

Suddenly he opened his eyes and recognized me.

"Did you see anything, Brother Leo?" he asked breathlessly.

"Yes, Father."

"Did you hear anything?"

"Yes."

"Do not reveal the secret, Brother Leo. Swear!"

"I swear. . . . How did you feel, Father Francis?"

"Afraid!"

"You weren't overcome with joy?"

"No, I was afraid!"

He touched my shoulder. "Get ready to leave now, Brother Leo. The journey is over; we are going to return to the Portiuncula. I shall die where I was born."

"Do not talk about death, Father Francis."

"And what else should men talk about, Brother Leo? About life? Be still and do not weep. We shall part for an instant, my brother, but then shall be reunited for all eternity. God bless Brother Death!"

I laid him down and bound his wounds with strips torn from my frock. After I had prostrated myself before his hands and feet, I left the shelter, weeping. Day was about to break.

I sat down in front of my hut, my tears flowing. The journey is over, I murmured to myself, the journey is over. Francis reached the highest peak of the ascent: he reached the Crucifixion. Man can go no higher. Now he has no further need of his body. He has arrived and is dismounting; he has arrived. . . . And me, what will become of me? Where will I go? I shall be lost!

Captain Wolf appeared with our daily alms. He was surprised to find me weeping.

"What's the matter?" he asked.

"Francis wants to return to his birthplace. I'm afraid, my brother, that he is going there to die."

Captain Wolf's face grew dark. "A bad sign, a bad sign. One breed of sheep I know of break their ropes the moment they sense death approaching, vault the walls of the sheepfold, and race off to their birthplace. . . . Poor Brother Francis!"

"Don't feel sad, my brother. Francis has no fear of death. He says it isn't the end but the beginning, and that a man's true life commences only after he dies."

"It might be the beginning for him, but for you and me it's the end. I've grown used to coming up to your hideaway to bring you a few scraps of bread. It made me happy: I felt I was doing a good deed. But now . . ."

He wiped his eyes.

319

"All right," he said, swallowing hard, "I'll go find a donkey for him to ride on, and a blanket to keep the pack-saddle from bruising him. Make him ready; I'll be back!"

He twirled round and began to descend the mountain. For a long time I could hear the stones as they shifted beneath his feet.

An hour later the donkey was standing in front of Francis' hut. A thick red blanket covered the saddle. Francis was in great pain, and we lifted him as carefully as we knew how. His blood, which had soaked through the strips I had used to bind his wounds, was flowing freely again.

"Brother Lamb," he said, placing his blood-soaked hand on the unruly head, "God grant that one day you and this donkey and the red blanket you brought to keep the saddle from bruising me may all enter Paradise together."

We began the descent, proceeding very very slowly. When we were halfway down, Francis signaled Captain Wolf to stop. Then he turned, lifted his arms, and bade farewell to Monte Alvernia.

"Beloved mountain, mountain trodden by God, I thank you for the good you have done me, for the wounds you have given me, for the sleepness nights, the terrors, the blood! It is said that when Christ was crucified, you, alone of all mountains, quaked and rived your heart in two. And your daughters the partridges tore out their feathers and wailed the death chant, their eyes turned toward Jerusalem. My heart is another partridge; it too has begun to wail and lament. Christ, crucified in the air above your rocks, has brought me a secret message, and I am leaving. I am leaving, dearest Alvernia. Farewell. Farewell, beloved. We shall never meet again. Farewell forever!"

We resumed the descent in silence. Even Captain Wolf's eyes were dimmed with tears, and he stumbled frequently.

In the surrounding villages, meanwhile, the peasants had leapt out of bed, startled by the intense brightness which had been visible at dawn. The bells began to ring. Everyone had seen Alvernia ablaze. Shouting, "Francis has been made a saint, Francis has been made a saint!" men, women and children set out to find him, and they took along the sick and infirm so that the new Saint could heal them with his touch.

The moment they glimpsed us approaching them, they all darted forward to touch Francis' hands, feet, and knees. But he kept his hands and feet tightly wrapped in his frock, hiding them so that the people would not see his wounds.

"Touch us, holy father," howled the sick. "Look at us, extend your hand, heal us!"

Forgetting himself for a moment, Francis brought his hand out from under his frock in order to bless the multitude. When the people saw the wound they bellowed madly. The women dashed forward with mantles outstretched to catch the drops; the men thrust in their hands and anointed their faces with blood. The villagers' expressions grew savage, and so did their souls. They longed to be able to tear the Saint limb from limb in order for each of them to claim a mouthful of his flesh, for they wanted to make him their own, to have him enter them so that they could become one with a saint—could be sanctified. Blind rage had overpowered them; their eyes were leaden, their lips ringed with froth. Sensing the danger, I stepped forward.

"In God's name, fellow Christians," I shouted, "let us continue. The Saint is in a great hurry to return to his native soil. If you want his blessing, make way!"

"He's not going to go! We won't let him!" shouted angry voices on every side. "Here's where he's going to leave his bones—here, so they can sanctify our village."

"And we'll build him a church, and people will come on pilgrimage from all over the world!"

"Hold him! Don't let him go! He's ours! Ours! Ours!"

I turned to Captain Wolf.

"My brother, I'm frightened. They want to take him from us. Help me!"

Francis had concealed his bloody hand beneath his frock again. He was waiting with bowed head, the sweat pouring from his brow. His eyes had once more become two running wounds.

"Have pity on him," I cried. "Don't you see him? He's bleeding!"

But the sight of additional blood only provoked the crowd that much more.

"He's ours! Ours! Ours!"

"We never had a saint in our village before. Now that God has sent us one, are we going to let him escape?"

"Bring some rope! Tie him up!"

This was too much for Captain Wolf. He seized a club from one of the old men and stepped forward, clutching the donkey's bridle.

"Make way, make way," he bellowed, "make way or I'll crack open your skulls! Don't forget, I'm Captain Wolf! Step aside!"

The men lost courage and backed out of his path, but the women pounced on Francis. Foaming with rage, they started to drag him by his frock, which ripped, exposing his bruised, skeleton-like body.

"My children, my children," murmured Francis, weeping.

The tiny donkey put forward its trembling front legs and began to kneel. Just as it was about to fall, Captain Wolf gave it a smack which made it stand up straight again. The crowd charged him, but he swung the club: there was the sound of a skull cracking.

"Back, back, sacrilegious thieves!" he cried, and he made his way forward, swinging the club up and down.

As soon as the sick and infirm beheld the saint leaving them, they began to shout and weep.

"How can you abandon us like this, Saint of God? Have you no pity? You cry, 'Love! Love!' Where is this love? Touch us, heal us!"

Francis kept his head turned toward them. He was gazing at them, blood and tears flowing from his eyes. "God . . . God . . ." he kept murmuring, unable to utter anything else.

At last it pleased the Lord that we should escape them. We reached the plain and began to breathe freely again.

"They wanted to gobble you up alive, Brother Francis," said Captain Wolf laughingly. "But they didn't, thanks to this holy cudgel. Bless it. With your permission, I'm going to take it along with the other things when I go to heaven."

Eventually we reached a village where we stopped to rest. It was necessary for me to wash Francis' wounds and to find some clean strips of cloth with which to bind them. There was a fountain in the center of the village. I began to attend to Francis while Captain Wolf went out to beg. Soon he returned with a piece of cloth. I tore it and bound the wounds in Francis' hands, feet, and right side.

"Are you in pain, Father Francis?"

He gave me a look of surprise. "In pain?" he asked. "Who is in pain? What is pain? I don't understand what you mean, Brother Leo."

And truly—I noticed it then for the first time—his face had become completely transformed. It was radiant with calmness, beatitude. A nimbus of light crowned his hair, and his hands and feet were sparkling.

I sat down at the edge of the fountain and watched Francis, watched him as he departed, vanished without even turning to look at me. God and God alone occupied his heart now. My journey was ended as well—finished! I was left midway. I would never be able to reach him. We would never meet again; I would never again journey at his side.

I sighed. Francis turned and looked at me for a long time, a bitter smile quivering round the edge of his lips.

"Brother Leo," he said finally, "can you find a piece of paper and a quill?"

I ran to the village priest and returned with the quill and paper.

"I've brought them, Father Francis."

"Write!"

I leaned over the paper and waited, quill in hand.

"Are you ready, Brother Leo?"

"Ready."

"Write!"

> *Thou art holy, Lord God. Thou art the God of gods, Who alone workest miracles.*
> *Thou art strong, Thou art great, Thou art most high!*
> *Thou art good, every good, the highest good.*
> *Thou art love, wisdom, humility, patience.*
> *Thou art beauty, certitude, peace, joy.*
> *Thou art our hope, Thou art justice, Thou art all our wealth.*
> *Thou art our protector, Thou art the guardian and defender.*
> *Thou art the great sweetness of our souls!*

As he dictated to me he became more and more carried away. First he began to tap with his hands and feet; then all of a sudden he attempted to stand up and dance. But his legs would not support him, and he sank back to the ground.

"What joy this is, what happiness!" he exclaimed. "The heavens have come down to earth. These beings all around me are not men, but stars. . . . Did you write everything down, Brother Leo? Everything?"

"Yes, Father Francis, everything," I replied, and as I said this I felt a serpent biting my heart. My soul was embittered, for I did not share the happiness he spoke about. I looked around me, but saw no one. Even Francis had left me, had gone far far away—forever.

"Write some more, Brother Leo. Write underneath, in capitals: THE LORD turn HIS countenance to thee, that thy face may be cleansed and radiant, BROTHER LEO. THE LORD place HIS hand upon thy heart, BROTHER LEO, and give thee peace.

"Did you write that?"

"Yes, Father Francis," I replied, my eyes filling with tears.

"Give me the paper and the quill. I want to add something myself."

He tried to clasp the quill, but he was unable to close his hand. With great effort he managed to trace a skull at the bottom of the paper, and above the skull a cross, and above the cross a star.

"Take this sheet and keep it always with you, Brother Leo. And whenever you are overcome with grief, remove it from beneath your frock and read it in order to remember me—to remember how much I loved you."

THE MORE I RECALL those days when we journeyed back to our native soil, the more certain am I that Giles was right: the saint does emit an odor which makes its way into the homes of men. Penetrating mountains and forests, it takes each man by surprise, overwhelming him with fear and anxiety. All his sins bound into his mind: every instance of cowardice, of villainy, of faintness of soul he thought he had forgotten, thought that time had erased. The jaws of hell suddenly open wide beneath his feet, and he, his heart in turmoil, sniffs the air, turns his face in the direction the odor is coming from, and sets out with trembling steps to find its source.

The friars—all who remained faithful—ran to the Portiuncula. Francis had lost almost all his blood. We laid him down in his hut, on the ground, and the brothers crowded around him, kissing him repeatedly and begging him without respite to describe how he had received his wounds, and the brilliance of the figure of Christ nailed upon the wings, and what were the secret words which the Son of God had confided to him. Francis, keeping his hands and feet hidden, wept and laughed in turn, so great was his joy. He had conquered pain: he felt that someone was in pain, but someone else, not him. He had already departed this world, and he looked upon all the rest of us with compassion.

Pilgrims from the large cities and from distant villages kept arriving continually, having been guided to our hut by the odor of sainthood. Some had diseases of the soul, some of the body. They touched Francis, kissed his feet, and he spoke to them using simple

325

words, but ones they had forgotten: love, concord, humility, hope, poverty. And these simple words, when pronounced by his lips, took on for the first time a deep significance full of mystery and certitude. The people were comforted. They were astonished to find how easy beatitude was, how close to them, and many returned to their homes so changed, so sweetened, that their families no longer recognized them. Thus more and more ran to drink a drop of the immortal water which flowed from the Saint's mouth.

One day Francis had closed his eyes: he was exhausted. It was terribly hot, and I, seated cross-legged next to him, was cooling him with a fan of sycamore leaves when an elderly, aristocratically dressed lady approached, walking on tiptoe in order not to disturb him. She knelt at his side and, without speaking, bent to kiss his hands and feet; then she caressingly grazed his hair, which was drenched with sweat. So tender was her caress that I looked up, trying to discover the identity of this majestic woman who was so tightly wrapped in her black wimple. She stared at Francis, did not take her eyes from him. Suddenly her lips moved:

"My child . . ." And she burst into tears.

I jumped to my feet. I had understood.

"Lady Pica, noble Lady Pica," I whispered.

She parted her wimple slightly, revealing her face. It was aged, full of wrinkles, deathly pale. She shook her head.

"Oh, Brother Leo, I delivered my son up to your care, and now look how you are returning him to me!"

"Not I, Lady Pica—God."

She lowered her head. "Yes," she murmured, "God . . ." and she fixed her tearful eyes once more upon her son.

Truly, this son, this darling son, was now nothing more than a tatter: one huge wound lying on the ground in a pool of blood.

"Is this my boy?" she whispered. "Is this my Francis?" She stared at him through her tears, struggling to recognize him.

Francis heard the whisper. Opening his eyes, he saw his mother and knew her immediately.

"Mother, Mother, you've come!" He held out his hands to her.

"My son . . . my father—I don't know what to call you any more —I kiss the five wounds which the Lord gave you. I have come to ask a favor. Remember the milk you drank from my breast, and do not refuse me."

326

"I do, I do, Mother; I remember everything, and I shall take all my memories with me and bring them to God so that He may sanctify them. What favor do you wish to ask?"

"Cut off my hair, call me Sister Pica; let me flee to San Damiano's. I have lost my husband, lost my son: I have no further use for the world."

"To have no further use for the world is not enough, Mother. You must have a use for God. You should say, 'I have lost my husband, lost my son—praise the Lord! But I have not lost God; I still possess everything, and I wish to enter San Damiano's not because I hate the world but because I love Almighty God."

"I wish to enter San Damiano's because I love Almighty God," repeated Lady Pica, struggling to restrain her sobs. "Give me your blessing, Father Francis!"

Francis raised himself up painfully. With my help he leaned back against the stone which served as his pillow.

"Have you distributed your belongings among the poor? Have you bowed, prostrated yourself before our noble Lady Poverty? Have you abandoned your magnificent house with a feeling of relief and joy, just as though you had recovered from a serious illness? Have you parted with everything?"

"Everything, everything, Father Francis."

"Then you have my blessing, Sister Pica," he said, placing his hand on his mother's head. "Go to Sister Clara's; she will cut off your hair and give you a frock. And farewell! We may never see each other again."

Lady Pica fell tearfully upon her son's breast and kissed it with reverence. Spreading her arms, she lifted him up, embraced him tightly, tenderly, as though he were an infant. Then she wrapped her black wimple securely around her again and set off in the direction of San Damiano's.

Francis glanced at me.

"Brother Leo, how can those who do not believe in God leave their mothers, leave them forever, without having their hearts break in two? How can they bear the sorrow, the unbearable sorrow of parting? Even the sight of an ordinary lamp flickering and about to die is enough to make one sick at heart. . . . What do you think, Brother Leo?"

I was completely bewildered. What could I say—that whoever

loves God does not love anything else, does not pity anything in the world; that his soul is burning, and that even mother, father, brothers and sisters are enveloped in its flames and consumed, as are joy, suffering, wealth—everything?

"I remember the time in Assisi," I offered by way of reply, "when the night watchman began to shout 'Fire!' It was midnight. The bells tolled; the half-naked inhabitants dashed into the streets. But it wasn't a fire that was burning, it was your soul. Your soul, Father Francis, and the whole of creation was being consumed within it. Look how your mother was just reduced to ashes."

He said nothing. Deathly pale, he kept looking at his hands and feet, biting his lips.

"Are you in pain, Father Francis?"

"Yes, someone is in pain, Brother Leo," he replied.

Exerting all his strength, he raised himself up.

"Let him suffer, let him groan in the flames. As for us, we shall hold our heads high! Do you remember the song the three children Hananiah, Mishael, and Azariah sang in the fiery furnace where they had been thrown by the Babylonian tyrant? Ready, little lion of God, let's clap our hands and sing it too. Oh, if I could only stand on my feet and dance! I'll begin; you keep time."

Clapping his hands, he commenced to sing in a firm, jubilant voice:

> All ye works of the Lord, bless the Lord: praise and exalt
>   Him forever.
> O all ye waters that are above the heavens, and all ye
>   powers of the Lord, bless the Lord: praise and exalt
>   Him forever.
> O ye sun and moon and ye stars of heaven, bless the Lord:
>   praise and exalt Him forever.
> O ye light and darkness, and ye nights and days, bless the
>   Lord: praise and exalt Him forever.
> O every shower and dew, and all ye spirits of God, bless
>   the Lord: praise and exalt Him forever.
> O ye fire and heat, and ye cold and warmth, bless the
>   Lord: praise and exalt Him forever.
> O ye dews and falling snow, and ye ice and cold, bless the
>   Lord: praise and exalt Him forever.

*O ye frost and snow, and ye lightnings and clouds, bless
the Lord: praise and exalt Him forever.*

*O let the earth bless the Lord: let it praise and exalt Him
forever.*

*O ye mountains and hills, and all things that spring up in
the earth, bless the Lord: praise and exalt Him forever.*

*O ye fountains, and ye seas and rivers, whales and all that
move in the waters, bless the Lord: praise and exalt
Him forever.*

He clapped his hands; his quivering feet swung back and forth of
their own accord, beyond his control. He wanted to dance but could
not. Never had I seen Francis so happy. The flame which licked
and devoured his face had turned to light. He had felt unburdened
ever since the celestial Christ had come down upon him, and now
his heart brimmed with assurance.

I remained at his side constantly, night and day. One morning as
I opened my eyes at dawn I saw him leaning against his stone
pillow, smiling.

"Your face is beaming, Father Francis. Did you have a pleasant
dream?"

"How can you expect dreams to make me smile, Brother Leo,
when you see the blood flowing from me like this? Until now I wept,
beat my breast, and cried out my sins to God. But now I understand: God holds a sponge. If I were asked to paint God's loving-
kindness, I would depict Him with a sponge in His hand. . . . All
sins will be erased, Brother Leo; all sinners will be saved—even
Satan himself, Brother Leo; for hell is nothing more than the antechamber of heaven."

"But then—" I began.

But Francis held out his hand and covered my mouth.

"Quiet!" he said. "Do not diminish the grandeur of God."

The earth's wheel continued to turn. The rains began, and Francis
closed his eyes in order to listen to the waters of heaven as they
descended to earth. His face glistening like a rain-washed stone, he
requested me to carry him to the doorway of the hut so that he
could hold out his palms and receive the drops.

329

"These are the last alms I shall ever beg," he said as he watched his palms fill with water. Bending forward, he drank joyously, gratefully.

In this state of uninterrupted joy his body continued to waste away, each day half of him sinking further into the earth while the other half mounted toward heaven. You could see unmistakably now that the two elements which formed him had begun to separate.

"Do not leave us yet, Father Francis," I cried to him one morning. "Your circle is still not complete. You always longed to worship at the Holy Sepulcher, and you never have."

Francis smiled. "Yes, Brother Leo, I was not deemed worthy of going to the Holy Sepulcher. But it does not matter, because the Holy Sepulcher is going to come to me, miserable sinner that I am."

The old, beloved brothers arrived continually from all quarters to bid farewell to their master and to bring him news of the regions where they had gone out to preach Love and Poverty. Many friars had been tortured and martyred in the wild forests of Germany. In France they were taken for heretics and thrashed mercilessly. In Hungary the shepherds set their dogs against them and the villagers pricked them with oxgoads. Elsewhere, the people had undressed them and left them to shiver in the snow.

Francis heard all this with radiant face. He deemed particularly blessed those brothers who had known the joy of persecution and the scorn of mankind.

"Which is the finest route to Paradise?" he kept asking. "The scorn of mankind. Which is the shortest? Death."

Bernard came, as did Father Silvester, Masseo, Juniper, Sior Pietro, Ruffino, Angelo, Pacifico. Sister Clara sent him a message: "Father Francis, all God's graces have descended upon you. Give me permission to come and worship the marks which they left upon your body." Francis replied: "Sister Clara, you do not have the slightest need to see or touch in order to believe. Close your eyes, my sister, and you shall see me."

"Why didn't you let her come?" I asked. "Don't you pity her? It would have done her a great deal of good."

"I do pity her, and that is precisely why I refused. She must grow accustomed to seeing me without my body, Brother Leo, and so must you and all who love me."

I averted my eyes so that he would not notice my tears. Invisible presences were not enough for me: as soon as I stopped seeing Francis I would be lost.

I think he divined my thoughts. He had begun to open his mouth and was about to comfort me, but at that moment Elias, the very last to appear, came to greet Francis and bid him farewell. He had just returned from a long tour which had produced vast amounts of gold. In Assisi the foundations had already been laid for a great monastery which was to consist of an imposing church with paintings, silver lamps and delicately carved stalls, a ring of cells, and a large library where the brothers could study, have discussions, and give lectures.

Francis placed his hand on the enterprising brother's head.

"God forgive me for saying so, Brother Elias, but it seems to me that you have misled our brotherhood. You expelled Poverty, our great treasure, and you granted dangerous liberties to the other virtues which were the original building blocks of our order. They were severe, pure; they made no compromise with ease or affluence. Now, so I hear, you are collecting funds to erect a monastery; and you have adorned the brothers' feet with sandals: no longer do they walk with bare soles upon bare soil. The wolf has entered our fold while I sit outside the Portiuncula like a chained dog, and bark. Where are you leading us, Brother Elias?"

"Where God pushes me. You know as well as I that everything happens because God wills it. The times have changed, and with them the heart of man has changed, and with this change in the heart of man, the virtues have changed as well. But you may rest at ease in the knowledge that I am guiding the order toward the spiritual domination of the world. Trust in me. The blood of our brothers has already begun to be spilled: it is watering the seed we have been sowing."

"I trust in God, and have no need of additional consolation. I am stupid, Brother Elias, illiterate; the whole of my life I never knew how to do anything except weep, dance, and sing God's glory. Now I can't do even that. All I am now, I tell you, is a barking dog chained outside our order. May God intervene and set things right again! I feel at ease and am not afraid of you, Brother Elias, because I am certain that this is exactly what He is going to do."

Elias kissed Francis' hand and departed hurriedly for Assisi in order to supervise the masons who were building the new monastery. As soon as he was gone, Pacifico, who had been present and had overheard all, approached Francis and said, "Father Francis, our hearts are very wide; words are very narrow, far too narrow to contain human feelings. What is the use then of talking? Give me permission to play the lute for you, for this is your true mouth, Father Francis: it is with the lute that you should speak to men. You don't know how to play? Well, let me teach you."

Crouching, he showed him the strings. His fingers ran up and down producing high and low notes, and Francis leaned forward, listening attentively to his instructor.

"Come every day and give me a lesson, Brother Pacifico. Ah, if only, before I die, I can say my final prayer with the lute! And now, sing a joyful song to cheer me."

Pacifico bent over his lute and began to play and sing. Once he had composed songs in praise of the beauty of his lady; now he praised the beauty of the Blessed Virgin Mary. The melody was the same, the words of praise the same; nothing had changed but the lady. Francis listened, softly humming the melody in his turn. The nimbus of light around his face grew brighter, and the hollows in his temples and cheeks filled with flames.

The days went by. Pacifico came each evening and Francis, like a young pupil, listened to him and exercised his fingers upon the strings. He was delighted to find that he was making progress: soon he would be able to speak to God and men with the lute.

One day a wild hare dashed up to him and burrowed beneath his frock. We knew the terrified creature must have been running for its life, because we heard the piercing cry of a fox in the distance.

Francis stroked the hare and spoke to it with such tenderness that I was astonished. He had never spoken so tenderly to a human being.

"Put your hand over its tiny heart, Brother Leo, to see how the poor thing is trembling. Its whole body is shaking. I'm sorry, Brother Fox, but I'm not going to let you eat this hare. God sent it to me so that I could save it."

The hare remained near him from that moment on, and the days when Francis was breathing his last, it crouched at his feet, quivering and refusing to eat.

The animals and birds loved him exceedingly, for they seemed to sense how much he loved them. One day he had been presented with a pheasant whose beauty he never tired of admiring.

"Raise your head, Brother Pheasant; give thanks to God for making you so beautiful," he used to say to it, whereupon the pheasant would unfold its wings and begin to strut in the sun like a great nobleman.

On another occasion—if I hadn't seen this with my own eyes I would never have believed it—an incensed wolf leaped out in front of us as we were strolling beneath the oaks of Alvernia. It was winter at the time, and the wolf was famished. Going up to it, Francis began to speak to it calmly, sweetly, as though it were a human being, a dear friend.

"Brother Wolf, great ruler of the forest, give us permission to walk a little beneath your trees. My companion here, who trembles and is afraid of you because he does not know you, is Brother Leo; I am Francis of Assisi, and we were talking about God, who is our Father, and your Father too, Brother Wolf. We beg of you not to interrupt our holy conversation."

When the wolf heard its brother's tranquil voice, it grew gentle and stepped aside, letting us pass. Francis calmly resumed our holy talk.

More than anything else, however, Francis loved light, fire, and water.

"How great God's kindness is, Brother Leo," he often said to me. "What miraculous things surround us! When the sun rises in the morning and brings the day, have you noticed how happily the birds sing, and how our hearts leap within our breasts, and how merrily the stones and waters laugh? And when night falls, how benevolently our sister Fire always comes. Sometimes she climbs up to our lamp and lights our room; sometimes she sits in the fireplace and cooks our food and keeps us warm in winter. And water: what a miracle that is too, Brother Leo! How it flows and gurgles, how it forms streams, rivers, and then empties into the ocean—singing! How it washes, rinses, cleanses everything! And when we are thirsty, how refreshing it is as it descends within us and waters our bowels! How well bound together are man's body and the world, man's soul and God! When I think of all these miracles, Brother Leo, I don't want to talk or walk any more; I want to sing and dance."

Of all the great feasts, he loved Christmas best. One year the holiday fell on Friday, and one of the new brothers, Morico by name,

333

did not want to eat meat. Francis invited him to sit down next to him at the table.

"When it is Christmas, Brother Morico," he said to him, "there is no such thing as Friday. If the walls could eat meat, I would give them such a day so that they too could celebrate the birth of Christ. But since they cannot eat the meat, I will use it to anoint them!"

Having said this, he took a piece of meat and daubed all four walls of the Portiuncula with its juice. Then he reseated himself contentedly at the table.

"If the king were my friend," he said, "I would ask him to command that on Christmas Day each person take some grain and scatter it throughout his courtyard and the streets for our brothers the birds, because it is winter, the earth is covered with snow, and they cannot find anything to eat. Also, that whoever has oxen, donkeys, or any other animals should wash them with warm water on this day and give them double rations out of love for Christ, who was born in a stable. Also, that the rich open their doors during this season and invite the poor in to eat; for on this day Christ was born—Christ, and joy, and dancing, and salvation!"

December had begun; Christmas was approaching. Francis counted the days, the hours, waiting anxiously for this great day of Christianity so that once again he could behold Christ as an infant child.

"This will be my final Christmas," he kept saying to me. "This year is the last time I shall see the infant Christ moving His tiny feet in the manger. Therefore, I must celebrate this Christmas with great devotion—I must say goodbye to it forever!"

He had a good friend in the city, a pious man named Sior Belita. He sent for him, and Belita came with great alacrity and kissed the holy, wounded hand.

"My brother," Francis said to him, "It would please me exceedingly if we could celebrate holy Christmas Eve together this year. Listen, therefore, to what I have in mind. Nearby in the forest you'll find a large cave. Would you be kind enough to place an ox and a small donkey in it on Christmas Eve, just as it was in Bethlehem? This is my last Christmas and I want to see how very humbly Christ was born in the stable, born to save mankind: to save me, sinner that I am."

"I'm at your service, Father Francis," replied the friend. "Everything will be done exactly as you wish."

He kissed Francis' hand and left.

"I will see Christ's birth," Francis said to me happily; "then I will see the Crucifixion, the Resurrection, and after that, I will die. Praise the Lord for giving me strength to enjoy the complete cycle: Birth, Crucifixion, Resurrection."

From that moment on, forgetting his pains and all his cares, Francis gave himself over to preparations for the Nativity.

"Brother Leo," he said to me, "you must help me celebrate my last Christmas joyfully and with deep and pious emotion."

He called for Giles.

"Brother Giles, you will be Joseph. Put a tuft of cotton beneath your chin to make a white beard, and take along a staff to lean on."

He sent Juniper to the mountain to bring him two shepherds. They came, one a robust old man, short and sunburned, the other young, his cheeks covered with blond fuzz.

"Brother shepherds," he instructed them, "on Christmas Eve you shall come to the cave which Sior Belita will point out to you, and you'll bring your lambs along with you. Do not be afraid: you won't have to do anything. You'll simply stand at the mouth of the cave leaning on your crooks and watching what goes on inside. That's all. You shall be the shepherds who see the newborn Christ."

He also sent a message to Clara: "Have your sister Agnes come to me. I have something to tell her."

"She will be the Virgin Mary," he said to me. "I chose her because her name is Agnes."

He sent me to the Portiuncula to fetch several young novices to portray the angels. They were to carry swaddling clothes and bands, and to sing "Glory to God in the highest, and on earth peace, good will among men." And Brother Pacifico was to be with them to play the lute; and Father Silvester would celebrate Mass.

On Christmas Eve Sior Belita sent word that everything was ready and that we should come. We set out in the middle of the night accompanied by several of the friars—Bernard, Sior Pietro, Masseo, Father Silvester. Pacifico marched at Francis' side, carrying his lute.

The sky was entirely clear, the air frosty. It was a peaceful night, with the stars so low that they almost touched the ground. Each one of us had a star above his head. Francis was walking with dancelike steps. Suddenly he turned:

"What joy this is, my brothers! What great happiness has been given to men! Do you realize what we are going to see? God as an infant! The Virgin Mary suckling God! The angels coming down to earth and chanting hosanna! Brother Pacifico, if you want my blessing take your lute from your shoulder and sing: 'Glory to God in the highest, and on earth peace, good will among men.'"

He leaned over to my ear. "Brother Leo, I cannot hold back my joy. Look how I'm walking: my feet do not hurt me any more. Last night I dreamed that the Virgin Mother placed her Child in my arms."

The peasants from all the surrounding villages had come with burning torches; the entire forest was splendidly illuminated. When we reached the cave, which was already crowded with people, Francis lowered his head and entered, the brothers following behind him. The manger was at the far end, lined with hay. An ox and a small donkey stood by quietly; they had eaten and were ruminating. Father Silvester placed himself in front of the manger and began to intone Mass just as if he had been before an altar. Francis, meanwhile, circled the crib on all fours, bleating like a lamb. And when Father Silvester came to the place in the Gospel where it says: "And she brought forth her firstborn son and wrapped him in swaddling clothes and laid him in a manger . . ." a bluish radiance spread over the wall of the cave and everyone saw Francis bend down and then stand up again holding a newborn babe in his arms.

The peasants bellowed and waved their torches insanely, while we all fell prone on the ground, unable to bear the miracle. I raised my head for an instant and saw the infant extend its tiny hands and stroke Francis' beard and cheeks, then smile at him, moving its diminutive feet. Francis, raising the child above his head, held him in front of the burning torches and cried: "Brothers, behold the Savior of the world!"

The peasants were beside themselves. They charged forward to touch the holy infant, but suddenly the blue radiance vanished, darkness spread over the manger, and no one saw Francis any longer. He had fled, taking the infant with him.

The peasants rushed outside with their torches and scattered throughout the wood. They searched and searched, but he was nowhere to be found. The heavens had begun to glow bluish white; the Morning Star, solitary in the eastern sky, gleamed and danced. The day had begun.

I found Francis outside his hut, kneeling, his face turned toward Bethlehem.

When I saw him the next day I was terrified. What I beheld was no longer a body; it was a pile of bones covered by a tattered frock. His lips were blue with cold.

"Father Francis," I said to him, kissing his hand, "let me gather some wood and light a fire for you."

He answered, "Go, Brother Leo, go throughout the world, and if you find a fire in every hut, every poor cottage, then come back and light one in my hearth. If even a single man in the world is shivering, I must shiver with him."

With the passage of time his wounds grew increasingly more painful. I often saw him doubled over, contorting his mouth in an effort to withstand the agony. He used to raise his head and glance at me, the same expression of beatitude always on his face.

"He's suffering," he would say to me, "he's suffering. . . ."

"Who?"

"Him!" And he would indicate his own breast, and hands, and feet.

One night, however, when a wood mouse slipped through the dilapidated door of the hut and began to lick Francis' bloody feet and then to bite them, he awoke with a start, and I heard him say ever so softly, as though he had been speaking to a child, "Brother Mouse, I am suffering! For the love of God, go away! I am suffering!"

One morning I found him shivering on his mat. He was completely naked.

"It's terribly cold, Father Francis," I cried. "Why did you get undressed?"

"I thought of my shivering brothers throughout the world," he said, his teeth chattering. "I am unable to warm them; therefore I decided to join them in being cold."

The next day he said to me, "I wonder what's happening to the friars who went out to preach. They've been on my mind day and night. A mouse, one of our many brothers in the woods, came last night and diverted my thoughts for a moment, but he was a good

337

mouse, and when I asked him to go away, he did. Now I sit here waiting. Waiting for what? For someone to come and bring me news."

The words were scarcely out of his mouth when lo! There was Juniper on the threshold, barefooted, covered with bruises, exultant. He was one of the naïvest and most beloved of our brotherhood, and during our first, heroic years he had often made us laugh with his jokes. One time, a brother who had fallen ill babbled in his delirium, "Oh, if I only had a pig's foot!" When Juniper heard this he raced at once to the forest, found a pig feeding on acorns, and cut off its foot; then, returning to the Portiuncula, he roasted the foot and gave it to the sick man to eat. Francis learned of this. "Don't you know you're not supposed to touch things that belong to other people?" he scolded him. "Why did you do it?"

"Because this pig's foot helped our brother. I wouldn't feel the slightest burden on my soul even if I had cut the feet off a hundred pigs."

"But the poor pig-keeper is weeping and wailing. He's searching all over the forest for the culprit."

"In that case, Brother Francis, I'll go of my own accord and find him. You can rest assured that we'll soon be the best of friends."

Running to the forest, he found the man and embraced him. "My brother," he said, "I'm the one who caught your pig and cut off its foot. Before you get angry, listen to me. God sent pigs into the world so that men could eat them. Someone I know fell ill and kept shrieking that he would never be cured unless he could eat a pig's foot. I felt sorry for the man, so I quickly brought the foot to him and roasted it. As soon as he ate it he got well, and now he's praying for the soul of the pig's owner and interceding with God for the forgiveness of his sins. Don't feel angry, therefore, but let us embrace: we are all brothers, all God's children. You did something pleasing to God—congratulations!—and I helped you do it. Come, kiss me!" The peasant, who at first had been white-hot with rage, found that his anger had subsided gradually, and now he fell into Juniper's arms and kissed him. "I forgive you," he said. "But for the love of God, don't do it again!"

When Francis heard Juniper relate his exchange with the pig-keeper, he laughed with all his heart. "What a pity," he exclaimed, "that we do not have a whole forest of Junipers like this one!"

338

Juniper wiped his mouth with the back of his hand. He must have had an important message for us, because his tiny eyes were sparkling. Keeping them fixed upon us, he began:

"I've just come from Rimini, Father Francis. What I saw and endured on my way there is almost impossible to describe. Apparently the villagers mistook me for you, because they ran—men and women alike—and crowded around me, stepping all over one another in their wild efforts to kiss my hand. They brought me the sick to be healed, but how could I heal them? I put my hand on their heads just as you do, but my thoughts were always on something else: namely, how to escape from the bellowing mob that was shouting 'Long live the Saint!' and pressing all about me, trying to kiss my feet. Well, one day I had a brilliant idea, and what do you think it was? As I was nearing a village just outside Rimini I learned that the multitude had set out again to receive me. So, what did I do? There were two laughing children nearby who were seesawing, one on each end of a plank they had laid across another plank. I ran to them at once and said, 'Children, I want to play too. Here, both of you sit on one end and I'll sit alone on the other and swing you up and down.' So, the three of us began to seesaw endlessly up and down, bursting with laughter. At this point the pilgrims arrived, headed by the priest holding the aspergillum in one hand and the Gospels bound in silver in the other. When they saw me playing and laughing, their expressions fell. They waited patiently for me to finish my game so that I could bless them and also heal several sick villagers they had brought with them. They waited and waited, but do you think I stopped seesawing—not on your life! 'This man isn't a saint, he's a lunatic,' they howled in a rage. 'Come, let's go!' So they went, which was just what I wanted them to do. I got off the seesaw immediately and continued on my way to Rimini."

Francis laughed. "You have my blessing, Brother Juniper," he said. "I'd rather we be taken for lunatics than for saints. That is the true meaning of holy Humility."

"And what did you do at Rimini, Brother Juniper?" I asked. "I imagine you still must have a great deal to tell us."

"Yes, a great deal, a great deal, my brother. A glorious miracle! I wouldn't have believed it if I hadn't seen it with my own eyes. You recall a pale novice we once had at the Portiuncula, don't you—a boy named Antonio? Well, God forgive me for saying this, but that novice has become a saint. Yes, yes, a saint! And he performs miracles! Do you remember how you preached one day to the birds, Father Francis? At Rimini he preached in exactly the same way to the fish. Don't laugh: I saw it with my own eyes. Antonio stood just where the river flows into the sea. You wouldn't have recognized him. He's grown taller and slimmer; his cheeks have become hollowed; his eyes are two black holes, making people mistake him for a blind man. And his hands! Lord Almighty, never in my life have I seen such long, slender, quick-moving fingers. He was holding a staff at the time, and his fingers encircled it twice! He stood, as I said, where the river flows into the sea, and behind him was a great crowd, heretics for the most part whom Antonio had often addressed in vain, saying, 'Follow me down to the shore and you shall see that the God I preach is the only true God. You shall see with your own eyes, and you shall believe.'

"Well, on this day they did follow him, and I went with them. Antonio leaned over, wet his fingers in the ocean, and made the sign of the cross. Then he waded into the water up to his knees and cried out in a loud voice, 'Brother Fishes of sea and river, I adjure you in the name of our heavenly Father to come and hear the word of the true God!'

"The moment he said these words, the sea grew turbulent, the river swelled, and the fish began to assemble. Some came from far away; others rose from the bottom: every kind of fish—perch, sea bass, dentexes, blackfish, sole, sharks, flying fish, swordfish, gray mullet, red mullets, sea scorpions, sea bream, giltheads. Regional fish, surf fish, predatory fish—how can I recall so many! The river stopped flowing, the ocean stood motionless, and the fish lined up, the small ones in front, the medium ones behind them, and the larger species further back in deep water, all with their heads raised above the surface so that they could hear. When all were in place, Antonio extended his hand and blessed them, then immediately began to preach in a loud voice: 'Brother Fish, I called you so that we could glorify our heavenly Father together. What joy He gave you, what gifts, what wealth! Water is a thrice-noble element—cool, clean, clear. When the sun shines and the sea is calm you rise to the surface and frolic in the spray; when a storm breaks out, you descend to the bottom where there is motionless calm, and you are happy. What suppleness, what colors, what beauty God gave you, Brother

Fishes! When the great flood took place and all the animals of the land drowned, only you swam calmly and securely in the swollen waters. And when the prophet Jonah fell into the sea, you provided him with a shelter and three days later you brought him back to the land. You are the water's brightest ornament. God loves you exceedingly and does not wish your race to die out. With the thousands and thousands of eggs that you lay, you are immortal. Lift your heads and give thanks to God. You have my blessing. . . . And now go, and the Lord be with you.'

"The fish opened their mouths and moved their lips. Perhaps they were singing a psalm, but I was unable to hear. Raising their tails happily in the air, they all left, churning up the ocean and river until both were white with spray. The terrified people fell at Antonio's feet. 'Forgive us, Brother Antonio,' they cried. 'You are right. The very fish listened to your voice; how then can we, we who are human beings, *not* listen to it? Step in front and lead us!' Antonio stepped out in front, therefore, and led us all joyfully back to Rimini, where we entered the cathedral and began to glorify the Lord."

This speech had caused Juniper to break out into a sweat. His whole body gleamed and flashed like that of a fish which has just been taken from the sea.

Francis raised his hand. He was extremely moved.

"All glory to God's name. I am dying; another is being born. God's seed upon the earth is immortal. I am exhausted, useless; my sight has grown dim; I am the setting sun. He is young, full of strength, joy, and fire; he is the rising sun. You must all salute him."

He waved his hand in the direction of Rimini.

"Welcome, Brother Antonio. I give my blessing and wish that you may attain the heights I was unable to attain."

We remained silent. I closed my eyes and saw one sun setting, another rising. A mixture of sadness and bliss flooded my heart. Opening my eyes again, I gazed at Francis with inexpressible tenderness. He was rapt in ecstasy, his head between his knees, and neither saw nor heard anything that was happening around him. He had left us.

Juniper winked at me.

"I'll go get some wood and light a fire," he said, leaning over to my ear.

341

"He doesn't want any, Brother Juniper. These last days he doesn't want his body to be warm. If you make a fire, he'll scold us."

"Let him. By that time he'll have warmed his bones."

As soon as he finished saying this he dashed outside and returned in a little while with an armful of wood which he arranged in the fireplace and lit. Francis remained submerged in profound beatitude, not hearing or seeing anything. The flames leapt up; the hut glowed with the reflections. I approached the hearth avidly and turned first my back, then my abdomen to the fire. After that I held out my hands, my feet, until my body was completely warm and my bones were soothed to the very marrow. Next, Juniper and I sat down in front of the fire and laughed surreptitiously. We were fully content, but we did not forget to throw a glance at Francis every now and then to see if by any chance he had felt the warmth and was getting up to scold us.

"You ought to use a little compulsion, Brother Leo," Juniper advised me. "Force him to eat. Pretend you don't understand, and light the fire at night when he's asleep. Mend his frock when he's not looking. Don't let him die. Didn't it ever occur to you that we'll never be able to find such a guide again, a guide who can lead us straight to heaven?"

"I can't, Brother Juniper. He won't allow it. I freeze and starve along with him."

"I admire you for sharing such a hard life, Brother Leo. It's beyond human strength. How can you do it?"

"I can't, Brother Juniper. I do more than I can, but it's out of pride. Not piety, pride. I'm ashamed at this point to turn back."

"Ashamed before whom?"

"Everyone: God, Francis, the people around me, and also myself."

"Don't you feel like eating a good meal now and then—on holidays, for example; or like drinking a sip of wine, or sleeping on a soft mattress? God, as you know, made all those things for man, and it's a sin not to accept them. As for me (why not speak frankly?) I live comfortably enough, glory be to God, and therefore each time I pray and give thanks to the Almighty my prayer issues not only from my heart, but also from my stomach, my warm hands and feet, my entire body. The whole secret is this, Brother Leo: to combine what's good with what's best for your own interests."

342

I smiled.

"Woe to us if you were our leader, Brother Juniper. We'd all end up well nourished—in hell!"

Juniper was opening his mouth to reply, but just then we heard Francis shift his position. We held our breath, our hearts thumping. Francis turned.

"What's this?" he cried as soon as he saw the fire. "Who lighted a fire? Bring water at once and put it out!"

"Father Francis, apostle of Love," said Juniper, embracing Francis' knees, "fire is our sister: why do you want to kill her? Don't you pity her, you who feel pity for the very ground you walk on? She too is God's daughter, and she wants to help us—that's why she came and seated herself in the hearth. Listen to how she cries. Don't you hear? 'Brother Francis,' she says, 'I too am one of God's creatures. Do not kill me!'"

Francis remained silent. Juniper's words had penetrated to his heart.

"Brother Juniper, you old swindler," he said finally with a laugh, "you've come to set us topsy-turvy with your pious jugglery."

He turned to the hearth.

"Sister Fire, forgive me. I shall not chase you from my hut; instead, I request you to come again."

When he had said this, he went to the doorway, as far as possible from the fire, and sat down.

Early the next morning Francis pushed me with his foot.

"Get up, Brother Leo. This hut is too warm; we're too comfortable here. Come, let's go to San Damiano's. Outside the convent there's a shelter made of branches; that is where I want to stay. But what about you? Will you be able to endure it? Take stock of your forces, Brother Leo. You can leave at any time; you can escape. Forgive me, little lion of God, for tormenting you so very much."

Yes, it was true that he tormented me, but he did so because his love for me was so very great.

"Wherever you go, I go too, Father Francis," I cried, jumping to my feet. "I've burned my bridges behind me; I can't turn back now."

"Well then, let's be off, Brother Leo. I have burned my bridges also. There is no turning back! Put your arm around my waist to keep me from falling. It's still not very light out."

The cold was biting, the sky dark blue; the entire swarm of stars had already been drowned in the tenuous morning brightness. Only Venus, still indestructible, happily awaited the sun so that it could vanish within its rays. The birds had not begun to chirp yet, but in the distance we heard a cock crow.

"The birds must go hungry in wintertime," I said. "That's why they don't sing. Could it be that men are just the same, Brother Francis? Could it be that we have to eat in order to have food to transform into prayer and song?"

Francis smiled.

"Your mind is constantly on food, Brother Leo. Everything you say is correct for those who do not believe in God. But for those who do, the opposite is the case: prayer, for them, is transformed into food, and their stomachs are filled."

The light increased as we were talking, the eastern sky turned rose, and the moment we stepped beneath a densely needled pine tree a songbird, feeling a glint fall upon its closed eyelids, awoke and began to twitter.

"Good morning, Sister Skylark!" cried Francis. "We are on our way to San Damiano's. Come, join us!"

The lark darted out from among the branches, shook her wings to rid them of their numbness, and all of a sudden flew up into the sky, singing merrily.

"The sky is her San Damiano's," said Francis. "Goodbye until we meet again!"

When we reached the convent we found the nuns still at matins. The lamps inside the church were burning. Advancing on tiptoe, we went to the little window of the sanctuary and stood outside to hear the high feminine voices warbling to the Lord.

"What joy this is, Brother Leo!" said Francis, tears welling up into his eyes. "The sun, the skylark, matins, the brides of Christ who are awake before anyone else and glorifying the Beloved—what joy! I can hear Sister Clara's voice above the rest."

The office completed, the nuns flowed out into the cloister, wrapped in their white wimples. The moment they saw Francis they uttered shrill, happy cries, like hungry doves at the sight of wheat. Sister Clara was the first to come forward. She took Francis' bloody hand, covering it with her tears.

344

"Father Francis . . ." she murmured, her voice stifled with emotion, "Father Francis . . ."

"Sister Clara, I would like to remain near you and the other sisters for a few days. I greet you and bid you farewell: I am departing. Holy Mother Superior, give me permission to stay in the shelter of branches which is outside your convent."

Sister Clara gazed at Francis, her large eyes overflowing with tears.

"Father Francis, the shelter and the convent and all the sisters are at your service. Command us."

Francis' aged mother appeared. She had grown exceedingly thin and was deathly pale from her vigils and fasts, but her face beamed with happiness. She stooped in her turn to kiss her son's hand, and he placed his palm on her gray hair and blessed her.

"Mother," he whispered, "Mother . . . Sister Pica . . ."

Two of the sisters wanted to run to put the hut in order, but Clara made them step aside. "I shall do it myself," she said. "Bring me a broom, a pitcher of water, the potted flowers I have in my cell; also a lamp, and the cage with the goldfinch that the bishop gave us the other day."

Francis was exhausted. He sank to the ground beneath the tiny window of the sanctuary, and waited. His mother, her heart filled with pain and pride, watched him from the corner of the courtyard where she had withdrawn. His lips, feet, and hands had turned blue with cold. The sisters brought a heavy wool blanket with which to cover him, but he tossed it aside and tried to stand up, only to find that he did not have the strengh. Two sisters ran to him. Supporting him under the arms, they brought him slowly, step by step, to the hut. Clara had laid a mat down for him, and on it a mattess well stuffed with straw; also a soft pillow. The sisters placed him on the mattress; then they departed, leaving the two of us alone once more.

I leaned over to his ear. "Do you want anything, Father Francis?"

"What could I possibly want, Brother Leo? What more could I want? I have everything."

He closed his eyes, nodding to me as though to bid me farewell.

That night he did not sleep a moment, but raved deliriously, his forehead, hands—his entire body—shooting forth flames. The following afternoon he finally opened his eyes.

345

"Brother Leo, instruct the sisters not to come to see me any more. Tell them I want to be alone and that I do not have need of anything. All I want now is quiet. Nothing else. No fire, no food—just quiet."

Seizing the pillow, he hurled it away from him.

"Take this and throw it outside, Brother Leo. The devil is inside it; he didn't let me sleep the whole night. Bring me a stone for a pillow."

He placed his burning hand in my palm.

"Brother Leo, my fellow voyager, fellow struggler: forgive me. . . ." Then he closed his eyes.

I went outside, sat down in front of the shelter, and wept—softly, with stifled sobs, lest he hear. Sister Clara came up to me.

"What can we do, Brother Leo? How can we keep him alive?"

"He doesn't want to stay alive, Sister Clara. He says the ascent is finished. Its peak is crucifixion, and he was crucified. Now he's waiting impatiently for only one thing: resurrection."

"And that means death, doesn't it, Brother Leo?"

"Yes, it means death."

Sister Clara sighed and bowed her head. Then, after a moment:

"Perhaps the goldfinch will keep him alive a little while longer. Did it sing all day yesterday?"

"No, Sister Clara. I imagine it was frightened."

"As soon as it gets over its fear and begins to sing, perhaps Father Francis will stop wanting to die so quickly."

I said nothing, but I knew extremely well that Francis was able to hear another, much sweeter song, an immortal warbling which came from far above the clouds, far above the stars, and which was calling him. His soul had already opened its cage in order to depart: to depart so that it could join the celestial choir.

On the third day his fever reached its height. His pale cheeks reddened; his lips became parched. He sprang up continually because in his delirium he kept seeing invisible presences. Suddenly he addressed me. It was nearly dawn.

"Brother Leo, where are you? I don't see you."

"Here at your side, Father Francis. Command me."

"Have you your quill and ink with you?"

"Always, Father Francis! Command me."

346

"Write!"

He had riveted his eyes upon the air and was trembling from his haste to dictate in time, before the vision left him.

"I'm listening, Father Francis."

"Write: I am a reed that bends in God's wind. I wait for Death, the Great Troubadour, to come and harvest me, cut holes in me, turn me into a fife. Thus, pressed between his lips, I shall go about singing in God's immortal reed-bed."

He sank down onto the mattress and lay still, face up, eyelids closed. But just as I was rising in order to extinguish the lamp so that it would not hurt his eyes, suddenly he sat up again.

"Brother Leo!" he called at the top of his lungs as though shouting for help, "Brother Leo, write:

"The black Archangel took me by the hand. 'Where are we going?' I asked. 'We are leaving the earth behind us,' he answered, placing his finger upon his lips. 'Close your eyes so that you will not see it and begin to shed tears.'

"I set sail," Francis continued without a pause. "Behind me was the green earth, in front of me the black endless sea, while above, in the heavens, the north star sped forward like a meteor. Lord, Thou hast my heart in Thy hand; Thou showest it the way, and it sails onward. Already the first bird of Paradise is visible."

His eyes were burning, his entire body pulsating. I waited, holding the quill in the air.

"Write! Where are you, Brother Leo? Write:

"When the Archangel expelled Adam and Eve from Paradise, our two Parents sat down on a clod of earth, neither of them speaking. The sun went down. The night rose from the earth filled with terror, descended from the sky filled with terror; a biting wind began to blow, and Eve snuggled against her husband's breast to grow warm. As soon as she felt better she clenched her small newborn fist, opened her mouth, and said, 'Thy will *not* be done, horrible old man!'"

Francis laughed. Doubtlessly he saw the First Creatures in the air before him, with Eve squeezing her newborn fist and threatening. But in the midst of his laughter, he was overcome with tears.

"Are you still here, Brother Leo? Write:

"It was spring when the Archangel Gabriel came down to earth.

347

What he saw frightened him. The earth is exceedingly beautiful—
the hussy! he said to himself; I had better not stay very long! A
carpenter ran out of his shop. 'This is Nazareth, my child,' he said.
'What are you looking for?' 'Mary's house.' The carpenter began to
tremble. 'And why do you have that cross in your hand, and those
nails, and the blood?' 'This isn't a cross, it's a lily.' 'Who sent you?'
'God.' A knife turned in the carpenter's heart. All is finished! he said
to himself as he opened his door, revealing a small courtyard, a
well, some basil in a flowerpot, and next to the well, a girl sewing
an infant's tiny gown. The Archangel hesitated for a moment on the
threshold, his eyes filled with tears."

Francis' eyes filled with tears also, just like the Archangel's. He
sighed; his heart was breaking in two.

"Poor, poor Mary," he murmured, "poor, sweet little mother whose
beloved child was robbed by death. . . . Lord, if all the tears that
men shed in a single year flowed at the same time, they would form
a river that would engulf Thy house. But Thou art omniscient, and
thus Thou makest them flow one by one."

These words frightened him, and as soon as he had uttered them
he implored me not to write them down. "They were words of the
devil," he said. "If you have already written them, Brother Leo,
cross them out—please!"

After a pause, he continued: "I still have one tiny song remaining
in my heart, Brother Leo. I don't want to take it with me to the
grave, so lift your quill, and write:

"When God had finally completed the creation of the world and
had washed the mud off his hands, he sat down beneath one of the
trees in Paradise, and closed his eyes. 'I am tired,' He murmured;
'why shouldn't I rest for a minute or two?' He commanded sleep to
visit him; but at that instant a goldfinch with red claws came,
perched above Him, and began to cry. 'There is no rest, no peace; do
not sleep! I shall sit above Thee night and day, crying, There is no
rest, no peace; do not sleep! I will not allow Thee to sleep, for I am
the human heart.'"

Francis fell down on his back, panting.

"How did you like it, Brother Leo?" he murmured.

I was at a loss. What could I say? How could the heart of man
speak to God so impertinently?

Francis divined my thought, and smiled.

"Do not be afraid, little lion of God. Yes, man's insolence is limitless, but that is the way God created our hearts; that is just what He wanted them to do—to stand up to Him and resist!"

ÐURING THOSE ÐAYS at San Damiano's his body suffered more than it ever had before, but his soul had never been plunged in such profound beatitude. Although none of his five wounds bled any longer, the pains had begun to spread treacherously within him. Blood flowed now only from his eyes: blood mixed with tears.

I spent the nights at his feet, lying awake with him, trying desperately to keep him from departing this world just yet. One day his ears ceased buzzing and he heard the goldfinch. He listened for a long time, his mouth hanging open, his eyes pinned on the cage. An expression of great rapture had spread across his face.

"What bird do I hear, what is this celestial music?" he asked me. "Are we in heaven already?"

He cocked his ear again and listened intently, his face constantly submerged in bliss.

"Oh, if you only knew what it was saying, Brother Leo!" he exclaimed joyously. "What a miracle is hidden within this tiny feathered breast!"

The goldfinch had grown accustomed to us now; each day it began to twitter at the very break of dawn. It would swell out its throat and fix its tiny round eyes on the light outside; and its beak would bleed, so extravagantly did the creature sing. Indeed, it became drunk with song. Sometimes it would stop abruptly and peck at the bars of its cage, overcome by a yearning to escape: it had just glimpsed a sparrow sitting in freedom on a branch outside, and it wished to join it. But before long it would hop back onto the strip of reed that was suspended in the middle of the cage, and resume its song.

350

Lady Pica used to come secretly to observe her son through the slits in the wall of interwoven branches. She would gaze at him for a long time, her palm over her mouth, and would then return in silence to her cell. And Sister Clara passed many nights of vigil on the threshold of the shelter, not daring to enter. She heard the moribund's joyful verses, for Francis had lately given himself up to song. His soul was gleeful, just like the goldfinch, and the old troubadour lays he had sung beneath closed windows in his youth, when he spent the nights roaming the city with his friends, came once more to his lips.

"If only Brother Pacifico were here to play the lute for me," he said again and again. "He's right when he says the lute is man's angelic mouth, because surely when the angels speak they must fly in the air and converse in song."

One morning he sat up in bed and clapped his hands with elation. "Do you know what I've been thinking all night long, Brother Leo?" he shouted to me. "That every piece of wood is a lute or violin; that it has a voice and glorifies the Lord. . . . If you want my blessing, Brother Leo, bring me two pieces of wood."

I brought them. He placed the first on his shoulder and slid the other over it with rapid bowlike motions. Seated on his mattress, he played and sang endlessly, beside himself with joy. His eyes were closed, his head thrown back: he was in ecstasy.

"Do you hear the pieces of wood, do you hear them singing?" he asked me. "Listen!"

At first I heard nothing but the two sticks rubbing and grating against each other. But gradually my ear became attuned, my soul awoke, and I began to hear an infinitely sweet melody coming from the two dry branches. In Francis' hands the mute wood had become a viol.

"Do you hear, Brother Leo? Do you hear? Cast aside your mind and leave your heart free to listen. When a person believes in God there is no such thing as a mute piece of wood, or pain unaccompanied by exultation, or ordinary everyday life without miracles!"

One day as he was playing his viol his face suddenly grew dark, as though a dense shadow had fallen over him. He stared through the open door with protruding eyes and uttered a cry—whether a happy cry or a doleful one I could not tell, for that cry had within it all the joys and sorrows of mankind. I turned in order to discover who he had seen, who had caused the outcry. But there was no one outside. In the deserted convent garden the last leaves were falling to the ground, swept off their branches by a powerful wind. The nuns were gathered to hear Mass. They were like an assembly of birds, and we heard their tender voices chanting the Lord's praises. But in the distance, in every village house, the frightened dogs were barking.

"What did you see, Father Francis?" I asked. "Who did you see? Why did you cry out?"

It was some time before he answered me. He had abandoned the two pieces of wood on the bed, and was still staring outside with gaping eyes.

"Who is it?" I asked again. "What do you see?"

His lips were moving. "O Brother Death . . . Brother Death . . ." he murmured over and over again, his arms spread wide as though he wished to embrace the apparition.

I said nothing. I understood: he had seen the black Archangel. The dogs had seen him too; that was why they were so afraid. Going outside in order to hide my tears, I circled the hut, but found no one. The hibernal sun had freed itself from the clouds that morning and had dispelled the frost which lay over the plain, making the winter laugh like spring. The sisters emerged from the chapel, scattered throughout the cloister, and convened again in the refectory to eat their breakfast: a mouthful of bread and a cup of water. As soon as Sister Clara saw me, she came close and asked in an uneasy tone, "Why are you weeping, Brother Leo? Father Francis—"

"Father Francis saw the black Archangel. He cried out, and then opened his arms to embrace him. . . ."

Sister Clara bit into the edge of her wimple to hold back her tears. "What did he say? Was he glad?"

"I don't know, Sister Clara. He kept murmuring, 'O Brother Death, O Brother Death . . .' That was all."

"Listen, Brother Leo," she said, lowering her voice, "there's one thing I'm still afraid of. You must be careful, because the last few days some inquisitive, disquieting men have been prowling round the convent. Wild men! One of the sisters recognized them: she says they are bandits from Perugia. The people there must have learned that Father Francis is gravely ill and have decided to send these bandits to snatch him away from us. There's no need for me to tell you what having a saint means to a city in terms of wealth. So, Brother Leo, be careful!"

Hiding her face, she left me hastily and was engulfed by the church.

I'll send word to the bishop, I said to myself. I'll tell him to dispatch soldiers from Assisi to guard Francis.

When I entered the hut I found Francis sitting up on his mattress, his back against the wall. His face appeared tranquil and content.

"Fetch your quill, Brother Leo," he said, happy that I had come. "I want you to record my final instructions, a pastoral letter that is to be read by all the brothers and all the sisters no matter where they are. When you finish, I shall affix my seal: a cross."

I took up the quill and knelt down next to him. He began to dictate, calmly, slowly, weighing each word:

"My brothers, my sisters: Today God sent his black Archangel to bring me the great invitation. I am departing. However, I could not bear the thought of going far from you without having first left you my final instructions. My children, may Poverty, Love, Chastity, and Obedience—God's four great daughters—be with you now and evermore! You must not forget, not even for an instant, that the black Archangel is at your sides, has been at your sides from the very day of your birth—waiting! Each moment you must say, This is my last hour, let me therefore be prepared. . . . And take care never to place your faith in man, but only in God. The body sickens; death approaches. Friends and relatives lean over the patient and say to him, 'Put your house in order, distribute your wealth, for you are dying.' And the poor man's wife, children, friends, and neighbors crowd round him and pretend to be weeping; and he, deluded by their wailing and lamentations, calls up all his strength and says, 'Yes, I have placed myself, body and soul, in your faithful hands, together with all my belongings.' Then, without losing a moment, the friends and relatives summon the priest to come and administer the sacrament to him. 'Do you wish to do penance for all your sins?' asks the priest. 'Yes, I do,' he replies. 'Do you wish to restore all that you unlawfully seized during your lifetime?' 'No, I can't do that!' 'Why not?' 'Because I've given all to my family and friends.' With this he loses the power of speech, and dies without having redeemed his sins. Then the devil, who has been hovering all the while above the man's pillow, laughing uproariously, takes immediate possession of

353

his soul and hurls it down into hell; and all his gifts, all the power, wealth, beauty, wisdom that he was so proud of—they all go to waste, plunging down with him into the abyss. Meanwhile the family and friends divide his goods, cursing him and saying, 'May his bones roast in tar and brimstone! He should have amassed more to leave to us.' And thus he is denied by both heaven and earth. What is left for him? The Inferno: there, in the boiling, bubbling tar, he is punished for all eternity.

"I, Brother Francis, your tiny servant, the great sinner, pray and beseech you, my brothers and sisters, in the name of Love, which is God Himself, and I kiss your feet, adjuring you to accept Christ's words with humility and love. And all those who accept these holy words and turn them into action and become examples to others, may they be blessed for all eternity!

"And to you, Brother Leo, my fellow voyager, greetings from your brother Francis. If you wish to have my blessing, my brother, do not forget the things we said on the road as we journeyed together. Try as much as you can, and in the way which is best suited to you, to please Christ and to follow in His footsteps; also to follow our noble Lady Poverty, and also holy Obedience. And whatever else you desire to ask me, ask it now, freely, while I still have lips and am able to speak. Farewell, my brothers and sisters, my children. Farewell, Brother Leo, my companion in voyage, my companion in struggle!"

He had grown tired. Closing his eyes, he curled up into a ball on the mattress. His pain must have been excruciating, for his face had suddenly become all contorted.

"Are you in pain, Brother Francis?" I asked.

He opened his eyes for an instant. "There is only one thing I am sure of, Brother Leo, and that is that I am happy—exultant! Victory! Victory! We have won, Brother Leo! From the day of my birth there was someone inside me who hated God, and now—how can I avoid rejoicing?—now he has vanished."

"Who, Father Francis?"

"The flesh," he replied, closing his eyes again, exhausted.

He was delirious that entire night. He kept seeing the Archangel and conversing with him, telling him reproachfully that he had delayed his coming far too long, that he—Francis—had been waiting for him for years. Why had he kept him so long in exile? Didn't he know that the earth had a seductive attraction for men, and that a blade of grass, a goldfinch, a lighted lamp, a sweet aroma were enough to make us never want to abandon this world of clay? Francis raved on and on in this reproachful manner, and Death must have answered him, because eventually he grew calm, ceased his complaints, and began to laugh.

The next morning his temples were on fire. He was plunged in a great torpor, unable to raise his eyelids, and his body had grown stiff. Frightened, I raced to find Sister Clara.

She was in the kitchen. "A good Christian has given us a chicken," she said to me. "He learned of Francis' illness and sent it to him as a gift. I was just preparing the broth: it will give him some strength."

"Lent has started, Sister Clara. He won't want to soil his lips with meat."

"If God decides not to take him right away, Brother Leo, he'll drink this broth in order to stay with us a little longer. Wait a moment so that you can bring it to him, and may God come to our aid!"

I held the cup of broth while Sister Clara added an egg yolk. Then I took it to him together with the chicken. I found Francis stretched out on his back, gasping for breath.

"Father Francis," I said, going up to him. "Sister Clara falls at your feet and implores you in the name of holy Love to drink this broth and not abandon your body just yet. . . . If you love me, Father Francis, open your mouth."

"In the name of holy Love . . . in the name of holy Love . . ." he whispered.

He opened his mouth, keeping his eyes still closed. He drank a sip, found it satisfying, opened his mouth again, and drank another sip and then another, until gradually he finished all the broth. Then I began to feed him a little meat. His mind must have been elsewhere: he was not aware of what he was eating, and he swallowed without resistance.

But while I was feeding him, an odd, breathless passer-by entered the hut and looked all around as though he had lost something and was searching for it.

"Hey, idiot, what are you looking for?" I shouted at him in a rage. "Where are your eyes? There's someone sick here."

"I beg your pardon, brother monk," he replied. "Isn't this Jerusa-

355

lem? I scented a sacred odor and said to myself, This is Jerusalem, let me enter and do worship. . . . But where is it? I don't see it."

Francis heard, and opened his eyes.

"You are insane, my brother," he said, smiling.

"No more insane than you," retorted the strange passer-by; "no, no more insane than you who wish to enter Paradise and who eat chicken during Lent."

Francis uttered a cry and fainted. I got up to chase away the brazen visitor, but he had vanished.

The next day Francis gave me a reproachful look.

"You deceived me, Brother Leo. You made me commit a mortal sin."

"I take it upon myself, Father Francis. May God punish me, not you."

"You can't take the sins of others upon yourself. Only God can do that. We human beings are responsible only for our own sins."

"God's loving-kindness is greater, Father Francis," I replied, recalling something he had once told me. "God's loving-kindness is greater than His justice; therefore it is in this that we must place our hopes."

"Yes, you are right," said Francis. "It is in God's loving-kindness that we must place our hopes. Woe to us, if He were only just!"

The days went by, with Francis suspended halfway between life and death. The brothers came to see him often; from time to time the bishop sent his deacon to inquire about the state of Francis' health and also to deliver a message requesting him to come to Assisi. "Come, my child," the bishop wrote, "come, stay in my house. Man's body is a sacred gift from God, and you are murdering it, acting as you are. Yes, you are committing murder, Francis, my child. You are transgressing God's mighty commandment: Thou shalt not kill!"

Francis always listened to the bishop's message without replying. But one day when the deacon had come to invite him once again, he turned to me and said, "Yes, the bishop is right: it is murder. I shall celebrate Easter at San Damiano's, and after that I shall stay at the bishop's palace. I want to see Assisi once more—to bid it farewell."

Holy Week came, and Francis devoted himself to remembrance of Christ's Passion. Each day he had me sit down at his side and read the Gospel to him. He followed Jesus' steps, marched just behind him, and was betrayed, condemned, scourged, and crucified with Him. On Good Friday his five wounds, which had been closed for such a long time, opened again; the little blood that remained to him began to flow. On the morning of Holy Saturday he recovered.

"Brother Leo," he said, grasping my hand, "if I, miserable sinner that I am, had been deemed worthy of becoming an Evangelist, I would not have had the lion next to me, nor the ox, nor the eagle, nor the angel. No, my companion would have been a lamb with a red ribbon around its neck, and on the ribbon would have been the legend: 'When will Easter come, Lord, so that Thou canst slaughter me?' "

On Easter Day, after the Resurrection, the sisters arrived with lighted candles to kiss his hand. He sat up and blessed them, extending his arms above their heads.

"My sisters," he whispered, extremely moved, "my sisters, my mothers, wise virgins, brides of Christ . . ."

He wept, and Sister Clara and Sister Pica and all the other nuns wept with him. The brightly illuminated hut was filled with wailing.

"Now we await *your* resurrection, Father Francis!" Sister Clara said to him. But he was sobbing loudly and did not hear.

Gifts—praise the Lord!—had flowed in from Assisi. I ate well and really felt that Christ had been resurrected on this day. Retiring early, I fell asleep at once.

"Do not blow out the lamp tonight," Francis had instructed me. "Let it burn all night long—it too must rejoice at Christ's Resurrection."

I slept, fully satisfied, and in my sleep I continued to experience the Resurrection deep down within me. I felt that every soul in this world must follow Christ's tracks to the best of his ability, sharing His Passion, Crucifixion, and then finally His Resurrection; because I realized—and the longer I lived with Francis, the more profoundly was I convinced of this—because I realized that the final fruit of death is immortality.

I was still asleep when the Lord brought light back to the world. The goldfinch had already awakened and begun to sing; but I,

357

completely given over to the joys of slumber, did not open my eyes. Suddenly I heard Francis' voice in my sleep. I sprang to my feet and discovered him sitting up in bed, singing to the accompaniment of his two pieces of wood, which he was playing again like a viol. I shall never forget the verses, and even more than the verses, the triumphant, joyful melody. So very many years have gone by, and yet I remember those verses perfectly: I seem to hear them this very moment as, old and decrepit, I sit in this peaceful monastery and write them down:

> Most High, omnipotent, good Lord,
> To Thee belong the praises, the glory, the honor and
>   every blessing.
> To Thee alone, Most High, are they suited,
> And no man is worthy of pronouncing Thy name.
>
> BE THOU PRAISED, my Lord, with all Thy creatures,
> Especially Sior Brother Sun,
> Who brings us the day, and through whom Thou givest
>   light;
> And he is beautiful and radiant with great splendor;
> He signifies Thee to us, Most High!
> BE THOU PRAISED, my Lord, for Sister Moon and the
>   stars;
> Thou hast formed them bright, precious and fair in the
>   sky.
> BE THOU PRAISED, my Lord, for Brother Wind
> And for air and cloud, calms and all weather Thou hast
>   granted us.
> BE THOU PRAISED, my Lord, for Sister Water,
> Who is humble and dear and pure.
> BE THOU PRAISED, my Lord, for Brother Fire,
> Through whom Thou dost illumine the night;
> And he is beautiful, strong, and merry.
> BE THOU PRAISED, my Lord, for our sister Mother Earth,
> Who sustains us and holds us to her breast
> And produces abundant fruits, flowers, and trees.
>
> Praise ye and bless my Lord; give thanks unto Him
> And serve Him with great humility.

I had crept to him ever so softly, afraid that if he heard me he might interrupt his song, and had listened with my arms thrown round his legs. Above us, the goldfinch stopped its peeping and listened too. Sun, moon, fire, and water entered the humble shelter, encircled Francis, and listened; and it seemed to me that Death entered with them also, last of all, and listened with bated breath. But Francis did not see anything or anyone. He sang with his head thrown back, and the prison bars gave way, and his soul prepared to flee.

God brought light to the world once more. The rising day found Francis leaning back against the wall, a smile upon his lips. He was exhausted: it was just as though the song had been his blood, as though he had been drained dry.

Toward midday he called me and said, "Brother Leo, I long to see Assisi again. Have two robust brothers—Juniper and Masseo—come to carry me in their arms. My legs are too weak: I have already walked for the last time."

I went outside and sent word to Juniper and Masseo at the Portiuncula. I also sent men to inform the bishop that Francis was coming and that he ought to dispatch an armed escort for us because the area was full of bandits from Perugia, wild men who were just waiting to carry Francis off.

When I re-entered the hut, I found Francis playing the viol again and rapturously singing the Laud of the previous night. As soon as he had finished, he cried, "Oh, I forgot to thank God for Sister Sickness."

Placing the two pieces of wood on the ground, he raised his hands to heaven.

> BE THOU PRAISED, *my Lord, for Sister Sickness.*
> *She is severe, and good; she takes pity on man*
> *And helps the soul to escape the flesh.*

I listened, forcibly restraining my tears. O my soul, I repeated again and again to myself, O my soul, say farewell to him, farewell forever. You will never see him again. . . . Farewell, farewell forever. . . .

It was evening when Juniper and Masseo arrived. They seated themselves in silence at Francis' feet. Sister Clara came, knelt,

359

kissed his hands, his feet, and sat down at his right, also in silence. Sister Pica entered, staggering. Her white hair was visible outside her wimple; she gathered it up, then prostrated herself before her son, and sat down in silence at his left. Francis, plunged in ecstasy, neither heard nor saw anything. He was lying on his back, his arms crossed over his breast, and his face was radiant with happiness.

Suddenly a feeble sob broke the hush, but Sister Pica bit her lips, and the sob vanished.

"He's sleeping," Juniper said softly. "We had better wake him and go. It's getting dark."

No one replied.

A springtime breeze entered through the doorway. The flowers in the courtyard had opened; their perfume suffused the little hut. A lamb appeared at the threshold, bleated mournfully, then scampered off. It must have been looking for its mother. None of us moved or spoke; we all had our eyes riveted upon Francis. Suddenly he appeared to me just like the figure of the dead Christ: it seemed that we had lowered Him from the cross, laid Him upon the ground which was all covered with springtime flowers, and begun to weep over His lifeless body.

As soon as it was dark out, Sister Clara rose. "Let us go, Sister Pica," she said. "We have made our farewells. The brothers will take him now. This is a good time, because night has come, and the wild men from Perugia will not be on the road waiting to snatch him from us."

Sister Pica got up, wiping her eyes.

"My child—" she began.

But Sister Clara put her arm around the mother's waist, and together, with unsteady steps, they crossed the threshold. All of a sudden I heard clamorous wailing in the courtyard: the two women were finally giving voice to their laments.

Francis opened his eyes and smiled when he saw the two brothers.

"Are we there?" he asked.

"We haven't even started yet, Father Francis," replied Juniper.

"And just now I was in Assisi," Francis sighed; "I was in the church of San Ruffino admiring the colorful stained-glass windows, and it seemed to me that I saw the Christ story recorded there. Our Savior had smashed the tombstone and was ascending to heaven grasping a white ribbon in His hand, and on this ribbon, written in azure letters, were the words *Pax et bonum!*"

I rose. "Let's go—in the name of the Lord!" I said.

Masseo and Juniper interlocked their hands to form a seat, upon which they placed Francis. He thrust an arm round each of the brothers' necks. We went outside.

"Is it nighttime?" he asked.

"Yes, Father Francis. The stars are out."

"How wonderful the air smells! Where are we?"

"In the courtyard of San Damiano's, Father Francis, and it's spring," answered Masseo. "Don't you want to say goodbye to the sisters?"

"Parting is bitter, Brother Masseo, extremely bitter. It will be better if we steal away like thieves."

We began the climb to Assisi. Two women were standng outside the cloister, under a tree. As soon as they saw us, one rushed forward with outstretched arms, but the other held her back. I heard a shrill cry beneath the tree; then everything became calm. We proceeded. I kept throwing anxious glances in all directions, on the chance that I might glimpse the Perugian mercenaries in the darkness. At a turn in the road five or six shadows sprang out in front of us, and arms glittered in the starlight. We're lost! was the first thought which came to my mind. I ran forward to investigate, and found, thank God, that they were the soldiers dispatched by the bishop. They ran up to Francis and kissed his hand.

"Why the weapons?" he asked in astonishment. "A curse upon them!"

"We were afraid that bandits from Perugia might seize you, Father Francis," answered one, the leader.

"Seize *me?* And what would they do with me?"

"Don't you know?" replied the leader with a chuckle. "A saint is a great treasure. Just think: festivals, candles, incense, thousands of pilgrims!"

"Brother Leo," cried Francis, as though calling for help, "Brother Leo, where are you? Did you hear what he said? Is it true?"

"People are capable of anything," I answered him. "It's possible to save oneself from Satan, Father Francis, but from men —never!"

"O God, take me!" Francis cried in despair; and he did not open his mouth again until we reached Assisi.

The bishop was standing in the doorway of the episcopal palace, waiting. He helped us lower Francis from the seat; then he leaned forward and kissed him on the forehead.

"Welcome, my child," he said. "Place your hopes in God. Your hour has not yet come."

"I do have my hopes in God, I do," answered Francis. "My hour *has* come."

The chamber in which Francis was laid had a large window which overlooked the roofs of Assisi. The entire city was visible, as was the olive grove, and also the gentle, domesticated plain below, with its vineyards and the slow river which crept snakelike through the meadows. By conjecture, you could observe the position of San Damiano's halfway down, and, further below, that of the Portiuncula.

When Francis sat up in bed the next morning and saw this vista which he had loved so dearly ever since his youth, he burst into tears.

"Mother . . ." he murmured, "Assisi, my mother . . . dearest Umbria . . ."

He had instructed me to lay my mat in a corner of the same room: we went to sleep and awoke together. Two swallows had built their nest under the eave, outside the window. Each morning at dawn the male began to fly about and twitter. Doubtlessly the female was sitting on the new eggs, incubating them, and the male was encouraging her by singing. Francis turned to me. "Brother Leo," he asked with great emotion, "is it really true that a person cannot raise his eyes, prick up his ears, without having them filled with miracles? Lift a stone and beneath it you will see an indestructible bit of life sitting in the moist darkness and serving the Lord: a tiny, humble caterpillar that is preparing to sprout wings, become a butterfly, and fly out into the sun. What else do we human beings do upon earth, if not this!"

While he was still speaking, we heard hooting and cursing in the street in front of the episcopal palace. A huge mob must have gathered: there was a great uproar, accompanied by the sound of heavy pounding on the door. Apparently someone had mounted a platform and begun to discourse to the crowd. The bishop's deacon entered our room.

"Do not be disturbed, Father Francis," he said. "The mayor of Assisi is at sword's points with the bishop, and each day he assembles the people, leads them here, and starts threatening. He has forbidden them to set foot in church."

Francis felt severely troubled. "This is shameful, shameful!" he cried. "We must make peace!"

As soon as the deacon had left, he turned to me. "Brother Leo, my hymn to God is never finished. Take your quill, please, and write."

I found the quill; he began to dictate to me:

> BE THOU PRAISED, *my Lord, for all who forgive their enemies out of abounding love for Thee.*
> *Blessed are those who endure injustice and persecution in peace, for the sake of their great love.*
> *Blessed are the peacemakers, for by Thee, Lord, they shall be crowned.*

He crossed himself. "Come, Brother Leo, help me get up. Support me; I want to appear at the door and speak to the people. . . . No, I won't speak to them; the two of us will stand next to each other and begin to sing these words which have just issued from our hearts."

I put my arm around him, and we crossed the courtyard. I opened the door. The rabid mob dashed forward in an attempt to enter, but halted the moment Francis came into view.

"My children," said Francis, blessing the multitude, "my children, God has instructed me to say something to you, a few kind words. For the love of Christ, allow me to speak."

He nodded to me. We both leaned against the street door, joined hands, and began to sing in loud voices:

> BE THOU PRAISED, *my Lord, for all who forgive their enemies out of abounding love for Thee.*
> *Blessed are those who endure injustice and persecution in peace, for the sake of their great love.*
> *Blessed are the peacemakers, for by Thee, Lord, they shall be crowned.*

The bishop had by this time appeared on the threshold. He was a venerable old man who regarded the populace with kindly eyes. Soon he began to sing, adding his voice to ours—and it was then that the miracle took place. The mayor made his way through the crowd, stepped forward, and knelt before the bishop.

"For the love of Christ," he said, "and for the sake of His servant Francis, I hereby forget our enmity, Bishop, and stand ready and willing to abide by your wishes."

The bishop was extremely moved. He bent down, raised up his adversary, and embraced him, covering him with kisses.

"My position obliges me to be humble, good, and to bring peace," he said. "But, alas! by nature I am easily angered. I implore you to forgive me."

The people knelt too and praised God; then everyone ran forward to kiss Francis, to kiss the hands and feet of the peacemaker.

When we went inside, Francis was happy and radiant. His abundant joy had made him forget his afflictions, and he was able to walk without pain.

"Do you know the tale about the prince and the sorceress, Brother Leo? Once upon a time there was a handsome prince, and an evil sorceress threw a curse over him, and he was transformed into a horrible beast that ate human beings. The people hated him. They armed themselves and set out in pursuit of him in order to kill him. Meanwhile, he grew more and more ferocious. But one day a compassionate young girl went up to him and kissed him on the mouth. All at once the horrible face melted away, and behind the wild beast appeared once more the handsome young prince. . . . The people, Brother Leo, are exactly like this bewitched prince."

Francis' new feat had tired him, however. He had mobilized all of his forces for an instant and had brought about the miracle. But once back in his room he collapsed onto his bed, unconscious. I summoned the deacon. He went for some rose vinegar, and we brought Francis to. The bishop came.

"I am going to call a doctor to look after you, Francis, my son," he said. "You are in my house, and I am responsible for you."

But Francis shook his head: he refused.

"You must respect life, Brother Francis," insisted the bishop; "not only the life of other men and of worms, but also your own. Life is the breath of God: you do not have the right to stifle it. In the name of holy Obedience, obey!"

Francis crossed his arms and did not speak. The doctor came—a quiet, jaundiced old man with fiery eyes. He undressed the patient, turned him over, turned him back again, listened carefully to his heart.

"With God's help he might get better," he said.

Francis shook his head. "And without God's help?"

"It's my opinion you shall be able to live until autumn, Father Francis. Beyond that, your future is in God's hands."

Francis remained silent for a moment, but then he lifted his arms to heaven. "In that case, I shall be ready to welcome you, Brother Death, with the first autumn rains!"

Turning to me, he said with a smile, "Isn't it right, Brother Leo, that we should also thank God for Brother Death? You agree, don't you? Take up your quill therefore, take it up once more, my much-buffeted companion, and write:

> BE THOU PRAISED, *my Lord, for Brother Death,*
> *Whom no living man can escape.*
> *Wretched are those who die in mortal sin,*
> *Blessed those, Lord, who keep Thy ten commandments.*
> *They do not fear Death; they love it.*

I made a fair copy of the entire Laud on a piece of paper and gave it to Francis so that he could affix his seal, the cross. He took the paper, looked at it, and shook his head.

"O Lord, I still had much to say," he murmured, "much to praise Thee for. But Thou knowest my heart and loins. Be Thou praised, therefore, for everything."

Taking the quill, he wrote: "BE THOU PRAISED, *my Lord, for everything!*" and then drew a large cross in the bottom margin of the paper.

"Finished!" he exclaimed. "I thank the Almighty for having granted me sufficient time. . . . And now, little lamb of God, send a man to the Portiuncula to tell Pacifico to come with his lute. I am nearing God and am exhausted; there is only one thing I want to do now, and that is to sing."

I dispatched the man, and toward evening Pacifico arrived with his lute. Francis greeted him with open arms.

"Welcome to God's troubadour, welcome to man's true mouth! Remove the lute from your shoulder. Here, take this piece of paper and sing the song that is written on it. I'll sing too, and so will this little lion of God next to me, and so will the four walls of our cell: stones, cement and paintings. All shall sing together!"

Before long our cell resounded with joyous, vociferous song. The window was open, the sun about to set; light dripped from the leaves of the trees. The bell of San Ruffino's began to toll for vespers, its sound spilling out with infinite sweetness into the air. Francis' voice grew louder and louder. He had begun to clap his hands; beneath his frock, the whole of his wounded, bruised body was dancing.

In the middle of all this, the door opened and in came the bishop, a scowl on his kindly face.

"If you want Christ's blessing, Francis, my son, do not sing. People pass by, stop at the sound of your voices, and then begin cursing again. They tell everyone that the bishop is drunk, that because he defeated the mayor he has given himself over to wild celebration."

But Francis was still carried away by the song's sweetness. "Bishop," he replied, "if my presence in your house is overburdensome to you, I shall leave. I sing because that is all I can do now. I am approaching God. How can you expect me not to rejoice and sing as I go to meet Him?"

"You are right, my child," replied the bishop, "but the others are not approaching God, and they do not understand. To them it seems scandalous. Sing, therefore, but in a low voice so that they will not hear you."

With these words, he left.

"Brother Pacifico," said Francis, "everyone is right from his own point of view. The bishop is right, and we are right also. Let's sing therefore in low voices so that we won't scandalize anyone. Give me the lute, teacher. I want to play too."

Taking the lute in his arms he began to play slowly, with painful fingers; and we, our voices extremely muffled, resumed our glorification of the Lord. When our need was fulfilled, Francis gave the lute back to Pacifico and closed his eyes. The singing had fatigued him. Pacifico started toward the door, walking on tiptoe.

"Do not leave Assisi," I said to him. "Francis may require you again tomorrow. He has already entered the kingdom of song."

But the next day Francis was overwhelmed by a new concern.

"We must not lose any time," he said to me early in the morning. "Before I die I want to write my testament for the brothers and sisters; I want to open up my life before them all, to confess my sins. Perhaps some soul, hearing how much I endured, how much I struggled, may be encouraged to continue along the uphill road. . . . Sharpen your quill, therefore, Brother Leo, and write."

That entire day I listened to Francis and wrote. I was deeply touched. Sometimes I had to stop in order to wipe my eyes; at other times Francis was the one who paused: he found the words too narrow for his emotion, and gave himself up to tears.

First he recounted his youth—how, dressed in silks and velvet, a red plume in his hat, he used to spend his nights going from party to party with his friends; how he stood beneath window after window to serenade his ladies. Next he told how arrogance had possessed him, how he had set out for the wars so that he could win glory by killing the enemy and then return in triumph to Assisi as a newly invested knight. Next, how one night he suddenly heard God's voice and grew afraid. "The Lord condescended to save me," he dictated, "to save me, the sinner Francis of Assisi, in the following manner: While I was still wallowing in sin, I felt an unconquerable aversion to lepers. God cried out, therefore, and tossed me in among them, commanding me to hug them, kiss them, to undress them and cleanse their wounds. And when I had hugged them, kissed them, and cleansed their wounds, the world seemed to change. What had formerly appeared so bitter to me was transformed: it became sweet, like honey. Not long after that I left the world, left this vain world and all its goods in order to dedicate myself heart and soul to God. And God gave me brothers and revealed to me by means of the Holy Gospel what Rule I should establish over my life and theirs. Those who agreed to come with me were obliged, before anything else, to distribute all their belongings to the poor. We possessed nothing but a single frock, patched inside and out, and a knotted cord; and we walked

367

barefooted. We were all simple and illiterate, each one obeying the other. And I worked with my hands, and I still firmly desire that all the brothers should learn an honest trade and should work, not to earn money but in order to set an example, and also to repel idleness. Only when we are unable to earn our living by working should we go from door to door and beg. God revealed to me this salutation: that we must always say *Pax et bonum!*"

The whole of that day and the next, Francis sat with closed eyes and related his entire life: all of the steep, terrible ascent he had mounted with his bloodstained feet, gasping for breath. He told of his father, who died unconsoled, his noble mother, who became a nun; of Sister Clara and all the brothers, one by one; of Dominic, the fiery Spanish missionary he had met at Rome; and finally of "Brother Jacopa," as he called the noblewoman who had fallen at his feet in the Eternal City and had donned the Franciscan robe beneath her own clothes, next to the skin. He also recalled the incident of the tiny lamb in Rome. A butcher was carrying it on his shoulder, taking it to be slaughtered. Francis was walking behind, and the terrified creature stared at him, stared at him and bleated as though asking for help. Francis' heart bled for the animal. Running to the butcher, he embraced him and cried, "In the name of Christ, my brother, in the name of Love, I adjure you not to slaughter this lamb!" The fierce butcher laughed uproariously. "And what do you expect me to do with it then?" he asked. "Give it to me, my brother. The Lord will record your good deed in His ledger and will present you with an immortal flock in the next world." "Oh oh," exclaimed the butcher with a sigh, "you aren't by any chance this Francis they talk about, are you? The one from Assisi, the miracle-worker?" "I am the sinner Francis of Assisi. But who am I to work miracles? I am simply a sinner, a sinner who weeps. I weep, my brother, and implore you not to slaughter this lamb!" "Take the beast," said the frightened butcher. "Here, I give him to you—free. You see, you've just performed another miracle!" He lowered the lamb from his shoulder. Francis carried it in his arms, brought it as a gift to Brother Jacopa; and it is said that ever since that day the animal never strayed far from her side: it even accompanied her to church and knelt in front of the icons like everyone else. . . .

Francis' entire life passed before his closed eyes. When Alvernia, the wild, holy mountain, rose up once more within his mind and it seemed that the Crucified Jesus fell upon him again in the form of a five-pronged thunderbolt, he cried out in a heart-rending voice, "Lord, Lord, I am a thief, a crucified thief. Place me on Thy right side!"

Toward evening he completed his testament and opened his eyes. "Brother Leo," he said, looking at me tenderly, "I have tormented you very much, my child; I have made you extremely tired. It is right that I should add the following words to the hymn which we have composed for the Lord:

> BE THOU PRAISED, *my Lord, for God's little lamb,*
> *God's little lion—for Brother Leo.*
> *He is obedient and patient; he climbed Thy ascent,*
> *Lord, accompanying me.*
> *But he is worthier than I am, Lord, because to do so*
> *he often had to fight against his nature, had to conquer it!*

I prostrated myself before him and kissed his feet. I wanted to speak, but my voice was stifled with sobs.

"I have just relived my entire life," said Francis. "I felt my afflictions all over again, Brother Leo, and am extremely weary. Call Brother Pacifico. Let's all three of us sing together to unburden my heart."

"The bishop will scold us again," I said.

"He is correct in scolding us, and we are correct in singing. Go call Pacifico."

The troubadour friar arrived.

"Ready, nightingale of God!" cried Francis happily. "All together now!"

At first the lute played quietly and we sang in low voices so that passers-by would not hear. But little by little we became enflamed; forgetting both the passers-by and the bishop, we sang out Francis' Hymn of Praise in gushing, triumphant voices. What joy that was! While Death stood behind the door we, carefree and unafraid, our heads thrown back as though we were twittering birds, transformed life and mortality into immortal song.

But at the very moment all three of us found ourselves in the seventh heaven, Brother Elias appeared on the threshold. A severe,

369

ill-humored expression was on his face. He had just returned from a new, lucrative circuit of the villages and as he was going about Assisi paying the workers who were constructing the imposing new monastery, he had walked by the bishop's palace, where he had heard singing, and among the voices had distinguished Francis'. Many passers-by had already halted in the middle of the street in order to listen. Some were moved to laughter, while others grew angry.

"Lately," one of them said to Elias, "you hear nothing but singing from the bishop's palace. You'd think it was a tavern."

Elias entered the room incensed. Francis saw him, and abruptly cut short his song.

"Brother Francis," said Elias, forcibly controlling his rage, "excuse me for saying this, but it is unfitting your fame as a saint for you to play the lute and sing so that everyone who passes can hear you. What will people say? What will they say of you, and of the order? Is this the strict, saintly life that we preach? Is this the manner in which we shall guide souls to Paradise?"

"And how else, Brother Elias?" asked Francis in a timid voice, like a child who has just been scolded by his teacher.

"By singing? I'm afraid this troubadour is responsible!" said Elias, and he pointed scornfully to Pacifico, who was trying in vain to hide the lute behind his back.

But the blood rose to Francis' cheeks.

"I am responsible! I am responsible for what Brother Pacifico does! And I am responsible for Brother Leo also, and for you, Brother Elias, and for the entire order! I am the one who shall render account to God for all of you. And if I sing, it is because God commanded me to sing. 'Francis,' He said to me, 'you are no longer of any use: Elias assumed your authority and threw you out of the brotherhood. Take the lute, therefore; retire into solitude, and sing!'"

"Ah, God commanded you to sing in solitude—you just said so yourself!" retorted Elias. "In solitude, and not here in the heart of Assisi, practically in the middle of the street. I'm sorry, Brother Francis, but I am the General of the order and I have my responsibilities."

Francis spread his arms, then brought them back to his side.

370

He wanted to reply; the press of words was strangling him. Finally he turned to me.

"Brother Leo, we are being driven away even from here . . . even from here. Where can we go? What shall become of us? Come, get up; we shall depart."

"Where to, Father Francis? It's dark out already."

"We are being driven away even from here . . . even from here . . ." he kept murmuring, opening and closing his arms in despair.

"Stay until morning, Brother Francis," said Elias. "No one is forcing you to leave; all you have to do is stop singing. Tomorrow morning, act as God inspires you."

He bowed, kissed Francis' hand, and left.

The terror-stricken Pacifico had slipped out in the interim. The two of us remained alone.

"What was it you said, Brother Leo?"

"Nothing, Father Francis. I didn't speak."

"Yes, you did. You said that whoever dwells among wolves must be a wolf and not a lamb. That's what you said, Brother Leo; that's what all sensible people say. But God presented me with a madness, a new madness, and I say that whoever dwells among wolves must be a lamb—and not care a jot if they eat him! What is the name, Brother Leo, of that part of us which is immortal?"

"The soul."

"Exactly—and that, Brother Leo, cannot be eaten!"

The next morning Francis awoke at dawn in a joyful mood. "Listen, Brother Leo," he said, "I don't need Pacifico or his lute any more; I don't need the two pieces of wood you brought me. Last night, for the very first time, I understood the real meaning of music and song. You were asleep and snoring, but this ramshackle being that people call Francis lay awake because of its pains. The poor fellow's blood had begun to form puddles on his mattress again; he was really suffering. . . . I heard the last people go by in the street; I heard dogs barking, doors and windows being closed; then quiet, motionless sweetness—unspeakable joy! All of a sudden there was someone playing the guitar beneath my window. The music lasted for a long time, and sometimes it was near me, sometimes it came from a short distance, sometimes from far far away, as though the guitarist were going back and forth between one end of the city and the other. Never in my life, Brother Leo, have I felt greater joy—no, not joy: beatitude. More than beatitude! It seemed to me that I was buried in God's bosom, that I had given myself up to Him completely."

Francis paused for a moment, and then:

"If that music had lasted only a little while longer, Brother Leo, I would have died of happiness."

Then, after another pause, he smiled, and added:

"Elias did not want me to play the lute or sing. Now God has sent me an angel to sing serenades beneath my window. Serves Elias right!"

He attempted to rise to his feet, but could not find the strength. "Come, help me, Brother Leo," he said. "Let's leave; let's go where we shall be free to sing—to our little hut near the Portiuncula."

I called Pacifico. We lifted Francis in our arms and carried him to the street door. The bishop was away, having gone out to make a circuit of the villages. The news that the Saint was leaving, was going back to the Portiuncula, spread like a flash from mouth to mouth, until it was known everywhere in the city; and as we proceeded through the narrow lanes, the men issued from their homes and workshops, the women ran to join them, and the children, waving branches of myrtle and laurel, darted past us to lead the procession.

We passed beneath the fortified gate, traversed the olive grove, and began the descent. It was August, extremely hot. The fig trees were heavy with fruit; clusters of grapes hung from the vines; the fields had been mowed; the plain smelled of parched grass and fig leaves yellowed by the sun.

"Go slowly, do not hurry," Francis begged. "You will see this beloved soil again; I will not. If you want my blessing, go slowly."

He was fighting with his beclouded eyes to see Assisi, the olive grove, the vineyards—everything—and to take them with him to heaven. When the beloved city had nearly disappeared behind us, Francis cried, "Stop! Let me see it for the last time and bid it goodbye."

Halting, we turned his face toward the city. The people behind us halted in their turn and stood in silence, waiting. Francis gazed,

gazed endlessly at the houses, churches, towers, and the half-ruined citadel which crowned them. Just then, the bells began to sound the death knell.

"Why are the bells tolling?" he asked.

"We don't know . . . we don't know . . ." we all answered him.

But everyone knew they were bidding farewell to Francis, who was going away to die. He, wiping his rapidly-failing eyes, struggled not to lose sight of Assisi and, behind it, of the olive-covered slopes of Mount Subasio with the caves where he had first taken refuge in order to call upon the Lord.

Raising his arm slowly, he traced a cross above the beloved city.

"Farewell, Mother Assisi," he murmured. "Be Thou praised, my Lord, for this graceful city with its houses, people, vine arbors, the pots of basil and marjoram beneath its windows; and with Sior Pietro Bernardone and Lady Pica; also their son Francis the little pauper. O Assisi, if I could only lift you up intact in my hand and deposit you at the feet of the Lord! But I cannot, I cannot, beloved —and so: farewell!"

Tears fell from his eyes; he lowered his head upon his breast, exhausted.

"Farewell," he whispered once again. "Farewell. . . ."

Behind us, the weeping people had begun to intone the dirge. We all set out together, walking hastily now, anxious to arrive. When we reached the hut we laid Francis gently on the ground: without our realizing it, he had fainted in our arms. The crowd dispersed; those brothers who were at the Portiuncula—Juniper, Ruffino, Masseo, Giles, Bernard—ran to kiss him, but he lay unconscious and did not feel their lips upon his hand.

One week passed, two, three. The vintage came and went, the vine leaves began to redden; the figs grew syrupy; the olives were glistening. The first cranes passed over our hut, sailing toward the south, and the swallows prepared once again to depart.

When Francis heard the cries overhead, he opened his eyes. "The cranes are taking the swallows south with them," he said.

He raised his arms toward the sky.

"Have a good trip, swallows, my sisters. Soon a large crane will come so that I too may depart."

Sometimes when he opened his eyes he used to lie still, his hand in mine; at other times I helped him to sit up, and he spoke to us of Poverty, Peace, and Love, his eternal ladies, while gazing tenderly at each of the five or six brothers who sat around him struggling not to miss a single word. These were his final instructions, we told ourselves; they were not only for us, but for all the friars who were absent, and for all the brothers and sisters yet to be born. It was our duty, therefore, to engrave them deeply in our minds so that they would not be lost.

"What is love, my brothers?" he asked, opening his arms as though he wished to embrace us. "What is love? It is not simply compassion, not simply kindness. In compassion there are two: the one who suffers and the one who feels compassion. In kindness there are two: the one who gives and the one who receives. But in love there is only one; the two join, unite, become inseparable. The 'I' and the 'you' vanish. To love means to lose oneself in the beloved."

One day he reached out and placed his hand in mine.

"Brother Leo, before I die I would like to see Brother Jacopa so that I may say goodbye to her. Do me this favor, please: take some paper and write: 'Brother Francis, God's little pauper, to Brother Jacopa: I have to inform you, dearest Jacopa, that the end of my life is drawing near. Therefore, if you wish to see me once again here upon this earth, lose no time, but as soon as you receive this message speed to the Portiuncula. If you delay even a little, you will not arrive in time to find me alive. Bring with you a coarsely woven shroud to wrap around my body; also candles for my funeral."

He turned to the brother who was kneeling at his side, and saw that it was Juniper.

"Brother Juniper, this is the last favor I shall ask of you. Take this message and—"

He fell suddenly silent. He had raised his head; he seemed to be listening to something. A sweet smile spread across his face.

"There is no need for you to go to Rome now, Brother Juniper, glory be to God! Thank you anyway."

As soon as he had said this he turned toward the entranceway. We all riveted our eyes upon the door as though we had been expecting someone.

It was then that we heard steps outside. I ran to see who it was, but before I could reach the door I let out a cry: Brother Jacopa was standing in front of me! The noblewoman entered, fell at Francis' feet, and began to kiss his wounds.

"Father Francis . . . Father Francis . . ." she whispered tearfully as she caressed his hands.

Francis placed his palm on her hair. "Welcome, welcome, Brother Jacopa. I am glad you came, very glad. . . . Who brought you the message?"

"The Blessed Virgin came to me in my sleep. 'Francis is dying,' she said. 'Run to him, and take the shroud you wove, and also candles for his funeral.'"

She laid the shroud at Francis' feet.

"I wove it with my own hands from the wool of the lamb you gave me."

Francis sat up. He looked at his feet and hands, fingered his sunken bloodstained chest—and sighed.

"Forgive me, Brother Donkey," he said; "forgive me, my old ramshackle body, for having tormented you so much."

He smiled bitterly.

"And you, my revered Mother Earth: you must forgive me also. You gave me a splendid, radiant body, and now look what mud and filth I am returning to you!"

But as he was speaking, his eyes suddenly protruded from their sockets. Extending his arm, he pointed toward the door.

"Look, there he is!"

"Who?"

"The Beggar! The Beggar, Brother Leo. He's at the door; he just lifted his pierced hand and greeted me. Now he's lowering the hood from his head— Oh, no! No!"

"Father Francis, Father Francis, stop trembling!"

"It's me, me, me! I see my face, the cross on the forehead, the scars from the white-hot iron on my temples. . . . He entered, he's coming nearer . . ."

Francis hid his eyes behind the sleeve of his robe.

"He's coming . . . coming . . ." he murmured, trembling. "Look, he's smiling happily and holding out his arms to me!"

He placed the other sleeve over his eyes now, but he still continued to see.

"He's here, *here*," he shrieked. "He just lay down next to me on my mat. There he is! Help, Brother Leo, help!"

Reaching out, he embraced me. Then he extended his hands and searched to the right, to the left; also behind my head.

375

"No one," he murmured. "No one!"

But a moment later, thoughtfully:

"The two of us have united, have become one. The journey is finished."

The end was indeed drawing near. The friars kept arriving from all directions to bid Francis goodbye. Elias raced from village to village assembling the inhabitants in order to announce that the Saint was dying and that everyone should be prepared to speed with lighted candles to the funeral. He had also made sure that the bishop would instruct the sexton of San Ruffino's to have the death knell tolled day and night. At San Damiano's the sisters knelt before the crucifix imploring God not to take Francis from them yet; and Captain Wolf descended his mountain, journeyed to the Portiuncula, and approached Francis on tiptoe, bringing him a gift of a basket of grapes and figs. Francis opened his eyes, and recognized him.

"Brother Lamb! Welcome! The wild hawks of Alvernia must have delivered the message that I was dying. Goodbye, my brother."

"It is not you who are dying, Father Francis," replied the savage brother; "it is not you, but us. Forgive me for everything I have done."

"God will forgive you, Brother Lamb, not I. If you are saved, everything will be saved with you, even the lambs you ate when you were a wolf."

Brother Wolf took the basket he had brought and placed it in the moribund's hands.

"Here are a few figs and grapes I brought so that you could say goodbye to them, Father Francis. You can eat them with a clear conscience: they weren't stolen!"

Francis laid his palm over the ripe fruit, rejoicing at the cool freshness. Then he plucked a grape from the cluster and placed it in his mouth. Next, he took a fig and sucked in the honey that was dripping from it.

"Goodbye, figs and grapes, my brothers. Goodbye for the last time. I shall never see you again!"

September drew to a close. One day early in October the sky darkened and the first autumn drizzles commenced to fall. A thin, tender mist unfurled above olive trees and pines: an inexpressible sweetness flooded the world, and the soil reclined fertile and content in the humid air. Francis opened his eyes. The hut was filled with brothers who had come from all directions, arriving early in the morning. Many had squatted down on the ground; others remained standing. They were all gazing at him, mutely, no one daring to break the hallowed silence. From time to time they wiped their eyes and stepped outside in order to breathe. Francis extended his arm, greeting them.

"You are departing, Father Francis," said Bernard, kneeling and kissing his hand; "you are departing; soon you shall ascend to heaven. Open your mouth for the last time and speak to us."

Francis shook his head.

"My children, my brothers, my fathers: whatever I had to say to you I have already said. Whatever blood I possessed in my heart, I have already given to you. Now I have no more words to speak or blood to give. If I had, God would keep me longer upon this earth."

"Don't you have anything, anything at all to say to us?" cried Giles from the corner where he was standing and weeping.

"Poverty, Peace, Love—nothing else, my brothers. . . . Poverty, Peace, Love."

He tried to sit up, but could not.

"Undress me, my brothers. Lay me naked upon the ground so that I may touch the earth and it may touch me."

Weeping, we undressed him, laid him upon the ground, and knelt around him. All of us sensed the presence of the Archangel above his body.

Sister Clara had come; unseen by any of us, she had been listening at the doorway. Suddenly we heard a sob. We turned and saw her huddled on the threshold, weeping, her face tightly wrapped in her wimple. All at once, everyone began to wail and lament.

"Why are you weeping, my brothers?" asked Francis, surprised. No one replied.

"Do you really believe this life to be so sweet? Where is your faith in the life everlasting, my brothers? Is it so very slight? Brother Death, you who are standing just beyond the door: forgive mankind. Men do not know your lofty message, and that is why they fear you."

He glanced around him.

377

"Where are you, Pacifico? Sound your lute, and let all of us sing the Hymn of Praise:

> BE THOU PRAISED, *my Lord, with all Thy creatures,*
> *Especially Sior Brother Sun* . . .

I joined the others, but as I sang, my mind began to wander. The hut vanished, as did the Portiuncula, Assisi—everything— and I found myself on an unknown stretch of land that was brilliantly green, and boundless. Francis lay in the middle, on the ground, his face turned toward heaven. He was breathing his last. A peaceful, tender drizzle was falling, and the mountain peaks in the distance were covered with mist. A delicious aroma rose from the freshly turned soil. Somewhere far away the ocean was sighing. Francis was alone, no one near him; but then suddenly the air seemed to congeal, and the twelve original brothers appeared in a circle around him, huddled over, their heads thrust within their cowls. No sound could be heard—none but their groans and wailing. I was among them, and as I raised my eyes and looked behind the twelve, I saw hundreds of thousands of tonsured friars, their hoods lowered; and they were chanting the Office of the Dead. Then I sat up on my knees and, looking further into the distance, beheld oxen, horses, dogs, flocks of sheep—all coming toward us, lamenting noisily. They placed themselves behind the friars and stood there with bowed heads. Then the wild animals—wolves, bears, foxes, jackals—emerged from the forest and lined up behind their tame brothers, and they too began to wail and lament. Suddenly thousands of winged creatures could be heard above me. I raised my eyes and watched the swarms of birds, birds of every kind, as they descended with screeching cries and perched around Francis; and a partridge began to pluck out its feathers and was the first among them to sound the dirge.

"My beloved Francis, my beloved Francis," I murmured, "all the birds and animals have come and are weeping; they have all come to your funeral, all your brothers. . . ."

Suddenly the heavens filled with flashes of blue, green, gold, and purple. I lifted my head. The air was thick with wings. Thousands and thousands of angels came and placed themselves round

378

the dying man, then folded their wings and waited with smiling faces, ready to carry off his soul. . . .

All at once the sound of heart-rending cries broke my reverie. Three women had fallen over Francis in an effort to keep him from departing. Sister Pica was holding his head in her arms, Sister Clara embracing and kissing his feet, while Brother Jacopa clutched his hand against her breast. The sun had set; outside, the rain continued to fall, softening, fissuring the earth. At that moment, we all saw two black wings above Francis.

His face was resplendent, his eyes wide open and fixed upon the air. Suddenly he stirred. Calling up all his strength, he turned and glanced slowly at each of us, one by one. His lips moved; he seemed to have some final word to say to us. I went close to him.

"Poverty, Peace, Love . . ."

His voice was muted and extremely frail, as though coming from far far away—from the other shore. I held my breath, trying to hear more. There was nothing.

Then, suddenly, we all fell upon his body, kissing it and wailing the dirge.

At the exact sacred instant I inscribed these final words, huddled over in my cell and overcome with tears at the memory of my beloved father, a tiny sparrow came to the window and began to tap on the pane. Its wings were drenched; it was cold. I got up to let it in.

And it was you, Father Francis; it was you, dressed as a tiny sparrow.